Chun-Chan Yeh was born in 1914 in a remote Chinese mountain village and is one of the few intellectuals in China today to have received a classical education. The region was an important revolutionary base and in 1929 Yeh went to Shanghai when his village was overrun by Nationalist troops. It was there that he encountered new ideas from the West and began his literary career, writing short stories and articles.

Chun-Chan Yeh pursued his literary activities in Japan (where he was imprisoned for 'harbouring dangerous thoughts'), China, Hong Kong and Chonqing. In 1944 he was invited by the British Ministry of Information to speak to the British people on Chinese efforts against Japanese invasion and after the war he went to Cambridge. There he furthered his relationship with many of Britain's leading cultural figures of the time.

He returned to Beijing in 1949 to work in the field of culture, editing a literary monthly in English and French, *Chinese Literature*. During the cultural revolution he was accused of 'having poisoned the mind of world people' and was relegated to cleaning toilets; he was not fully rehabilitated until the arrest of the Gang of Four. Since then he has devoted his time to his own writing and to promoting new cultural exchanges between East and West through International PEN.

The trilogy *Quiet are the Mountains* consists of three novels: *The Mountain Village*, *The Open Fields* and *A Distant Journey*. The first was written in English in 1946 while the author was in Cambridge and was published to great acclaim in 1947. The other two were written in Chinese in 1984 and 1986, after Chun-Chan Yeh had had the opportunity to revisit the village region of his childhood, the background of the trilogy.

ff

A
DISTANT
JOURNEY

Chun-Chan Yeh

Translated by Stephen Hallett

faber and faber
LONDON·BOSTON

First published in 1989
by Faber and Faber Limited
3 Queen Square London WC1N 3AU

Photoset by Wilmaset, Birkenhead, Wirral
Printed in Great Britain by
Richard Clay Ltd, Bungay, Suffolk

British Library Cataloguing in Publication Data is available

ISBN 0–571–14173–0

CHAPTER 1

The evening Uncle Pan and I arrived at Aunt Sunflower's house a volley of firecrackers resounded throughout the village, just as if Spring Festival had arrived a month early. Uncle Pan went excitedly into Mother's bedroom, which was serving temporarily as a delivery room for O Ran and her chubby little 'ox-herd baby', as the child had already become known. After he had had a look at O Ran and the baby, he came back into the main room where he found Mother, Aunt Sunflower and Sister Apricot busily stitching clothes and nappies for the infant. Almost speechless with happiness, his wrinkled face was wreathed in smiles, and his eyes, which had been so tearful on his return, now shone with pure delight.

'Can I do anything helpful?' he asked the three mothers, adding with a note of apology, 'I'm afraid my hands are too rough and clumsy to handle a needle.'

'Yes, there is something you could do,' said Mother, pointing at the family altar at the end of the room, on which, in addition to the usual offerings to the ancestors, a dish of freshly cooked spiced red eggs had been placed to welcome the birth of the new child. 'You could shell a few of those. The ancestors have already had a taste.'

Mother had not appeared so happy and relaxed for ages. And I knew that Uncle Pan must be hungry, as he had only had one meal the previous day, and not so much as a mouthful of water that day. I quickly cracked five red eggs for him.

1

Sitting on a three-legged stool, he took the eggs. But his eyes remained fixed on our family shrine.

'Ma'am,' he said haltingly, 'how can you still go on believing in the ancestors at this time?'

Mother's face at once became grave.

'What? Do you mean that by making revolution you can cast aside the ancestors?' she said. 'Without their protection do you really imagine you would have kept so safe until now? And do you think O Ran would have given birth to such a healthy baby – and a boy at that! We must ask the ancestors to protect him throughout his childhood. He's your grandson as well, you know. Surely you care about him?'

Uncle Pan lowered his head. The word 'grandson' had caught his imagination. He raised his head and said more cheerfully, 'Ma'm, is what you say really true? Yes, I suppose you could call him my grandson. I watched O Ran grow up and always treated her as if she were my own daughter. As for Lao Liu, well, I always liked to listen to his stories. And now, even if he is a comrade, I like to see how skilful he is at his work and I always think of him more as my own son-in-law. Isn't that so, Ma'am?'

Mother nodded in agreement, but Aunt Sunflower and Sister Apricot both laughed.

'So what plans do you have for your grandson's future?' Aunt Sunflower asked playfully. 'Do you think he'll be an ox-herd, or become a revolutionary, like you two?'

Uncle Pan made a slight grimace.

'Of course he'll be an ox-herd. We're all farming people, after all – making revolution is just a necessity of the moment. By the time he grows up there won't be any need for it. By then the country will belong to everyone and he'll be the master of his land. How wonderful to be your own master!'

'Well, in that case we should call him "Kuaile" [Happiness]. We were just trying to think up a name for him,' Sister Apricot said. 'He's the newcomer here and he really ought to have a name!'

Uncle Pan nodded repeatedly and said with approval, 'Yes, that's right. I think that "Kuaile" sounds as good a name as any. I've only ever been really happy once in my life, and that was when I heard that the peasants had seized the county town. And now an old bachelor like me has a grandson. What do you say to that, Ma'am?'

'That's quite right,' Mother said, smiling. 'As well as any other reasons, we can call him Kuaile in your honour, Uncle Pan.'

'I'm so happy,' Uncle Pan said, standing up. 'But all this is a heavy responsibility for me. I really must work harder than before – for the sake of the next generation! I'd better get back to town soon. Quite enough time has been lost already.'

Without even staying to eat his spiced eggs, Uncle Pan stuffed them into the front of his coat and walked out into the dusk, muttering as he went, 'I really must let Lao Liu know that he's got a chubby little son – he very nearly ended up an old bachelor too!'

The sound of firecrackers could still be heard, though fainter and more intermittent than before. Dusk was already turning into night. Knowing how heavy Uncle Pan's responsibilities were, and how seriously he always took them, the three mothers watched him leave in silence, but we all feared for his safety on the road, as he was no longer a young man and his eyesight was not what it had once been. Sister Apricot shook Little Baldy, who had already fallen asleep on her lap, and also got up to go. I went with her, as I had to go and report my activities over the past few days to Grandpa Whiskers and Ho Shuoru.

Since Lao Liu and I had both been away from the village, Ho Shuoru did not have very much work to occupy him at that moment. I imagined that he must be sitting in his house feeling pretty edgy. But as soon as I got to his house I realized that it was empty, and probably had been for several days. My suspicions were confirmed by a voice from behind.

'Ho Shuoru's been gone for a few days!'

Looking round, I saw Grandpa Whiskers standing behind me.

'Grandpa,' I said, 'I just wanted to report my activities over the last few days to you. You must have wondered what happened to me.'

'Of course we did,' Grandpa Whiskers replied. 'I've only just returned from the county town myself. Jiqing has already told me about you, so there's no need for you to report. Did you know that I've also joined the Peasant Self-defence Corps, as a temporary member. I won't really be able to fight, but I can always cheer them on.'

'And where has Ho Shuoru gone?' I asked.

'The day after you left, Lao Liu suddenly appeared and took Ho Shuoru with him in a great hurry,' said Grandpa Whiskers. 'As he was leaving he became really excited and said that at last he had something useful to do. He said he'd been getting restless and felt guilty about living such a quiet life in Red Hill Village.'

'What? Has he also joined the Peasant Self-defence Corps?'

'No,' said Grandpa Whiskers. 'Ho Shuoru isn't a peasant. He's an intellectual and must stick to what he's good at: doing propaganda work with Lao Liu and making up songs. When Lao Liu set up the provisional Propaganda Committee he sent the words of his songs to all the Self-defence Corps, to raise their spirits. Don't you imagine it was easy for us to take over the county town. We needed all the encouragement we could get!'

'When will he be able to get back here? I need to see him.'

'I'm afraid he won't be back for a while,' Grandpa Whiskers replied, shaking his head. 'He's become even more hot-headed than Lao Liu these days.' Then, lowering his voice, he continued earnestly, 'He's joined the revolution, you know. Over the past few days many activists have asked to join the movement – and he was among the first to apply.'

'Do you mean to say he's taken the oath?' I asked.

'Yes. He's become a comrade. Lao Liu and Jiqing were his sponsors.'

'So he won't be needing my help any more?'

'That's the way it looks,' Grandpa Whiskers replied with a smile. 'He's no longer a young master – he's become a proletarian fighter! But you'd better stay around to receive your new instructions. No doubt one of us will hear soon enough.'

It seemed I really would be able to have a few days' rest. Grandpa Whiskers still hadn't had his supper, and despite his excitement he looked weary. His fluffy white hair made his face appear all the more sallow and haggard. He needed a rest even more than I did.

While Sister Apricot put Little Baldy to bed, I went into the kitchen to light the stove and boil some water for his wash. After settling the child, Sister Apricot came in and started cooking some food for him. Seeing that there was not much more I could do, I decided to return to my mother's house.

When I arrived, I found Mother as cheerful and excited as ever, and still up and about, although Aunt Sunflower had already returned to her own room. Indeed passing Aunt Sunflower's room on my way home I had even heard a gentle sound of snoring coming from her half-open door. She really was a healthy soul, our Aunt Sunflower. Even if the heavens had collapsed, she wouldn't have felt discomfited! Though Uncle Zizhong and Jiqing had both been away for days, this did not stop her from sleeping soundly, probably as a result of years of practice. She seemed totally undisturbed by all the banging and clamouring which was going on outside her door and quite content to get on with her normal, quiet life in this out-of-the-way village. It was probably because of this that Uncle Zizhong and Jiqing were able to feel easy about carrying on with their activities away from home.

Mother, too, seemed to have been affected by Aunt Sunflower's calm and did not seem too bothered by the bangs and shouts, which could still be heard from time to time. But she did not feel like sleeping; as the night drew on she grew more and more lively. One moment she was busy stitching the baby's clothes, the next she would stop her work and listen out for any sound from the inner room.

It seemed that O Ran was feeling restless and was reluctant to rest in bed to recover the strength she had lost during the birth. We could hear the creaking of her bed as she turned over. Her restlessness probably disturbed the child and he started crying. Suddenly, the sound of a lullaby drifted in from the next room:

> Little Kuaile, Little Kuaile,
> Sleep soundly.
> When you wake,
> Your daddy will play with you . . .

The voice seemed so deep, gentle and filled with motherly love that we both found it hard to believe that it could really be O Ran who was singing. A smile appeared on my mother's face, so soft and gentle that I hardly believed my eyes. Then she said softly, 'You see. She heard every word we were saying earlier on. She's even calling the child by the name Uncle Pan gave him. From now on we'll all be really happy – even if it is a bit early for such fantasies!'

'They're no longer fantasies,' I said. 'Just look how confident Uncle Pan is.'

'Yes. He seems to have got younger,' said Mother, 'and young people are always full of hope . . . O Ran must be feeling tired. I can't hear her any more. And Kuaile has stopped crying. Shouldn't we give her something to eat?'

I was silent, not knowing what was best. Mother went on talking, more to herself than to me. 'Yes, she really should have something to eat. Mothers need more food after giving birth, to recover their strength.' She went over to the cooking range and heated up a bowl of noodles. Then she carefully carried it through to O Ran's room, while I followed behind.

6

O Ran at once struck a match and lit the oil lamp by her bed. She did not look in the least bit tired – in fact, she seemed particularly fresh and alert.

'You've already taken too much trouble, Mama,' she said. 'If you go on looking after me like this, you'll tire yourself out. And especially at such an exciting time, when there is so much to do, I really feel bad about lying here only thinking of myself.'

A more sombre mood suddenly seemed to cloud my mother's face, which for the first time in ages, had looked relaxed and free from anxiety. None the less she smiled gently and said, 'Just eat these noodles – and not too fast, mind. I'll only feel happy if I see you eating properly.'

Mother watched her silently as she ate, and would leave only when she had seen for herself that she had finished her food. I also stood there quietly. O Ran had no choice but to eat. I remembered how good her appetite had been as a child. She could never get enough to eat, no matter how much she devoured. I couldn't think why she had now become so refined, absently thinking about something else as she slowly ate her food. In the lamplight her face, despite being some-what drawn, appeared whiter, and the smallpox scabs she had developed as a child seemed less noticeable. A few days in bed had really transformed her into a beauty! Mother seemed to have noticed this too. As she watched O Ran, her eyes shone with rare pleasure.

O Ran ate up her food conscientiously, not leaving so much as a drop of soup at the bottom of the bowl. She also seemed to have noticed the change in Mother's countenance and this had increased her own sense of well-being. But when she handed the bowl back to Mother, she said, with a resolute expression, 'I think I'll be able to get up tomorrow. I must hurry back to town – I can't become a deserter from the revolution!'

Mother's smile at once disappeared and she became grave.

'What nonsense!' she said. 'Uncle Pan was only just saying that the revolution is for the sake of the next generation. How could you throw aside such a beautiful baby? And who's going to feed him?'

There was nothing O Ran could say. To avoid my mother's glance she lowered her head and looked at Kuaile, who was still sleeping peacefully. An oppressive silence settled on the room. As we left O Ran, Mother said, 'I'm just an old-fashioned woman and if I've said anything out of place, it would be best you forget it. But I've been a mother myself and I do have a sense of responsibility. I can't let you go until you've finished your month's recuperation.'

Mother had never spoken like this before. It seemed that O Ran was only just beginning to understand Mother's way of thinking; O Ran had, after all, been brought up and doted on by Mother, just as if she had been her own daughter. So it followed that she should see O Ran's child as her own flesh and blood. There was no more that O Ran could say. For the time being she would just have to accept Mother's orders.

But in her heart of hearts O Ran was feeling more restless than ever. She desperately wanted to know what had happened since the peasants had taken over the county town. The uprising was only a means to an end and there was still plenty of vital work to be done. At such a critical time as this she must be involved in the activities, even though she had little idea as to what work the leaders would assign her. Only Lao Liu could tell her and she wished desperately that this husband of hers, who was so vitally involved in propaganda work, would return to see her. Uncle Pan would already have told him that he had become a father. If he couldn't get back to see his son, it must just be because he was too busy. The thought of this made O Ran more restless than ever.

But one day, as O Ran was standing staring out of the window, we suddenly heard her clap her hands in delight. There was only one thing that could have made her so cheerful at that moment. Running outside we saw, as we had guessed, that Lao Liu had come back. Despite his wasted, ragged look and the old gown – more suited to the milder weather of early

8

autumn – that he was wearing, he still walked with that characteristic lightness of step and still had the appearance of a story-teller. Seeing my mother, he made a deep bow and said, 'My deepest thanks to you, Mama. If it hadn't been for your care, I would never have been able to continue my work with such an easy mind.'

'Two more days,' Mother replied, 'and O Ran would have become sick with worry. What on earth could have kept you that busy?'

Before Lao Liu had a chance to reply, the sound of O Ran's voice came from inside the house. Brushing aside all courtesy for the moment, he rushed indoors. When he saw O Ran he stopped dead, as if he couldn't recognize her.

'Heavens! What's suddenly made you so beautiful?' he exclaimed. 'You've turned into a stunning young girl!'

'I'm no longer a girl,' O Ran said, giving him a poke. 'I'm a mother now. Quick, take a look at our child!'

They went together into O Ran's room, leaving us waiting outside. We could hear Lao Liu crying out in surprise.

'Ah! The little fellow really is beautiful – just like you, O Ran. He's certainly been born at the right time – he'll never have to starve or suffer humiliation or repression. He's going to have a wonderful life!'

'That's why Uncle Pan chose the name "Kuaile" for him,' said O Ran.

'I know. Uncle Pan has already told me all about it. Kuaile is a good name.' Then, raising his voice, as if he were reciting a poem, Lao Liu went on, 'I will not allow him to follow in my footsteps and become a story-teller. In the old days that was only something intellectuals did when they had no other way out. We will send him to university to study culture and science. He will become a pillar of the nation, an advanced builder of socialism. Oh, what a splendid time for him to be born!'

For once, Lao Liu's eloquence stirred my mother's heart and she cried, 'Lao Liu, what's all that about? I've never heard such beautiful words from you before! What is so wonderful about these times? Tell us, quickly!'

Lao Liu came out with the child in his arms, his eyes screwed up in delight as he watched his fat little Kuaile. Mother took the child from him, so that he could concentrate on the question she had asked.

'Hasn't Grandpa Whiskers told you?' he asked. 'Oh no, I suppose he couldn't have done, as he doesn't yet know himself. The Democratic Government of Workers and Peasants yesterday announced its administrative programme, which is being sent to all villages for discussion, and must be carried out to the letter.'

'What? The Workers' and Peasants' Government also has an administrative programme?' my mother asked in surprise. 'What sort of programme is that?'

'Haven't I just said?' Lao Liu replied, 'It is an administrative programme.' Then, just as he used to tell stories in the past, he slowly and clearly began to recite: 'In order to carry out the revolution on the land, the workers and peasants must arm themselves so as to overthrow the landlords and evil gentry and establish their own regime; to attain freedom and democracy, the lives of the labouring masses must be improved, the eight-hour day must be implemented and wages increased; trade and commerce must be developed and small traders protected; uphold the principles of Soviet socialism and oppose the imperialists' invasion of China.'

Despite the clarity and eloquence of Lao Liu's speech, my mother remained as much in the dark as ever. She just mumbled to herself over and over again, 'A Democratic Government of Workers and Peasants . . . I've never heard of such a thing in all my life . . .'

'Of course you've never heard of it,' Lao Liu explained. 'This is the first government in thousands of years in which ordinary folk have been the masters. Its leader isn't an emperor or a president, but a chairman, elected by the ordinary people – Comrade Pan Xudong. We also have our own army. Mama, did you know that the Peasant Self-defence Corps has now been turned into the official army of the Democratic Government? It is called the First Army, and Pan Zaixing has been elected its commander, while Wang Jiansheng is its political commissar and party representative. In future, when we have more guns and ammunition, we will set up a Second and a Third Army . . . With an army, we can protect our political power. The government will at once divide the land amongst the peasants. The founder of the original Nationalist Party, Dr Sun Yatsen's promise that 'the toilers will possess their land' will at last become a reality. China's most fundamental problem is the question of land, and once this problem has been solved and political power consolidated, then Utopia won't be far away . . .'

As he reached the end of his recitation, Lao Liu's voice suddenly developed into a crescendo and then fell away, ending with a prolonged 'Aaah . . .' of emotion, as if he had already entered his Utopia. Although Mother still did not appreciate the full significance of this eulogy, she could not fail to be moved by Lao Liu's enthusiasm, and she remained speechless with wonder. It was O Ran who broke the silence.

'Everything has happened so quickly and I feel as if I have been left far behind. Lao Liu, I must return with you to the county town.'

Only then did my mother come to her senses and stared from Lao Liu to O Ran, fixing her gaze on her smooth, white face.

'No,' she said, 'not before you've had your month's recuperation. Even with big events like these, you mustn't endanger the child's health. He can't go without his mother's milk. And in any case, didn't you say that "the revolution is for the next generation"?'

There was not much O Ran or Lao Liu could say to this line of reasoning. Lowering their heads, they fell silent for a while. Then Lao Liu spoke.

'O Ran, there's some truth in what Mother says. In any case, the Democratic Government is at present occupied with establishing its political power and making a plan for the redistribution of land. Women's work will have to wait a while. But there's no need to worry. You'll be notified as soon as you're needed. Just pass your month quietly. At least I can get on with my work with an easy mind, knowing that the child is well. And I can do the work of two people alone – no, three people! What do you say?'

A faint smile appeared on O Ran's soft white face.

'All right!' she conceded.

'Good. We'll leave it at that, then,' Lao Liu said. Then, turning to me, he added, 'Oh yes, I nearly forgot. Ho Shuoru is now working for the government, and so naturally he won't be needing your services any more. But Wang Jiansheng needs you, so you'd better return with me tonight.'

Mother's eyes, which had brightened only a moment before, dimmed once again, but she remained silent. Lao Liu, O Ran and I exchanged glances, but we said nothing. To escape this awkward silence, Mother disappeared hurriedly into the kitchen. She wanted to make us some supper quickly, so that we could set out as early as possible, in time for me to report for work at the Democratic Government the following day.

When we were taking leave of Mother and O Ran, Lao Liu said, with forced cheerfulness, 'Mama, as soon as everything is settled I'll come and take you to town to see the changes. O Ran will come with you – and, of course, Kuaile.'

'Yes,' said O Ran, 'we'll certainly come. The earlier the better!'

Only my mother remained silent. She simply stroked my face with deep, inexpressible emotion.

Uncle Zizhong was staying in a single room in town, which a bamboo craftsman had temporarily cleared out for him. The only furniture in the room was a plank bed, an old table and a bamboo rack full of documents. This room, for the time being, had to serve as both bedroom and office, for the Democratic

Government had already put him in charge of its office work. During our first day at the county town we stayed with Uncle Zizhong. Even though he was now a member of the Propaganda Committee, Lao Liu still had to make do with an improvised wooden bed for an office, shared by turns with Ho Shuoru. There was no way I could squeeze in there as well.

Uncle Zizhong, however, was hoping I would spend a day or so with him. When Lao Liu took me to his place it was getting light and he was already up. Uncle Zizhong at once told me to get into his bed while it was still warm and have a good day's rest, as the following day I would have to begin a hectic new schedule. Although I felt desperately anxious to begin my new work without a moment's delay, in the end I just had to do as he said, and to tell the truth, I was feeling rather tired after our night's journey.

After a long sleep I woke to find it was already dusk. Uncle Zizhong had just come back after a busy day's work. He looked tired and had probably gone without food, as he brought with him two dried-up pancakes.

He bit into one of them and handed the other to me.

'This is your supper for today,' he said. 'Have a drink of water and it'll help fill out your stomach. This pancake will have to last you till tomorrow afternoon.'

He ate very quickly, though I, naturally enough, ate even faster, as my teeth were good and I was feeling really hungry. After he had noisily drunk some cold tea from the spout of the teapot, he took me off to see Wang Jiansheng. The newly appointed Political Commissar to the First Army looked drawn and pale through lack of sleep, but I quickly discovered that he was in excellent spirits. He greeted me with a broad smile and a hearty slap on the shoulder, just as if we were old friends.

'So we're to work together again, are we?' he said. 'We all have a great admiration for how fast you run and how well you find your way in the dark – and nobody appreciates you more than me!'

'So you'll be wanting me to run night errands again?' I

13

asked. I felt much more at ease now that I had seen Wang Jiansheng's cheerful mood.

'Comrade Zizhong will tell you himself,' he replied. 'But in general you shouldn't be needed much over the next two days.' Then, changing the subject, he asked with concern, 'How are Sister Apricot and Little Baldy doing? Do they miss me?'

'You go home so rarely that they're already quite used to life on their own,' I said. 'They're both fine and there's no need for you to worry about them.'

Wang Jiansheng cast a sideways glance at Uncle Zizhong and then said meaningfully, 'You're only telling me not to worry so as to set my mind at rest. But even with Aunt Sunflower to keep them company, I'm afraid there must be times when they feel lonely, especially at night, when nobody else is around. Sometimes I just can't help feeling like this, even though the thought is often pushed out of my mind by my work and the difficult conditions we have here.'

Uncle Zizhong smiled and said, 'Ah, for once you're telling the truth, Jiansheng!'

Wang Jiansheng made a grimace and retorted, 'Could I ever tell a lie? I'm only human, after all. And I know that as a husband and a father I haven't been as responsible as I should have been. But now I've got an even greater responsibility, and so that's just the way it will have to be. How about you, then?'

Uncle Zizhong retracted his smile.

'Me?' he said. 'My plight is really much the same as yours. I still can't get back home. It's just as well that Sunflower, like your Apricot, is already quite used to managing without a husband like me. Oh, these times . . .'

It was Wang Jiansheng's turn to smile now.

'It won't be long before our lives begin to return to normal,' he said calmly. 'No – all the peasants' lives will begin to return to normal, otherwise how will we be able to build the new society and establish socialism? But for the time being we have to bear these abnormal conditions, for the sake of creating normality in future. Isn't that right?'

Uncle Zizhong nodded.

'Yes,' he said, 'the new era has only just begun and may at first be even tougher than the old one. But let's leave it at that. When Chunsheng has finished his work over the next few days I'll send him over to you, I promise.'

Slapping one another on the shoulder, we left and returned to Uncle Zizhong's 'office-cum-bedroom', where Uncle Zizhong poured me out a bowl of cold tea. This was the only refreshment either of us had that evening. Before starting on his night's work he chatted with me for a while, telling me how the Da Sheng Tang Drugstore was still running, but now under the management of the old man who used to be its doorkeeper. Uncle Zizhong himself had to go there from time to time to make sure everything was going smoothly, as medicine was an essential commodity which the people could not do without. There was even a chance that the place might expand in the future. He also told me that the leaders of the Peasant Self-defence Corps, who had taken part in the uprising, were now formally enrolled in the new army.

'You can also consider yourself a member of the army,' he said in conclusion. 'From now on, you must strictly obey orders and follow revolutionary discipline. Now, go and get some sleep! Sweet Potato is coming here first thing tomorrow morning and Uncle Pan will be here later. This will be the start of your new work and they will tell you what to do.'

The next morning, before it was quite light, a quiet knocking woke me up. Uncle Zizhong was still busy working by lamplight on his documents. He opened the door quickly. Uncle Pan came in, while Sweet Potato stood outside still carrying the shoulder-pole he always used for delivering letters, and which now prevented him from squeezing in through the door.

Uncle Pan handed me an envelope and said. 'This is a report from Comrade Pan Xudong to the Provincial Party Committee in "The Big City" down the river. He is too busy at the moment to go there in person and doesn't want to burden Sweet Potato with every important document, so you must share some of his work. Tuck it into your shirt and take good care of it. Try to keep out of trouble. Now, be on your way and get back quickly!'

He then handed me a little cloth bag and explained, 'This is your food for the journey.'

I put my hand inside the bag and found a few fried pancakes.

'Let's go!' said Sweet Potato urgently from outside the door.

Uncle Zizhong yawned, feeling quite numb with exhaustion. He put out the lamp, did up his shirt and lay down on the bed without uttering so much as a word. Then he pulled the bedding that I had just used over him. Uncle Pan quietly shut the door and said goodbye to Sweet Potato and me.

When we had left the city gate Sweet Potato at last broke the silence.

'Apart from delivering that report, we must also go to Comrade Ho Shuoru's house,' he told me.

'To his house?' I asked in surprise. I at once started wondering how on earth I could explain my sudden reappearance to Ho Shuoru's father and the rest of his family. 'Do I have to go with you?' I asked.

'But of course,' Sweet Potato replied. 'No matter where we go, we must always go together. This is an essential precaution. If anything should happen to one of us, then the other will know and can at once tell the organization.'

'But how can we face them?' I asked. 'We've taken away their son, and quite a few of their possessions too . . .'

'We don't just want to visit them,' Sweet Potato said, 'we want to get even more things from them, because there are some things only they can get hold of. We also need to stay at their place for a few days, as it's safer there than anywhere else. When I went to "The Big City" a few days ago I stayed with them then.'

'Didn't they try to detain you or report you to the reactionaries?' I asked.

'On the contrary, they were very hospitable.'

'That sounds very odd!' I said. 'How come you're so good at getting their trust and goodwill?'

'It's got nothing to do with me, it's all thanks to the skill of their son, Ho Shuoru,' Sweet Potato explained. 'Ho Shuoru wrote several long letters to his father explaining the whole situation to him. I delivered them myself. He told him that our Party intends to treat him very well and that there is no need for the family to feel anxious. He also said that the Party is really working for the ordinary people of China and wants to make the country rich and strong, so that the people can enjoy proud and dignified lives, without suffering oppression, humiliation and discrimination. He said that he now knows that the purpose of his life is to work for the happiness of all the common people and so he at last has a use for his learning. He also said that he now feels very proud and happy and he really hopes that his family can feel the same. At the very least, he hopes that they can sympathize with him and support him in his work . . .'

'So from what you've seen, do you think they sympathize with him?' I interrupted.

Sweet Potato was silent for a while. Then he continued. 'Ho Shuoru's father told me that as this was how things stood, he would feel easy so long as his son was content. But he also realized the dangers involved and the strict need for secrecy. They'll put it about that Ho Shuoru has gone to Shanghai to attend a missionary university there. And of course they'll never breath a word to anyone about us.'

'Aren't they afraid?'

'What's the use of being afraid?' Sweet Potato retorted. 'These days there are so many things to be afraid of! At any moment the Blue and Red Gang might come and extort money from them. They could be killed at the mere touch of a trigger. So in comparison we're a pretty safe bet, as well as bringing them news that their son is safe. What does it matter if they give us a bit of help? And now, with the Democratic Government installed, Ho Shuoru is even safer than before. Ho Ludong can already see that it's all right to have dealings with us – as long as nothing leaks out.'

'So what help is he going to give us this time?'

'You don't imagine we'd come all this way for nothing, do you? Especially not at a dangerous time like this! Didn't Lao Liu tell you? Not long ago, Ho Ludong gave us a printing machine and a telegraph transmitter, both of which are worn out and need new parts. At the moment both machines are urgently needed, and so we've got to get the spare parts from Ho Ludong.'

I laughed. 'Oh, so we'll be fetching them directly from his house this time, will we? And not picking them up at Zhong-guanyi Bridge, like before?'

Sweet Potato laughed too.

'That's all past,' he said. 'This time he's got to entertain us at home! I tell you, when we get to his house tomorrow, we can have a change of diet! Running errands really isn't so bad these days!'

Our laughter helped to ease the tedium of our long journey.

During our stay with Ho Ludong, the only hardship we suffered was not being able to enter the house openly through the front door. Instead, for safety's sake, we had to go in through a side door. Ho Ludong had already heard some news of my family from Sweet Potato and he seemed genuinely sympathetic. He even seemed to have forgiven my brother, Zhao Jue. In the past this old-fashioned merchant had had a strong antipathy towards any form of politics. But now even he began to express political opinions to us. Just as Sweet Potato had promised, he gave us a warm welcome on the evening of our arrival, treating us to a sumptuous meal and even a jug of wine. But for me what was really special about this reception was that he treated me like a guest of equal standing. I even detected a note of respectfulness, as if he now regarded me as an emissary from the Democratic Government.

After supper he took us into Ho Shuoru's little study to drink tea. As he had not invited any other members of the family to join us, the atmosphere was very cordial and private. He first asked me for the latest news from the village, in particular for news about his son. I told him all about how I had been his son's assistant, keeping from him only the news that Ho Shuoru had become a 'comrade'.

'Ah, it really is another world!' he said with a sigh. 'And to think that he is already quite used to your way of life and even feels happy there!' Then, lowering his voice, he continued, 'The newspapers here give the impression that you are all a dreadful scourge. Chiang Kai-shek reacted particularly strongly to the establishment of your Democratic Government of Workers and Peasants. He said in a speech that you are already carrying out an organized policy for the common ownership of property and women. He says that he will not tolerate it any longer and will wipe out all the "bandits"!'

'Who are the "bandits", anyway?' Sweet Potato interrupted angrily. 'I'm a messenger, and I've come across most types of people in my time. And I tell you, those fellows in the Blue and Red Gang, which Chiang Kai-shek was once a member of, will stop at nothing: assassination, selling women, running opium dens, kidnapping, blackmail . . . Now it is time for us to wipe out these gangsters – we've now got our own government and so we've also got the power to do something!'

'I'm afraid we don't have that power.' Ho Ludong sighed. 'When it comes down to it we are really at their mercy.'

Ho Ludong was no doubt remembering the time he himself had been blackmailed by the Blue and Red Gang. He became lost in thought and, so as not to disturb his meditation, we both remained silent for a while. Then he took a sip of tea and, opening the drawer in Ho Shuoru's desk, took out that day's newspaper, pointing to the headline about Chiang Kai-shek's speech.

'Look at this!' he said.

We both looked at the newspaper he was holding, but our attention was at once drawn by two items of news which he had not mentioned. The first concerned the Japanese, British and American consuls to this city, who had paid a special visit to the Provincial Governor, expressing their deep concern about the present situation in the countryside. They required that the Chinese authorities take immediate steps to safeguard the lives and property of foreign nationals resident in the province and to guarantee their special commercial privileges (i.e. the right to dump their goods in the Chinese countryside without being subject to taxation). Finally, they suggested that they might provide aid, when and if it was needed. The second piece of news was about how the 'gentry of this province' had sent a petition to Chiang Kai-shek urging him to protect national unity and take immediate measures to annihilate the 'bandits'. Among the signatories were three of the despotic landlords from our own district: Duan Lianchen, Chumin and Mao Dehou.

Pointing to the three names, Sweet Potato said, 'They're pretty quick off the mark! It only takes them a few days to band together and work out their own plan.'

'That's right. They're all getting cold feet,' Ho Ludong said. 'And when they're nervous, that is bound to mean trouble for all the youngsters in town. There will be yet another wave of executions. Thanks be to the ancestors that our Ho Shuoru is safe with you!'

Our evening's conversation thus ended amid the sighs of this old manager, who would now be put out of business. There was nothing more for him to say and, yawning, he invited us to go and have a rest. As we were leaving, he told us that if we needed anything from him, he would 'do his utmost' to fulfil our wishes.

The next morning Sweet Potato took me off to meet Master Qiu, a middle-aged man from the Provisional Office of the Provincial Party Committee, who was staying above a tailor's shop in a little alley-way, then he left me, to see to his own business. As he had already introduced me, there was no need for me to produce any sort of identification. In any case, the document I brought with me was ample proof of my identity. Master Qiu was wearing an old padded jacket with a long blue gown over it. His hair already had a few strands of white and his eyes were deep set. At first glance he looked like an ordinary tailor, but on closer inspection he gave the impression of being keen-witted and intellectual.

He opened the letter I had brought him and after glancing at it asked me about our journey.

'Did you meet with any trouble on the way?' he asked.

'No,' I replied. 'The insurrection has already had an enormous effect and the new government has been established so quickly that the reactionaries have fled and their lackeys have gone into hiding . . .'

'The situation will not last long,' he replied. 'We mustn't slacken our vigilance. Are you staying at Ho Ludong's place with Comrade Sweet Potato?'

I nodded.

'Yes. It is very safe there,' I said. 'He is being very friendly to us.'

'Yes, but when it comes to it he is still a merchant,' Master Qiu said. 'His real concern is making money. In this respect he is still closer to Chiang Kai-shek.'

'But his son is with us!' I argued. 'In that respect, at least, he is closer to us.'

'How did Ho Shuoru react to the uprising?'

'He's been very active and his application to join the Party has already been approved.'

'Well, that just means that he has turned his back on the family – not that his family has undergone any fundamental change of attitude. The tide of reaction has already begun and we must still be careful about Ho Ludong. Fortunately, he's already been put out of business . . .'

I couldn't help feeling somewhat reluctant to accept the logical conclusion of Master Qiu's reasoning. I would just have to wait for events to speak for themselves. But my main concern was the new 'tide of reaction' he talked of. I knew very well what this implied. My brother, Zhao Jue, had been driven to Shanghai by just such an episode and his friend, Huang Zhuqing, a poet of great promise, had been shot.

'Yes,' I said, 'Ho Ludong was only saying yesterday that there would soon be another wave of killings, but it seems he was already behind the times.'

'He certainly was,' Master Qiu replied, nodding. 'The two warlords of the Guangxi faction have already established themselves in this province and in order to secure their position – especially in this city, which is their base – they just go around killing people quite indiscriminately. Now Chiang Kai-shek has signed an agreement allowing him to manipulate them. And because of this, the imperialists, who were just beginning to get cold feet, are starting to feel more secure again . . . Well, you might as well go out and have a look around town now. I'll pass this letter on to my superiors at once. You'll probably have to wait a couple of days for a reply from the Provincial Committee, so I'll meet you back here the day after tomorrow.'

As soon as I got outside I came across a group of soldiers, with rifles at the ready, dragging some students and other youngsters off to the suburbs. Passers-by remained blank and expressionless at this spectacle, but in their eyes one could sense their terror and bitterness. Only one white-haired old man with a walking stick came up to me and, lowering his voice, gave me a word of warning.

'Hide yourself, quickly!' he whispered. 'Once their blood's up they could pick up anyone as a communist. I'm afraid these poor youngsters are all off to the execution ground!'

Darting behind the old man, I stole a glance at the young

people going past, hands tied behind their backs. Some looked angry, some had their heads bowed in thought, others just looked vacant. It was obvious that none of them had any idea yet of the 'crime' for which they were being convicted. Suddenly, a loud and furious cry arose from their midst.

'Down with Chiang Kai-shek! Down with the warlords! Down with imperialism! Long live the Chinese people!'

This shout took both soldiers and passers-by completely by surprise. Everyone was dumbstruck and stopped dead in their tracks. The prisoners all came to a halt too, and the soldiers escorting them, being utterly at a loss, could only resort to beating them about the head and body with their rifles. At that moment, however, a group of men pulling heavy carts happened to pass by; their indignation aroused by the scene, they at once dropped their ropes, rushed forward and wrested the rifles from the savage hands of the soldiers. The commander was just about to draw his revolver when it was snatched from him and thrown up on to the roof of a nearby shop. At once, a crowd gathered, blocking the traffic, and amid the confusion the prisoners managed to slip their ropes and disappear into the throng. I also took the opportunity to slip away.

I quickly made for Ho Ludong's shop, which still displayed the sign 'CELEBRATING PROSPERITY', although it had already closed down. To avoid trouble I went round to the kitchen and slipped in through the back entrance. Then I made straight for Ho Shuoru's study, where Sweet Potato and I had been staying. Just as I was about to go in, I heard voices inside. Ho Ludong was discussing something with a woman and I could hear her pleading with him for some information. Ho Ludong's voice was almost as agitated, as he explained that he was unable to help her and begged her to leave at once to avoid trouble for both of them.

I was hovering outside the door of the study when the woman came out, forlorn and dejected. Seeing me, Ho Ludong said, 'Oh, so you're back. This lady says that she knows your brother and needs his address urgently. I've no idea where he is. Since he left us we haven't had a word from him.'

'I'm afraid I don't know either,' I said. Then, turning to the woman, I asked, 'What is your name?'

'Peng Wanzhen.'

I gave a start. The name sounded very familiar to me. I looked at her, desperately trying to remember where I had heard the name before. She had a gaunt appearance and her delicate features looked dull and colourless. She must have been about twenty-three or four and although she seemed cultured, she did not have the air of a student and looked old for her years. What connection could my brother have with a woman like this? He had never mentioned such a friend before.

As I was racking my brains, she cast me a friendly, tragic smile, displaying an immaculate row of teeth. I felt a pang of sympathy for her at once and, quite spontaneously, smiled back. As her smile broadened, I could see a glint of hope in her sad, soulful eyes.

'Are you Zhao Jue's younger brother?' she asked excitedly. 'Have you ever heard the name Huang Zhuqing? He was my husband, and a good friend of your brother's. Not long after we married he . . . sacrificed himself . . .'

Of course I had heard of him! After Mother and I had moved to the city, Huang Zhuqing, then a young middle-school teacher, had come to us with news of my brother, and not long after that my brother himself had turned up. I also remembered the posters announcing Huang Zhuqing's execution, in which the reactionaries had accused him of being a leading member of the Communist Party. For an instant his honest, innocent face flashed into my mind.

'I heard that you were sick with TB,' I said.

'People who have suffered hardship can survive anything,' she replied, her smile gradually fading. 'I managed to get an effective prescription from a kind-hearted doctor. After taking

24

the medicine I stopped coughing blood and the fever gradually went away. I think I'm all right now.'

'So why do you need to find my brother?' I asked.

'Haven't you seen what is going on now?' she said. 'At the moment I'm living with a cousin of Zhuqing's – a poor and honest schoolmaster. A few days ago he was arrested and so far there's been no news of him. I doubt whether he'll be any luckier than Zhuqing. Next it'll be my turn – but I have no good reason to sacrifice myself. I want to get away from here as quickly as possible, but I have no contacts anywhere. Knowing that your brother had gone far away from here, I thought that maybe I could find him and ask him for help. He and Zhuqing were close friends, after all . . .'

Her voice trailed off, ending almost in a sob. Ho Ludong stood silently to one side, an ashen, dejected look on his face. He glanced furtively from me to Peng Wanzhen without uttering a word. I also remained silent, though I sensed the urgency of the situation. Ho Ludong no doubt felt the same, and the silence which descended on the three of us seemed very awkward. In the end I just said the first thing that came into my mind.

'Since he went to Shanghai we have had no news from my brother. And after losing Zhuqing there has been no way for him to communicate with us. But if you want to get away from here you could always go to my mother's place. Even though she's never met you, I'm sure that she remembers who you are. Our village is pretty remote, though, and life there is tough . . .'

'That doesn't worry me,' she replied. 'I just can't stand the terror here any longer . . .'

'Well then . . . ?' I asked.

'I'll go!' she said firmly. 'I'll go there at once!'

'I'll be going back there in a couple of days,' I said. 'Will you be able to come with us then?'

'Yes, of course,' she said.

Ho Ludong heaved a sigh of relief. He seemed also to

approve of this plan. I would never have imagined that this moderately wealthy, money-minded old merchant could ever become so sensitive and sympathetic. The current changes and upheavals had left their mark on him, too.

'Going in and out of this house can be a problem,' he said. 'If you've decided to go to the countryside with Chunsheng, you'd be safest staying here until you leave. You can use our younger son's bedroom for the time being.'

Then he left us together to let us talk about our past experiences. Before long, Sweet Potato came back, having completed his business. After he had heard about Peng Wanzhen's circumstances, he agreed with my suggestion.

'You've really grown up a lot!' he said to me, slapping me heartily on the shoulder.

Two days later Master Qiu gave me the reply from the Provincial Committee. Sweet Potato had already finished all his business and Ho Ludong had supplied all the spare parts we needed for the telegraph and printing machines. We slipped out of the back door of Ho Ludong's 'CELEBRATING PROSPERITY' shop just as the sky was growing light and quietly left the city. Peng Wanzhen came with us. If anyone questioned us, we would just say she was a distant cousin.

CHAPTER 2

When Sweet Potato and I got back to the county town with our new travelling companion, Peng Wanzhen, the first people we came across were Lao Liu and Ho Shuoru. The sun was just setting behind the hills and the two of them were pacing around outside the town walls like a couple of surveyors. As soon as they spotted us they waved and beckoned us over.

'Lao Liu!' I called out. 'You must be feeling cheerful – still able to find time to enjoy the sunset!'

'You must be feeling even more cheerful to talk like that,' he replied as we drew near. 'The government is planning a great celebration for the masses, you see, so we're trying to work out how best to maximize the propaganda effort. How did you get on?'

'We didn't have any accidents along the way,' Sweet Potato said, 'and we've even brought a new friend back with us – she's called Peng Wanzhen and she is very fond of literature. She also says she is a friend of Chunsheng's brother.' Sweet Potato pointed at Peng Wanzhen and then said to her, 'Lao Liu used to be our local story-teller. And this is Ho Shuoru, the best educated among us. Ho Ludong, whom you met in the city, is his father.'

Peng Wanzhen nodded her head silently, a faint smile on her lips. Both Lao Liu and Ho Shuoru seemed rather dazed by her sudden appearance and just stood there as if transfixed by her. Maybe the sight of her in this unlikely setting had triggered Lao Liu's story-telling imagination. Ho Shuoru's thoughts, however, remained completely unfathomable. Both of them, it seemed; had been stunned into silence.

I gave them a general explanation of Peng Wanzhen's situation and of my mother's concern for her. This seemed to bring Lao Liu and Ho Shuoru out of their trance and they started looking her up and down, just as a film director might size up a potential actress for a new role.

'As soon as I've reported to Uncle Zizhong and Uncle Pan, I'll take her up to Mother's place,' I said. 'Then I'd better look for Grandpa Whiskers to see if he can find somewhere for her to stay at Red Hill Village.'

'What's the hurry?' Lao Liu said, a little brusquely. 'There are plenty of places to stay in town, and we need someone else to help us right now. We're up to our necks in work. How could we let someone with her learning go?'

Ho Shuoru congratulated Lao Liu on his sense of responsibility and his commitment to expanding the propaganda work. Then, to reaffirm his own revolutionary zeal, he announced resolutely, 'Miss Peng has arrived at just the right time. We really need someone with a literary education to join us in our propaganda work. I hope you won't refuse, Miss Peng, will you? We'll be able to find you somewhere to live in town. And I promise to take you to see Chunsheng's mother as soon as we've sorted out your work.'

Peng Wanzhen seemed quite unprepared for this unexpected turn of events and the sudden display of warmth and friendship from Ho Shuoru and Lao Liu. Not knowing how best to reply, she just stood there, smiling silently. But her smile said more than any words.

'You two go quickly and report on your work,' Lao Liu said with a wave of his hand. 'Don't worry, we'll take care of Miss Peng.'

Regardless of whether or not Peng Wanzhen agreed, he waved once again to send us on our way. Then, as an afterthought, he stopped me and asked: 'Did you manage to bring back the spare parts we need for our work?'

'Yes,' I replied. 'They're in the wicker basket. Ho Ludong was very helpful – he even entertained us in his house for a few days.'

Lao Liu and Ho Shuoru both clapped their hands in admiration. But at this moment it seemed that Peng Wanzhen was more important to them than any spare parts. As if they feared that I might try to grab her back, they quickly set off with her towards their own workplace, shouting back to us as they went, 'Just hand the things over to Uncle Zizhong for clearance and then get them sent on to us.'

Sweet Potato took up his carrying-pole and I followed him. When I reached Uncle Zizhong's makeshift office I found Uncle Pan and Chang Je-an there too. They had just come over from Mazhen county to discuss their work, but they also wanted to hear our news, as they had guessed we should be back around this time.

Having finished my first assignment, my work now passed formally into the hands of Wang Jiansheng. He really needed someone at his side to help him, as he and Pan Zaixing between them commanded all the militia protecting the area under the control of the Democratic Government. Since some of their activities needed to be carried out at night, my special knack of finding my way in the dark was put to good use. Apart from acting as scout during the night, I had a whole range of duties during the day too, such as taking down notes at meetings and reminding them the night before of the following day's work.

The first meeting he took me to was a work discussion between the leaders of various departments. It took place at the old county administrative offices, which were now the headquarters of the Democratic Government of Workers and Peasants. As usual the meeting was chaired by Pan Xudong, whose attitude was grave but confident.

'We must proceed swiftly with our task of consolidating the position of the new government,' he said. 'There's no time to be lost!' He swept his glance around the people sitting before him, who were all watching him intently. Then he took a fat envelope from the rough cloth bag which served as his attaché case. I at once recognized it as the letter I had brought from Master Qiu.

Unfolding the document, he went on, 'Let me once again give you the gist of the Provincial Party Committee's instructions, so that we can decide on our immediate course of action. Firstly, we must expand the work already started regarding the redistribution of land. We mustn't act rashly and must make sure we do not leave any loop-holes. Secondly, in some areas there are still remnants of the landlords' forces, such as the Red Spear Society and the Order Preservation Corps. There's no doubt that they are still operating underground and they must be wiped out completely. Thirdly, we must strengthen our propaganda and bring our policies to the hearts of the people, to become a movement of mass consciousness. Fourthly, we must strive to extend our influence to other counties and even to surrounding provinces. Finally, because of the radical developments in this region, the leaders of the Provincial Party Committee are unable to cope adequately with the new situation. The Central Committee has therefore instructed that a Special Regional Committee be set up here, linked directly to the centre . . .'

Pan Xudong paused for a moment. Then, seeing everyone gazing at him with rapt attention, he raised his voice a little to express his own opinion.

'You see! Here we are, having been scorned for years as stick-in-the-muds, and look what we've produced! The newspapers which Comrade Sweet Potato and Chunsheng brought back with them say it all: we've really managed to put the wind up everyone from landlords Chumin, Duan Lianchen and Mao Dehou right up to Chiang Kai-shek himself. The foreign powers are getting nervous too, which shows that our movement is assuming international proportions. The Central Committee's instruction that we should set up a Special Regional Committee should strengthen our sense of responsibility and demands that we improve our work. We must recruit more people to our ranks and encourage more and more peasants to join our army . . .'

At this, Lao Liu was unable to control his excitement and, speaking in his capacity as a member of the Propaganda Committee, he said, 'I would like to report that another comrade has just joined our department. She is very talented and her name is Peng Wanzhen. She writes beautiful characters and can produce a good article . . .'

'That's excellent.' Pan Xudong said. 'For historical reasons most of our peasant friends have been unable to study and many are illiterate. We need the help of intellectuals. Let us welcome her. Now, does anyone have any other comments?'

As nobody else had anything to add, the meeting ended at that. Leaders of the various departments went their own ways and began at once to make preparations for the selection of candidates for the Special Regional Committee of which Pan Xudong had spoken. Wang Jiansheng and Pan Zaixing had already established a 'military headquarters' in an old pawnshop in town, the owner of which had long since fled. The Security Department, organized by Uncle Pan, was also located there. As this building was considered particularly sturdy, it was also used for storing ammunition – not that there was very much ammunition to store.

When Wang Jiansheng took me to the 'headquarters' I saw that Chang Je-an was already waiting for us there, probably to discuss the military situation in our two counties. As I had anticipated, the discussion quickly turned to the problem of arms and ammunition, in particular how to make equitable use of the limited supplies available. This was indeed a most pressing problem, since no matter how large our armies, everything would ultimately depend on whether or not they were properly armed. Uncle Pan took part in these discussions too, as his work was also dependent to a large extent on the supply of arms.

'Although we're supposed, at least in name, to be the First Army,' Pan Zaixing said, 'we still have less than 300 guns between us, including those originally belonging to the various landlord forces and those taken from the county armies and the old government garrisons. About a third of the guns are old Hanyang rifles and half are second-hand guns which the Japanese sold to the warlords, many of which don't work at all. There are also quite a few shotguns and hunting rifles, which have a very limited range. The ammunition situation isn't very much better, either. We have about 4,000 rounds in all, and much of this is unusable. So far we've already sent out two units, one, under the command of Jiqing, has gone to the southern districts, the other, under Pan Mingxun, has gone to the northern districts to wipe out the last traces of reactionary control. It's a tough job for them. Naturally enough, the forces which remain in the county town are very much depleted, though we still have a great deal to do . . .'

'Nevertheless,' Chang Je-an insisted, 'we mustn't let this weaken our resolve to increase our numbers. At the moment we're just in the process of setting up a Second Army at Mazhen county, which will incorporate, the local ninth unit of the Peasant Volunteer Force. Already a good number of able-bodied men have joined up from the villages. The only problem is that we cannot announce our presence there openly, as there is an enemy garrison posted in the county town; so we have to do most of our work there at night. Guns are of course essential to this kind of work. At the moment we're still far weaker than our opponents and it would be quite unrealistic to try to seize their arms. So we're still dependent on supplies from here.'

Pan Zaixing cupped his large hands, roughened by a lifetime's labour in the fields, over his weather-beaten face, as if he were trying to squeeze out some solution to our present predicament. Uncle Pan looked equally perplexed. Never in his wildest dreams had he imagined that he, an uneducated old yokel, would ever have to bear the responsibilities of a security chief.

'The urgent task we have to face is clear enough,' he said, 'and that is going all out to get hold of more weapons. The main source will still have to be the landlords and county gentry, who have stashed most of their guns underground. We must try and dig them all out. This way we can kill two birds with one stone, by increasing our supplies and wiping out the threat of the landlords.'

'It may sound pretty easy,' put in Wang Jiansheng, 'but in practice it's a hard job. They've grown cautious with experience and are not likely to leave their weapons lying around. If you want to find them, you've got to mobilize the masses to keep an eye on things and make it difficult for the landlords to hide their guns away. This is something we can't afford to ignore. If we stop relying on the masses our task will be near impossible.'

'Well, in that case, Lao Liu's work is going to be more important than ever,' Uncle Pan said, 'and he now has a very valuable assistant – a young woman who used to be a student. He and Ho Shuoru have been full of it lately, getting up before dawn each morning . . . They have only been working together for three days and already they have produced scores of leaflets, broadsheets and posters on that printing press of theirs. The outside of the town walls is now plastered with a dizzying array of posters! Lao Liu says that as soon as he's finished training his new assistant, he plans to put together a book of revolutionary songs, praising the new government and inspiring the masses. Once his songs become popular they're bound to have a big influence on people's thinking.'

'It seems that nothing escapes your notice, Uncle Pan!' Wang Jiansheng said, for the first time allowing a smile to light up his solemn face. He seemed quite heartened by this new development.

'Well, that's my job,' Uncle Pan replied. 'But I'm really just an old country bumpkin. I've only learned to read a few characters. I really admire people like them.'

'The next generation will all be able to read and write,' Chang Je-an said. 'That's what all our efforts are about now. But to get back to the original subject: the last time we made a night raid into the county town we managed to pick up a good batch of modern weapons. So it seems as if we'll have to look towards Chiang Kai-shek's forces for our supplies in future.'

'So you mean that our next target is to be the regiment based at Mazhen county town?' Uncle Pan asked.

Chang Je-an glanced round us all without replying.

'That's right,' Pan Zaixing suddenly exclaimed, slapping his thigh excitedly. 'We can grab whatever we want from them! How do you suggest we prepare for this, Comrade Je-an? Obviously, their forces are very strong. They've already become the local bastion of reaction and sooner or later they must be rooted out. Their one regiment alone can supply enough arms for three of ours!'

'Yes, they must be rooted out,' Chang Je-an agreed, though he gave no hint of how this was to be achieved.

Wang Jiansheng, eager to speak but hesitating to find the right words, said, 'You'd better establish your Second Army properly before taking any action. I've already discussed this with Pan Xudong, who says we should give half of the weapons captured in the uprising to you. Tomorrow night we'll send them over.'

At this a small smile played on Chang Je-an's lips.

'Well, in that case we'll be able to start up some small-scale guerrilla activities,' he said, 'and we can also start attacking their small patrols by day. As long as our armies can co-operate well, we're sure of rooting them out sooner or later.'

Thus everyone agreed that our forces' next aim should be the obliteration of the Nationalist forces* in Mazhen County.

* That is, the forces of Chiang Kai-shek, who styled himself the supreme leader of Kuomintang, the Nationalist Party.

'We're the official army of the Democratic Government Workers and Peasants,' Wang Jiansheng said, 'so our next objective should be more ambitious than in the past. I agree with the opinion of everyone here and I'll take this as our main discussion, to be reported to the Special Regional Committee.'

Since everyone seemed in agreement there was no further discussion, and Pan Zaixing got up to go. Chang Je-an was anxious to get back to Mazhen to organize people to transport arms and ammunition. Wang Jiansheng signalled to me that he was leaving and began hurrying on his way. He still had some important work to complete, particularly the plan to redistribute land amongst the peasants. But before he reached the door he was stopped by Uncle Pan, who came up to him and whispered, 'I know you're very busy at the moment, but you must try and find time to meet someone . . .'

'Who?' Wang Jiansheng asked in surprise.

'You'll know when you meet them,' Uncle Pan replied. 'I've arranged it all and I'll be responsible for everything. Just try and get all your work finished before dark.'

Without waiting for Wang Jiansheng to pursue the matter any further, Uncle Pan hurried on his way. Wang Jiansheng gazed vacantly for a moment at the aged, yet apparently rejuvenated figure of Uncle Pan disappearing into the distance. Then he started off with me for the old county government offices, which were now the headquarters of the Democratic Government.

That evening, while we were having supper in the old kitchen, now enlarged to make a canteen, we heard a familiar voice calling us from outside.

'Jiansheng! See who's here!'

Raising my head I looked out of the window and saw Uncle Zizhong standing there. He usually looked grave and thoughtful, but his habitual frown seemed to have disappeared and he was smiling. Clearly the heavy responsibilities and anxieties of the past had at last lifted. Wang Jiansheng seemed to be

35

infected by this obvious sense of well-being and appeared happy and relaxed. He quickly went to the window and looked out, but then he retreated a few steps and a slight shadow passed over his face. Uncle Zizhong turned round and beckoned to two women and a child to enter the room. Wang Jiansheng turned pale with surprise. He was obviously quite unprepared for these unexpected guests and the fact that Uncle Zizhong had brought them made him even more startled.

'None of us has had time to go and visit them, so they've come here to look for us instead!' Uncle Zizhong explained.

Wang Jiansheng seemed to revive slightly from his initial shock, but his face remained blank.

'Aren't you pleased?' the older of the two women asked with a smile. 'You're all so busy these days that you don't seem to be interested in your families any more.'

'Aunt Sunflower, had I known you were coming I would have found time to meet you,' Wang Jiansheng said. Then, with a slight note of complaint, he added, 'but this really isn't a very good time.'

'I'm afraid that this state of affairs is all too common for us, Jiansheng,' Uncle Zizhong said in a conciliatory manner, 'but that isn't to say that we can completely ignore our families. I often feel rather bad about it.'

This was the first time Wang Jiansheng had heard any expression of real emotion from Uncle Zizhong. He had always thought that this committed Party organizer, who, while working in the Da Sheng Tang Drugstore, had always been involved in one kind of covert operation or another, was one of those people whose mind was dominated purely by reason and not by emotion. He may not have felt particularly apologetic about his own actions, but he did have a sense of the emotion Uncle Zizhong had kept hidden so far in his inner self. Lowering his head slightly, he gazed in silence at his young wife and his son, Little Baldy. Sister Apricot, aware of

36

his gaze, lowered her head too. Wang Jiansheng looked even more ill at ease.

'You mustn't blame Apricot. It was Uncle Pan who told us to come here,' Aunt Sunflower explained, a slight note of protest in her voice. 'Even an old bachelor like Uncle Pan seems to understand more about the meaning of family life than you do. Even though Zizhong had no idea I was coming here, he at least showed some pleasure at our arrival, dropped what he was doing and brought us to see you. These really should be happy times, shouldn't they? Everything's changing in town. Can you blame us for wanting to come and see it for ourselves?'

Wang Jiansheng remained silent.

'Jiansheng, you mustn't feel so put out by my sudden appearance,' Sister Apricot said. 'I just wanted to make sure you were all right. You really have got thinner, but you seem to be in good spirits. That makes me feel a lot better . . . Well, I suppose Baldy and I had better return to Red Hill Village tonight . . .'

She glanced outside. The moon was already rising above the eastern hills. Then she pulled Little Baldy to Wang Jiansheng's side and patted his little head.

'Say "papa",' she said. 'You often think of your papa at home, don't you?'

Little Baldy looked up at Wang Jiansheng and then lowered his head. He no longer seemed to recognize his father and felt uncomfortable in his presence.

'Come!' Aunt Sunflower exclaimed. 'This is your father!'

Little Baldy's lips quivered. But before he had a chance to speak, Wang Jiansheng picked him up and held him tightly in his arms. I could see tears glistening in Wang Jiansheng's expressionless eyes, but he held them back and merely whispered to himself, 'Poor child . . . You are so thin. I haven't been looking after you properly. And now you hardly recognize me . . .'

'You mustn't blame yourself,' Sister Apricot comforted him.

'You have so much to do. I understand. Little Baldy will understand in the future too.'

At this point Uncle Zizhong broke in, 'All right, that's enough! Now you must all be hungry and the food's all getting cold.' Then he shouted to the kitchen, 'Comrade cook! We've got guests today. Fry five eggs for us and charge it to my account! I'm sorry to keep you longer at your work!'

'That's a good idea!' Wang Jiansheng said. 'Tonight we'll celebrate our reunion, symbolized by the full moon. We haven't had a meal like this for ages . . .' His voice sounded a little more relaxed than before.

After this he said no more about the matter, but concentrated all his energies on feeding his son. His wife also remained silent about her plans to return to the village that night. Most of the conversation revolved around domestic matters, with a few comical stories thrown in. Their dinner table was a reflection of the general sense of peace and calm which now reigned over the town. By the time they had finished eating, the moon had already climbed well above the distant range of hills to the east. Aunt Sunflower suggested that Wang Jiansheng should take Little Baldy outside for a stroll in the moonlight. Meanwhile, she and Uncle Zizhong went off to his office, which doubled up as his bedroom. On his way out, Uncle Zizhong said to Wang Jiansheng, 'Why don't you and your wife go and have a look at the posters and slogans all over town. Even if she can't understand the slogans, Sister Apricot will at least be able to get some idea of the great changes which have taken place in our town. They are all the work of Lao Liu and Ho Shuoru, but now we've also got a new woman scholar to help our cause and their work is becoming more and more inspired.'

After Aunt Sunflower and Zizhong had left I began to feel somewhat in the way and went off to Uncle Pan's place. He had now set up a bed for himself in the office of the old shop and had made some space on his bed for me to sleep there too. This 'temporary' state of affairs, though, might last for any length of time, as living space was in short supply. We could not occupy the houses of ordinary townsfolk and it might be a long time before we could undertake any construction work.

Just as I was about to set out for Wang Jiansheng's place to begin my day's work, Pockmarks the Sixth, who used to be the manager of a fried dough-stick stall in Tanjiahe, suddenly appeared at our door. Seeing me, he patted my shoulder warmly and said, 'It's ages since I last saw you. I was just thinking of you the other day . . .'

When he laughed, the pea-sized pock-marks clustered together, making his face look like the skin of a gourd.

'Where have you been all this time?' he asked.

'I've been here all the time,' I said, pointing to our bed. 'I'm sharing the place with Uncle Pan. How about you?'

'I'm still making fried dough-sticks,' he said. 'But now I've been promoted to manager of the county dough-stick shop! The old manager, Cuiba, got a better job somewhere else. I couldn't leave, although, I must say, I do miss Tanjiahe. So, how's Uncle Pan?'

'He's very busy and has already gone to work. Do you need to see him about something?'

Pockmarks the Sixth lowered his voice and whispered in my ear, 'We caught a spy last night! I need to discuss it with Uncle Pan.'

Hearing the word 'spy', I felt both a sense of alarm and curiosity. Could anyone really dare come to the county town to spy on us?

'I'll go and get Uncle Pan at once,' I replied. 'You wait here. I'll be as quick as I can.'

'We've already locked the spy up and there's no way he can escape,' he said. 'But in times like these we can't afford to take any risks and we must deal with him quickly.'

I came across Uncle Pan on the way to the government offices. He was talking to Wang Jiansheng. The latter's second-ary job was officer-in-chief of the People's Committee, but in fact he spent most of his time helping Pan Xudong with various kinds of administrative work. In this way Pan Xudong could devote his time to more pressing matters. He had temporarily delegated military work to Pan Zaixing and Liu Dawang, while he himself gave his attention to trying to revive the Peasants' Union and making preparations for the meeting of worker, peasant and soldier deputies which was shortly to take place. Since most of Wang Jiansheng's work was closely related to that of Uncle Pan, they spent a lot of time together exchanging ideas. When I told Uncle Pan why I had come looking for him, Wang Jiansheng immediately pricked up his ears and we all returned to the old pawnshop.

'We caught the spy early yesterday evening,' Pockmarks the Sixth told them. 'He came to my stall to buy fried dough-sticks. I had sold out of them, so he asked for some pancakes. He looked very hungry. I gave him two pancakes. When he stretched out his hand I saw that his skin was rather smooth, though the tips of his fingers were stained yellow. I guessed that he must be an opium addict. He certainly didn't look like a peasant or a craftsman. He wasn't likely to be a shop-assistant either. So I sent someone to follow him. As he ate his pancakes, he kept looking around, and when he reached the east gate he turned round and crept back as if he were looking for somewhere to hide. He probably wanted to come out again after dark. At this point, the comrade who was following him called a nearby militia man, who picked him up. We've got him under lock and key for the moment. I didn't report this at once, firstly because it was too late, and secondly because we wanted to find out something about him ourselves. We can't push everything on to you . . .'

'Have you questioned him yet?' Wang Jiansheng asked.

'We interrogated him almost all night,' Pockmarks the Sixth replied.

'Who interrogated him?' said Uncle Pan.

'Jiqing,' Pockmarks the Sixth replied. 'He had come over to see him, so I asked him to stay on to question the fellow. Jiqing is a pretty calm youngster on the whole, but a thing like this can really set him off. As soon as he saw the captive, he had the feeling he's seen him before somewhere, though he wasn't quite sure. When he started asking questions, the wretched fellow refused to answer. Then Jiqing really lost is cool and hit him in the face. He fell on the floor and passed out.'

'Did he really pass out or was he just having you on?' Uncle Pan asked. 'I've never heard of a slap on the face having that sort of effect.'

'Have you forgotten? Jiqing used to be a blacksmith,' Pockmarks the Sixth said. 'He had to be strong enough to hammer iron into shape. But anyway, the fellow didn't die from the blow. He came round after a while, and this time he was better behaved. When he looked up and saw the veins standing out on Jiqing's arms he gave a shudder and told us where he was from. It turned out that he belonged to *Bao* Chief Liu Qiyu's gang.'

'Is Liu Qiyu still around?' Wang Jiansheng asked.

'Liu himself has already fled. But in the meantime he had sent this fellow to come and spy on us.'

'So what were his plans?' Uncle Pan asked.

'He couldn't get round to telling us, as he suddenly got a desperate craving for opium and collapsed on the floor, tears streaming from his eyes. All we could do was lock him up again for the time being.'

'We must get on with the interrogation at once,' Wang Jiansheng said. 'We'll all go together. Go and tell Jiqing to start questioning him again.'

While Pockmarks the Sixth fetched Jiqing, we went to wait at the back of his fried dough-stick shop. This was regular meeting place for us. Before long, Pockmarks the Sixth and Jiqing came along. Jiqing went straight to a little storeroom next to the latrine, now set aside specially for holding suspicious persons. As soon as Jiqing dragged the spy in I had a feeling I'd seen him before somewhere. Then I realized that he had once visited our village with Liu Qiyu to ask Grandpa

Whiskers about the kind of songs we were singing in our village. He looked much the same as before, though he seemed pretty weak. And now, after suffering this desperate craving for opium, he looked more pathetic than ever, like a half-starved dog. As he looked at Jiqing he did not move, but his whole body trembled violently.

'What was your plan when you came to spy on us?' Jiqing roared, as he clenched his fist. 'Tell us the truth, or else you'll get a taste of my fist!'

The spy raised his hand in terror, as if to try to block a blow from Jiqing's fist. But after a moment he again collapsed on the floor and we could barely hear him breathing.

'This is useless,' Wang Jiansheng said. 'What can we do? He's got another craving for opium.'

Uncle Pan lowered his head in thought.

'Jiqing, search his clothes,' he said after a while. 'Make sure you check the linings carefully.'

Jiqing turned the spy over and undid his clothes, beneath which the bones stood out sharply on his wasted body. The cold air at once set him trembling violently, though his eyes remained open and still gleamed with a flicker of light. After a thorough search of his clothes, the only thing Jiqing discovered was a little snuff bottle, which he handed to Pockmarks the Sixth. Inside were several little black pellets, which Pockmarks the Sixth held in front of the prisoner's face.

'What are these?' he asked.

'I've forgotten. I've completely forgotten about it,' the prisoner replied. 'That blow on my face yesterday left me quite confused. I can't remember a thing now.'

Pockmarks the Sixth held the pellets beneath his nose, sniffed them and gave a laugh. Then he stood up, went over to the table and poured out some cold tea. He said to Jiqing, 'Open his mouth. I want to perform a little operation!'

Jiqing sat the prisoner up and forced a piece of wood in his mouth to keep it open. Then Pockmarks the Sixth took two of the pellets, put them in the prisoner's mouth and washed them down his throat with some cold tea.

'That's it,' he announced. 'You can take that piece of wood out now. Those little black pellets are opium tablets. There are still four left. I'll keep them for him. He should be fine in a moment, and then we can get on with our interrogation.'

Just as he had predicted, the prisoner recovered before long and stood up. He watched the four strapping men who stood around him. When his gaze fell on Jiqing he once again began to shudder. He would have been glad for the ground to open up and swallow him alive.

'There's no point you trying to hide anything from us,' Uncle Pan said. 'You can't escape from here. The most pressing question for you just now is whether or not you want to live! Is it really worth sacrificing your life for that master of yours? I'm only telling you the truth in order to help you save your own skin.'

At this point Jiqing waved his fist once more and began hammering the table, causing the teacup to leap about and eventually to roll to the edge of the table.

Then, suddenly, the prisoner rolled his eyes and snivelled. 'Yes, of course I want to live! There's no reason I should die for them. They have never been very good to me. They know that I need money to smoke opium, but once they're done with me they just cast me aside like an old shoe. I've had enough of it! None of them was willing to risk coming to town, so they forced me to come, saying that since I was a bachelor, it didn't matter so much what happened to me. They promised me a big reward if I succeeded – maybe they would even find me a wife!'

'Who are "they"?' Uncle Pan asked.

At this the prisoner once again became evasive until Jiqing roared and again raised his massive fist.

'All right, all right, I'll tell you . . . They are Chumin, Duan Lianchen and 'The King of Hell' Mao Dehou . . .'

'So those devils are on the rampage once again,' Wang

Jiansheng said to Uncle Pan. 'It's probably because we've been dividing up their land and they're getting scared.' Then he looked the prisoner straight in the eye and raised his voice.

'Where are they now?'

'I don't know. Liu Qiyu went to see them and then told me to come to town.'

'So where's Liu Qiyu?' Pockmarks the Sixth asked.

Again the prisoner kept silent, merely glancing furtively at the surrounding company. Jiqing strode over to him and shook his fist violently in the wretched fellow's face. Then he pinched his left ear between his fingers, forcing him to twist his head to one side and cry out in pain.

'I'll tell you, I'll tell you! He's waiting for me at Ghost Cliff Gate.'

Ghost Cliff Gate was a place deep in the mountains some forty *li* from the county town. It was a place that most people had heard of, but very few had actually ventured there. Wang Jiansheng at once became alert and shot a meaningful glance at the rest of us; we all started as if we had received an electric shock.

'So he's there alone, is he?' Wang Jiansheng asked. 'Isn't he afraid of being attacked by jackals or, for that matter, having his soul stolen by ghosts?'

'Well, he's not quite alone . . .' Having uttered half the sentence, he swallowed the rest of it and then peered at us slyly, trying to decide whether or not we had noticed his indiscretion. Jiqing began pounding the table again and the teacup leapt an inch into the air. He looked severely straight at the startled prisoner, who lowered his head and mumbled, 'There are a few others . . .'

'What others?' Jiqing asked furiously, raising his fist again. 'If you tell us a single lie, I'll kill you!'

'I wouldn't dare!' replied the prisoner, casting an anxious glance at Jiqing. His face already looked red and swollen. 'They're some of the disbanded forces of the landlords' Order Preservation Corps. Liu Qiyu has secretly gathered some of

44

them together again and they're hiding up at Ghost Cliff Gate . . .'

He again paused to glance at the expression on each of our faces. At his, Pockmarks the Sixth stood up, gave him a kick on the backside and then went out to the front room to fetch a large stick for threshing grain. Tapping the prisoner on the forehead he said, 'So, they sent you here in order to spy on us before preparing for their night raid on the town. Isn't that right?'

Not daring to answer, the prisoner simply lowered his head.

'Well,' Wang Jiansheng said, 'It looks as if you're pretty stupid, allowing them to send you off to your death here! It would be an easy matter for us to beat you to death, but I think it'd be a waste of our energy. So we'll let you live, providing you do something in return to show that you appreciate it.'

Then, turning to Pockmarks the Sixth, he said, 'You can take him away now. He hasn't eaten yet, so if you've got some fresh fried dough-sticks, give him some and make sure he eats enough to get his strength back.'

At this the prisoner started kowtowing. Banging his head loudly on the floor, he said, 'Thank you! Thank you for your mercy! Just tell me what to do and I'll do it!'

After Pockmarks the Sixth had taken the prisoner away Uncle Pan said to Wang Jiansheng, 'I see what you're after. This is too good an opportunity to be missed. We'll deal with him tonight.' Then, he added, for the sake of Jiqing and me, 'You'd both better stay here, as there are still things that need to be discussed.'

Realizing what Uncle Pan meant, Wang Jiansheng smiled and went on his way. I knew that he still had a full day's work ahead of him.

Autumn was already turning into winter and the days were growing shorter. By five o'clock in the evening dusk was already beginning to fall. Pan Zaixing had organized an armed force of fifty men, led by Jiqing. Pan Zaixing himself had to stay behind to keep an eye on things in town, so he appointed

45

me to accompany Jiqing. When we set out it was already so dark that all we could see were the silhouettes of the trees and hills. At the head of our brigade, apart from Jiqing and myself, was the spy, whom we had taken along to act as our guide. We had to march briskly, and to make sure that he was able to do so, Pockmarks the Sixth had allowed him to swallow a couple of the opium tablets he carried around with him. Now he seemed much revived and could quite easily keep up with our pace.

We reached Ghost Cliff Gate just before midnight. Situated in a narrow valley between a range of bare hills, the place was, in fact nothing but a small cave opening onto the valley, which was littered with rocks and stones. Not a blade of grass grew there or on the surrounding hills and the only things that seemed to survive were a few solitary pines. The lack of fertile soil meant that no one lived near there and few people took any interest in the place. The entrance to the valley was fairly wide and we stopped there for a while to assess the lie of the land. Despite the murky darkness, we were able to see a few rocks further up the valley glistening in the starlight. We could now tell that the description of the place given to us by the spy was quite accurate.

'You're quite sure they are sleeping in the cave?' Jiqing asked him again. 'Can so many people really sleep in there?'

'Yes, at a squeeze,' the spy replied. 'It's even possible to squeeze in a few more. I've slept several nights there myself.'

'Is Liu Qiyu really their leader?' Jiqing asked.

'They all used to belong to the Order Preservation Corps and Liu Qiyu is the only person who can feed them and keep them together. Who else could be their leader?'

'All right then,' Jiqing said. 'You go and fetch Liu Qiyu out. And if you try to trick us, you know how we'll deal with you!'

Jiqing ordered me and three others to follow the spy at a distance and keep an eye on what he did, while he himself divided the force into three sections: one lying in wait on each side of the valley and the third guarding the entrance.

The spy walked towards the Ghost Cliff Gate, with us following stealthily behind, hidden by the darkness. Then, I heard voices drifting over from the entrance to the cave.

'So you're back!' somebody snapped. 'Commander Liu Qiyu has been waiting for your news. He was afraid that you'd got into trouble.'

'You're on guard duty tonight, are you?' the spy said. 'Go and fetch Commander Liu quickly so that I can give him my report.'

'Didn't you hear that splashing sound just now?' the guard asked. 'He just went out to relieve himself!'

At this I noticed a shadow to the left of the cave entrance. The spy quickly went over there and in a moment we heard another conversation drift towards us.

'Commander, I hurried back as quickly as I could. I managed to slip over the town wall at dusk. Before leaving I managed to get a good look at various parts of the town and at the four gates. I couldn't see any defences at all. There aren't many of them and they hardly have any guns between them.'

'That's excellent.' Commander Liu replied. 'All our men have had a good sleep and if we set out now, we should be able to get there before sunrise. Then we'll be able to catch them off their guard and wipe them out in one go, before they even have a chance to open their eyes!' Raising his voice he then shouted to the guard, 'Go into the cave and tell everyone to get up quickly, take their guns and come outside to receive their orders. We mustn't lose a minute!'

The 'commander' took a long time relieving himself. Even after giving his orders he still had not finished. I waited for the guard to disappear into the cave, and then quickly led the three men accompanying me up to where the 'commander' was standing. Before he had even had time to do up his trousers, I had got him round the throat, while another comrade silenced him with a hand over his mouth. Then we dragged him to the bottom of the valley. Jiqing, seeing what had happened, came down the hillside to meet us and at once gave Liu Qiyu a hard pinch on the back of the neck with his huge rough fingers. The 'commander' writhed in pain, just like Sun Wukong with the metal band on his head.* But since a hand was held firmly over his mouth, he could not utter a sound.

'Liu Qiyu, just you listen to me,' Jiqing said. 'We've got you now and there's no point even thinking of trying to escape! Your only way out now is to do something to atone for your crimes. Bring that evil band of yours out of the cave and tell them to lay down their arms. All right?'

Liu Qiyu was unable to say yes, as Jiqing continued to grip the back of his head and a hand was still clamped over his mouth. But Jiqing, sensing his compliance, shifted his grip and held him firmly by the scruff of the neck. Then he told us to take our hands away from Liu's mouth.

The 'commander' started speaking at once, almost involuntarily. 'I'll do it!' he cried.

Just as he had uttered this life-saving plea, his little band of men began to emerge from the entrance to the cave. When they were all together, the 'commander' began to issue new orders.

'Lay down your arms for the time being and come and listen to what I have to say!'

When the men reached him, they discovered a large, rough-looking fellow standing behind their commander, still holding him firmly by the scruff of his neck with one hand. Realizing instantly that things looked bad, some of the men turned to try and make an escape. But it was already too late. The men lying in wait on the hillsides rushed down and before they knew it had taken possession of all their rifles. 'Commander' Liu and

---

* Sun Wukong, the Monkey King, is a popular figure in Chinese mythology. In the famous *Journey to the West* he appears as a disciple to the Buddhist priest Tang Seng (Tripitaka). Whenever he gets up to his tricks, Tang Seng need only recite a magic formula and a metal band around Sun Wukong's head tightens, causing him excruciating pain.

his men were reduced to nothing but a motley, good-for-nothing gang, powerless without their weapons.

Having successfully completed our mission, we at once returned to the town. When we arrived, we locked our captives up in the Temple to the Fire God, and began questioning them about their connection with other secret landlord organizations. Liu Qiyu himself was interrogated separately by Uncle Pan, in order to discover more about the activities of the three landlords, Chumin, Duan Lianchen and Mao Dehou. Pan Zaixing at once set to work checking the guns and ammunition we had captured. Before long he was able to report his findings to Wang Jiansheng.

Wang Jiansheng lost no time in reporting the whole affair to Pan Xudong. The Special Regional Committee at once decided to expand its armed forces and set up a new battalion in the southern part of the county. Li Chengbao was appointed commander of this 'battalion', which actually had about fifty or sixty soldiers, as they only had this number of rifles. This was much the same situation as in other battalions.

The Special Regional Committee was very satisfied with our operation, as not a single bullet had been lost. Moreover, our success in luring the enemy out to the bottom of the valley and catching them unawares was a valuable lesson.

'The cave was so small and so crowded,' said Pan Xudong, representing the Special Regional Committee, 'that if you had started fighting there there would inevitably have been casualties on our side. You might even have had to resort to using your guns. Guns and ammunition are our most valuable possessions and we must treasure them like gold! Of course, there are times when we must use them. This is an armed struggle, after all, isn't it? It is precisely because of this struggle that we must preserve our weapons. The things we want to achieve are the very things which the landlords most bitterly oppose. We must get on with the task of redistributing the land. Comrade Jiansheng, you can now devote your energies to this task.'

Now Wang Jiansheng's new task became ever more demanding. That afternoon, Sister Apricot and Little Baldy left him to return to the village. Wang Jiansheng was too busy to see them off and so he asked me to walk part of the way with them instead. I accompanied them out of the town as far as the main road leading to Tanjiahe. From there they could find their own way home. When we parted, I said to Sister Apricot, 'Jiansheng asked me to tell you not to worry too much about him. He promises that he'll come and visit you as soon as he has the time, or bring you over to town again for a day or two.'

He really had said this to me and I had sensed that he felt uneasy passing all his family responsibilities over to his wife. Sister Apricot remained silent and merely wiped her eyes on her sleeve, which made them red, but she held back her tears. Finally she gave a deep sigh and said to herself, 'Will we ever be able to have a proper family life?'

CHAPTER 3

The notices announcing the Democratic Government's plans for land reform and its decision to expropriate the property of corrupt officials and landlords had been posted up for several days. These notices were issued in the name of Pan Xudong, who was now provisional chairman of the government. Everywhere, the notices attracted eager crowds. The Peasants' Union, which had been decimated during Chiang Kai-shek's wave of attacks on the Communist Party, now began to revive. The Democratic Government released whomsoever it could to assist in the re-establishment of the Peasants' Union. In this way it could also ensure the proper implementation of its policies. A spirit of excitement spread throughout the villages, very similar to the joyous atmosphere leading up to New Year.

But despite this, there was still a fair number of people who felt unmoved or resentful about all the excitement. Among them were the landlords Chumin, Duan Lianchen and Mao Dehou, who still wielded considerable force, and whose interests were represented by Chiang Kai-shek's government. This was all reported in the Nationalist newspapers; the latest copies had been obtained by scouts sent out by Uncle Pan. The papers announced that Chumin, Duan Lianchen and Mao Dehou had appointed themselves 'representatives of the people' and had sent a plea to the Nationalist Party to dispatch troops to 'wipe out the bandits'. Chiang Kai-shek, enraged by the news, at once ordered that forces should be mobilized to 'put an end to the uprising and restore national unity.'

From one point of view, this news was merely a reflection of the nervousness felt by Chiang Kai-shek and his supporters. The following day Pan Xudong held a meeting in which he outlined these points.

'This is a sign of further action to come,' he said. 'We managed to catch one spy, but far from being the end, I'm afraid this is only the start of our problems.'

'But we haven't been asleep all this time,' Uncle Pan said. 'I've been watching their movements all along. I would now like to report an important matter. Chang Je-an has just sent a messenger from Mazhen county. At the moment he's resting at my place. He wants me to tell the Special Regional Committee that the Nationalist forces at Mazhen county have been forcing the local villagers to make grass shoes* for them, as if they were preparing to march. They couldn't be preparing to withdraw to the Provincial Capital . . .'

Pan Xudong listened silently to this news without any sign of emotion. He swept us with his gaze as he did when there was a grave state of affairs. Pan Zaixing, Uncle Zizhong, Wang Jiansheng and others obviously felt the gravity of this news as well and glanced at one another without uttering a word. The silence was finally broken by Wang Jiansheng.

'There's no question that they are preparing to set out,' he said. 'But the real question is: where are they heading? Our government is at present engaged in destroying the basis of Chiang Kai-shek's support. So there's little doubt that their forces must be heading in our direction. They want to recapture this town, and Chumin's plea to the Nationalists was merely the start of this campaign.'

'I agree,' Pan Xudong said, nodding in agreement. 'What do you think, Comrade Zaixing?'

---

* Shoes woven out of straw, generally worn by peasants at work or soldiers on the march.

'I suggest that we enforce a curfew in the town before nightfall. The enemy have one division based in Mazhen county. Even if they only send a single regiment, it'll be as much as we can cope with. Altogether we have less than three hundred guns. They are several times stronger than us. In addition, people like Liu Qiyu and their followers are bound to come out of hiding again and cause trouble around the county.'

'But we can't just ignore them,' Uncle Pan and Uncle Zizhong put in.

'I know that,' said Pan Zaixing, 'but dealing with them is yet another burden for our already limited forces. However,' he went on, with added emphasis, 'we can't afford to give up the county town. Without the town we can no longer have our Democratic Government. What would the masses say to that? And what about Chang Je-an? The only reason he can continue his underground activities in Mazhen county is because he has us behind him.'

Pan Xudong's expression became even graver at this point. His silence was infectious and nobody uttered a word for a while. It was as if we were all waiting for him to solve an impossible riddle. Then Liu Dawang suddenly ran in, quite out of breath. He had originally been allocated to the First Army as a staff officer, but because of the mass movement amongst the peasants, he had been sent instead to the countryside to help organize the peasant volunteers. He looked agitated, and all eyes turned to look at him.

'We've caught two more spies!' he burst out. 'Both of them were sent here from the enemy's stronghold. After interrogation they eventually came out with the true story: Chumin and his gang are already gathering their remaining forces to back up the Nationalists' attack.'

At this point, Pan Xudong finally began to speak.

'This, and the news brought back by Je-an's scout, only go to show that the Nationalist commanders in Mazhen are preparing for a massive onslaught, aimed at destroying us and our government. Is Je-an's scout still here?'

'Yes,' Uncle Pan replied. 'But he'll leave as soon as he's eaten.'

'Good.' said Pan Xudong. 'I think we should enforce a curfew in the town at 4.30 this afternoon and at the same time mobilize the army and people throughout the county. I shall leave Wang Jiansheng in charge of military affairs, while Pan Zaixing will concentrate on the defence of the town. Does anyone have any comments?'

Probably because of the urgency of the situation, everyone felt anxious to get moving and at once complied with Pan Xudong's suggestions.

'Good.' Pan Xudong repeated. 'If there are no other comments, we'll take this as a collective decision and start carrying it out at once. Uncle Pan, could you and Zizhong ask Chang Je-an's scout to take this message to Mazhen county right away? Je-an should at once begin organizing the local peasant militia to sabotage the Nationalist forces – just as they did when we took the county town. They should start preparing at the same time that we begin enforcing the curfew.'

After this, we left and went our separate ways.

At a time like that, when it seemed that war might break out at any moment, my work as Wang Jiansheng's messenger placed even greater demands on my legs than usual. I was only really able to have a break from this job after half past four, when dusk began to fall and the city gates closed. Pan Zaixing himself kept the key to the gates and nobody was allowed to open them without his consent. Once the gates closed, I was free to take part in the defence operations. We only had about a hundred guns available for the defence of the town. Fifteen men were posted at each gate and the remaining forces were divided into two divisions: one posted on top of the wall to watch for the enemy and the other keeping guard in the streets. All the men kept their guns at the ready to give the appearance of strength and prevent anyone causing trouble in the town. I spent my time with Jiqing and three skilled marksmen, pacing the wall and looking out for incidents which should be reported to Pan Zaixing and Wang Jiansheng.

By about nine o'clock in the evening it was so dark that you could hardly see your hand. In the distance I could hear dogs barking, intermingled with a noise like a night watchman sounding the time on his bamboo clappers. But something about it told me that it was in fact the peasant volunteers' signal, warning the local people that enemies had been seen in the vicinity. After an hour or so, just as I had thought, I began to hear voices, at first very faint but growing louder as they approached. Then, all of a sudden they stopped. The sound of clappers and the barking had ceased too and the silence seemed intense.

'Listen!' Jiqing whispered. 'I thought I heard someone below the walls.'

He was just about to light a match to peer down when I grabbed his arm and whispered, 'I thought you had more experience than that! You don't want to give us away to the enemy, do you? I can see well in the dark. Let me have a look.'

Looking down, I saw two shadows creeping around beneath the wall. They were peering up towards the top of the wall with mouths agape. I pointed them out to Jiqing, who at once realized that they must be enemy spies. Quite coolly, he took stock of the two men. Then he took out two small knives and threw them at their gaping mouths. All we heard were two cries of pain and the sound of bodies falling to the ground. Then silence returned once again.

That the Nationalists were now sending spies on reconnaissance errands was only further proof that they were preparing to attack. I immediately ran off to Pan Zaixing and Wang Jiansheng's headquarters to report the incident.

'So it seems that Chang Je-an's underground forces cannot prevent the enemy from launching an attack on us,' Wang

Jiansheng said, more to himself than to us. 'They're on their way! We must go all out to defend ourselves against their attack.'

He then ordered Pan Zaixing to go out and inspect the defence preparations, while he himself went off to the Special Regional Committee to report to Pan Xudong. He asked me to stay in his headquarters meanwhile and report anything urgent to him at once.

That night, not one of the men engaged in defending the town was able to sleep a wink. But, perhaps because they had already realized we were on the alert, the Nationalist forces did not dare launch an attack, so the night passed peacefully without further incident.

Just as dawn was breaking, and a glow could be seen on the eastern horizon, Wang Jiansheng returned from the Special Regional Committee offices. He confirmed that the Nationalist attack was still imminent and that we must not be off our guard for an instant. He told me to go and find Pan Zaixing at once and pass this message on to him. I went out and found him not far from the north gate, inspecting the guards. Just then I noticed a man with two baskets suspended from a carrying-pole balanced on his shoulder. He asked the guard to open the gate as he said he wanted to leave the town. Pan Zaixing came over and told me to go and find out what was going on. If necessary, he said, the man should be arrested.

'I'm the cook for the volunteer force,' the carrier said, 'and I need to go out to buy turnips.'

'That's fine,' I replied. 'Just wait a bit. The time for the gates to open has changed. Now they open at eight o'clock. You just rest a while.'

I motioned to the guards to keep an eye on him until I had reported the matter to Uncle Pan, who would no doubt send someone to question the man. I then continued with Pan Zaixing on his inspection of the gates, and we came across a similar incident at the south gate. A man carrying a bundle over his shoulder said that he needed to leave the town early, as he wanted to set off on his way to the Big City, many miles down-river. When he asked the guards to open the gates, they told him that they could not, under any circumstances, open them before eight o'clock, and would he please wait until then. The man turned to leave, but the guards stopped him and told him to sit down on a nearby stone, so they could keep an eye on him.

'Well, you must admit they've done pretty well, sending in all those spies,' Pan Zaixing said. 'They obviously reckoned that we were too busy – and too inexperienced – to notice them all. Well, it seems they were at least partly right, otherwise how could so many spies have slipped in? And they even dare to ask us to open the gates early! Perhaps those spies are really their advance guard, and they have already positioned their forces just outside, ready to storm the town as soon as the gates are opened . . .'

'You're right!' I said, suddenly realizing the truth in his argument. 'Last night while I was up on the wall I heard the sound of the volunteers beating warning signals on their clappers. But before long the sound stopped. Perhaps the Nationalist forces moved across last night, trampling and killing our outer defences as they went!'

'Aya! How could we have been so careless?' Pan Zaixing said, but before he had finished speaking, we heard a volley of gunfire coming from outside the gates. It was only twenty past six and, as Pan Zaixing had predicted, the enemy were already just outside the gates and were beginning their assault on the town. We immediately climbed up on to the walls and saw that the enemy were attacking the west and south gates – concentrating their main force against the latter. There were nearly 100 men trying to break through there, at the weakest part of the wall. Pan Zaixing looked down and cried out in horror.

'It looks as if they want to wipe us out in one go! They must be at least ten times stronger than us!'

He hurried back down to the foot of the wall and quickly made his way to the south gate to take command of the guards

57

who were trying to defend it. At his instructions, I remained on the wall to keep a watch on the Nationalist forces, ready to report any new developments. Meanwhile, I asked four volunteers of about my own age to pass on information to the various commanders.

The enemy forces multiplied rapidly at the south gate. It was clear that they had massed their main force at this point. I could see them shooting wildly into the town to provide cover for their assault force, which was rapidly climbing the wall on ladders. Then I saw Wang Jiansheng at the head of Commander Pan Mingxun's thirty-strong battalion rushing towards the south gate. Pan Mingxun leapt up on to the wall and opened fire, just as the first of the enemy soldiers were climbing over the top of the wall. Three members of the assault force fell from their ladders and rolled to the ground. Then Wang Jiansheng climbed up behind Pan Mingxun and, taking cover behind the battlements, he sized up the Nationalist commander below, who was shouting and gesticulating madly at his troops. He took aim with his revolver, moved his finger to the trigger and fired at the commander's forehead. The commander fell to the ground instantly and the assault force at once ceased its attempts to mount the wall.

Then, not far from me, one of Pan Mingxun's men threw a hand grenade out over the wall. The grenade was old and failed to explode, but despite this, the enemy clearly felt that their position was too vulnerable and they began to retreat.

All remained peaceful until about three o'clock that afternoon, when the enemy again launched a mad assault on the town. This time they concentrated on the west gate, and instead of attempting to climb the walls, they attacked the gate itself. They piled straw against the gate and tried to set fire to it. As the gate was covered with a layer of iron, it did not catch fire easily. What was more, the straw, which they had plundered from nearby farms, did not make a good blaze and burnt out within minutes.

When we realized what they were doing, we concentrated

our defences on the west gate. Although we had very few hand grenades, it was decided that the situation was grave enough for all of them to be used against the enemy. Whenever they neared the wall, they were greeted by a hail of grenades. This continued until nightfall, when they finally decided to pull back and camp in a circle around the town.

By this time, the two agents sent in by the landlords, in collusion with the enemy army, had not only been exposed, but were safely under lock and key. But there must have been a few more agents lurking in the town whom we hadn't yet discovered. The lull in the fighting gave them the opportunity to spread rumours about how the gates would be burnt down sooner or later, and how it would be better to let the civilians out of the town before there was fighting in the streets.

Faced with this, Pan Xudong decided to take advantage of the temporary truce to hold an emergency meeting. Several important measures were agreed: we would encourage the citizens of the town to report all enemy agents; we would send people to talk to all the townsfolk and prevent them from panicking; the newly established Workers' Scouts and Citizens' Volunteer Brigade would be fully mobilized to help defend the town walls; and the four gates were to be bricked up on our side and the gate towers kept supplied with water to put out the fires. That evening, the townspeople discovered three more enemy agents. The situation was so desperate that, the defence headquarters decided to have them executed at once.

The following morning, just as day was breaking, the Nationalists renewed their assault on the town. Their soldiers had managed to get hold of dry cotton stalks and pine branches from neighbouring peasant homesteads. This time, they concentrated their efforts on the north gate. Our guards climbed up and threw a grenade from the gate tower. It exploded in the midst of the Nationalist soldiers who were busy carrying branches. The branches caught fire, burning many of the soldiers, who scattered in terror. The guards on the gate, taking advantage of the confusion, started shooting and killed a handful of enemy soldiers. At this the Nationalists' forces fell to pieces and they could do nothing but retreat and once again form a circle around the town.

Meanwhile, inside the town morale was very high. Our defence strategy was working well, and all the enemy agents had been rounded up. There was an atmosphere of confidence, displayed on almost every face, and the townsfolk took tea and cakes to the guards to keep their spirits up. Lao Liu and his assistant Ho Shuoru were particularly active, going around thanking people who had brought things to the guards. Wherever they went they made little impromptu speeches about the epic revolutionary spirit of the people. Ho Shuoru, who was usually rather shy in front of so many people, became infected by Lao Liu's enthusiasm. In his excitement, he would break in with a few simple words of encouragement, unable to hold back his emotions any longer.

In all this commotion there was only one person who appeared completely unruffled. This was Peng Wanzhen, who joined us in the street, attracted by the noise and acitivity. Walking along behind Lao Liu and Ho Shuoru, she seemed quietly moved by their passion and vigour. Perhaps she was thinking about how her husband, Huang Zhuqing, would have participated in this struggle had he still been at her side. There was no doubt that she felt deeply affected by these great events, but because of the memories they evoked, she was unable to express her feelings. Instead, she wrote down what was happening, as she was convinced of its historical significance. When she was making these notes she appeared even more unruffled than usual. In contrast to the activity and excitement around her, Ho Shuoru thought she looked exceptionally beautiful.

She would occasionally pass Ho Shuoru a little slip of paper. After reading the note, Ho Shuoru would put it carefully away in his breast pocket and nod cheerfully at Peng Wanzhen, before continuing with lofty words of praise and encouragement to the townsfolk. Peng Wanzhen's notes no doubt recorded the crowd's reaction and would be useful for future propaganda work. She had really thrown herself into this work with great enthusiasm, even though she kept a low profile. Her silent encouragement was a constant source of inspiration for Ho Shuoru, whose words flowed with more vigour than ever.

Pan Zaixing and Pan Xudong also felt elated when they saw them together.

'Isn't it wonderful to see how well such educated people can co-operate with country folk like us?' Pan Zaixing commented.

'People with learning are better able to see the truth,' Pan Xudong replied, 'so they are quicker in changing their outlook. Ho Shuoru has really come a long way – though Peng Wanzhen seems to have adapted herself even more quickly.'

'What a fine team we've got!'

At this moment yet another burst of gunfire echoed from the top of the wall, followed by a loud explosion, as another hand grenade was thrown down at the enemy soldiers. Pan Zaixing stopped to listen and then went on, 'On the whole everything's going well. The only real problem is our shortage of guns and ammunition. The longer we have to fight, the less ammunition we have – but whatever happens, we must go on defending the town . . .'

Uncle Pan, who was inspecting the defence operations, happened to be passing.

'There's no need to worry,' he said. 'Tonight I'm sending two scouts out to inform all our forces on duty in other districts of the situation here, and tell them to return here at once to support us.'

'Who are you going to send?' Wang Jiansheng asked. 'They'd better be the most sharp-witted we've got!'

'One of them is Feng Xinshun from Pheasant Nest,' Uncle Pan replied. 'I had him transferred here when I was short of people. He's ready to undertake top-secret work and because he looks so clumsy, nobody is likely to suspect him. The other

61

is Hao Baomin, a youngster who has just finished his training. He's sharp and alert and he and Feng should make a good team, like father and son. They've both been quick and efficient in the past.'

'How are they going to get out, with the town so tightly surrounded?' Pan Zaixing asked.

'There's always a way!' Uncle Pan replied. 'We could let them down over the wall with a rope.'

'That's one way,' Pan Xudong said. 'But we must think of every possibility . . . If only we could tell our other forces to come back quickly, we could open up the gates ourselves and begin a counter-attack from two sides.' A smile of hope spread across his face at the thought.

I left them and returned to my duties at the other end of town. The weak winter sun was already slanting towards the west and a chilly evening breeze began to blow, bringing a slight feeling of melancholy. I found Jiqing busy surveying the movements of the Nationalist forces.

Pointing at a heap of earth outside the walls, he said, 'Look, the enemy are busy digging cooking pits. It looks as if they plan to sit it out until we starve to death! They know that we're short of ammunition and they'll just try to wear us down. I can't think what we can do to speed things up a bit . . .'

Keeping his eyes trained on the Nationalist soldiers setting up camp in the distance, he became thoughtful for a while. Their cooking pits were soon finished and we could see the flickering of camp-fires.

Suddenly Jiqing came out of his trance and whispered through his teeth, 'Right, you sons of turtles! You just see if we don't deal with you sooner or later!'

We watched the sun sinking below the horizon. The land-scape before us turned black as lacquer, broken only by the occasional flicker of light from the enemy camp. In order to give the impression that we were stronger than we really were, we had placed lamps along the battlements. The Nationalists could not see our soldiers, as they were hidden behind the battlements, but they would get the impression that we were highly organized and well prepared. In addition, we kept all our 'guns' pointing outwards – though in fact quite a number of them were wooden replicas intended to fool the enemy. We were on 'standing duty' until dawn and had to eat our supper on the wall. We were about to eat some pancakes sent up by the townsfolk, when Wang Jiansheng appeared with a patrol made up of three members of the Workers' Scouts. He was going round inspecting the defences while keeping on the look out for any new movements in the enemy camp. He patted us both warmly on the shoulder.

'Aren't you feeling sleepy?' he asked. 'Keeping awake can be a struggle in itself!'

'We're not in the least bit sleepy,' I replied. 'In fact, we're feeling pretty energetic. It's you who should have a sleep. Don't worry. If anything happens, I'll report it to you at once. So why don't you go and have a rest?'

'I'm afraid there's little chance of that tonight,' Wang Jiansheng replied. 'I've got to keep alert, just like you. It may look as if the Nationalists are keeping quiet, but who knows what plans they've got? This might just be the calm before the storm. We can't afford to be off our guard for a minute!'

Then he and his patrol went on their way.

As night drew on, the stars appeared one by one, making it possible to pick out the outlines of silent shapes in the dark landscape. We began to make out shadows moving towards us, first in little groups but then in a great mass of men, moving step by step towards the wall. We knew what this meant. The Nationalists were closing in, in order to make a final assault upon the Democratic Government of Workers and Peasants. At once the town seemed electrified, as everyone prepared themselves for the fight.

Just as we had thought, the Nationalists began their attack, concentrating this time on the north gate – right beneath where Jiqing was standing. Under cover of darkness, they began piling kindling against the gates, while letting off their rifles in several different places to divert our attention. To save our scarce ammunition, we ordered our men to hold out as long as possible without firing, while the Workers' Scouts led them in the ancient chorus 'Ah . . . he . . . Ah . . . he!' which used to be sung during inter-clan fights to scare the opposing side. The town people came out to join in the shouting. The roar seemed to shake the hills and engulf the entire town.

Jiqing, however, seemed unmoved by this uproar and kept silent as ever. Clenching his fists, he carefully assessed the position of the enemy soldiers who were piling wood against the gates. Then, taking out a hand grenade which he had kept in reserve, he threw it into their midst. There was a loud explosion, for an instant drowning the sounds of shooting and chanting, and I could see flesh and blood flying in all directions.

After the explosion, the Nationalists stopped shooting, as if they were waiting for something. In this split-second silence, we suddenly became aware of another sound, at the enemy's rear. It was a roar, even greater than the last, like a mighty wave moving in on the enemy.

The roar became louder and louder, turning into an earth-shaking thundering. Then we heard the thud of guns and cannon. The Nationalist troops, quite unprepared for this turn of events, were thrown into a frenzy. As the roaring at their rear drew closer and closer, their panic grew. At this moment, Pan Zaixing appeared on the gate-tower, clutching a pistol.

'Open the gates!' he ordered the guards. 'Pursue the enemy!'

The gates were opened and our forces, together with members of the Workers' Scouts, flooded out, clutching any weapons they could lay their hands on. The enemy, already in disorder, and, with no will to fight, hastily drew back, each soldier trying to save his own life. Our own chanting joined with the roar behind the enemy, who were so terrified they surrendered immediately. Our fighters, excited by their success, took more interst in the guns dropped by the retreating soldiers than in the soldiers themselves. As they stopped to grab the abandoned weapons, most of the enemy soldiers managed to escape.

The same thing happened with the peasant forces who had been pursuing the Nationalists from behind. We only realized this after the battle was over, by which time it was already too late. If only we had taken the Nationalist soldiers prisoner, the number of guns captured would have been far greater. As it was, our total haul of guns was little over a hundred.

This 'attack from both sides' happened partly by chance and partly by design. We learned that the Nationalist forces had caused immense suffering to the local peasants in the area around the town, stealing their grain, pigs, goats and firewood, and even molesting their women. The peasants, infuriated by these abuses, got together and organized a volunteer force which eventually joined up with our armies on duty in other parts of the county. At the same time, by chance, Chang Je-an's troops from Mazhen county were in hot pursuit of the Nationalists, but were unable to intercept them due to their vastly superior forces. However, they soon joined up with the newly formed volunteer force, and Chang Je-an himself was immediately appointed Commander-in-Chief. His first decision was to change their tactics, and instead of making minor incursions from the rear, they would launch a sudden major assault from behind. The result, as we saw, was that the Nationalists were thrown into complete disarray and their attack on our town came to nothing.

That afternoon, the Democratic Government organized a great victory celebration for the masses. An atmosphere of excitement and rejoicing filled the whole town. The only person who seemed less than exuberant was Uncle Pan, who squatted beneath a tree and did not utter a word. It emerged that one of the scouts he had sent out the previous night, Hao Baomin, had been discovered while trying to get through the enemy encirclement and had been killed on the spot. Uncle Pan was mourning him. I went over to him, fully understanding how he must feel, but I could find no words to comfort him. In the end, the best I could do was repeat a sentence I had once heard Pan Xudong utter. 'If you want to make revolution, sacrifice is unavoidable . . .'

Eventually, however, the sounds of rejoicing drew Uncle Pan out of his depression and, with an effort, he managed to brighten up a little. Screwing up his eyes, he watched Ho Shuoru, the intellectual from The Big City, waving his hand in the air and joining in the shouting with the town people and the peasants. Peng Wanzhen, standing motionless at his side, was as calm and quiet as ever.

'You go over and talk to them,' Uncle Pan said. 'See what they think of it all. You needn't worry about me – I'd rather just sit quietly beneath this tree.'

I found Ho Shuoru and Peng Wanzhen, heads lowered, deep in some private conversation. It seemed they had a lot to say to one another. The crowds were now beginning to disperse, but the two of them stood there, showing no sign of leaving. As I came up, they smiled at me. Ho Shuoru patted me warmly on the shoulder, as if I were his younger brother. Our relationship had been transformed and we were now true 'comrades'. Peng Wanzhen, too, already thought of me as a close friend and the two of them continued their conversation, unperturbed by my presence.

'When I was in the city, I could never have imagined such a thing as this,' Ho Shuoru said. 'Now the tables have really been turned!'

'Yes, but this is quite a natural development,' Peng Wanzhen replied. 'Had it not been for the brutality of Chiang Kaishek and the warlords, I don't think things would have happened so quickly.'

'Nevertheless,' Ho Shuoru went on, 'the masses are so highly motivated that I can't help feeling excited myself. Just now, when I raised my hand and shouted those slogans, I had no idea what I was doing – I was just swept along by the crowd! this is another thing I'd never imagined before.'

'Well, I feel rather as if I were in a dream too,' Peng Wanzhen said. 'Except that this dream is different from yours. I can see myself in the dream and however hard I try, I can't bring myself to raise my hand or shout slogans. This dream is just a lesson for me. And the fact that you and I have been together throughout is in itself a dream. Don't you think so?'

This conversation seemed most mysterious and abstruse to me and I had the feeling that it was not really meant for my ears. Just as I was about to slip away, Peng Wanzhen, sensing my discomfort, stopped me and said, 'Don't go. I've been hoping to have a chance to talk to you. I'm afraid that ever since I got involved in this work with Lao Liu and Ho Shuoru, I've had no time to think about you. It's really bad of me . . .'

I laughed and replied, 'Do you mean you still worry about such things at a time like this?'

'However busy we are, we shouldn't forget our feelings,' she replied. 'At least, I can't! I've never seen your mother, but Zhuqing used to speak of her most warmly. I really should go and visit her and let her know how I've been getting on.'

'I know she thinks a lot about you, even though you've never met,' I said.

'Well,' Peng suggested, 'maybe I should go and see her right away.'

'What a good idea!' I said. 'She'll be delighted!'

'Now that the fighting's over, there shouldn't be so much to do for the time being,' she went on. 'I'm sure you can manage without me for a while, can't you, Shuoru?'

'We certainly cannot!' Ho Shuoru replied. 'Your work is quite indispensable! But, on the other hand, I agree that you should go and see Chunsheng's mother. And I'm sure that Lao Liu will agree too.'

'Well, in that case,' I said, 'I'll take you up there myself. Mother is bound to be worried about me after all that has happened. You can also rest a few days in Red Hill Village.'

'I think that would be good,' Ho Shuoru agreed. 'But there is one thing I insist on, and that is that I accompany her myself.

I'm already quite familiar with Wanzhen's needs. Her health isn't all that good, you see, and she really should have someone to look after her.'

Peng Wanzhen could not help casting a meaningful smile at Ho Shuoru. Then she nodded and said, 'You're right. There's nobody who can look after me as well as you. I'm afraid I'm really too weak to cope with all this alone.'

'There are always ways of coping!' Ho Shuoru said with determination.

We left for Red Hill Village that very afternoon and went to see my mother and Grandpa Whiskers, the old man of whom everyone always talked so affectionately.

After being forced to retreat, the thousand-odd Nationalist soldiers fled back to Mazhen county. Chang Je-an led the enlarged peasant forces in pursuit of the enemy, chasing them right up to the edge of the county town. The soldiers of the garrison, who had stayed to guard the town, were frightened by the sorry state of their returning comrades and dared not come out.

Chang Je-an took this opportunity to greatly expand the scale of the peasant movement in Mazhen by co-ordinating his movement with the underground organization, which partly came out into the open. The result of this was that the area controlled by the Democratic Government of Workers and Peasants effectively doubled in size. Government officials and citizens of our county town began to feel more secure. This feeling was summed up well by the ditty, 'One of Chiang Kai-shek's regiments dares not fight us; two regiments cannot break in; they would never find enough people for a whole division!'

This saying became popular almost overnight. It not only reassured the citizens of the county town, but also helped to set at ease the minds of the peasants throughout the county. This did not escape Pan Xudong, who paid a special visit to Wang Jiansheng.

'I'm afraid,' he said, 'that this ditty might have the effect of numbing the senses. Extra vigilance is essential, especially when it comes to your task of organizing the redistribution of land, which is very likely to be opposed by the landlords.'

'Yes,' Wang Jiansheng replied, 'I've been thinking about this problem too. I'm planning to hand over my military responsibilities to Pan Zaixing for the time being, so that I can go and supervise the redistribution of land myself.'

The next day, before Wang Jiansheng set out for the villages to supervise this work, Sweet Potato arrived back from 'The Big City', carrying copies of several provincial newspapers. These reported that 'Chiang Kai-shek was shocked and furious when he received news of the successes scored by the Democratic Government of Workers and Peasants and he swore to pull it out by the roots'. In the past, he had underestimated the strength of the peasant forces and so he had now decided to allocate larger forces to the attainment of this end.

That afternoon, before he went to the countryside, Wang Jiansheng took me to visit Uncle Zizhong and Uncle Pan to see if they had any more information. It so happened that they had just been listening to the report from a young scout from the countryside. The scout was covered from head to foot in dust and his eyelids were dropping as if he had travelled through the night without sleep.

Uncle Zizhong sent him off to have a good meal and a proper sleep. Then, turning to us, he said, 'Will you be going to the countryside?'

'Yes,' Wang Jiansheng replied. 'Now that things are more stable we must make the most of the chance and press ahead with our land distribution work. Last night Pan Xudong and I discussed this and came to a decision. Most peasants have joined the revolution in hope that it might solve the problem of land, so this must be the Democratic Government's first priority.'

'That's right!' Uncle Zizhong replied. 'All our efforts are aimed at bringing about the right conditions for this. But the struggle has barely begun. That scout whose report we were listening to was sent here from Mazhen county by Chang Je-an. Apparently, enemy troops are now on their way from the Provincial Capital to Mazhen county. Chiang Kai-shek is planning a large-scale attack. Never before in Chinese history has there been a government of workers and peasants, with its own army and a policy of land distribution like our own. This is bound to have a huge effect on the whole country – perhaps even on the whole world! How can Chiang Kai-shek possibly sleep soundly any more?'

Wang Jiansheng gave a start when he heard this news and muttered to himself, 'Well, it looks as if we won't be able to go to the countryside for the time being after all . . .' Turning to me, he said, 'Quickly go and fetch Pan Zaixing and Liu Dawang so that I can discuss the situation with them and make some plans.'

Up to now Liu Dawang had been busy providing supplies for our forces. Wang Jiansheng's request that he come and talk to us showed how seriously he was taking the military situation.

'First I'll go over to the headquarters to tell Pan Xudong that Pan Zaixing and Liu Dawang will be along shortly,' I said.

Uncle Pan and I left together. Just as we were going out, I turned my head to see Wang Jiansheng and Uncle Zizhong staring blankly at one another. Both men seemed to be posing the question: what should the next move be?

CHAPTER 4

During the emergency meeting chaired by Pan Xudong it was decided that for the time being Wang Jiansheng should not go to the countryside, but should remain in the town to set up a new defence committee. Wang Jiansheng, Pan Zaixing and Liu Dawang, the three members of this committee, would now be on duty day and night and I, of course, would have to be with them. The scout sent by Chang Je-an should return at once to Mazhen to convey our decision, so that Chang Je-an could take what measures he could to halt the progress of the Nationalist troops.

This time, however, the Nationalists started their campaign before we had had time to make proper preparations. They made the first move, proving that Chiang Kai-shek was anxious to have us wiped out as quickly as possible. That very night, when I was on duty, I suddenly heard the sound of shooting outside the town. Wang Jiansheng and Pan Zaixing were busy discussing their defence strategy by the light of an oil lamp. As soon as they heard the shooting, they stopped talking and listened intently for a few seconds. Intermingled with this sound was the heavy thud of cannon, resounding like distant thunder.

'It looks as if Chiang Kai-shek has sent a big army this time,' Pan Zaixing said. 'No ordinary army would have those sort of guns!'

They paused to listen a few seconds longer. Then Wang

Jiansheng said, 'Yes, you're right. It sounds as if it's one of the main Nationalist armies. After their defeat when they tried to besiege us, they must have decided to try to finish us off!'

As if to emphasize Wang Jiansheng's words, the sound of cannon now became even louder.

Pan Zaixing pulled out his revolver and rushed out, closely followed by Wang Jiansheng and myself, grabbing our guns as we went. There was already a frenzy of activity in the streets as our troops and the Workers' Scouts picked up their weapons and headed out of town in the direction of the disturbance. Pan Zaixing took control of the situation and had reinforcements sent to the guards at all four gates. The Workers' Scouts were meanwhile scrambling up on to the walls to observe the movements of the Nationalist troops. All members of the Democratic Government ran to the points of the wall which had the least defences, to reinforce the soldiers and Workers' Scouts. Shopkeepers, awakened by the noise, threw open their doors and rushed out with lamps, candles and tea, lighting the dark streets so that the defence brigades could find their way.

From their vantage point on the wall, Pan Zaixing and Wang Jiansheng watched the progress of the enemy troops and gave their orders. I stood at their side, helping to pass on their commands. All around the town the ground was black with enemy troops – it seemed we were completely surrounded. In the distance we could see the flicker of flames, which lit up the sky with clouds of red smoke.

'See those fires over there?' Wang Jiansheng said. 'They're killing the peasants and burning down the villages, so as to wipe out the Peasant Volunteers. That way there will be no one left to help us defend the town!'

At this moment, Pan Xudong arrived with Uncle Pan and Liu Dawang. Glancing at the spectacle before us, Pan Xudong said, 'This time Chiang Kai-shek has really made up his mind to beat us! This army must be at least twice the size of the last. Well, let him try his best – we'll see if he can wipe us out!'

No sooner had he spoken than a shell hit the ramparts close by, and we had to rush for cover. Then Pan Xudong took another look out to assess the situation. By this time, the Nationalist strategy was evident: their main point of attack was to be our south gate, where they were concentrating their assault force and their heavy artillery. Pan Zaixing and Liu Dawang rushed down to direct the reinforcement of the south gate Pan Xudong and Wang Jiansheng also left their positions on the wall to command the overall defence of the town.

The enemy fire was intensifying. Flames could already be seen just outside the gates. This time, the Nationalists were not trying to burn down the gates, but were burning the houses of all the people living around the town, as if they were carrying out a scorched earth policy. By waging war against the local people and laying the land to waste, the revolution would be halted in its tracks.

Now they started shelling the town from the south gate. Shops and stalls were wrecked and a large number of civilians were injured. The angry shouts of the townsfolk soon turned into cries of pain and anguish. There was only one primitive clinic in the town and it was ill-equipped to cope with all the casualties. People began panicking and disorder spread rapidly. By about four o'clock, when day began to break, the situation was well out of control.

At this point, in order to prevent further civilian casualties and to conserve what was left of our strength, Pan Xudong decided to pull out our entire forces and retreat to Tanjiahe while it was still dark. There were very few of our troop at Tanjiahe at that time and they had probably gone unnoticed by the Nationalists. When Wang Jiansheng announced this decision, Lao Liu mustered his propaganda team to explain the wisdom of this move to the people. Both townsfolk and soldiers quickly realized that this was the only way we could prevent the enemy from wiping us out completely.

Now that we had a plan of action, everyone's spirits revived and we all set to work. Pan Zaixing was in command of the break-out. He led a small but fearless team of fighters to open the way. Our sources told us that the Nationalists were weakest at the north gate, so we concentrated our attention there, leaving a few of our soldiers at the other gates to distract the enemy's attention. During this apparent lull in the fighting, the guards at the north gate suddenly threw the gates open. Pan Zaixing and his break-out brigade swept each side of the gate with gunfire, opening up the way for us. Our forces poured out behind them, slashing to left and right with their bayonets. Before long, however, the way was blocked by Nationalist soldiers and we had to resort to hand-to-hand combat. Our break-out became so dangerous and difficult that every step we took was paved with sacrifice.

After breaking through, Pan Zaixing and his team returned to the fray to assist the soldiers and civilians still caught in the fighting. They did this six times and eventually managed to get Wang Jiansheng, me and some members of the Democratic Government to safety. Their forays, however, soon attracted the attention of the Nationalist soldiers, who concentrated their fire on Pan Zaixing himself. As the bullets struck home, blood poured from his chest. Undaunted, clutching one hand to his chest, he kept firing, until the two enemy soldiers on his heels had been shot down.

In order to disperse the fire of the enemy troops, we split up into groups and started heading in different directions. Wang Jiansheng and I stuck together to take care of Pan Zaixing. In front of us was a small temple. We rushed behind it to take cover from the bullets. Not far from this temple was a little wood. We managed to make our way towards it unnoticed by the enemy.

By this time Pan Zaixing was too weak to walk any further and we needed to think fast if we were to save his life. Our original plan to go to Tanjiahe was now impossible. Carrying Pan Zaixing between us, Wang Jiansheng and I came to the foot of a little hill. Close by was a long, narrow gorge. By this time the sound of firing seemed far away. We followed a little rain-washed, pebble-strewn path along the edge of the gorge. It was hard going because the path was choked with grass and bushes, but at least they provided cover from the enemy. The gorge became narrower and narrower until it finally petered out and we found ourselves surrounded by high hills. We started climbing. The hills here were bare, and save for an occasional hawk circling overhead, not a living creature was to be seen. The fighting seemed a distant thing of the past – our only real concern now was Pan Zaixing's condition. Mustering all his remaining strength, he made not so much as a murmur as we carried him up those hills. But his face was already white and there was little doubt that he was nearing his last breath.

Somewhere around midday, we reached the bottom of a steep cliff jutting out from the hillside. Not far from here, amongst a group of pine trees, we discovered two little grass huts. Thinking that they must be inhabited, we made our way towards them.

As we had expected, there was a family living there. Looking us up and down, they seemed to guess that something had been happening in the town and that we were somehow involved . Without asking any questions, they made a bed for Pan Zaixing in their inner room and let the three of us rest there. A middle-aged woman, her skin dark and chapped, hurriedly brought us warm water to wash Pan Zaixing's wounds. Lying on the bed, Pan Zaixing made no sound of suffering, though it was obvious from his face that it took great determination to bear the pain. He stared at us as if he had something to say, but could not bring the words to his lips.

The head of the household, whose skin was as brown and weathered as his wife's, stood to one side watching us. When he saw Pan Zaixing's pained, yet steadfast countenance, he too seemed to feel something of the pain. Rubbing his hands together, he seemed at a bit of a loss.

'Do you have any medicine to stop the pain, friend?' Wang Jiansheng asked.

'I'm a charcoal-burner,' the fellow replied. 'I only ever go out in winter to sell charcoal, so I'm afraid I don't have anything like that. But this has its advantages. The Nationalists know that we're poor and don't bother us at all. We're just like wild hares up here – nobody really takes any notice of us.'

'What? So you know about how the Nationalists make the poor suffer?' Wang Jiansheng asked. 'I thought you just said that they didn't bother about this mountain area.'

'That's right,' the man replied, 'but in winter I still have to go to town to sell my charcoal. Most people can't afford it and the officials always insist on low prices. And as for the soldiers – they just take your charcoal without paying for it!'

At this the woman, who had not uttered a word until now, suddenly started talking excitedly.

'A long time ago a young fortune-teller came up here. He came especially to tell the fortunes of poor people. He talked a lot about the Nationalists and their officials and told us that so long as they were in power, the poor would never be able to improve their lot. He really spoke a lot of sense! Later he came to visit us twice and stayed overnight. This time, he told us that there was a revolutionary party which was meant to help the poor . . .'

'That's right!' the charcoal-burner went on. 'Not long ago I went to town to sell charcoal and found that the revolutionaries had taken over there. They were a lot more honest and polite than the Nationalists. But because of this, it was said that the Nationalists planned to send an army to beat them. You must be revolutionaries escaping from the Nationalist soldiers!'

Rather than answering him directly, Wang Jiansheng asked a question.

'Do you know the name of that young fortune-teller?' he asked.

'Later, when we got to know him better, he told us his name,' the woman replied. 'His family name was Chang . . . but I can't remember what his given name was.'

Wang Jiansheng nodded. I, too, guessed that this might have been Chang Je-an. It was as if a weight had been taken off our minds – we were now, at last, in a safe place.

'If you don't have any medicine in the house,' Wang Jiansheng said, 'do you think you might be able to find us a doctor?'

After thinking for a while, the charcoal-burner exclaimed, 'Yes, there is one! Brother Qui Mingtai specializes in curing wounds. I'll go and fetch him at once! He'll have medicine from the town. Just wait here and I'll go right away!'

As he was about to leave, he turned to his wife and said, 'There's some brown sugar in that earthenware pot on the family altar. Make some sugar-water for the patient. There are also a couple of sweet potatoes in the fire. Give them to our guests – they must be hungry.'

Neither of us felt like eating. We just stayed at Pan Zaixing's side, watching over him – watching his eyes which, though immobile, seemed full of meaning and expression; his face suddenly seemed to have lost its colour. Thoughts surged through our heads and words flooded to our lips, but we lacked strength to utter them.

All Wang Jiansheng could say was, 'This is just a temporary measure. We'll beat them in the end . . . we'll definitely beat them!'

Pan Zaixing's mouth quivered as if he was about to say something. Unable to bring the words to his lips, he smiled faintly. I could guess what he had wanted to say: yes, we will certainly beat them!

By two or three o'clock that afternoon Doctor Qui Mingtai, the 'doctor who specialized in curing wounds' arrived. He was a short man, as thin and wasted as the charcoal-burner, but his deep set eyes, small as black beans and typical of the hill people, seemed alive with concentrated energy. He made straight for the inner room and his sharp little eyes flew to Pan Zaixing. No doubt the charcoal-burner had already briefed him on Pan Zaixing's condition and he at once squatted by his side to examine the wound.

'Quickly bring me some water, Sister Jia Hongcai,' he said, turning to the charcoal-burner's wife. Then, continuing with his examination, he muttered to himself, 'The bastards! They're really vicious . . .'

Cursing the Nationalists under his breath, he took a pair of scissors, a needle and thread and three little packets of herbal medicine out of his cloth bag. When the charcoal-burner's wife brought in a bowl of warm water, he started dabbing the wounds with cotton wool. By this time, Pan Zaixing had lost consciousness. His eyes were closed and his face had turned yellow. Doctor Qui Mingtai stopped his work and he stood up as if dazed.

'He's already cold,' he whispered. 'He's lost too much blood. Even if I'd come earlier, there wouldn't have been much I could have done for him . . . Oh, those bastards!'

Packing up his bag, he got ready to leave, but Wang Jiansheng stopped him and said, 'I'm sorry to have brought you all this way. We must give you some sort of payment. Just tell us where you live and we'll see that your fee is sent to you.'

'But I haven't even cured the wound,' the doctor protested. 'How can I think of receiving any payment? And even if I had been able to find a cure, I wouldn't have wanted any payment from you. You are from the revolutionary army – and this wounded man looks like an officer.'

'Yes,' I said, 'he is an officer of the revolutionary army. He was wounded last night while leading a break-out force from the town.'

'But he was really a poor tenant farmer,' Wang Jiansheng explained. 'When the Peasants' Union was formed he became an activist in the movement. Later, when Chiang Kai-shek and the landlords started hitting back, he was under threat of arrest and decided to join the revolution. He was a very able person and did some really important work. Later, after learning to read, he was even more valuable and so he became an officer in the revolutionary army.'

'Oh! What an exceptional person!' the doctor exclaimed. 'I really admire people like him. My father was also a tenant farmer. I didn't want to follow in his footsteps, which is why I found myself a teacher and learnt herbal medicine. Since there were no other doctors in this area, my work is of some use to people here.'

'I also came to this valley and became a charcoal-burner so as to escape the life of a tenant farmer,' the charcoal-burner said. 'This officer was really one of us – he died for our cause. I admire him too.'

Standing before Pan Zaixing, he clasped his hands together and lowered his head as if praying that his spirit might go up to heaven . . . Then his wife and Doctor Qiu followed suit. Without realizing it, Wang Jiansheng and I did so too, though both of us felt sure that Pan Zaixing would much rather his spirit stayed in the world of men, where so many suffering people still needed his help.

After finishing his prayer, Doctor Qui Mingtai took his leave.

'I heard that those bastards have been burning down houses and killing peasants on the plains. Quite a few people have fled to the hills and a number of them are wounded. I must get back to attend to them.'

'But please leave us your address before you go,' Wang Jiansheng insisted. 'We can't talk of any payment for the time being, but maybe we'll need your help again in the future.'

'Of course,' Doctor Qiu replied. 'The place where I live is much like Brother Jia Hongcai's – not in the least remarkable. It's called White Stone.'

'That isn't really a proper name,' Jia Hongcai explained. 'It's just called that because his grass hut is built next to a big rock. Other people call this place Black Charcoal Hole for the same reason. People call these mountains the Daji Mountains. All the people living here are poor folk like ourselves.'

'Well, goodbye then!' Doctor Qiu said to us. 'Goodbye, Brother Hongcai!' It seemed that he really had urgent work to attend to.

Jia Hongcai took out some of his own clean clothes and changed Pan Zaixing's dirty, blood-stained tunic. Then, taking down the doors dividing the two room of his house, he used them to make a coffin. As dusk was falling, we buried Pan Zaixing in a little thicket not far from Black Charcoal Hole. We returned in silence to Jia Hongcai's hut, unwilling to utter a word, and sat around until nightfall. Then, under cover of darkness, we bid farewell to the charcoal-burner and his wife and set on our way, hoping to be able to meet up with the rest of our forces at Tanjiahe, where the Special Regional Committee had decided to take refuge.

We arrived at Tanjiahe just after daybreak and went straight to the Yuewang Temple, which had been our headquarters in the past. This little town only had about ten members of the Peasant Volunteer Force to keep order. After the Democratic Government of Workers and Peasants had been established, most of the revolutionaries from this area had moved to the county town and since then liaison work in Tanjiahe had been left in the hands of Grandpa Whiskers. Pockmarks the Sixth, who used to run the dough-stick stall, had from time to time acted as messenger between Tanjiahe and the county town. When we arrived we found only three people there: Pan Xudong, Uncle Zizhong and Uncle Pan. All of them, apart from Uncle Pan, had suffered minor wounds, though none of them allowed this to affect their work. All other government workers and soldiers had been dispersed by the enemy and our original plan to meet up here had failed. When Pan Xudong saw us, he clasped our hands tightly without uttering a word. Even when Wang Jiansheng told him the news about Pan Zaixing, his face remained expressionless. Uncle Zizhong, Uncle Pan and Grandpa Whiskers remained equally silent, as if silence was the most suitable comment of all. Everyone felt confused and bewildered and it was impossible to put our thoughts into words. In the end, however, Pan Xudong broke the silence.

'You've both had a rough time,' he said, turning to Wang Jiansheng and me. 'But at least you've made it here. We still have no idea what has become of our other comrades – though I'm sure they will try their best to meet up with us. But you must both be exhausted after your night's march. Quickly go and have something to eat and then get some sleep.'

My eyelids did feel rather heavy and my legs were very tired. I imagined that Wang Jiansheng must be feeling much the same. Grandpa Whiskers quickly brought us two rice cakes and a pot of tea. At the time, this simple meal seemed like a delicious feast. As the tea made the rice cakes expand in our stomachs, a drowsiness began to settle over us. Unable to fight it any longer, I fell asleep at the table.

Before long, however, I was awakened by the sound of gunshots from outside. Opening my eyes, I saw Pan Xudong, Wang Jiansheng and Uncle Zizhong deep in discussion. Hearing the gunshots, they quickly climbed the stairs at the back of the temple to look out and see what was happening. I followed them and saw nothing but a plume of black smoke rising from a distant point to the south.

'That must be the Nationalists heading this way,' Wang Jiansheng said. 'They're burning houses as they go!'

'They're not going to allow us a moment's rest!' Uncle Zizhong said. 'They're going to mop up all their opponents and turn this place into a wasteland. We'd better move on at once.'

'But we must first tell the people of Tanjiahe to get on the move too,' Pan Xudong said. 'The more dispersed we are the better. We have no way to defend ourselves, so we can't just wait around to be slaughtered by the Nationalists!'

Everyone agreed with this and, led by Uncle Pan, we all went out to warn the townsfolk of the approaching enemy army. After half an hour, the townsfolk were beginning to leave their homes and we followed them. However, we were slowed down a little by Grandpa Whiskers, who had sprained his ankle when we captured the county town.

'Don't worry about me,' he said. 'Don't forget that I'm a "*Jia* chief" – a petty official of the Nationalists! I know this area like the back of my hand and can easily find somewhere to hide away. Now get on your way as quick as you can!'

We had no choice but to leave him behind. But we were then faced with the problem of where to go.

'North!' Pan Xudong said. 'We'd better head north towards the Lianyun Mountains. The mountains are high and covered in thick forests, and there isn't much fertile land. Being such a poor area, it is unlikely that the Nationalists have paid much attention to it. We have considered this place as a possible refuge before. We can try to reassemble our dissipated forces there.'

Uncle Pan beat a final warning on the temple gong. The townsfolk, young and old, streamed out of the town to seek safety in the hills. We left Tanjiahe amid the shouts of the crowd, Uncle Pan still beating the gong, and headed north along a little mountain path. We felt the revolvers at our waists. They gave us a feeling of security, even though we were rather short of ammunition.

'We can carry on with our work here. The conditions aren't bad.' These are the first words Pan Xudong said to us on our arrival at the Lianyun Mountains. His voice sounded a little less tense than when we left Tanjiahe. Sitting down beneath an ancient maple tree we all heaved a sigh of relief. Now we could at last slacken our pace a little. We were surrounded by mountains and it felt very peaceful. The hills were covered in low bushes, with only an occasional plot of cultivated land, no doubt because the hills were too stony and the soil too poor for the local people to eke out a living here. The only fertile places were at the bottom of the valleys, where soil had been washed down by the mountain streams. This soil, however, could support no more than a handful of people. Those who did live here were extremely poor, so government officials had never bothered to pay much attention to them.

'It's not a bad place,' Wang Jiansheng commented, a note of relief in his voice, 'but we're not going to find much to eat. Once things calm down you can't help feeling hungry!'

Wang Jiansheng was right. I not only felt hungry, but my whole body was aching with exhaustion. The others must have been feeling much the same.

'There's a solution to every problem.' Uncle Zizhong said lightly. 'There must be wild berries around here. Or we could look for some wild water chestnuts in the valley. It's just a matter of looking for them.'

This suggestion helped to renew a little of our strength.

'Well, one thing is certain,' Pan Xudong said more seriously, 'we'll have to stay here for the time being. So we must find some way to solve the problem of food. We'll have to wait until the others arrive – they are almost certain to head this way to escape the Nationalist massacres.'

We all knew that Pan Xudong was right. After two sleepless days and nights, our strained and tired bodies were lulled into drowsiness by our rather relaxed exchange of ideas. For the moment, we had to set aside the problem of finding food, to gather our strength once again and set off up the mountainside to find a cave where we could sleep. This time, we were at last able to have a proper rest, sleeping until late the following morning.

The sun that day seemed particularly bright, as if welcoming us to this barren, but peaceful mountain area. The hills, bare as they were, were not quite devoid of life. Small birds darted amongst the bushes, delighting in the bright sunlight and chirping incessantly. Some gave out strange calls of alarm, as if frightened by our sudden presence. High above us hawks were slowly girating, apparently undisturbed by us, intent as they were on possible prey to be found on the ground below. They, too, were acting out a kind of struggle, although, unlike ours, it involved merely the day to day problem of survival.

For the time being, however, we were faced with the same basic struggle for survival as these wild creatures. We could hear our stomachs crying out in protest and our mouths felt parched. We had neither the energy nor the time, like the hawks circling above our heads, to hunt for living prey. All we could do was go down to the stream in the valley and wash away the grime and weariness of the last few days. Then we started searching for things to eat beside the stream. Just as Uncle Zizhong had predicted, we quickly found some wild water chestnuts, though they were too small to satisfy our hunger. And to make things worse, the fresh mountain air had sharpened our appetites; hunger became our persistent and insatiable enemy.

I was not sure whether Uncle Zizhong, Wang Jiansheng, Uncle Pan and Pan Xudong felt the same way as I did, but after searching for a while beside the stream, they too set off up the hillside. Higher up, the air felt much cooler and it was quite windy. We had on the clothes we were wearing when we had left the county town, and, apart from the guns at our sides, we had no other possessions. Our thin shadows on the ground seemed to heighten my hunger. It seemed that the problem of food was not one that could be solved in a day or two, but would involve an enormous amount of self-tempering. Putting it this way to myself, I began to feel considerably less hungry, maybe because I knew that there were more pressing problems ahead than mere hunger.

When we had found enough wild berries to fill at least a small corner of our stomachs, Pan Xudong called us over to let us know that Liu Dawang and fifteen others had just arrived. Shortly afterwards, Lao Liu and several other members of the Democratic Government appeared. During the meeting which followed, Pan Xudong made a careful analysis of the new situation, reaching the conclusion that 'the enemy was strong and we were weak'. From the military aspect alone, the Nationalists were many times stronger than us. Moreover, they had the cities under their control and the compradors, landlords and even the imperialists behind them. Because of this, they could mobilize their soldiers very quickly and their forces were well armed.

'Our own forces are small enough as it is,' Wang Jiansheng said, 'but on top of that they have largely been dispersed.'

'The main problem as I see it,' Uncle Zizhong said, 'is what our next move is going to be.'

'Yes,' Lao Liu put in. 'And we need to make our next move right away, otherwise we're going to find it hard to survive at all.'

Up to now Uncle Pan, the oldest among us, had appeared desperately weary. Now, however, his eyes suddenly flashed with renewed vigour. 'It isn't just a question of our survival,' he said. The future of the revolution is at stake! It's a question of how the Nationalist armies are eventually to be wiped out!'

Pan Xudong and Wang Jiansheng nodded in agreement.

'Yes,' Pan Xudong said. 'And that relates directly to the immediate problem. However powerful the Nationalist forces, we must destroy them.'

Continuing our discussion along these lines, our attention was drawn away from the hunger of our stomachs to the survival of the revolution. After talking for about two hours we resolved that from now on we would not only strive to reassert the power of the Democratic Government, but we would widen its influence and build up an army really capable of guaranteeing its existence. The key issue was the question of political power and much of our discussion was devoted to this matter. For the time being we had lost power. It had been lost over night and it was essential to find out exactly why. 'The enemy is strong and we are weak' could not be the only explanation. So long as the Nationalists received the support of the reactionary and imperialist factions, this state of affairs could persist for a long time to come. We all came to the logical conclusion that the only way ahead was to concentrate on building up our political power in the countryside, rather than in the towns. Our own experience was proof enough of this.

Having lost the town, our political base was destroyed. Moreover, given the power of the Nationalist armies, the towns were very hard to defend.

Summarizing our views, Pan Xudong said, 'Starting right here, we must begin to organize and mobilize the masses. In this way, we can make this into our moutain base and rebuild the Democratic Government of Workers and Peasants. We must not contemplate re-establishing control over the towns until we have laid a very solid foundation. Otherwise we will become an easy target for the Nationalist armies again. On the other hand, we can begin to surround, and maybe, conditions permitting even take over some of the Nationalist-controlled towns from the countryside. For example, we might surround and capture the Nationalist base at Mazhen county. This way, we can begin to take the initative again.'

There was no immediate response to this suggestion, probably because the question being addressed related to the very survival of the revolution and thus, at the moment, was too grave to contemplate. Silence descended on us for a while, broken eventually by Uncle Pan.

'As I see it, this is the way it should be. When we took over the county town, our uprising started in the countryside, didn't it? Now that Chiang Kai-shek has become so powerful, it makes sense for us to give up the town for the time being. Once we have really re-established ourselves in the countryside, we can then consider recapturing the towns.'

'Yes,' Wang Jiansheng continued. 'And then we can start not only taking over the county towns, but we can surround the cities and work towards national revolution.'

'Yes, that is inevitable!' Pan Xudong said, confirming what the others had just said. 'But because of this, we must now change our tactics.'

Nobody else had anything to add and the silence which followed was an expression of everyone's agreement with Pan Xudong's view. From the grave expression on each face, it seemed that everyone was eager to get on with the task ahead.

The next day we divided up to go around the area and start working with the local people. Although this was a pretty bleak place, there were a few scattered communities. They were not totally cut off from the outside world either, as from time to time the local people would have to go down to the town to sell firewood and local produce in exchange for oil, tobacco, needles, thread and other necessities. They, too, were subject to oppression and crippling taxation. They were our people – the masses upon whom we were based. Following this line of thought, I remembered the young student who had taken refuge in our house one dark night and had later become a political commissar, before being killed by the landlord Chumin; I also thought of Chang Je-an, who had worked disguised as a fortune-teller. They had started their revolutionary work from scratch in the countryside. Now it seemed as if history was repeating itself – though this time the setting was a bare mountain area and I myself was involved. I could not help seeing a little humour in the situation.

Since Pan Zaixing's death, Wang Jiansheng's chief task was the reconstruction of our armed force. The fifteen rifles which Liu Dawang and his men had managed to bring with them now accounted for most of our weapons. But so as to avoid further set-backs, the armed soldiers no longer operated together. They, too, were split into two sections – one led by Liu Dawang and the other staying with Wang Jiansheng, to provide protection for the recently established Special Regional Committee. According to Pan Xudong, these two sections could, if necessary, be further subdivided. As before, I acted as messenger. For the most part, my work was decided by Wang Jiansheng. But naturally I still needed to keep close contact with all the others, especially with Uncle Pan, who continued his security work. Our work here was considerably more arduous than it had been in the past. I, for one, was especially aware of this. The terrain was rough and there were often dangerous paths to negotiate. We were now very spread out, making communication difficult. I had to know where everyone was so that the various groups could co-ordinate their activities.

So I was kept busy both day and night and I became even more skilful at finding my way. I had to find my way even if there was no path to follow and be able to locate people even when they were well hidden. This was necessary not only for the continuation of our work, but our very survival depended on it. We could not spend our time searching for wild fruits and berries when there was such pressing work to be done. We had to seek the support of the masses, for without them we could not survive.

I soon discovered that the people living around here were not as few as I had at first imagined. Because of their extreme poverty, many of these people lived in grass huts built up against the rocks. This saved on building materials and helped to protect the occupants from the wind and rain. Because of this, these people could not settle together in villages like those on the plains and there would be no more than two or three families living in any one place. Furthermore, the lack of fertile land in this area made it essential for these people to live in tiny dispersed communities. Gradually I discovered that the area had not been totally ignored by Nationalist officials after all. Aware of the considerable number of labouring people who lived here, they would send people here once or twice a year to collect various taxes and subscriptions. Neither had this area been totally ignored during the rise of the peasant unions on the plains. One day I had to deliver letters to Uncle Zizhong and Uncle Pan who were staying in two caves far away. On my way back I met a young woodcutter. We got chatting and he told me that a fortune-teller called Chang had once been to visit their district. The two of them had become friends and the fortune-teller had encouraged him to get the hill people to co-operate to form a union.

'After a while there was no more sign of him. I heard that he was very busy with his work on the plains. We're too spread out up here and most places are hard to reach. I had no idea how to go about it anyway, so nothing ever came of the union. Later, some other people arrived here carrying guns. They called themselves the . . . the Order Preservation Corps. They wanted to know whether any revolutionaries had been this way.'

'So what did you tell them?' I asked.

'What could I tell them?' the young woodcutter replied. 'I just said that this was a very poor place and the only people who ever came here were officials sent twice a year to collect money. They just called me a muddle-headed oaf and didn't ask any more questions.'

'Did they leave here completely?' I asked.

'They went down to the foothills where they stayed,' he replied. 'Once, when I went down to sell firewood, I saw even more of them living in huts they had built by the roadside. They wanted to charge me a toll to go past. I asked them who had sent them here and they answered that they had been sent by someone called Chumin from the county government. They said they had set up a "line of defence" to protect us from disturbance by bandits – that was why they wanted me to pay.'

My heart missed a beat. This was an unexpected piece of news. We must have passed through their 'line of defence' on our way up here, though we did not encounter a single garrison. Perhaps they had run away in fright after Wang the Lion had been crushed. But there was no doubt that they would now be trying to reconstruct their line, because in order to wipe out the Revolutionary Party, it was essential for Chiang Kai-shek's forces to work with Chumin's own army. The two were inseparable.

'What is your name, Uncle?' I asked him. 'Where do you live?'

'People call me Mountain Runner,' he replied. 'You know what a mountain runner is? It's a hare. When I'm up on the mountain cutting firewood I have to run all over the place looking for the right stuff – just like a hare. I don't live far from here.

He pointed his chin in the direction of a little grass hut built up against the rocks ahead.

'And how about you?' he asked. 'Where are you from? How come I haven't seen you before?'

'I'm from the plains,' I said, 'and I haven't been in this area long.'

Mountain Runner looked me up and down, an expression of alarm on his face. 'Could you be working for the Revolutionary Party? I've heard that they are trying to help the poor.'

I nodded and gave a slight smile. 'That's right! We've come here to help the poor people and to stop the officials from extorting your money. But you mustn't let the Order Preservation Corps know, not at any cost!'

Mountain Runner rolled his eyes as if unable to believe his ears. But after a short while he managed to control his excitement and said, 'How could I tell them that I know a revolutionary? That would just be looking for trouble!'

'You're right,' I replied. 'We're both on the same side and we mustn't let ourselves be used by those officials. I'll come to see you again if I get the chance.'

After leaving him, I returned to the cave which I was sharing with Wang Jiansheng. When I arrived I found Pan Xudong, Lao Liu and Liu Dawang there, discussing something with Wang Jiansheng. Not wanting to disturb them, I sat down to one side and listened to what they were saying.

'There really isn't much we can do about that "line of defence" of their's,' Liu Dawang was saying. 'We've only got those few guns and we could not hold out against them for long. On the other hand, we must keep a careful eye on their movements. If we are going to rebuild our army, we must find some way of getting hold of their guns!'

Hearing this, I couldn't help feeling a bit surprised: so Liu Dawang already knew about the 'line of defence'! Liu Dawang seemed to find out everything – he really was a dab hand at scouting.

'But we mustn't alarm them!' Wang Jiansheng said. 'The best would be if they came up into the hills. Let them deliver their guns to our front door!'

Pan Xudong made no reply, but instead turned to me and said, 'Did you manage to do what we asked you? Anything happen on the way?'

'I met a woodcutter called Mountain Runner,' I replied, 'and had a short chat with him.'

'What did he tell you?' Pan Xudong asked.

'He told me the same as Uncle Liu Dawang was just saying: that the reactionaries have set up a "line of defence" below the mountains.'

Then I gave them a full account of the conversation I had had with Mountain Runner.

'We must make good use of this contact,' Pan Xudong said when I had finished. 'It's exactly these kind of labouring people we need to mobilize to establish a base.'

'In fact,' Lao Liu broke in, 'the labouring people here are already beginning to mobilize themselves. They already have some idea of the Nationalist outrages and they know that there are revolutionaries in the mountains. They're on our side.'

'How do they know about us?' Wang Jiansheng asked.

'I've been telling them,' Lao Liu said honestly. 'Both Zizhong and Uncle Pan have been telling them too. The people up here in the hills have even harder lives than the people on the plains. And there are no landlords around here, so what is there to be afraid of? In any case, this is the only way we can really speed up our propaganda work.'

'What?' I asked in surprise. 'Have you already been spreading the message?'

'This is my work,' Lao Liu replied. 'We can't wait around for ever, you know. When I first meet someone I get chatting about this and that and then say that I'm a doctor, or a fortune-teller, or a story-teller. A remote place like this is really short of doctors, and fortune-tellers and story-tellers are always welcome. Then, after getting more familiar with them, I tell

91

them who I really am – that I'm a member of the Revolutionary Party and am here to speak for them and work for them. You get around a lot, sending messages here and there – have you never heard them singing?'

'Yes,' I said. 'I once heard a young woodcutter in a little hollow singing. At the time I thought it very strange.'

'Why, what was he singing?' Pan Xudong asked, his interest aroused. 'See if you can remember the words.'

'Yes, I can remember it exactly. It was a sort of jingle:'

> 'Oh sigh, we toilers of the land!
> Our stomachs empty, our backs are bare.
> All men are raised by mother's hand,
> Yet equality is all too rare.
> Why, oh why, are there rich and poor?
> The rich men say it's their natural right.
> We toilers work from dawn to dusk,
> Yet to keep alive is a constant fight.
> I tell you, do not be deceived,
> This exploitation's a deadly plight!'

When I had finished my recitation, everyone looked meaningfully at Lao Liu. Guessing their thoughts, he at once said, 'Yes, I made up that jingle. They really seem to like it and learnt to sing it very quickly.'

At this, Pan Xudong smiled and said, 'That's fine, comrade. But there's one thing you've forgotten: there aren't any rich people up here in the hills, so the people wouldn't know about exploitation!'

'Yes,' Lao Liu argued, 'but there are rich people – landlords – beyond the hills. The old officials are basically no different from the landlords, as they send armed messengers up here several times a year to extort whatever money they can from the local people. All the hill people are as poor as can be imagined and they've always been bullied by the authorities. Who can say this isn't exploitation? In fact, it is worse than exploitation – it's out and out robbery! But the real problem, I tell them, is that the rich people and old officials are now working hand in glove with the Nationalists, killing people and burning down their houses. And if they get into the hills, they will commit the same sort of outrages here. The Order Preservation Corps are just their vanguard and it won't be long before they try to wreak havoc up here.'

'Do they believe what you say?' Wang Jiansheng asked.

'If they didn't believe me, why should they sing my songs with such enthusiasm?' Lao Liu said persuasively. 'They even sing when they're cutting wood, isn't that right, Chunsheng? To tell the truth, I've already got myself quite a number of young disciples who want to learn to sing. That way they can find expression for all the suffering in their lives. They have also promised to let us know at once if the Nationalists enter the area, so as to help us beat them.'

'That's excellent!' Pan Xudong said, resuming a more serious expression. 'This is a good way to mobilize the masses. Once we have the masses behind us we'll have a more solid base. Then we can start our work in earnest!'

'That's excellent!' Uncle Pan said too. 'You've not only got a natural gift for composing moving songs, but you at once get to work spreading them around! And you've got students too! Good. Just let me meet these followers of yours.'

'If you'll come out with me tomorrow,' Lao Liu said, 'they'll be sure to give you a warm welcome.'

When everyone was ready to leave and go their own ways, Uncle Pan seemed so excited by what he had heard that he decided to remain for a while. Lao Liu stayed to talk to him. For me, this felt like the first family get-together since before all the recent upheavals – even though both my mother and O Ran were still at Red Hill Village and we knew nothing of their fate. Wang Jiansheng seemed to understand our thoughts and went off to find some wild sweet potatoes which he boiled until they were soft and tender. He also baked a few wild chillies to add a bit of flavour. This was the best meal we had

had for days and it helped to raise our spirits even higher. We sat around chatting late into the night. A mountain breeze began to blow, whistling fiercely through the woods. Strange to say, this sound actually added to the sense of warmth and comfort inside our cave.

The next day Uncle Pan went off with Lao Liu to meet his new followers. Uncle Zizhong had told me that he wanted to meet Mountain Runner, so I went to show him the way. We found Mountain Runner in his hut. Uncle Zizhong, as a young man, had been no better off than Mountain Runner, so the two of them had plenty to talk about, almost as if they were old friends. They sat shoulder to shoulder on a rock beneath a tree, chatting very intimately to one another. I had to leave as soon as I had made the introductions, as I knew that Wang Jiansheng was waiting for me back at the cave.

Two days later, on a heavy, overcast afternoon threatening snow, Wang Jiansheng and I sat in our cave, having completed our day's tasks. We had decided to hold a meeting here, as our cave was bigger than most and was fairly central. We were waiting for Pan Xudong, Liu Dawang, Uncle Zizhong and Uncle Pan. This was to be a meeting of all members of the Democratic Government and therefore promised to be quite important. By four o'clock it had already begun to grow dark and the participants began to arrive. The first was Lao Liu, who brought with him five young hill people. Just behind him came Uncle Zizhong, who arrived with Mountain Runner. They were followed by all the other members of our government.

'This is Big Tree Lu,' Lao Liu said, introducing a stout and sturdy young man. 'He is my first student. He really can sing! He also has quite a few students of his own.'

'Are these his students?' Pan Xudong asked, looking at the other four.

Lao Liu nodded and introduced them to us.

'Good!' Pan Xudong said. 'So now that everyone knows one

another, we should have some sort of ceremony to welcome our new members. We also have a number of important matters to discuss, so we'd better start right away.'

'As this is the first such ceremony we have had in this mountain area,' Pan Xudong continued, 'we all attach particular importance to it. From today onwards this region will see big changes. I hope these six new comrades understand the full significance of this.'

Pan Xudong thus presided over the acceptance of these six hill people into our revolutionary organization, while Lao Liu and Uncle Zizhong acted as sponsors for the new comrades.

After the completion of this ceremony, Pan Xudong continued to chair the meeting, discussing our campaign to mobilize the hill people and establish peasant unions. The meeting continued until late into the evening and it was decided to begin organizing the hill people as quickly as possible. As to the form this organization should take, it was decided that although few of the hill people were actually peasant farmers, it made sense to keep the name 'peasant union' so as to show that this organization was part of the peasant movement. An executive body of this peasant union was set up there and then, led by Big Tree Lu. At the same time, the first branch of the revolutionary organization in this mountain area was established, led by the six young men who had just joined up. The activities of the peasant union would henceforth be under the command of this branch.

The close of our meeting thus marked the start of fresh activities. It was upon this new base that our revolutionary army was to be rebuilt.

Eventually everyone began to leave, though it seemed as if we all had plenty more to discuss. Pan Xudong himself was always like this. When the meeting had been formally closed, he relaxed and addressed Lao Liu in a more lively and humorous manner.

'Now you can have a change of job, Lao Liu!' he joked. 'You

don't need to spend all your time running around singing your songs any more.'

'What you say is only half true, my dear chairman!' Lao Liu replied. 'There's a limit to how much I can achieve on my own. I also need to have students – ten, twenty, thirty of them – so that the mountains are filled with my songs. I can give up singing songs myself, but I still need to be able to train youngsters to sing. There really is natural genius amongst them, you know. I also have to compose songs for them – beautiful, moving songs. It's a real pity that Ho Shuoru and Peng Wanzhen aren't here too. They're much better at composing songs than I am.'

Lao Liu's voice suddenly trailed off as he remembered his two comrades. No one knew what had become of them. I, too, was moved and thought of my family back at Red Hill Village. Pan Xudong, guessing our thoughts, said no more. He was no doubt thinking about our old base, which we had taken such pains to build up and which was now lost to the enemy. Accompanied by Liu Dawang, Uncle Pan, Uncle Zizhong and the six young hill people, he set out back to his own cave. Lao Liu wanted to stay at our place for the night. Fetching some dry leaves to sleep on, he settled down between Wang Jian-sheng and me. We all needed to revive our spirits in order to be prepared for the next day's work. That was even more important than thinking about our families and friends.

A number of soldiers and government workers from our old base eventually managed to make it to the mountains. With the establishment of the Peasant Union there it was now possible for Uncle Pan (who was in charge of security) and Uncle Zizhong (who looked after organizational work) to begin to recruit new scouts to keep an eye on the movements of the Order Preservation Corps and even spy out the land in the enemy-occupied areas. By this time Chiang Kai-shek was mustering his forces for an attack to clear the area of the revolutionary movement once and for all. With Chumin, who represented the interests of the landlords, the Nationalists, based in Mazhen county, set about strengthening the Order Preservation Corps in readiness for this final assault. The Order Preservation Corps now worked together with the Nationalist armies in their campaign of suppression and extermination. Our scattered forces, including the troops at Mazhen county led by Chang Je-an, were almost completely destroyed. As to Chang Je-an himself, we had no idea what fate had befallen him. There had been widespread massacres of revolutionaries and many villages had been burnt down. And this was only the start of the campaign. Determined to preserve their rule, Chumin and his associates, backed by Chiang Kai-shek's armies, set about strengthening their 'line of defence' so as to prevent revolutionaries from escaping the net and disturbing the 'peace and purity' of the mountain areas. They did not yet realize that the peasant movement had already spread to almost every corner of the mountains.

One afternoon Wang Jiansheng came back from an emergency meeting with Pan Xudong and said, 'We've got a new task to carry out! You will have to come along with Liu Dawang and me, as you're best at finding your way in the dark and these mountain paths can be quite treacherous by night.'

'Is this some sort of military operation?' I asked.

'Yes,' he replied. 'This will be our first assignment since coming up to the mountains and it's essential we carry it out well.'

'What about Liu Dawang?' I asked. 'He's got the only guns we have left.'

'He's already given us half his guns,' Wang Jiansheng replied. 'We'll be travelling at the same time as him, but we'll take different routes. Our soldiers are just outside – you can see them from here.'

I went outside with him. Pointing to a piece of level ground behind some bushes he said, 'Do you see them? They're just getting ready to go.'

'Yes,' I said. 'And Big Tree Lu is there as well. Is he coming too?'

Wang Jiansheng nodded. 'Of course. He's most familiar with the terrain, so he'll be acting as our guide. You must try and work together and learn from him. Mountain Runner and a young hunter called Sun Nan are going with Liu Dawang. Sun Nan is also a member of the branch. We'll all be heading to places below the mountains and with the state of the mountain paths, it is likely to take us at least a night to get there. It's essential that we get moving right away so as to start our operation before daybreak. Still, we should be quite good at this sort of thing by now!'

Big Tree Lu came over to us from behind the bushes. Having briefed his eight soldiers on the details of our mission, he was now ready to escort us. We set off at once. The others were dressed as peasants, though their clothes were as ragged as could be imagined. Their meagre diet of wild fruit and the hard life in the mountains had practically reduced all of them to skeletons. But now that they were faced with an urgent task, they seemed in very high spirits. They knew full well that what lay ahead could cost them their lives, but they all realized that its successful completion could lead to the betterment of everyone else's life.

Our march was hampered by the need to take wild and difficult paths, to avoid being spotted by the enemy; our rifles made us look suspicious to any passer-by. The only one without a gun was Big Tree Lu, though he was not empty-handed: he carried a large club. This arduous journey devoured much of our time and energy and it was well after midnight before we reached the foot of the mountains.

'Their "line of defence" is just ahead of us,' whispered Big Tree Lu, pointing to a dark, square object below us. 'That black thing is the sentry post. They check everyone passing on their way to the mountains. They also check us if we come down from the mountains. There used to be seven or eight armed sentries there, but then they suddenly disappeared – probably because you wiped out the Order Preservation Corps and the Red Spear Society, like Lao Liu was telling us. But over the last few days they have been coming back again and there must be twice the number there used to be.'

'Have you checked the details?' Wang Jiansheng asked. 'Just think carefully and tell us the exact situation.'

'The report I gave you this morning was accurate,' Big Tree Lu said. 'I hid right behind that big rock and got a very clear view. They came in and went out several times and I counted exactly fifteen people.'

'That was a day ago,' Wang Jiansheng said, 'I just hope that there are still the same number of people there.'

'But we've only got eight guns,' one soldier commented.

'Yes,' another put in, 'but we've always had fewer guns than the enemy – sometimes far fewer. That's just the way things are!'

'Right,' Wang Jiansheng said. 'Let's get to work. We're now pretty close to the enemy so we had better step lightly. Whatever happens, we mustn't let ourselves be seen.'

'I'll first try to get a closer look,' Big Tree Lu said. 'You can get yourselves ready in the meantime.'

He set off quickly down the hillside, while we followed at a distance. Our eight soldiers then spread out to form a circle around the sentry tower. Big Tree Lu picked his way step by step towards the black building. When he got close he squatted down to watch for any movement. We also drew closer in order to protect him in case he was seen. Then, suddenly, we heard a door creak followed by the sound of trickling water. Big Tree Lu pounced and we heard a coarse voice.

'Who's that?'

In an instant the voice was muffled and then ceased altogether. We went up and found a member of the Order Preservation Corps, who had got up to relieve himself. Little did he know what was awaiting him outside. Big Tree Lu had one hand over his mouth and the other on his throat. He had probably used a bit too much force, as the fellow appeared to have stopped breathing. But his cry had alerted the others sleeping in the building.

'What? What's going on?' voices said inside.

Big Tree Lu threw down the lifeless body and picked up his big club. Then he quietly positioned himself next to the door. Our eight soldiers meanwhile divided into two groups and lay in ambush close by, sealing off the exit. The door of the sentry post was very narrow and only one person could get through at a time. As a soldier emerged, Big Tree Lu raised his club and brought it down on the fellow's head, knocking him to the ground. Our soliders were equally efficient, immediately pulling the body aside and hitting the man on the head with their rifle butts to make sure he was fully unconscious. This was repeated several times, though not always with the same results. Three times Big Tree Lu's club missed its mark. Instead of falling unconscious to the ground, the victim escaped with a bad bruise, but because he was rather dazed, it was relatively easy for us to catch him.

Our operation was on the whole quite smooth and successful. But the thing which made Wang Jiansheng happiest was the discovery that Big Tree Lu was a most able and imaginative young man. This also gave us a new insight into the potential strength of these mountain people.

Big Tree Lu waited by the door to make sure that no one else was coming out. Then he suggested to Wang Jiansheng that we should go inside and take a look.

'Of course we should take a look,' Wang Jiansheng replied. 'We still need to find out what they plan to do around here.'

I lit a torch and, led by Big Tree Lu, we went inside. Meanwhile our soldiers kept a careful eye on the members of the Order Preservation Corps. We found the room empty. I felt the quilts spread out on the long wooden board. They were still slightly warm. On the only table we discovered a written 'plan of action'. Holding the torch, Wang Jiansheng scrutinized the document and read out the parts he thought important.

' "The bandits must at all costs be prevented from entering the mountains . . . It is of utmost importance that we carry out investigations of all the households to recruit able-bodied young men for the Red Spear Society, strengthen our military capacity and ensure the maintenance of order." '

'Who issued that order?' I put in hurriedly, having realized its implications. 'It looks as if they are making long-term plans!'

'It is issued by the army command at the county town and Chumin's Order Preservation Corps, which has just been revived,' Wang Jiansheng said. 'It looks as if Chumin has come back in the wake of the Nationalists and plans to re-establish his little empire once again.'

'So they think they can use us hill people against our own comrades?' Big Tree Lu said behind us. 'Do they take us for fools or something? Well, we'll see about that! Just let them come and investigate us and let them see what secrets they can unearth!'

We found three guns leaning against the wall in a corner of the room – probably left by the last three guards when they rushed out of the building. In the same corner we also found a case of ammunition.

'This is really a bit of luck!' Wang Jiansheng said with a grin. 'With the dozen or so rifles outside we've just about got enough to make a whole squad!'

'We could make a company, a battalion, a regiment or anything we like!' Big Tree Lu said excitedly. 'We've got enough able-bodied men and it won't take them long to learn how to handle these rifles.'

Then he quickly picked up the three rifles, put them over his shoulder and stopped to pick up the ammunition box.

'Just wait a moment,' Wang Jiansheng said. 'We must first rearrange the bedding and put the documents back in their original place so that it looks as if nothing has happened. We don't want to make things too obvious for Chumin and his gang!'

'Yes!' Big Tree Lu replied, putting down the rifles and doing as Wang Jiansheng had instructed. 'When they get here Chumin's men will probably think they've just gone off into the hills to recruit people for the Red Spears!'

'There's just one problem,' Wang Jiansheng said, looking around the room. 'It's easy enough to tidy this place up, but what are we going to do with those fellows outside?'

'Let me take care of them,' Big Tree Lu said. 'Why not put them to work doing something useful for a change? There's a piece of hillside that we need opening up and we're short of labour. We could put them to work on that. They won't have a gun between them so there's no danger of them running away.'

Then he picked up the rifles and left the room, followed by Wang Jiansheng who carried the case of ammunition. I made one final check of the room, to ensure that no trace of our visit remained. When we got outside our soldiers reported that seven of the captives had serious head wounds and were still unconscious. Five others had come round and were trying to get up and run away. At the moment our soldiers were holding them down with their feet. Some of them were having their hands tied behind their backs ready for our return journey.

'Half way up the hillside there is a cliff,' Big Tree Lu said. 'We can carry those seven useless ones up there and throw them down into the deep gully. Then no one will know about them. We'll take the other five with us. There's plenty of room for them to rest in our sheep pens!'

We were all most impressed with Big Tree Lu's quick-thinking and at once agreed with his suggestions. However, it took us several hours to carry this out and by the time we had got back up into the mountains with the five captives, it was already beginning to get light. Big Tree Lu took them into a maze-like, rock-strewn cave from which they could not escape. Wang Jiansheng gave him all the guns and ammunition which we had just captured and told him to start instructing the hill people in their use. He also told our soldiers to join him to help train them.

We returned to the cave where we had arranged to meet Pan Xudong. Liu Dawang, too, had just returned with his men. They had attacked a guard post on another part of the 'line of defence', but, according to Liu Dawang, their strategy had been different. The guards there had gone to bed late and there was still a light burning in the building. They had crept close to one of the windows and peeped in through a crack. Inside they saw seven guards smoking opium and playing mah-jong. Their guns were still hanging up on the wall. Smashing the window, some of Liu Dawang's men had fired into the room while others broke down the door and stormed the room. They found three of the guards were already dead while the other four surrendered without a fight. Mountain Runner had made very much the same suggestion as Big Tree Lu: they had tidied up the guard house to make it appear that nothing had happened, even wiping up all the blood-stains. After getting back to Pan Xudong's cave, which now served as our headquarters, Liu Dawang gave us a brief report, in which he appeared to make something of a self-criticism.

'I'm afraid I had to use up a few bullets,' he said regretfully.

'There are times when you cannot avoid using bullets,' Pan Xudong said with a smile. 'But of course you mustn't waste them. A few bullets in exchange for all those guns and ammunitioni is well worth it!'

Pan Xudong then suggested that we should now rebuild our First Army, using the captured guns and ammunition to set up a new brigade. Wang Jiansheng appointed Big Tree Lu as commander, Mountain Runner as second-in-command and Sun Nan as political commissar. Their immediate task was to expand our forces in the mountains and continue attacking guard posts of the Order Preservation Corps to capture more arms.

Our activities in the mountains were of course kept strictly secret from those living on the plains, and the Order Preservation Corps was completely baffled by the peculiar state of affairs. Amongst the hill people a new feeling of confidence began to grow, now that we had guns and ammunition to fight with. They felt less ready to accept the bullying tactics of the officials. This was principally a result of the new organization they had established, which had now developed into a proper Peasants' Union. Our unsettled life of eating wild fruit and living in caves was coming to an end, as it became possible for us to reveal our true identity. The hill people welcomed us, invited us to live in their homes, and provided us with valuable information and guaranteed our safety.

But we knew that the Nationalists and landlords were busy making trouble down on the plains, killing and burning wherever they went. The ordinary people there had already been influenced by the revolution and we could not allow the enemy to continue their wanton killing and destroy all we had achieved. We needed to revive our work there. The first step was to assess the true situation, get in touch with our supporters who had been dispersed, and then begin our task over again. After several discussions, we all decided that Uncle Pan and I should be the first to go down, as Uncle Pan was a poor old peasant and it would be easy for him to fool the enemy. I was familiar with the lie of the land and there would be no danger of us getting lost.

'You must try your best to set up a network of contacts and find out more about what is going on,' Pan Xudong told us as we were about to leave. 'When we've re-established a base we can begin to spread out again. Once you've been there, the masses will come to realize that the revolution is still alive. This is the very best form of counter-attack we can make at present.'

So, for the time being, we left the mountains which had become so familiar to us.

CHAPTER 5

Uncle Pan now went under the guise of a 'cow master', as the local people used to call their veterinary doctors. This was a most suitable disguise, as Uncle Pan was an expert in cows and oxen, having raised them himself. He knew at a glance what disease a cow might have and he could even prescribe remedies. Furthermore, a 'cow master' required no special disguise, save an old blue full-length gown. I went disguised as an odd-jobber in search of work. This, too, required nothing but a bit of dirt on my face to make me appear convincing.

'You mustn't only look around but must ask questions too,' Uncle Pan urged me, as we parted at the foot of the mountains. 'But make sure you only ask people who seem reliable. Don't just start talking to anyone you meet – that could land you in trouble.'

Even though Uncle Pan had become far more daring, he remained cautious in his actions. This time, however, his caution was an expression of his concern for me and of his hope that I would perform my duty safely.

I decided to head in the direction of Tanjiahe. This was the place in which I felt most at home, and its people were like members of my own family. I felt a longing to see them again. But I had a difficult journey ahead of me. I walked for hours and hours through hilly country and by nightfall had only covered about half the distance. Finding a dilapidated little temple at the bottom of a hill, I lay down for the night behind the altar. Bare as the place was, my resting place was secluded and I passed a peaceful night, untroubled by nightmares.

I set off again early the next morning, and after walking for three hours, I reached the main road leading to the county town. This had once been a more populous area, but I discovered that almost all the villages on both sides of the road had been burnt down, with nothing left but a few charred walls. There were hardly any people to be seen in the fields and I guessed that most of the villagers must have fled to the hills and had not yet returned. Although the fighting had now stopped, the killings still continued, and to be on the safe side I decided to avoid the main road and make a diversion through a low range of hills. Near a large burial mound in a valley I came across two women and a young man sitting on the ground with a look of desolation on their faces. Next to them were two cooking pots, a basket full of paper money and a broken wooden door. My curiosity aroused, I walked up to get a closer view of them.

As I came up, the young man suddenly noticed and asked in surprise. 'Hey! Aren't you the one who sold dough-sticks? What are you doing around here at times like these?'

I gave a start as I realized the inadequacy of my disguise. Uncle Pan's warnings had not been without good cause. Yet from the young man's tone of voice I felt that he was friendly and sincere and that it would not matter if I chatted with him a while. I went up and squatted down next to them. The older of the two women looked as if she might be the mother-in-law, and the younger her daughter-in-law. Seeing their rags and their anxious, drawn faces, I felt more at ease and began talking with them.

'Where can you sell dough-sticks now?' I said. 'My home has been burnt down and I've got nowhere to go. I'm just hoping to do a few odd jobs for a bowl or two of rice.'

'Young man,' the older woman said, turning to me, 'you are still too innocent! Can't you see what is going on around you. They call this a "bandit zone" and many youngsters have been executed for banditry. Where do you think you'll find any odd jobs – unless you go to help the Order Preservation Corps?'

At this moment the younger woman started crying, mumbling through her sobs, 'All they know is killing and executing!'

'So can you avoid execution by joining the Order Preservation Corps?' I asked.

'It's not as simple as that any longer,' the young man said, confirming the older woman's words. 'Haven't you heard what's going on now? If you're not already in the old *Bao* chief's good books and haven't got friends in the Blue and Red Gang, you'll never stand a chance of getting into the Order Preservation Corps. You'll be lucky if you're not picked up straight away and executed for banditry. You can go and see for yourself in the town. The head of the Order Preservation Corps there is either an old *Bao* chief or an opium-smoking member of the Blue and Red Gang.'

'I want to go and have a look for myself,' I said, trying to gauge their reaction. 'Maybe some of the shopkeepers there will need some odd jobs doing – carrying goods or fetching water.'

'Do you want to get yourself killed or something, young brother?' the old woman said sharply. 'My home has been looted and none of us have enough to eat. My elder son also wanted to go to town to find odd jobs, but before long he was picked up and accused of being a spy for the bandits. He's due to be executed any time now. Do you want the same to happen to you?'

'They're going to execute your son?' I asked. 'How do you know that?'

'They sent people to our house for money,' the young woman sobbed. 'They said that we could buy his life for 200 silver dollars. But where are we supposed to find that sort of money? In the end they reduced it to 100 – but even that is more than we can manage. My husband is to be executed today. They're running out of space to lock people up. Now we're just waiting to get his body.'

I gave a shudder and felt cold sweat run down my body. I had never imagined that such a state of terror would have developed already. I did not know what to say. Looking at this family, I felt my heart break. The old woman, seeing my reaction, gave a sigh and said, 'All we can do for him now is give him the best burial we can manage. What else can poor folk like us do? Young brother, I wonder if you could give us some help . . .'

Guessing what she was thinking, I said, 'Help you to fetch the body, you mean?'

'You can see for yourself,' she said, 'only my young son has any strength. I can't expect my daughter-in-law to carry anything in her state. And as for me,' she sighed, 'I'm so starved that I can barely walk. If you would help us with this, it would be a great act of kindness. You can stay in our house tonight to avoid running into the Order Preservation Corps.'

The only reply I could make was to nod my head in agreement.

'They hold two executions a day,' the young man said. 'Once in the morning and once in the afternoon, regardless of the weather. We can go there soon.'

I had no more courage to talk to them. I now understood everything. All I could do was wait with them silently. Before long we heard a crack of gunfire coming from the town, at which the young woman fell on the ground in a fit of crying. Her mother-in-law tried to pick her up, resting her head on her lap. Strangely, there was not a tear in the old woman's eyes – no doubt her tears had run dry. Perhaps she had already learnt to accept what fate had in store and felt that tears no longer had any meaning. She merely said flatly to her younger son, 'You can go now. Those executioners are probably going off to have their supper.'

The young man glanced at me. I understood what he meant.

'All right, let's go,' I said. Then turning to the two women I said, 'You wait here. There's no need for you to go with us. We'll be quicker on our own.'

They agreed silently to my suggestion and the young man and I picked up the old door and headed in the direction of the sound of firing. We reached the execution ground just as dusk was falling. It was an old threshing-ground on a little hillside just outside the town. Now, of course, there were no longer any rice stalks to be seen. All we found were the bodies of the thirteen young men who had just been executed. They lay there silently, as if no longer part of this world. Only a few wild dogs seemed to pay any attention to them, sniffing around the bodies to find out which one would make a good dinner. It seemed that the dogs had already fallen into an instinctive routine, based on the daily executions in the town. As soon as they heard the gunfire, they would rush here in search of fresh meat.

The young man eventually found his brother's body and after hoisting it on to the old door, we carried it back to the burial ground where his family was waiting. Half his head had been blown away, and when they saw this the two women dared not look at him and were so terror-stricken that even their sobbing ceased. The young man and I at once set to work digging a long trench beside the burial mound. We placed both the body and the old door in the new grave and then filled it with earth. They told me that the other grave was that of his father, who had been a farmer half the year and the other half had travelled around with a carrying-pole, mending pots and pans.

After burning paper money in honour of the dead, the old woman, true to her word, insisted that I should stay with them for the night. I could guess what their home must be like and it was difficult to refuse her offer; indeed, I felt reluctant to leave the three of them. But, under the circumstances, I thought it wiser to go on, as there was nothing more I could do to help. I assured them that I was quite used to travelling at night and that no misfortune would befall me. Just before I set off, I thought I had better try to light a little flame of hope in their hearts. I told them that although the Nationalists and the Order Preservation Corps seemed to be riding high at the moment, it would not be long before the revolutionary forces returned to protect the interests of the common people. Then I went on my way, making a detour around Tanjiahe and heading in the direction of Red Hill Village. I had no wish to end up in the Nationalist-controlled town. I thought of my mother, Aunt Sunflower, Sister Apricot, Grandpa Whiskers, O Ran and her newborn child, and decided that I would be able to learn more about the present situation from them than I would on my own.

It was already getting light by the time I neared the lonely little village. Not knowing what changes might have taken place there, I dared not enter the village directly. Instead, I made my way round to the White Stone Stream below the hills east of the village, pushed through the bushes on its bank and sat down on a rock. I was feeling tired and needed a rest and a drink of water.

What I needed most was a good nap; my eyelids grew heavy. Eventually I could no longer keep them open. I had no idea when I fell asleep or how long I slept, but by the time the sound of footsteps woke me up, the sun was already high in the sky. I saw a middle-aged peasant with a carrying-pole, a piece of rope and a machete approaching me. My instinctive reaction was to get up and run away, but experience had taught me that caution was safer, so I remained where I was. I cast an unconcerned glance in the man's direction. He was just gaping at me in surprise. Both of us sensed that we had met before, but neither was certain where.

'Er . . . do I know you?' I asked.

'I . . . I think so,' he replied. 'Do you know Meixiang?'

I suddenly remembered that Meixiang was Aunt Sunflower's daughter. She had been married to someone who lived far away and so rarely returned to the village. I had only met her once, very briefly, at Aunt Sunflower's. Had he not mentioned her name, I would never have remembered her.

'I've seen her once,' I said, 'but I've never talked to her, so I can hardly remember her.'

'But I can remember who you are,' he said. 'You're a busy person – like Jiqing. I saw you that time I brought Meixiang to her mother's place. What are you doing here now?'

'What are *you* doing here?' I retorted. 'You live miles from here, don't you?'

'I've come here to cut firewood,' Meixiang's husband said. 'We don't have any firewood left at our place.'

Then he put his mouth against my ear and whispered, 'Did you know that we've now moved to Red Hill Village?'

'Are you staying at Aunt Sunflower's?' I asked quickly.

'She's already left,' he said. 'Your mother and O Ran have gone too. So have Grandpa Whiskers and Sister Apricot. That man called . . . Ho Shuoru and his girlfriend, Peng Wanzhen, came here just after the county town fell, but they also left with the others.'

I felt my heart sink and a black shadow enveloped me.

'Were they taken away by the Nationalists?' I asked. 'How could they have all gone?'

'They've all gone!' he confirmed. 'Grandpa Whiskers came here to take them away.'

Only then did I feel a slight sense of relief. I could feel sure that no harm would come to them so long as they were being looked after by Grandpa Whiskers.

'Where did he take them?' I asked.

'How should I know?' Meixiang's husband said. 'He didn't tell a soul. Even my mother-in-law wouldn't tell us where she was going. She just told us to live in her house. Our house had just been burnt down by the Nationalists – in fact our whole village was burnt down. Only this village, being off the beaten track, escaped. As we had nowhere else to go, we decided to come here. We brought some other relations with us, who are now staying in Grandpa Whiskers' house.'

'What if the Nationalists and the Order Preservation Corps find out?' I asked.

'They're too busy to worry about us,' he replied. 'They're more interested in the big villages. Apparently only *Bao* Chief Liu Qiyu and his opium-smoking accomplices know about this place. But now there's a new *Bao* chief and all he knows is that this is a poor place with nothing much to offer. So long as the few remaining youngsters join up in the Order Preservation Corps there won't be any trouble.'

'Have they joined?' I asked.

Shaking his head, he said, 'They keep putting it off. They go and hide in the hills each day after breakfast. What can the Order Preservation Corps expect if they go around killing and seizing people like that? If they really want them to join, they'll just have to go and look for them in the hills. If you'd got here any later, I'd have been hiding up there too. All we can do is keep avoiding them until the revolutionaries at last come back and drive them away.'

At this point he lowered his voice even further and said, 'We're all waiting anxiously for the Revolutionary Party to come back. You'd better go up to the hills too. If they see you, you'll be in big trouble.'

'Just wait. The revolutionaries will be back sooner or later,' I whispered. Thank you for your warning. I'll know what to do if I need to hide. Anyway, Liu Qiyu and his accomplices aren't likely to return.'

'How do you know?' he asked with interest, his eyes lighting up.

'I heard that the revolutionaries dealt with them,' I said. 'They were sent off to meet the devil just before the Nationalists staged their come back. You needn't worry!'

'Is that why you came back here?' he asked.

'No,' I replied. 'I was just passing by and I wanted to see my mother and O Ran. But since they have already left, I won't go into the village. I must be on my way. Please give Sister Meixiang my greeting. See you some other time.'

As I was leaving, he shouted to me, 'If you find out where they're staying, please run back and tell us. Meixiang really worries about them!'

Knowing that they would be safe with Grandpa Whiskers, I decided first to go up to Pheasant Nest to take a look. The only person left there was Uncle Pan's old scout, Feng Xinshun, who was unlikely to have attracted anyone's attention. Perhaps he would be able to give me some information. Turning to the hills, I followed a little path in the direction of Pheasant Nest.

This little hamlet had once been our meeting place but now it really seemed to have been forgotten by the rest of the world. It was quite deserted, and the only sound came from the stream which bubbled down the hillside behind the thatched huts. After the establishment of the Democratic Government of Workers and Peasants all our activities had become open and above ground. This place had already served its historical purpose and after Wang Xianzheng's death, when the only person remaining here was old Feng Xinshun, it was no longer of any use to us. Despite this, I thought that perhaps some of our supporters had returned here after the Nationalist attack to spend a night or two and find something to eat. Just to be on the safe side, I did not go straight in, but waited for a while beneath a large tree about fifty paces away to see if there was any sign of life.

There was a lonely stillness all around, intensified by the sound of running water. I stood there for a long while, but detected no movement. I was filled with apprehension. Was it safe to go and have a look? I was trying to make up my mind when a figure suddenly emerged from the hut, carrying a tin bucket and walking a little unsteadily. After a moment I recognized him as Feng Xinshun. He glanced up at the sky and ahead of him to see whether there was anyone there and then headed in the direction of the brook. I jumped out from behind the tree and surprised him.

He gave a start, but when he saw it was me he calmed down and asked, 'What on earth are you doing here?'

'I've come to see you,' I said. 'Is there anyone else in your house?'

'No, not a soul,' he replied. 'I don't know whether it's because of hunger or because my clothes are too thin, but I feel cold all over and I don't have any strength left. My legs are terribly stiff.'

'That is probably because you haven't been eating enough,' I said. 'Haven't you anything to eat at home?'

Feng Xinshun was silent for a moment. Then he said, 'I'm just on my way to fetch some water and try to find a few wild water chestnuts.'

'I'll go with you,' I said.

I took the bucket and we sat down for a while on the trunk of a willow next to the stream. Being such a secluded place, I thought it safe to talk and began telling him briefly what had happened to Pan Xudong and the rest of us. Then I went to look for wild water chestnuts in the soft soil beside the stream, giving the old man a chance to rest. I washed off mud and gave him a few chestnuts. After a few mouthfuls of water and something to eat he at last began to liven up a little.

'Well,' he said, 'you've certainly come to the right place. They would never bother with a decrepit old man like me, who could never be of use to the Order Preservation Corps. You'll be quite safe resting here for a couple of days.'

'That would be too long,' I said. 'Has anyone at all been up here?'

'Yes, Sweet Potato.'

'Sweet Potato?' I asked in surprise. 'How could he get here?'

'He can easily run as fast as you and he's as slippery as a loach,' Feng Xinshun replied. 'He really knows how to operate underground. Right now he's busy trying to get in contact with all our people, though this is a tough job to do on his own, without any leadership.'

'Dear Sweet Potato!' I said. 'Even at a time like this he

remembers to put his work first! Is he coming up here again? I'd really like to see him.'

'It's hard to say,' he replied. 'He wants to go further afield this time to try and make contact with other people who have been dispersed. He was even talking about going as far as "The Big City" to report to our leaders. He said that some of our people have gone to other counties not so badly affected by the Nationalists' burning and killing, to try to start up new activities there.'

'He's always been good at finding a way out,' I said. 'And now he seems to be more resourceful than ever. It's a real pity I won't be able to see him. Do you feel safe enough up here? If not, you could always come and join us at our new base in the mountains – though it would mean climbing some rather difficult mountain paths.'

'Just look at the state I'm in!' Feng Xinshun replied. 'I'm afraid I'd never make it. In any case, who is going to bother with an old man like me? Don't worry about me. The day before yesterday a hunter came this way chasing a wild pig. The pig ran round here and then disappeared into the creek behind the village. Afterwards the hunter came in to have a smoke and a chat and he told me that Chumin and those other old landlords have set up the Red Spear Society again. The Red Spears need to recruit more able-bodied men, so for the time being it looks as if they will stop their killing and burning.'

'I see. Well, in that case I'd better be on my way. I can't stop in one place too long. Is there anything you would like me to tell Pan Xudong?' I asked.

'I'd just like you to tell him what I have told you,' he replied. 'Tell him that I hope you all return quickly. And don't worry: that hunter I was telling you about has plenty of friends round about and if anything happens he is sure to come and tell me at once.'

Before I left I went to pick some wild fruit from the hillside near by so that Feng Xinshun would have something to eat over the next few days. Once he had regained a little of his strength, he would be able to go and pick fruit for himself. I suddenly remembered the charcoal-burner, Jia Hongcai, who lived in that hollow in the Daji Mountains. He had given us a lot of help when we had found ourselves in difficulty. I wanted to go and see him and find out whether or not any of our people had passed his way.

Again I chose to follow a small, rarely used path and arrived safely at Jia Hongcai's place. When I got there, he and his wife had just finished burning a large pile of wood. The best charcoal was to be sent to the town, and the rest to the villages to sell. When he saw me he looked very surprised, stopped his work at once and invited me into his house to drink some tea. Refusing the invitation for the moment, I set about helping him with his work.

'Does anyone buy charcoal at times like these?' I was curious to know.

'You wouldn't have thought so, would you?' Jia Hongcai replied. 'But if I don't sell, we'll starve, so I just have to take the risk. I recently carried a big load to Baiguo town. In the past there were never any soldiers stationed there, but this time there were. There were even guards at the town gates and when I saw them I turned back, hoping they wouldn't see me. Unfortunately, they did and accosted me. They wanted to steal all my charcoal, but then an officer's batman who was passing stopped them and said, 'If you don't pay him for it this time, he won't bring any more. In this cold weather the officers' barracks must have charcoal to burn.' So he took me into town and made me unload the charcoal outside a grain store. I suppose this store was being used as their head-quarters. Then he gave me some money and told me to come again, promising to pay me if I did.'

'They seem to be having a comfortable time,' I said, 'burning charcoal to keep themselves warm. It looks as if they are planning to settle here for quite a while.'

'Who knows?' he said. 'Anyway, they are newcomers here. They speak with northern accents. I've heard that the original troops who captured the county town have now been replaced by new troops – most of them are northerners. The officers aren't only dependent on their fires, they also like to eat hotpot. Every night they have a hotpot and drink wine, so they need to burn quite a lot of charcoal.'

'Well, that's good,' I said. 'At least you have somewhere to sell your charcoal, so you can buy food. Let's just hope that they eat more hotpot and burn more and more charcoal. You seem to have made quite a lot today. Why don't you take some more down to town so that you can earn more money? I'll help you carry a load. You can say that I'm your helper. What do you think?'

Jia Hongcai looked startled by my suggestion. 'W-w-what?' he stammered. 'Do you really dare to go?'

'Why, what is there to be afraid of if I go along as your helper?' I said. 'I haven't had a proper meal for several days. Once you have sold your charcoal and bought some rice, I can also benefit from it!'

At this, a faint smile crept over his lips and his anxiety vanished. 'You're really straight!' he laughed. 'I like talking to you. Of course you can come, if you really aren't afraid. But don't forget that one load of charcoal weighs a hundred *jin*. It's about fifty *li* to the town and we'll have to walk quickly.'

'You might find that I can walk faster than you,' I joked. 'Especially with a decent meal lying ahead of me!'

That night I stayed at Jia Hongcai's house. My bed was just a pile of straw, but I slept very soundly. I woke up at the third cock crow. Jia Hongcai was already up and, without even stopping to wash, we loaded up our charcoal and set off for the town.

We arrived at Baiguo town at midday. Just as Jia Hongcai had said, we unloaded our bundles outside the grain store and were paid straight away by the officer's batman. As our charcoal had been for the officers, the soldiers dared not molest us and we were left fairly free to wander around the town. This was a good opportunity for me to get a more detailed impression of what was going on in the streets. This little town, which had never experienced a military presence, was now brimming with troops, who were billeted in practically every shop or tavern. But the soldiers did not look like real soldiers. They staggered down the streets in little groups, gambling or smoking opium. It seemed from their numbers that there must be almost an entire battalion there. This struck me as a peculiar state of affairs for such a small town.

We had entered through the north gate, so I suggested that we leave through the south gate to get a clearer picture of the troops stationed here. But Jia Hongcai seemed a little reluctant.

'I never go through the south gate. It is not that I mind walking further, but if you go there you can see the problem for yourself.'

'What is so special about the south gate?' I asked.

'There's a piece of low-lying ground just outside. They use it as an execution ground and I prefer to avoid it.'

'Who do they execute there?' I asked.

'Usually poor peasants or craftsmen,' he replied, 'and usually for no better reason than that they are young. Living in a remote part of the mountains, I rarely have contact with outsiders, so the soldiers don't suspect me. But if I were to go there and take a look they might get suspicious and that could be the end of me.'

'Just this once,' I persisted. 'We'll take a quick look and then go. They are not likely to notice us if we're careful.'

'All right, all right!' Jia Hongcai said a little impatiently. 'If you really must, we'll go along this once.'

When we went through the south gate Jia Hongcai quickened his step so as to pass the place as quickly as possible. The hasty glance I stole gave a fearful impression. On a little earthen mound next to the piece of low-lying land was a large wooden cross with a middle-aged man nailed to it. It looked as if he had been dead for a few days, as the skin on his face had already shrivelled up in the wind. Jia Hongcai started to walk even faster, with barely a glance in the dead man's direction. From then on he remained silent. I, too, fell silent.

We walked for a long time with our heads bowed, like two strangers. Only when we reached the mountains did Jia Hongcai stop walking. He looked up at the sky and I noticed beads of cold sweat on his brow.

'Such brutality!' he muttered to himself with a sigh. 'Why on earth do they have to use this method to kill people? What a slow, painful way to die!'

'They probably want to scare the peasants,' I said, 'so that they no longer dare to cause trouble for the landlords.'

'That is not necessarily the reason,' Jia Hongcai replied. 'When they catch someone they suspect, their main idea is to get money out of him. If they can't find any, they'll execute him there and then. But if the suspect refuses to pay up and tries to argue with them, then they'll really make him suffer!'

'Talking of money,' I said, 'don't you have that money you made from the charcoal with you? That money came from them.'

Jia Hongcai gave a shudder and returned to his senses. He started walking silently up the hill, head down. He was probably thinking about the money he had earned from the Nationalists. That had been dangerous! What if they changed their minds next time and insisted on having their money back? He could not repay them. And even if he could pay, they might still decide to nail him up on the cross. Could you expect any sort of fair treatment from those beasts? They could do whatever they liked. It was too dangerous!

Half way up the hill he could no longer hold back his feelings. He turned to me and said, 'I cannot go on burning charcoal. Poor people can't afford it and no good can come from selling to those people. So many people have suffered at their hands. Isn't it just helping them to go on stoking their fires and heating their hotpots? I've never done anything wrong in all my life – neither have any of my ancestors. How could I begin doing wrong now?'

He was then silent for a while. I did not know what to say and so the two of us continued on our way without speaking. Then his feelings erupted again and he said, 'But how are we going to live? Everyone in the hills is so poor!'

His obvious predicament moved me and I decided to talk to him more openly.

'But you're not the only people to be suffering,' I said. 'You know this very well already. The problem is that they don't even allow us to get on with our lives, miserable as they already are. Just think of that poor man we saw nailed to the cross . . .'

Silence reigned again. Jia Hongcai plodded on for a short distance and then suddenly stopped and stared at me, his eyes bloodshot.

'What sort of world is this?' he cried. 'Is there no justice anywhere?'

'There is justice,' I said, 'but only we know how to find it! What we are doing right now is trying to restore justice and prevent them from committing inhumane acts.'

'How can you prevent them?' he asked.

'By wiping them out!' I replied. 'At the moment they're doing their best to wipe out all the honest, hardworking people. Can we really allow them to do this?'

'Wipe them out . . . wipe them out!' Jia Hongcai repeated to himself excitedly. 'But how can that be possible?'

'That is both a complicated and a simple matter,' I said. 'It would take a long time for me to explain it all to you. The most important thing is for the labouring people to unite. The rest, I shall explain to you slowly . . .'

Jia Hongcai then listened in silence as I began to describe our plans to him. By the time we reached his house it was already dark. His wife cooked us some porridge and dried yam leaves. After our meal we continued our discussion, while his wife sat on one side listening to what we were saying. We talked deep into the night and by the time we had finished and went to bed, Jia Hongcai had a general grasp of the work we had done so far and of the nature and aims of the movement to which we belonged. When he asked to join our organization I promised to act as his referee. The next day I formally accepted his application on behalf of the organization. Then I told him that I thought I should return to the Lianyun Mountains to give an initial report of my findings in the Nationalist-controlled areas.

That afternoon I set out. Jia Hongcai and his wife went with me for a short distance to see me off. As we parted I said, to hearten them, 'You will be seeing some of our comrades around here before long. Maybe I'll be able to come myself. Our aim is not only to eliminate those inhuman armies but to build a more beautiful world for the future!'

By the time I returned to our base in the Lianyun Mountains the Peasants' Union was well established. It even had several branches, with its headquarters in Big Tree Lu's house. When I got there I found many young people going in and out, while our newly established armed forces were training a little distance away. But there was no sign of Pan Xudong, Uncle Zizhong, Lao Liu or Wang Jiansheng. Even Big Tree Lu was nowhere to be found. Only Sun Nan was there; he had just returned from a training course in shooting and guerrilla tactics run by Liu Dawang, and now he, in turn, was training a volunteer corps of hill people, and he was always kept busy until nightfall. I went to see him to get some idea of the developments that had taken place while I had been away. I found him living temporarily in a little straw hut next to Big Tree Lu's house.

'Where has everyone gone?' I asked.

'Do you expect everyone to stay here when there's so much to be done?' he said. 'We hill people now have our own organization, the women have theirs, the volunteers have their training courses. Everyone needs to be involved in this. They are all very spread out. But don't worry: the leaders usually meet here and they are sure to come here before long.

Just wait a while – you can take the opportunity to get a good rest.'

'I don't need a rest,' I said. 'You're all so busy. Do you really expect me to sit about doing nothing? Has Uncle Pan come back yet?'

'I haven't heard any news of him,' Sun Nan said. 'But I'll let you know as soon as he gets here.'

'And Liu Dawang? Shouldn't he be with you?'

'Now that our volunteer forces are being set up so quickly, more and more commanders need training. He always has a lot of places to visit.'

'But how can we have so many volunteer corps with so few guns?' I asked.

'Haven't you heard?' Sun Nan asked. 'All our recent night excursions have been aimed at getting hold of guns. So far we have raided five guard posts on their "line of defence", capturing over a hundred guns. If one volunteer corps uses five guns, how many corps do you think we can set up? See how busy we've been all this time!'

'What? You mean it is really that easy to launch night raids on Chumin's forces and get hold of their guns?'

'Well,' he replied with a smile, 'it is still a bit of a problem. We discussed this a couple of days ago. Chumin is bound to feel nervous when he finds out. But up until now his forces have cut off the mountain areas so effectively and had such a tight grip on the areas they control that no one suspects that the revolution could have reached here – much less that we would start raiding their guard-houses. Anyway, we've left all their guard-houses as they were, though with no trace of men or guns. What can they do? We now have many volunteers and quite a few scouts, so there is no way the enemy prisoners can get out and tell Chumin what's been going on. The result is that their "line of defence", which was originally intended to seal off the mountains, has in fact sealed them off. So let's just keep them guessing!'

Sun Nan could barely restrain his laughter as he described

this situation to me. But then he suddenly cried out in surprise, 'Look! They're back. That's really lucky!'

Looking up, I saw Pan Xudong, Wang Jiansheng, Uncle Zizhong, Liu Dawang, Big Tree Lu and Lao Liu coming towards us. Then I also noticed Uncle Pan following them. Delighted by this piece of luck, I ran over to them.

'We were just talking about you!' Uncle Pan said, patting my shoulder heartily. 'I was telling them that I was quite sure you wouldn't fall into any trouble. I have just got back myself and I happened to meet the others on the way. And so here you are, safe and sound as I promised! Well, let's go inside and give our reports together.'

Big Tree Lu's house was now not only the headquarters of the Peasants' Union but also the place where we held most of our meetings. Uncle Pan and I followed the others inside and sat down on a bench by the wall. Despite their obvious pleasure at seeing us, Pan Xudong and the others remained grave and solemn. This was probably because of the heavy responsibility which weighed on their shoulders – they all looked very tired. Without so much as an informal greeting, they sat down to listen in silence as we gave our reports. Uncle Pan asked me to speak first and I told them in detail what I had seen and heard. After I had finished neither Pan Xudong nor the others made any comment. They simply asked Uncle Pan to relate his findings.

'After Chunsheng and I had separated,' Uncle Pan said, 'he went off to find out about the general situation and the reaction of the masses. Meanwhile, I went off to try and make contact with some of our people and start rebuilding our local information network.'

Uncle Pan went on to tell how he had managed to locate some of our dispersed soldiers and officials and how they had discussed plans to resume and expand their work. His account was very precise and methodical and after he had finished he summarized his findings as follows:

'More than half our fighters and personnel sacrificed their

lives during our break-out from the Nationalist encirclement of the county town. Chang Je-an's underground force in Mazhen county was almost completely destroyed by the Nationalists. But Chang Je-an himself managed to escape and went into hiding in our county, where he got in contact with Pan Mingxun, Jiqing and a small number of survivors from our original forces. He has now taken them up to Changshan Mountains, where they are beginning new operations. Meanwhile, he told our underground workers to continue looking for our people and to make sure they kept up guerrilla activities in our old bases. I also met Sweet Potato. He's really shrewd and experienced. He had already found Huang Yongfa and Jin Bailong and had told them to get in touch with Li Chengbao and Wang Jingxian, who had remained in hiding in Mazhen county. They planned to revive our forces and set to work remotivating the masses . . .'

'This looks like a replay of what we did before,' Uncle Zizhong said, 'except that this time the conditions are very much harder. Maybe they will serve as good experience for us.'

'Well,' Wang Jiansheng said, 'you can't really call it just another replay. This time the masses have been influenced by the revolution. All the burnings and killings that have been going on can only serve to heighten their consciousness. This could actually encourage morale.'

'But the question is: how, under the present circumstances, do we exploit this state of affairs and begin our operations again?' Pan Xudong asked. 'This is something we must think about most carefully. How has Chang Je-an managed since they moved up to the Changshan Mountains? We haven't had any operations among the local people there before.'

'That's probably the reason he chose to move there,' Uncle Pan said. 'Sweet Potato has been in touch with him and has made a secret visit up there. According to him, the Changshan Mountains cover a large area and, being on the border of three provinces, no one pays much attention to them. The military leaders of each of the three provinces dare not send their forces there for fear of causing a dispute. And the provincial officials keep away from the area, to avoid encroaching on the territory of their neighbours. So most of the power lies in the hands of local landlords and gentry, who rely mainly on the Red Spear Societies they have set up for themselves. They have effectively made themselves a little kingdom, but in order to protect it they have to use all their cunning to buy off the provincial leaders. This is difficult for them, but they must do so if they are to keep their region safe from outside interference. They are constantly having arguments and making compromises with the provincial leaders. This is really to our advantage. And although there is a Red Spear Society in the area, there are no proper military forces. This is also helpful to us.'

Pan Xudong seemed deep in thought. The rest of us remained silent so as to allow him to think things out.

'This really is a new state of affairs,' he finally said. 'It should help to inspire us. We are still extremely weak compared to the enemy and cannot yet afford to try and fight them directly. It looks as if we made a serious error of judgement in trying to hold the county town – our forces were practically annihilated by the Nationalists. This has been a crucial lesson for us. But our most important base still lies in the hearts of the masses. We mustn't desert them for a moment. Their support must continue to grow from day to day – otherwise we can never hope to make any real progress. The Changshan Mountains seem to be a good place to begin our work afresh.'

'So do you think we should move over there and join up with Chang Je-an?' Wang Jiansheng asked. 'By concentrating our strength there we could set up a powerful new base from which to carry out further operations. The Changshan Mountains are not too far from here, so it would be possible to co-ordinate our work and expand the area we control.'

Uncle Pan nodded in agreement. 'I also think we should move there,' he said. 'I know that area – part of it is in the province where my family comes from, and one of the neighbouring provinces is not far from where Wang Jingxian and Li Chengbao have been operating.'

'But we mustn't give up the base we have set up here,' Liu Dawang said. 'We must carry on expanding and strengthening it.'

'And Chunsheng has also been sowing the seeds of revolution in the Daji Mountains,' Lao Liu said. 'We must try to develop that area too.'

'I agree,' Big Tree Lu said. 'We must carry on with our work amongst the hill people.'

At this, Pan Xudong's grave expression lifted a little and he said, 'Yes. I agree with all of you! I think it would be a good idea to move to the Changshan Mountains. This will expand our area of influence. The conditions there sound very suitable for the establishment of a new base. This way we will be able to do as Comrade Wang Jiansheng suggests – connect the three mountain areas and gradually surround the area under Nationalist control. To begin with we could send a few people to the Changshan Mountains to help set things up.'

'I'd like to stay in the Lianyun Mountains,' Liu Dawang said. 'The volunteers here still need training. Who knows when the Nationalists might launch a sudden attack on us.'

'But you won't be able to manage here alone,' Uncle Zizhong said. 'I'd like to stay here too. We must also pay attention to the work over in the Daji Mountains. Jia Hongcai will be needing our help.'

'Since Chang Je-an has already started operations in the Changshan Mountains, I think I should first go back to the Nationalist-controlled area,' Wang Jiansheng said. 'We must do all we can to rebuild our forces there and organize the masses. We mustn't let the people think that we have been wiped out by the enemy.'

'I'll also go back there,' Lao Liu said, and then added with a note of indignation, 'We've already done so much propaganda work there. If the people think the Nationalists have wiped us out in one go, they can't have very much confidence in us!'

'I understand your feelings,' Pan Xudong said, 'and I agree with all you say. We can take this as our decision. But now that the areas we operate in are growing, we will need someone to co-ordinate all our operations. I suggest that Wang Jiansheng should take this responsibility, working with Chang Je-an to co-ordinate our work in the new and old areas. Once our armies are stronger, we will be able to start more effective political work.'

Wang Jiansheng shook his head and said, 'Well, I think that the development of our armed forces is now the most pressing issue. This calls for very special leadership. I think you would be best suited for this. I can act as your assistant and resume my position as political commissar. Of course, I will still be involved in military affairs – especially after I return to our old base areas. Then I'll have to start building up our forces independently, just as Chang Je-an has had to do. But the overall leadership will still be up to you.'

Everyone applauded Wang Jiansheng's remarks and there seemed to be a renewed sense of excitement and optimism. The applause marked the close of our meeting.

Seeing that nobody else wanted to speak, Wang Jiansheng turned to me and said, 'Chunsheng, I really admire your skill at finding your way. How about coming with me to the Nationalist areas?'

'Fine!' I replied, my thoughts at once turning to Grandpa Whiskers, my mother, O Ran, Aunt Sunflower, Sister Apricot, Ho Shuoru and Peng Wanzhen, all of whom were still in the occupied area. 'That's fine!'

'Well, this will be our strategy for the present,' Pan Xudong said. 'But we must first report this to the leaders of the party. Uncle Pan . . .'

'I've already thought of that,' Uncle Pan said. 'I will tell Sweet Potato to go to "The Big City". Apart from reporting to Master Qiu there, he could also go and see Ho Ludong if necessary.'

'That won't be necessary for the moment,' Pan Xudong said.

'We will move over to the Changshan Mountains soon – all of us except Liu Dawang and Uncle Zizhong. Once we've established a base there, each of us can set about our respective tasks.'

'I'll take care of the practical arrangements for our move,' Uncle Pan suggested. 'Now that we've made the decision, we can set off tomorrow.'

'Good!' Pan Xudong said.

CHAPTER 6

Our move to the Changshan Mountains turned out to be yet another 'break-out', as it involved passing through the area under Nationalist occupation. It took us four full days to reach our destination. We got little sleep during the journey, as we travelled by night and held our meetings during the day. The people whom Uncle Pan had contacted during his excursion into the Nationalist areas had begun to organize underground resistance and arm the masses, right under the noses of the Nationalists. Far from being dissuaded from their task by the enemy's campaign of killing and burning, they were inspired to work even harder for their cause. For them, the return of members of the Special Regional Committee was like the return of long-lost relatives, and naturally there were no end of things to be discussed.

So most of our time during the day was spent in discussions. Pan Xudong was pleasantly surprised to discover that these bitter times had produced exceptional talent in the underground movement. A young carpenter called Zheng Xiang-yong had become something of a popular hero: every time the Nationalists and the Order Preservation Corps came to the village to press-gang people or loot their houses, he would take the women, children, the old and weak up to the mountains for safety. He had also organized the young men to ambush the enemy using fake wooden guns which they had made themselves, scaring them and taking away their rifles.

By now he had a fighting force of some twenty armed men, who dispersed during the day to do their usual work in the fields, but got together at night to harass the enemy, making them feel nervous and insecure.

Other men had similarly set up fighting forces to resist the enemy. One was Yu Minghan, a bricklayer by trade. At night he and his apprentices would raid the barracks of the Order Preservation Corps. While everyone inside was sound asleep, they would make a large hole in the wall, walk straight in and take the guns and ammunition lying at the foot of each bed. Like Zheng Xiangyong, Yu Minghan and his men would work in the fields during the day and operate only by night. Between the two of them, they had the basis for a real guerrilla force.

'Well, it seems as if you are now in a position to do more than just operate at night,' Pan Xudong said after hearing their reports during a secret meeting. 'You could begin fighting an open guerrilla war. If you could harass the enemy during their daytime operations, it would really help to spread the revolution, encourage the people and frighten the enemy. It would also be of great service to our political work.'

'But on your own,' Wang Jiansheng put in, 'there is a limit to what you can do. We must start setting up an underground network so that forces in different areas can co-ordinate their activities. You might think it strange, but since the Nationalist outrages our area of influence has actually expanded and we now control a large part of the mountainous region!'

'Yes,' said Pan Xudong, 'and as our military operations expand, they grow more and more complex. We must therefore make adjustments to our strategy. Wang Jiansheng, you should still come to the Changshan Mountains with us to decide upon a joint plan of action with Chang Je-an. If necessary, you can always return here later . . .'

'You're right,' Uncle Pan said. 'If the Changshan Mountains are to be our base, we should have our headquarters there and our main leaders should be there too. Leave the work here to me. Our scouts can keep you regularly informed of our movements – and if for some reason we lose contact for a while, it won't matter. We're quite used to operating independently. Just so long as the overall strategy is the same.'

'I think that for the moment I should stay down here too,' Lao Liu said. 'I work best under difficult conditions. My propaganda could help Zheng Xiangyong and Yu Minghan with their military operations, as well as Uncle Pan's organizational work. Through propaganda, we can again mobilize the masses!'

'Good!' Pan Xudong said. 'Operating right under the noses of such a cruel enemy will at least drive out any romantic ideas you might have!'

Having taken the initial steps to rebuild our operations in the old area, we now made for the Changshan Mountains. I acted as Wang Jiansheng's scout. Since it was already late evening, Pan Xudong asked a local scout called Wang to show us the way. This gave me a good opportunity to become familiar with this stretch of the road, along which I would frequently need to travel in future. Lao Liu and Uncle Pan stood beneath an oak tree waving to us and wishing us a good journey as we left.

'I'll be seeing you both again soon!' I said.

'Of course,' Lao Liu replied. 'No matter where our work takes us, we'll never lose contact. That's part of our instinct as revolutionaries.'

Uncle Pan said nothing, but just stood there beneath the tree waving slowly at us. After taking some steps in the direction of the mountains I turned round once again to see Uncle Pan still waving at us, slowly and mechanically . . .

Our guide knew this area intimately and took the shortest route possible. He knew many people living in the Changshan Mountains and he was soon able to find out the whereabouts of Chang Je-an. He was a coppersmith by trade and normally travelled around with a carrying-pole repairing household utensils. He had been around all the neighbouring counties, and had made plenty of friends. Just at the mention of the name Wang the Coppersmith, people would be eager to help, whether or not they had met him before. Before our arrival he had come up to the area as a scout, and now he took us directly to a place called the Temple of the Three Gods.

This temple stood at the top of a hill. To its west was a small village lying in a narrow valley. No doubt the temple served as the place of worship for this village and other neighbouring mountain hamlets. Despite its modest appearance, the Temple of the Three Gods commanded a superb strategic position high on the hill, with panoramic views over the landscape below. It did, of course, have its disadvantages. Given the Nationalists' current campaign of suppression, the temple could easily become an obvious target. We scrutinized the ancient, wind-blown edifice from a safe distance before drawing nearer.

Reading our thoughts, Wang the Coppersmith said, 'I've already come here once. That time, I put down my carrying-pole to take a closer look. Quite a lot of people were going in and out and I guessed that something must be going on inside. At the time, though, I didn't want to reveal my real identity, so I didn't go in. Later, I heard from an old wood-cutter that a scholar had come from a neighbouring county. He was a specialist in reading the stars and telling people's fortunes. I guessed at once that this "fortune-teller" might be Chang Je-an. Uncle Pan once told me how he disguised himself as a fortune-teller – and even as a woman. Well, you all know him, so now's the time to see whether it really is him or not.'

'Hm!' Pan Xudong sounded a bit uncertain.

Just then a middle-aged peasant came out of the temple and said to us, 'What do you want?'

'We come from a neighbouring province,' Wang Jiansheng replied. 'We know the astrologer who is staying here and would like to see him.'

The man looked us up and down for a while and then said,

'He isn't telling fortunes at the moment – he's busy with other work. Wait here and I'll go and ask him.'

He turned to go back into the temple. After a short while a thin young man appeared at the entrance. Shading his eyes with his hands, he stared at us and then ran over to where we were standing. He shook Pan Xudong and Wang Jiansheng warmly by the hand and patted me on the shoulder.

'Well, young man,' he said, 'you've seen quite a few changes! What do you think of it all?'

'Je-an, you're really quite amazing!' Pan Xudong said, 'Coming here to live in a sacred place like this! You haven't decided to become a monk, have you?'

'Look at the length of his hair,' Wang Jiansheng said with a laugh. 'And his beard is at least three inches long. He could only become a Taoist!'

We all started laughing at this. Then we followed Chang Je-an into the temple. After resting a while and drinking a cup of tea, Wang the Coppersmith said that he must be leaving. He wanted to get back as quickly as possible to be sure of finding Uncle Pan before he moved on.

'You're a really responsible comrade,' Chang Je-an praised him. 'You've certainly proved yourself this time. In future we will be seeing more of one another. Now that you know where we are based, you can come up here whenever necessary.'

Then, going into the kitchen next to the gate, he fetched two baked rice balls for Wang's return journey. I walked down the hill with him. I was deeply impressed by his skill as a scout and told him that I wanted to learn from him.

'It's been really good meeting you, my lad!' he said as we parted. 'I know how fond Uncle Pan is of you. I've been one of his scouts for a long time now, so I'm sure we'll be good friends in future.'

I went back to the temple and decided to take a look around. In the main hall quite a number of ancient spears and knives were standing against the wall as if in preparation for battle. I found Pan Xudong, Chang Je-an and Wang Jiansheng in the east wing calmly discussing something. Catching sight of me, Wang Jiansheng beckoned me over. He was always keen that I should listen to their discussions so I would know what work was in hand. The discussion, it seemed, had just started. Chang Je-an was talking about the work they were doing in the Changshan Mountains.

'This area is under the control of several different landlords, each of whom has his own sphere of influence as well as his own armed militia – namely, the Red Spears. They form their own alliances and have their own disputes, but none of them can become the overlord because the Red Spear Societies in this area are entirely made up of peasants, armed with the most primitive of weapons. Even their leaders are peasants. The landlords have persuaded them that by joining the Red Spears they can protect their homes from the bandits. Many renegade soldiers have come up to these hills as a result of skirmishes between the armies of warlords from the three provinces, and most have turned to banditry. I once came up here just before the Great Revolution in 1926. This place was far from the main centre of activity, so after looking around for a while I left. However, I made several friends amongst the local peasants, though the struggle which was being waged in the rest of the province left no time to develop things here or set up a peasant union. Seeing that this area looked "peaceful", the reactionaries have not bothered to pay much attention to it. This, of course, gave us an ideal opportunity to step in. After the fighting in Mazhen county and we had been dispersed, I remembered this mountainous area and hurried up here. Luckily, the friends I had made were ready to help me and at once found me somewhere to stay . . .'

'Did they give you shelter in their homes?' Wang Jiansheng asked.

Chang Je-an shook his head and said with a laugh, 'Can't you see where I'm living now? This place was empty. It used to have some monks a long time ago, but the local villages could no longer afford to support them. I was able to come here and act as a fortune-teller. My clients include landlords and local gentry. They seem pretty impressed by my knowledge of reading and writing and my fluent tongue. They even invited me to join their Red Spear Society to act as a secretary!'

Pan Xudong and Wang Jiansheng laughed.

'So you're now an officer in the Red Spear Society, are you?' Pan Xudong asked. 'In that case, we've saved you a lot of trouble by coming to you voluntarily as "prisoners of war"!'

'Well,' Chang Je-an laughed, 'I'll treat you as guests anyway. And I hope you'll help me make the Red Spears even better than before!' Then, lowering his voice, he became more serious and said, 'You remember how before, when Chumin's Red Spear Society and the Order Preservation Corps worked with the Nationalists to attack us, it was the mutiny within the Red Spears which eventually turned the situation to our advantage.'

'That's right,' Wang Jiansheng said, growing noticeably excited. 'I was there at the time. From then on, we grew rapidly in strength and because of this the uprising which followed was successful.'

'Right!' Chang Je-an went on. 'So why shouldn't we turn the Red Spears here to our advantage too? They are made up of peasants and it's really just a matter of who controls them. In the hands of the reactionaries, they can only have a negative role. But in the hands of the revolutionaries they will push history forward. I'm pleased to say that most of the peasants in the Red Spears around this temple already understand this. This place is now their headquarters. Didn't you notice all the people coming in and out when you arrived? They are all very friendly to me and as a result I can sit here in peace and safety talking to you. I'd originally planned to look for you myself to discuss our plans. But here you are anyway!'

Pan Xudong and Wang Jiansheng smiled cheerfully.

'We'd already heard that you had started afresh up here,' Pan Xudong said, 'and that is why we decided to come. But we never imagined the speed of developments here. One thing, though: what do the landlords and local gentry think about all this? They can't be resting too easy in their beds at night.'

'To tell the truth,' Chang Je-an replied, 'they're not really aware of what's going on here. The peasants can be relied on to keep things secret and they have also guaranteed our safety. Now that you have come, we are stronger than before and can quickly get on with the task of transforming the Red Spear Society. Once we've won over the Red Spears, the landlords and gentry will be powerless to do anything against us. Even if they discover what we have been doing, it won't matter in the slightest.'

'And then we can destroy them in one go!' Wang Jiansheng added. 'How simple it all seems!'

Pan Xudong, however, shook his head a little doubtfully and said, 'In the past we suffered set-backs because we looked at things too simply. Now we can learn from the past. Our activities here are just beginning. We need a period of stability so that we can review our policies. It looks as if the landlords and gentry around here are not yet in collusion with the reactionary government and its armies. So long as this state of affairs continues, we can find ways to make them feel safe for the time being. For example, we could delay our implementation of land redistribution, providing that they reduce rents and lower interest so as to improve the lives of the peasants. At the very least we can neutralize them. All they need do is understand the benefits of maintaining stability in this region and then both sides can make the necessary compromises. Then we'll have a firm foothold here.'

Chang Je-an and Wang Jiansheng suddenly became silent. They exchanged glances with Pan Xudong, neither knowing what to say. This silence made the three friends, at last reunited after such severe hardships, feel strangely ill at ease. Chang Je-an, the host on this occasion, felt particularly uncomfortable. It was finally Wang Jiansheng who, sensing the tension in the air, broke the silence.

'Compromise?' he said. 'You mean reach a compromise

with the landlords and gentry? I must say that I would feel very suspicious of any such compromise. You remember what both the national and international revolutionary organizations have said. At a time of intense class struggle like this how could we possibly think of compromising with the enemy class?'

Chang Je-an remained silent, but he threw a questioning glance at Pan Xudong.

Feeling that some sort of explanation was essential, Pan Xudong said, 'You're right. We are working under the leadership of national and international organizations. But they are both far away and the situation in our region is changing by the day. We must adapt our policies to the realities which exist here. Our aims do not change, but the means we use must be flexible. Isn't Je-an doing precisely that by acting under the guise of an astrologer up here? On the surface, it looks as though he is just disseminating superstition, but in reality he is helping to spread the revolution. Of course we must consider what means we use, but the effect is the most important thing of all.'

Chang Je-an and Wang Jiansheng were again silent but after a while they were both unable to suppress a chuckle.

'Well, I'm not all that fond of fortune-telling!' Chang Je-an laughed.

With their laughter the atmosphere relaxed again.

'Yes,' Wang Jiansheng said. 'We are responsible for the progress of the revolution. The first task ahead of us is to rebuild a base. We should consider every possibility in order to achieve this goal and make use of all this region has to offer. Once we have a base, we can begin to rebuild our political power and then our work in all areas will become more effective.'

This time it was Pan Xudong's turn to smile. A grin spread across his weathered face.

'Yes,' he said. 'Political power – that's one of the most important things. We were not wrong in setting up our government before, but our plans were a bit unrealistic. It was not realistic to try to set up our base in the county town while the enemy was so much stronger than we were. Now we must change our strategy. Starting in this area, we must mobilize the masses and expand our armed forces. Once we have a really solid base, we can expand into surrounding areas. Then, no matter how big Chiang Kai-shek's armies are, we'll be able to handle them.'

Although this was no more than an impromptu discussion, it helped us to review our past experience and make a blueprint for our work in this area. Everyone began to feel excited, which made us forget our hunger. However, Chang Je-an brought us back to the present.

'You must all be feeling tired and hungry,' he said. 'Now I've got something to welcome you properly: white rice. Come into the dining hall!'

He led us into the dining hall. White rice! This was something we had not even dared to dream of. And a real dining hall! Chang Je-an had really established himself in the Changshan Mountains. With this as our base, we would certainly be able to put Pan Xudong's blueprint into action.

Our new work kept us very busy. My legs were put to constant use and found little rest. I had to run to the Daji Mountains, the Lianyun Mountains and even as far as Mazhen county, sending messages to Uncle Pan, Jia Hongcai, Liu Dawang, Big Tree Lu, Li Chengbao and others. Then I would bring news from them back to Pan Xudong and Chang Je-an. This meant that most of my work involved passing through areas controlled by the Nationalists and the Order Preservation Corps. My task was thus a very dangerous one, though with the help of our underground workers I was able to keep well informed of the enemy's movements, and since I usually travelled by night, I managed to avoid detection. In fact, I could quite easily have travelled during the day, as I received the constant assistance and protection of our supporters.

This situation was crucially connected to the expansion of our guerrilla activities. Since our forces were now engaging more and more frequently with the enemy, we now had a better idea of their real strength. Although they seemed formidable, it turned out that the Nationalist troops and the Order Preservation Corps were powerless without their weapons. Our main aim was to deprive them of their weapons, and every time we did this it added to our strength and increased the morale of our fighters. Even Big Tree Lu and Sun Nan's troops up in the Lianyun Mountains had tasted this new experience. They were no longer satisfied with simply raiding the Order Preservation Corps along the 'line of defence'. They now began to try their luck with the Nationalist bases further afield, as they possessed more modern weapons than the Order Preservation Corps. They had already made one such attempt, with encouraging success.

Once I was asked to send a letter to Liu Dawang, who had remained in the Lianyun Mountains. Being practically illiterate, he told me to take this verbal message back to our new headquarters:

'Although these guerrilla activities are still on a fairly small scale, they have caused a considerable stir amongst the masses, both in the mountains and down on the plains. Although the enemy is still better armed and is superior to us in numbers, the masses now regard them differently. They live in fear of the enemy's weapons, but scorn the enemy soldiers themselves. In contrast, the masses are fully behind us, as they realize that our forces are their forces as well. Recently Uncle Pan got in touch with us from the old base area. Our guerrilla activities will now expand more rapidly, as we are already beginning to co-ordinate our strategy.'

On returning to the Temple of the Three Gods I reported all I had found out to Pan Xudong, Wang Jiansheng and Chang Je-an. The temple had become our headquarters. We now had a considerable network of contacts covering different areas, so I was not the only person to deliver regular reports here. Uncle

Pan had assigned Wang the Coppersmith to report from the old base area. Uncle Zizhong found a wood-cutter nicknamed Half Wild Man to send messages from the Daji Mountains. Li Chengbao, who had once been the commander of the ninth branch of the Peasant Volunteer Force in Mazhen county, also commissioned someone to deliver messages from there. After the break-out from the county town, Pan Mingxun and Jiqing, who had been in the seventh branch, had taken a few guns and begun setting up a small force in neighbouring Shangsheng county. They were now beginning to engage in fresh guerrilla activities. They had also managed to get in contact with Uncle Pan and our headquarters and by now had a messenger to keep us regularly informed of their news. Sweet Potato, too, was in contact with the Temple of the Three Gods. He delivered reports from 'The Big City'. My main task, therefore, was to deliver messages from the headquarters to the various areas in which we were operating, making me one thread in a large network of contacts.

Lao Liu was another important thread in this network. He had taken up his old trade again and went around with his clappers telling stories. He grew a little beard and got hold of a very old, worn gown. With his weather-worn face, aged by hunger, he now looked like a character out of the pages of a history book. Nobody suspected that he had been the head of propaganda for the Democratic Government of Workers and Peasants. His field of activity stretched from the Lianyun Mountains to the old base area, across to the Daji Mountains, and even as far as Mazhen and Shangsheng counties.

One day, when I was sending a message to Uncle Pan, I passed through a little village at the foot of some hills, and I heard the sound of drumming. Hiding behind a tree, I looked out to see what was going on. There was Lao Liu, telling stories in which a revolutionary message was hidden. To avoid revealing our real purpose, I crept away before Lao Liu or anyone else noticed me. Later, Uncle Pan gave me a report from Lao Liu to take back to the headquarters, in which he described his propaganda work.

'Our forces in the Lianyun Mountains are becoming stronger,' Pan Xudong said, summing up the report I had just delivered, 'and Chumin's Order Preservation Corps at the foot of the mountains are gradually being whittled away. But they are not likely to give in that easily. As soon as they discover that the Lianyun Mountains, which they believed were "clean", now have a revolutionary force, they are bound to feel nervous and angry; they might well get together with the Nationalist armies to launch another extermination campaign. We must be prepared for such an eventuality.'

'I agree,' Wang Jiansheng said. 'But this could be a good opportunity to destroy the Nationalists – we could certainly use their guns.'

'We can't afford to engage with them directly this time,' Chang Je-an said. 'They are dozens of times stronger than us. We must avoid making the same mistake as last time, when we took over the county town and were surrounded.'

A smile appeared on Pan Xudong's face.

'Well,' he said, 'now there's no town for us to defend. Nor do we have any plans to try and hold a town in the future. I agree with what you say: that we should wipe out the Nationalist forces. But we can only do this bit by bit.'

'But we must make a co-ordinated effort,' Wang Jiansheng put in. 'The enemy will be unable to resist our assaults from all sides.'

'This is the only way we can achieve victory,' Chang Je-an agreed, 'given our limited numbers.'

Pan Xudong nodded and was thoughtful for a while.

'In that case we should begin to take the initiative,' he said. 'We should start making preparations without delay and send messages to organizers in different areas, telling them to begin a co-ordinated mobilization.'

It was up to me to go out and inform our forces in other areas of this decision. My first destination was the Lianyun Mountains and the first person I had to report to was Liu Dawang. Wang Jiansheng told me to go off and get a good rest so as to renew my energies for that evening's march. I slept soundly in his bed. At dusk I left the hills and headed for the Lianyun Mountains.

At the third cockcrow I reached the little hidden village where Uncle Pan was staying. I had decided to rest there a while and tell him the decision made by headquarters, so that he, in turn, could spread the message to other local organizers. Before I had reached the mud hut where Uncle Pan had been staying, a middle-aged peasant jumped out from behind a nearby ash tree. Recognizing me at once, he cheerfully led me indoors. Uncle Pan was talking with five young men, who included the carpenter, Zheng Xiangyong, and the bricklayer, Yu Minghan. Their guerrilla forces around the old base area had successfully raided the Order Preservation Corps in a number of places, capturing about 100 guns. They had used these to set up five brigades of guerrillas. These five young men were the commanders of the brigades. I told them about the decision of the Special Regional Committee.

'This is exactly what we were planning to do,' Uncle Pan said. 'Since we have proved ourselves capable of destroying the landlords' Order Preservation Corps, we'll certainly be able to wipe out the Nationalist troops.'

'Wipe them out bit by bit,' Zheng Xiangyong said. 'That seems a very sound idea. Ants can turn bones to dust, so long as they keep on gnawing away!'

'But we could use different tactics in different places,' Yu Minghan suggested. 'We don't always need to wait until they are asleep before we attack. We can attack them even while they are carrying out exercises. We already have a strategy for doing this. We recently got news from our scouts that the Nationalist troops in Tanjiahe are busy making opium pellets. This means that they are probably getting ready to launch an offensive, as they can't take their opium pipes as well as their rifles when they're marching, so they need opium pellets to chew as they go. Chiang Kai-shek sent these recruits here from Szechuan province, and they're all hooked on opium.'

Uncle Pan was silent for a moment. Then he raised his head and said, 'They might be planning an attack on the Lianyun Mountains. People from Szechuan are short and stocky and are good at climbing mountains.' He turned to me and said, 'Don't forget to inform Liu Dawang and Big Tree Lu of this new state of affairs so that they can begin making preparations. We'll keep an eye on the Nationalists from here. As soon as they start heading for the mountains, we'll follow them.'

This new information meant time was of the essence, and I had to set out for the Lianyun Mountains at once. I hurriedly drank a mouthful of water and ate a piece of cake. As I was leaving, Uncle Pan gave me a couple of rice cakes for my journey.

'It'll soon be light,' he said, 'so you'd better stick to smaller paths.'

His concern warmed me, and my legs no longer ached. I was already familiar with the various paths leading to the Lianyun Mountains and, choosing a direct but relatively difficult route, I managed to reach Big Tree Lu's place by midnight. Big Tree Lu seemed delighted to see me. As soon as I gave him my message, he went off to fetch Liu Dawang and several newly appointed commanders. Over the past few days they had managed to capture nearly 100 guns from the Order Preservation Corps and so had been able to set up five new guerrilla brigades. Now they began to discuss the message I had brought from the Special Regional Committee, as well as the news of the Nationalists' new offensive.

'Our own scouts report the same situation as described by Uncle Pan,' Sun Nan said. 'They are definitely heading in this direction.'

'We'll have to find out how many of them there are,' Big Tree

Lu said. 'This'll be the first time our guerrillas have had to fight the proper enemy forces.'

'We must be guided by the decisions of the headquarters and wipe them out completely,' Liu Dawang said. 'We mustn't let them come up into the mountains. It's already poor enough up here and the last thing the hill people need is to be interfered with by bandits.'

Everyone was silent after he had spoken and I felt a nervous tension in the air.

'What can I do?' I said, breaking the silence. 'I know the roads down there really well and I'm a good runner.'

'You've already done enough running for the time being,' Liu Dawang said. 'You need a good sleep. My bed is empty and you're welcome to use it. There'll be plenty for you to do later. I'll tell you when you've had a proper sleep.'

Everyone looked at me, encouraging me to go off and have a sleep. I really did need to sleep. I had been finding it hard to concentrate as I listened to their discussion. In Liu Dawang's room I slumped down on his straw bed and in a moment was fast asleep.

I slept right through until the following afternoon and if it hadn't been for the sound of voices outside, I could quite easily have gone on sleeping. Outside was a group of young men, each carrying a rifle. Liu Dawang was telling them their plan of action. I immediately realized that their scouts must have brought news that the Nationalists were already heading for the mountains.

Finishing his directive, Liu Dawang turned to me and said, 'Now we need your help. We're going to set out tonight and you should come along to carry messages between our various brigades. But first have something to eat with the rest of us – and make sure you eat enough!'

This time we had the most luxurious of meals – sweet potatoes. Around midnight, the six guerrilla brigades set off on different routes down the mountain, planning to meet at a place called Nantiangou. This was really a valley from which one could go up into the mountains. The foothills sloped gently down to it and the valley covered about four or five *li* before opening up into the plain. Nearby, a guardhouse of the Order Preservation Corps kept watch over this valley, but it had recently been secretly ransacked by Big Tree Lu's guerrillas and not a soul remained. However, the building had been left untouched and nothing appeared to be amiss.

By the time we reached this valley the sky was already beginning to grow light. Between us, we had about 115 guns. This was the largest force I had seen since we had left the county town and I couldn't help feeling a sense of excitement. Looking up, I noticed on the hillsides above the valley many men were moving through the undergrowth, their bodies silhouetted against the pink light of early morning. Carrying ancient spears, pikes and hunting muskets, they appeared and disappeared among the bushes. They were even more numerous than our forces in the valley and I realized at once that they must all be members of the recently established Peasant Union.

Liu Dawang divided our armed soldiers into three sections. One, led by him, lay in ambush at the foot of the slope. Another, led by Sun Nan, hid on a hillside halfway down the valley. The third, led by Big Tree Lu, lay in wait at the entrance to the valley. There was also a small group made up of seven youngsters, including myself. Apart from our revolvers, each of us carried a little cloth bag full of fire crackers. We were all fast and agile, and adept at reconnaissance work. Our task was to keep well hidden at various points along the side of the valley. Because of my speed and skill at finding the way, I was assigned to a point close to the opening of the valley, from which I was able to obtain a good view of the main road.

When everyone else had taken up their positions, the hills suddenly became still, as if under the influence of some strange magic. Not a single figure could now be detected on the hillsides or in the valley and a deathly silence settled over the entire place. I, alone, ran down the valley to take up my appointed position. I could hear my footsteps as I ran and my breathing sounded loud in my ears. Although my position was the most hazardous of all, I had no time to feel any sense of fear. In any case, I was used to facing danger by now.

I squatted down behind some bushes at a point where the road turned in towards the valley. My main aim was to keep an eye on this road, which joined many other roads and paths leading to various towns and villages. I had to keep an especially close watch on the road leading from Tanjiahe. Squatting there alone on a flat piece of rock, far from feeling lonely or nervous, I was filled with a reassuring sense of calm and confidence. In these days of war and upheaval it seemed a rare pleasure to be able to sit alone, quietly enjoying the beauty of nature. Looking at the silhouettes of the trees and the distant mountains, the sky above tinged by the light of early morning, my mind began a little reverie of its own: when I grew old, and had completed all the work I had in front of me, I would return to this place and live here in a grass hut for the last few years of my life. Remembering all the experiences I had had in my life, I would quietly pass from this world among these hills and trees. Having entered the world as flesh and blood, I would then leave it peacefully and return to the still soil. This way I would enter eternity.

While these thoughts of eternity were passing through my mind, the sky in the east grew lighter and early-morning clouds appeared, lit up by the sun. The road before me shone like a white streak across the undulating landscape; like other roads in this area, it was covered with white gravel. This brought me back to my senses and I remembered with a start that I was preparing for battle. Instinctively I felt the revolver at my waist. I knew that if the Nationalists did come, it would be up to me to fire the first shot. Gathering my wits, I strained my eyes to search for any sign of movement ahead.

Just as the sun appeared above the tops of the mountains to the east, I glimpsed a cloud of dust rising from the road in the distance. Then, through the dust, I gradually made out figures, their outlines growing clearer and clearer. At first glance their numbers seemed endless and I felt my body tense, not with fear, but in anticipation of what was to follow. I waited until they drew near enough, and the sky grew light enough for me to get a clear picture of them. The battle would have to begin soon, and it was up to me to set it in motion. Running out of the bushes, I waved my revolver at the enemy and, without waiting for them to shout or open fire, I fired the first shot. No sooner had the shot rung out than I dived back into the bushes and crept along the valley, keeping myself well hidden against the hillside. The soldiers tried to give chase and started firing, but with no target in sight, all they could do was shout, 'Hey! Catch him . . . catch him! Rebel agent . . .'

I let off two more shots into the air, leading them on into the valley. These shots were also a signal for our guerillas who were lying in ambush, and for the other scouts along the valley, who let off their firecrackers, which sounded very similar to a volley of gunfire. This was to give the enemy the impression that there was nothing more than a small group of soldiers – remnants of the break-out force from the county town – hiding in the valley. The enemy, thinking that their judgement had been proved correct, rushed up the valley to mop up these 'remnants' of the communist rebel army.

By the time their front line had almost reached the first foothills, I had climbed up to where Liu Dawang was waiting. We not only had to prevent them from entering the mountains, we also had to make sure we wiped them out. With our limited numbers and scarce ammunition we could not afford to fight them face to face, and therefore had to rely on our accurate marksmanship. In other words, we had to pick off their commanders, who were clearly distinguishable by the two leather straps they wore across their chests. From their vantage points on the hillsides, our soldiers were able to shoot at their targets with great accuracy and each bullet hit its mark. Seeing their commanders falling at their feet, those opium-smoking Nationalist soldiers turned into an undisciplined rabble, each fleeing to save his own skin.

Then the guerrillas hiding in the middle and lower sections of the valley began to open fire, picking off the remaining commanders from among the rest of the advancing troops. The enemy had no chance whatsoever of opening fire and, taking advantage of their confusion, the members of the Peasants' Union hidden along both sides of the valley started a deafening, earth-shaking roar. Their stones pelted down, thicker than hail, upon the enemy, whose soldiers began to flee in panic, trying to protect their heads with their hands.

This mad rush for safety was exacerbated by the enemy soldiers' craving for opium. Unable to reach for their pellets, they trampled one another as they fled. Quite a number were crushed to death and lay in heaps on the floor of the valley, hindering the flight of others. Within about an hour, half of the Nationalists had been wiped out along this short stretch of the valley. The remaining half fled out of the valley and back in the direction of Tanjiahe. Liu Dawang decided to reorganize our forces to give chase, leaving the Nationalist prisoners and their captured weapons in the hands of the Peasants' Union, whose men had by now run down the hillside to round up the soldiers who had not managed to get away.

About 200 Nationalist soldiers escaped in all and we could spare less than 100 men to give chase. Had they decided to turn round and attack us, we would have incurred serious casualties – especially in this open country where there was nowhere to take refuge. But it was obvious from their panic-stricken flight that they had no such intention. Mustering our courage and strength, we managed to chase them some ten *li*. However, the energy from the sweet potatoes we had eaten the night before had its limits and after a while we began to slow down. In addition, we had to pick up all the Nationalist rifles we found scattered along the way, and eventually the enemy soldiers began to disappear into the distance.

Seeing that our pursuit has slackened, the Nationalist soldiers suddenly turned round and tried taking a few shots at us. We returned their fire and although the crack of rifles could be heard for a while, the distance between us was too great and neither side sustained any casualties.

All of a sudden a roar rose up some distance ahead of the enemy.

'That must be our guerrillas trying to cut them off,' Liu Dawang said to me. 'Go quickly and find out what's happening!'

By climbing a nearby hill, I got a good view of what was happening up ahead. The Nationalists had stopped firing and were fleeing in all directions. The roar grew even louder and before long I was able to make out a large peasant force coming towards us. As they drew nearer, I could not believe my eyes: Uncle Pan himself was leading this force, shouting as he went, 'Don't let any enemy soldiers go! Don't lose a single enemy gun!'

Liu Dawang did not have to wait for me to return with my report. He knew full well what was happening up ahead, as he himself had planned this strategy in advance. Just then, the guerrillas led by Big Tree Lu and Sun Nan joined our rear, concentrating our forces still further. Seeing that there was no longer any point resisting, the Nationalist soldiers fled into the bush on all sides. Now it was our turn to 'surround and exterminate' the enemy. The three guerrilla brigades under Liu Dawang's command closed in on three sides, while Uncle Pan's Peasant Volunteers continued to press down ahead. The enemy were now left without a single route of escape and became nothing more than 'a turtle in a hole'. Needless to say, we took them all alive and not a gun, nor even a single bullet, was lost.

Later, when we counted the number of guns captured, we discovered we had taken 178 rifles, as well as 3,004 rounds of ammunition. With the guns we had captured in the valley, this made a total of over 500 guns and a huge amount of ammunition.

As we were beginning to regroup into our respective brigades, I overheard Uncle Pan and Liu Dawang talking about the battle.

'Our scouts had been keeping a close watch on the Nationalist troops,' Uncle Pan was saying. 'As soon as they set out for Tanjiahe, we began to get organized. Knowing that they must be heading for the Lianyun Mountains, we took a path across the hills and lay in wait for them. Keeping well hidden, we watched them pass. We knew that they wouldn't get far and, sure enough, they soon came fleeing back! We had no more than about fifty old guns between us and could only hope to block them once they were already in retreat.'

'Well,' Liu Dawang said, 'this time they've given us enough guns to arm an entire battalion. By our usual reckoning, 100 guns are enough to arm a battalion, which means we could practically set up a whole regiment! One regiment of ours would be able to cope with two divisions of Chiang Kai-shek's troops!'

The two men laughed heartily at the thought. By now the sun was beginning to curve down towards the western horizon.

'I think I'd better be getting back to the Changshan Mountains to tell them what's been happening,' I said. 'Do you have any new instructions for me before I go?'

'You should have something to eat before you go,' Uncle Pan said.

'It doesn't matter,' I replied. 'I'll run through the night. When I'm running I don't feel hungry.'

Uncle Pan patted my stomach lightly. It gave a hollow sound. He let out a small sigh, but said nothing more.

'Yes,' Liu Dawang said, 'you should set out right away. You've seen everything that happened here – you took part in the action yourself. You know what to report to the headquarters. The only message I have is that we will now plan a major expansion of our forces. I'll discuss the details with Uncle Pan tonight.'

'Yes,' Uncle Pan agreed. 'And this expansion will include the Daji Mountains. Jia Hongcai's scout, Half Wild Man is here right now. I'll send him off at once to ask Jia Hongcai to find out how many guerrillas he can organize there. We can let them have some of the guns we have just captured. We also plan to take over Tanjiahe as soon as possible, as only the Order Preservation Corps is left there. We can take them completely by surprise!'

I said goodbye to them and went on my way. After walking for about half an hour under cover of twilight, I looked up to see the sky filled with stars and there was a bright full moon. They seemed to wink at me in cheerful greeting, like old, long-forgotten friends. I felt a sense of well-being at our reunion.

CHAPTER 7

I arrived back at the Temple of the Three Gods in the Chang-shan Mountains late the following afternoon, just as the day was drawing to a close. The three remaining members of the Special Regional Committee, Pan Xudong, Chang Je-an and Wang Jiansheng, were deep in discussion. As soon as they saw me they broke off their conversation and listened eagerly to my report. As I finished talking about the situation in the old base areas, I suddenly felt my head start spinning and my legs grow weak. I steadied myself against the wall behind my stool as confusion clouded my mind.

Wang Jiansheng leaned over to support me and said quietly in my ear, 'You're just hungry, Chunsheng. You can't have eaten for two days – and you probably haven't had a proper sleep either!'

Without waiting for a reply, he helped me up, led me into the kitchen and made me a bowl of porridge with wild vegetables. Although my mind still felt rather hazy, I managed to drink all the porridge in one go. Wang Jiansheng pressed his hand to my forehead and said, 'You have a slight fever – just the result of exhaustion. You'd better go and get a good sleep right away.'

He led me into the little room next to the kitchen, used for storing wood. This was where I usually slept while I was in the Changshan Mountains. Zheng Xiangyong had cleared a small space for me here, just large enough for a wooden door, which served as my bed. As soon as I lay down I fell fast asleep and slept for the whole of the next day and night.

When I woke I became aware of someone sitting by my side. I opened my eyes slowly and saw that it was Wang Jiansheng.

'You still seem to have a bit of a fever,' he said. 'You've probably just caught a cold.'

'It's nothing,' I replied, rolling over and sitting up. 'As soon as I start running I'll sweat it all out and I'll be fine.'

'But you've been doing too much running lately,' he said. 'People aren't made of steel, after all, and there's a limit to what you can do. You see . . . you can't even stand up properly. Your legs still need a few day's rest.'

'I can't rest,' I insisted. 'All sorts of things must be going on out there right now. I couldn't bear to sit around here doing nothing!'

'Well, you'll just have to bear it!' he replied. 'Even greater things will be happening and if you don't give those legs of yours a good rest now, I'm afraid they won't be able to take part in anything that happens in the future. And then you'd feel even more frustrated! You must rest now in preparation for more important work later.'

'What's going to happen?' I asked eagerly. 'Tell me quickly – then I'll be able to rest more easily!'

'So you want me to give you a "report"?' Wang Jiansheng said with a grin. 'All right then! I'd planned to spend some time chatting with you anyway. The news you brought back has made everyone feel very excited. But in reality, this is just the start of the new turn of events. Just after you fell asleep some even more exciting news arrived from other messengers reporting from different areas. Now we have a much more complete communications network, so in the future you may not need to spend so much time running around and will be able to work more closely with me.'

'What exciting news?' I asked impatiently. 'Tell me every-thing!'

'There's no need for you to know all of this,' Wang Jiansheng replied. 'All you should be thinking about now is resting and you shouldn't bother your brain with anything else!'

'I'm not a machine,' I argued. 'If I don't know the full situation, how can I be expected to carry out my duties as a messenger? I could run into real danger . . .'

Wang Jiansheng once again stretched out his hand and felt my forehead.

'You're quite right,' he said. 'I just want you to have a proper rest. You'll know everything sooner or later anyway. Liu Dawang and Uncle Pan chased the few remaining Nationalist soldiers all the way to Tanjiahe, taking the Order Preservation Corps there completely by surprise. Like an eagle catching a rabbit, they swooped down and grabbed all their weapons. The number of guns at our disposal is now growing by the day. The most important thing, of course, is to eventually wipe out Chiang Kai-shek and the landlords and bureaucrats whom he represents, heightening the people's confidence in the revolution, so as to lay a basis for our land reforms. Once the land is returned to the peasants, we will have changed the course of thousands of years of history.'

'But we'll first have to destroy Chiang Kai-shek's armies,' I said. 'Without doing this our other policies can never succeed.'

'Correct!' Wang Jiansheng replied. 'But we can't wait until Chiang Kai-shek's armies have been completely eliminated before beginning to change the structure of society. Neither can we wait until we've changed society before eliminating his armies – that would be impossible.' Then, lowering his voice, Wang Jiansheng went on more earnestly: 'Jiqing and Pan Mingxun in Shangsheng county, and Li Chengbao and Wang Jingxian in Mazhen county are moving gradually in this direction. They are having a lot of success wiping out the Order Preservation Corps and before long they plan to wipe out the local Nationalist forces. They are all co-ordinating their efforts so as to close in from two sides.'

'So is the Special Regional Committee now planning to develop things a stage further?' I asked.

Wang Jiansheng nodded.

'Our forces in Mazhen, Shangsheng and in the old base areas have been growing very quickly and so we'll soon be able to start large-scale operations. With the support of the masses there, we now have the right conditions in which to operate.'

'What sort of large-scale operation?' I asked. 'I want to be part of it!'

Wang Jiansheng smiled and again felt my temperature.

'Of course you'll be part of it,' he assured me. 'And you'll be carrying out the same duties as usual – as a messenger. But now you must rest, so as to be able to do your work properly.'

His smile broadened into a grin, making it clear that he did not wish to discuss the situation in any more detail. He was often like this, always reluctant to discuss matters that were still in the pipeline.

'Sweet Potato is doing his usual work,' he said evasively. 'He's already been up here with instructions from above given to him by Master Qiu. The leaders have approved our plans.'

'Does this mean that our whole organization is now ready to start a fresh offensive?' I asked. 'But surely . . .'

Wang Jiansheng had already stood up to leave, but he stopped and said, 'But surely what?'

'During our break-out we lost a lot of people,' I said. 'Now we've gradually got in contact with most of those who survived. But I really can't lie around here while there are still people waiting to be contacted.'

Wang Jiansheng was silent for a while.

'Oh, I see,' he said. 'You're thinking about Ho Shuoru and Peng Wanzhen. There's been no news of them yet. And there is also Grandpa Whiskers, your mother, Aunt Sunflower and O Ran, isn't there?'

'You're right,' I said. 'And there's one other person you've forgotten – Lao Liu. We haven't heard anything from him recently. Even Uncle Pan has lost touch with him. Now that things are happening so quickly I must make sure that he's kept informed.'

Wang Jiansheng nodded and said, 'Yes. We really need him now. We could also do with Ho Shuoru and Peng Wanzhen's help. Our propaganda work must go hand in hand with the rest of our operations. We need more written propaganda. You're quite right – we must get them up here.'

Now it was my turn to be silent.

'And there's also O Ran's baby . . .' Wang Jiansheng added.

'And Sister Apricot and Little Baldy,' I said, noticing the grave and thoughtful expression on his face.

Wang Jiansheng patted his head, turning slightly pale.

'You mustn't think that I don't care about them,' he said, his voice growing a little unsteady. 'I'll do all I can to find them. It's just that with such pressing work, none of us has had the time to think of personal matters.'

'I don't have nearly as many responsibilities to cope with as you,' I said. 'So I have more time to think about my family. I really must find them – and not only because they're my relations.'

'You're right,' he said. 'This isn't just a personal matter. All of us in the Special Regional Committee are concerned about them.'

'Well, in that case I'd better be going right away,' I said, grabbing this opportunity. 'I'll be back as quickly as I can. This won't effect any work you give me in future.'

Seeing how determined I was, Wang Jiansheng said no more about the matter. Taking his silence as consent, I immediately made preparations to leave.

This time I decided to go down the south side of the mountain. Here there was an area of rolling hills stretching south-west towards the three neighbouring counties. The area was bare and stony and there was little fertile land. Because of this, there were no big landlords like Chumin here. The small landlords lacked the resources to get together and organize any force on the scale of Chumin's Order Preservation Corps. The most they could manage were small bands of peasants like the Red Spear Societies, whose task was 'the defence of our homes'. In reality these organizations had now come under the influence of Chang Je-an and were already little less than branches of the Peasant Volunteers. The landlords and gentry, however, seemed to be unaware of this transformation and the threat it represented, as so far the peasants had not demanded any redistribution of land and had simply requested a reduction in rents and interest.

Because of this situation I was able to pass through this region in complete safety. Occasionally I would meet a peasant on the road – maybe even a member of the Red Spears – and he would wave or exchange a few greetings. But as I entered the old base area I felt a change in the atmosphere. I saw quite a number of women and old people heading in the direction I had come from, their few possessions on their backs. This suggested that the Nationalists were still burning villages. I came across an old couple with a child of four or five walking along a stream in the direction of the hills.

'Grandpa,' I said, 'you're not from the hills, are you? Do you have relatives here?'

The old couple looked tired and took the opportunity to rest for a while next to an old pine tree.

'I have a distant relation in the hills,' the old man said. 'We haven't been in touch for ages, but now that times are so hard we have no choice but to ask him for shelter.'

I could tell at once from his accent that he was from the old base area.

'Why do you need to take shelter?' I asked.

'Three battalions came to our district,' he replied. 'They took over three towns and the Order Preservation Corps took control of the bigger villages. But they hadn't expected to still find guerrillas in the countryside. There are even guerrillas in such remote places as the Lianyun Mountains. They come down by night to raid the guardhouses of the Order Preservation Corps. All their guns – and even the men – disappear without a trace. The Nationalists sent a battalion to the mountains to wipe them out, but they ran straight into an ambush at the foot of the hills and all their guns were taken by the guerrillas. I heard that the provincial heads were furious and are sending a whole lot more soldiers here. The Order Preservation Corps are backed up by the Nationalists and have been taking revenge on us ordinary people – burning, killing . . . Now our grandson is our family's only hope, so we want to take him somewhere safe.'

'How can you manage to climb the hills at your age?' I asked. 'Where are your son and daughter-in-law?'

The old couple did not answer.

'Where are you from?' the old man asked instead. 'You sound like someone from our area.'

'You're right,' I replied. 'I'm also from the plains, but I've been up in the hills for a while now. The peasants in our village joined the Peasant Volunteers and were chased by the Nationalist troops. I managed to escape to the hills.'

'Oh, I see,' the old man said. 'My son joined the Peasant Volunteers too. Now he's in the guerrillas, which is why he couldn't come with us. My daughter-in law is with him and can't come either. Only the two of us were left with nothing to do, so we decided to bring the boy up here to shelter for a while.'

'I was just on my way down to see what was happening,' I said. 'I'm still young, so maybe there's something useful I can do there.'

'That's right,' he replied. 'It's up to you youngsters to try to put things right. How can we let them go on killing and burning like that?'

Then, with his old wife and grandson, he went on his way up into the hills. What he had just told me was a timely warning and I began to be more wary as I continued on my way towards the old base area, taking the least conspicuous route I could find. The sun was already dropping below the horizon and darkness was falling fast. I heaved a sigh of relief, as I felt quite safe travelling by night. But suddenly, just as I had jumped across a ditch, a man leapt out from behind me, grabbed me round the neck and put a hand over my mouth. Without a word, he pulled me into a hollow in the hillside and, taking a rope from his belt, bound my hands tightly behind my back. Then, holding on to the rope, he marched me ahead of him deeper into the wild valley. This was the first time I had ever been captured. I did not feel particularly frightened, but was ashamed at having fallen prey so easily.

After passing through the valley we came to an even more desolate area of hills. As we went along, I tried to size up my captor. In the dark I could not make out any details of his face, but from the swiftness of his footsteps he did not sound like an agent of the Order Preservation Corps. More likely, he was a hunter or a labourer.

Hoping to find out what he wanted, I said, 'You're pretty strong. I couldn't even move when you grabbed me round the neck!'

'If you'd moved, you'd have had it!' he replied. 'My fists are tougher than hammers. I could easily have flattened your skull!'

'If you'd done that, I wouldn't be chatting to you now,' I replied. 'I really admire your courage. But I'm afraid you've caught the wrong man this time. You're not an agent of the Order Preservation Corps by any chance?'

'Me? An agent of the Order Preservation Corps!' he said. 'My job is to grab people like you! What do you get from the Order Preservation Corps, snooping around here at night, doing their dirty work for them?'

I did my utmost to hold back my feelings of disgust at having been mistaken for an enemy agent.

'I'm afraid you're wrong there!' I said. 'With people like you around at night, not even armed members of the Order

Preservation Corps dare to come out – let alone their agents! I'm afraid you've really made a mistake this time.'

'So who are you then?' he said even more fiercely, raising his fists.

'Who are you?' I shouted back.

Neither of us was prepared to answer this question directly. I decided that I'd better do something before he started his fists raining blows on my head. I said, almost amiably, 'For all you know we might both be on the same side. Just loosen the ropes. I promise I won't try to escape. I'll go wherever you want me to.'

'All right then!' he said, lowering his fists. But he did not loosen the ropes.

We walked a long way, reaching a little mud village at daybreak. Behind some bushes at the edge of the hamlet stood a small millhouse. My captor pushed me in through its half-open door. Inside several peasants were sitting around talking in the weak light of an oil lamp.

'I found this fellow snooping around out there,' he said, breaking into their conversation. 'He seemed pretty suspicious, so I nabbed him.'

An elderly man stared at me for a moment and then stood up and loosened my ropes.

'Chunsheng!' Uncle Pan cried. 'Well . . . you do look a bit like an enemy agent!' Then he turned to my captor and said. 'He's a messenger from the headquarters in the Changshan Mountains. Well done! You're really keeping on the alert!'

'Yes,' I added. 'And he moves so fast! He had me in an instant. I really admire him!'

While we were talking, my captor, either from embarrassment or for some other reason, left the room and did not reappear. Later I learned that he was a kilnsman called Yao-jiang.

'What is your errand this time?' Uncle Pan asked. 'Tell me quickly. As you can see, we're in the middle of a meeting here. I'm just on my way to another area to organize things there.'

160

'The Special Regional Committee is just about to start a large-scale mobilization,' I replied. 'You should be getting detailed instructions before long. I'm on my way to try and trace our family and friends in the old base area.'

'Well,' Uncle Pan said cheerfully, 'You've come at just the right moment. We had news of O Ran only yesterday. She's gone off to the mountain area in Xinyi county to get things going up there. Now she's busy trying to make contact with organizations in other counties. You can tell her what has been going on here and pass on her news to the Special Regional Committee. She should also have news of Grandpa Whiskers. We must get in touch with all of them as soon as possible. We really need their help now. We must also find Lao Liu. There's no need for him to go on doing propaganda work alone. Once you find O Ran, it should be easy enough to find him. Xinyi county is in another province, but it isn't too far from here. The place where she is . . .' he patted his head for a moment. 'Oh, yes, it's called Rice Valley. It's said to be close to Camel Hill. Most people know Camel Hill and you'll have no problem finding it. Well, it's getting late and I must be moving on.'

'I'll go with you,' I said. 'I have to be extra careful if I travel by day.'

The two of us left the little hamlet. After walking together for a short distance we went our separate ways. Uncle Pan went towards the Daji Mountains; I headed for Xinyi county. It was very lucky I had been grabbed that night – otherwise I would never have found Uncle Pan so quickly. The information he had given me would save me a lot of extra running over the next few days.

Xinyi county, being in a neighbouring province, came under the control of a different military commander. Although the various military leaders of these neighbouring provinces all recognized Chiang Kai-shek as the supreme leader, and their armies were all part of the central Nationalist armed forces, they in fact remained quite independent and did not generally tread on one another's toes. This division in their areas of influence worked to our advantage. We could secretly move back and forth with relative freedom, and their troops rarely dared to pursue us over the provincial boundaries. Under these circumstances it was quite easy for O Ran to move to the area around Camel Hill to begin new operations.

Camel Hill was only about one hundred *li* from where I was now, and going at my usual pace I should have been able to reach it in about a day. However, the road was quite new to me and if I travelled alone by night, I would quite likely lose my way. I therefore decided to travel during the day, sticking to the smaller, more lonely hill paths. Despite this the ravages of the Nationalist terror were constantly in evidence. There were very few people working in the fields – the young men had probably fled to the hills to hide or entered the underground. Only when I neared the area around Camel Hill did the atmosphere begin to change. The Nationalist armies and Order Preservation Corps from our old base area probably kept away from this border zone for fear of causing friction with the neighbouring province. This area certainly had the feel of a territory over which neither side exercised control. Here, there were people working in the fields and walking along the roads. I was just another passer-by and nobody took any notice of me.

In the distance I even heard the sound of singing. Out of curiosity, and because I no longer felt the need to keep hidden, I decided to head in the direction of the singing. As I drew closer I began to make out the words of the song.

> The landlords have not given in,
> Crushing revolutionary men,
> They've paid out money to buy two demons,
> To do the job for them.
>
> From the north there's Li Kebao,
> From the south there's Xia Duyin,

They've brought with them two bandit bands,
To do the poor folks in.

They're as cruel as can be,
Of killing they never tire,
They'll stab you with their knives,
And then tie you up with wire.

The villagers flee to the hills,
But their eyes become no drier;
In the distance they see their homes,
Belching smoke from the enemy's fire.

Our homes are all burnt to the ground,
With the grain which we reaped in the fall;
They're trying to do all they can,
To burn all and kill all and loot all.

Wives ask their old men to say,
How can they live in this way?
For a family young and old,
Is there nowhere safe they can stay?

The husbands answer quite true,
That worry alone won't do;
The revolutionary army will come here soon,
And the enemy will get their due.

The poor must at last unite,
And with the strength of all our hands,
We'll push out those landlords and evil gentry,
And wipe out their bandit bands.

We'll take back the reigns of power,
Again build a peasants' government;
Then at last our lives will be changed . . .

The two names mentioned in the song were at once familiar to me: they were the two warlords who at that time ruled over our province. It had been they who, following Chiang Kai-shek's orders, had dispatched two armies to our old base area. As I drew nearer I could see a throng of people crowded round the singer. They all looked very serious, as if attending some sort of ceremony. And from the words of the song it was quite clear what sort of 'ceremony' this must be. I quickly sensed that the people here were very friendly and, without hesitation, I stepped straight into their midst. Nevertheless, I wondered why they should be singing such a song, as apparently this area had so far escaped the scourge of the 'bandit armies'. They looked at me without suspicion. Probably they thought I had just come along to take part in their ceremony.

It turned out that it was a funeral ceremony and in the centre of the crowd I saw a newly built tomb. The tomb had no inscription on it, so at first I had no idea who lay in it. Once the singing had stopped, I asked an old peasant at my side to tell me what was going on.

'The man being buried was a story-teller,' he replied. 'He came from the south and used to stay here a day or two at a time telling stories. Everyone who heard him wants to attend his funeral. See? There are more and more people coming and no one wants to leave. That song you just heard was one he made up just before he died.'

'It's a very moving song,' I said, though I felt my heart sink, as I was overcome by a sense of dread. 'Who was this story-teller?'

'His name was Zhang Quanyi,' the old man replied. 'He really knew how to move our hearts, as he always told true stories. That's why we miss him so much now that he's gone.'

'But why are you singing this particular song?' I asked.

'Because of the way he died!' a young peasant put in. 'He died a terrible death! Really terrible! They're too cruel for words . . .'

I stared at them in horror. I knew at once that Zhang Quanyi

164

was not the story-teller's real name. Sensing my reaction, the two men gave further vent to their emotions. The younger man clenched his fists and fixed me with a bloodshot stare.

'It happened the night before last at a place about twenty *li* south of here. He went to tell stories in a little hill village, where he meant to stay the night. There was a poor peasant living there who had been unable to pay back a loan to the local landlord, so the landlord had taken his wife as a "deposit". The man and his family were as miserable as could be imagined. So Zhang Quanyi at once made up a poem about them. Everyone was so moved when they heard it that they all decided to go off and seek revenge. Then he made up another song – the one you just heard – and before long they had all learnt it. What nobody knew at the time was that one of the landlord's spies was in their midst, listening to every word! That night he went back and informed the landlord, who at once sent his bandit soldiers to grab Zhang Quanyi, while everyone else was still asleep in their houses. By the time we found out there was no sign of anyone – and it was too dark to see anything. The next day we sent people off to go and find out what had happened and try to rescue him. But it was already too late!'

Suddenly my eyes saw black and I had to struggle to steady myself.

'Did they kill him?' I asked.

'Haven't you seen his grave?' the old man replied, sparks of anger in his eyes. 'The area south of here is under their control and they can do whatever they like there.'

'The people we sent said that when the soldiers dragged him off to the execution ground, he kept shouting and cursing them,' the younger man said. 'He called them robbers and bandits and then sang a revolutionary song. They were furious and cut out his tongue, and then they beat him to death on the spot, like a pack of wild animals. Later that night, some local peasants got his body and brought it up to the hills. Then we buried him here. He really was a great man and all of us have

165

come to pay our respects. That's why we are now singing the last song he composed . . .'

Now I knew the whole story. No words could express the feelings that welled up inside me at that moment. I just repeated the young peasant's words mechanically.

'Yes. He was a great man.'

'We wanted to put up a monument to him,' the older man said. 'A great monument. But they can still come across here whenever they want and smash it to pieces. They'd even go so far as digging up his body . . .'

'You're right, Uncle,' I said. 'Now that he's gone let him rest in peace throughout these troubled times. His life was quite hard enough . . .'

I left them and continued on my way. After a few hours' walk I crossed the provincial boundary and entered Xinyi county. There had not been any killing or burning in this area as Chiang Kai-shek had not yet discovered any of our forces and had not issued orders to dispatch troops here. Nor had the local landlords organized an Order Preservation Corps; they still depended entirely on the Red Spear Societies, which were largely made up of peasants. Camel Hill was a notoriously poverty-stricken area in this county. Most people had heard of it, though few ever paid a visit there. And Rice Valley – the name was itself an irony – was the poorest place in this district. It took me over a day to get there, though I finally found the place without too much trouble.

As expected, I found O Ran working in the area, though she was not actually living here. Few of us, at that time, had a fixed place of abode. Uncle Pan had given me a password which I was to use when I found a certain fortune-teller. I quickly found this man, who lived at a permanent address, and he took me off to a little hamlet a short way from Rice Valley. We arrived at the house of a man who made glutinous rice sweets, and there, in his back yard, I found not only O Ran, but Ho Shuoru and Peng Wanzhen as well.

'So here you all are!' I cried in surprise. 'When did you get here?'

'As soon as the news that we'd lost the county town reached us in Red Hill Village,' she replied, 'Grandpa Whiskers led us off to the north-west. We kept on moving, trying to keep ahead of the Nationalists as their campaign of killing and burning spread. So eventually we ended up here.'

'Have you been here all this time?' I asked, instinctively wondering about their safety. 'What's the owner of this place like?'

'Old Dong's very reliable,' Ho Shuoru assured me. 'He might just be a confectioner, but in fact he's got a real artistic eye. He's a great fan of Lao Liu's. Every time Lao Liu comes up here, he makes sure he hears all his stories. He can even recite most of them off by heart.'

'It was Lao Liu's stories that converted him to our way of thinking,' Peng Wanzhen said. 'Now he's on our side, so we can live here quite safely.'

'Well,' O Ran explained, 'you can't exactly say that we're living here. This is just a place to stay – a meeting place. You probably don't know that we've just got in contact with the Temple of the Three Gods. Our messenger, Huang Erhao, has just got back from there with some very important instructions. We'll now have a clearer idea of the work we should be doing here. You must have left the temple a few days ago. If you'd set out a bit later you could have met Huang Erhao there and saved yourself the journey. There's such a lot of work to be done!'

'However busy, I'd have found time to come here to see you,' I said. 'I've been very worried about you all! We've all been anxious about you, so they readily agreed to let me come and look for you. Did Lao Liu really come up here?'

'Of course he did,' Ho Shuoru said, 'otherwise we'd never have been able to stop here. It was he who set things going, but he decided that there was even more pressing work to be done in the old base area – keeping up the morale and will of the people there under the shadow of the enemy. He kept up his story-telling, as he could operate more effectively and safely that way.'

'But he must have been exposed to severe danger,' I said. 'Didn't he worry about that?'

'You wouldn't really understand that,' Peng Wanzhen said with a smile. 'He's a poet, a romantic. His entire work is a poem, a great epic poem. And such a poem cannot be written sitting inside a room. He needs to be in the thick of things, confronted by danger on all sides. Only then does he feel truly inspired, truly heroic! I know what he feels. It's all part of his artistic temperament!'

'Well,' O Ran said, 'I don't know anything about art. But I do know that what Lao Liu is really working for is the future happiness of all the working people. And I know that future will be pure and beautiful. That is why I didn't discourage him from going back to the old base area. If he must go, I said, let him go!'

'You're right,' Ho Shuoru said. 'If it wasn't for him, I doubt whether we'd be able to stay here now – especially you and me. That's right, isn't it, Wanzhen?'

Peng Wanzhen lowered her head, her cheeks growing a little flushed, and nodded shyly in agreement. At this, O Ran couldn't hold back a smile.

'Oh, didn't you know?' she asked me. 'They've already got married. Old Dong's place isn't very big and, what with all his glutinous rice, he could only give us one room, too small for the three of us. I'm always on the move and they, being townsfolk, needed a quiet place in which to work. But of course they couldn't live together without getting married. I was both their go-between and the witness at their wedding. Well, that's what I call romance!'

'Yes,' I said. 'And it's also Lao Liu's romanticism come true! It is the best way we can remember him!'

I suddenly began trembling all over. I sensed that what I had said was not quite appropriate and had touched a sensitive spot in O Ran. So far, however, O Ran's feeling was purely intuitive and had no basis in fact. I felt perplexed, unable to make up my mind whether to tell them about the funeral I had attended on my way. Finally, I decided to keep quiet about it and, changing the subject, asked, 'And how's the baby?'

'Mother's looking after him,' she replied.

'Where's Mother?'

'She's with Aunt Sunflower and Sister Apricot. They're still in the old base area, miles away from here. If you want to see them, you'll have to head back into our province. They're at a place called Buffalo Hill, in the district of Seven Stars. There's a broken-down old nunnery there called the Temple to the Nine Goddesses. The hills there are stony and hardly anything grows. The only people living there are a few hunters and woodcutters, who are so poor that no one really bothers with them. Grandpa Whiskers got a local hunter to help them settle in the temple. I came straight on here after spending a couple of days up there. This place used to be virgin territory. Luckily, Lao Liu had already got things started, so it wasn't long before we had set up a small branch of the Peasants' Union. This quickly developed into a proper Peasants' Union, and now there are unions springing up all over the place! But without Ho Shuoru and Peng Wanzhen I'd have had an almost impossible task. Their propaganda work has been invaluable. And now that we've got new instructions from the headquarters we'll be busier than ever. We're getting ready to move.'

I knew what she meant by the word 'move' and I realized that I must not waste a minute if I was to go and visit Grandpa Whiskers, my mother and the others before our next mobilization began. Then my mind turned back to Lao Liu and I again felt upset. Holding back my feelings, I tried to look as cheerful as I could and got ready to go. O Ran saw me to the door.

'Since I left them,' she said, 'I haven't had a moment to pay them a visit. At times like these we have no control over our personal lives. I hope they will forgive me.'

Huang Erhao, their messenger, showed me on the right

road. He was typical of many hill people: short and stocky and even quicker than me when walking up mountain paths. However, he was forced to moderate his pace, as O Ran, Peng Wanzhen and Ho Shuoru accompanied us some of the way, chatting about their work as they went.

'I wonder,' Ho Shuoru said as we parted, 'whether you could still get hold of a printing machine for us? Without one there's really a limit to what we can do. We work mainly with our brains and our pens, you see – not like Lao Liu, who is such a skilful speaker!'

'It's possible,' I said. 'Sweet Potato has again started making regular visits to "The Big City".'

'Well, in that case I'll write to my father and ask him to buy us another one. If you see Lao Liu, ask him to come up here as soon as possible so that we can discuss how to renew our propaganda work.'

'Well . . .' I started, but again held back. 'Well . . . you needn't go any further with me. You should be getting back. I know my way from here. Goodbye.'

I walked away quickly. After quite a distance I turned round and saw all four of them, standing on the hillside, still waving goodbye.

The Temple to the Nine Goddesses was not easy to find. Had it not been for the detailed description O Ran had given me, I might not have found it at all, even if I had passed close by it. It was hidden in a thicket and its walls and black tiles were thickly covered in moss. From the outside it was practically indistinguishable from the trees and bushes and only once you had penetrated the encircling greenery did it become more visible. Fortunately, a little strip of bare ground surrounded the building, separating it from the encroaching woods. The first person I saw on nearing the temple was Sister Apricot with her child, Little Baldy, playing at her side. She did not notice me as I approached, as she was engrossed in planting something on the narrow strip of land around the temple. A cat was dozing in the sunlight which fell onto the ground beside her, its shafts penetrated the thick canopy of branches. The cat must have noticed me, for it suddenly stood up, stretched its back and miaowed. Sister Apricot looked up, and Little Baldy ran to her, pressing himself against her.

'Sister Apricot!' I called. 'Little Baldy!'

She looked at me in surprise, instinctively putting a finger to her lips to warn me not to shout so loud.

'Oh, Chunsheng!' she cried, running over to me with a smile on her pale, sunken face. 'What a surprise! We've been thinking about you every day. How did you get here?' Then, lowering her voice, she said to Little Baldy, 'Quick! Go and fetch Granny and Aunty. But don't tell them who's here. And bring two stools out with you!'

I watched Little Baldy disappear into the temple and then turned to look at Sister Apricot. I really did feel as if I had dropped from the sky! This place was so quiet. I could barely believe that I was still in the real world.

'It was O Ran who told me how to get here,' I said. 'But it was pretty hard to find. You are certainly out of the way here!'

'That is why we came here,' she replied. 'We've been hiding in so many places since we started out. Here, at last, we seem to be safe from the Nationalist troops and the Order Preservation Corps. Thanks to Grandpa Whiskers, we're finally able to stop for breath . . .'

As she was speaking, Aunt Sunflower and my mother came out of the temple. My mother was carrying Kuaile, O Ran's baby, in her arms. When she saw me she stopped in her tracks, unable to utter a word. She stood there, staring at me for a while, her old eyes moistening, though not a tear rolled down her cheeks. Then she handed Kuaile to me and her tearful face broke into a smile.

'Look!' she said. 'Here's the youngest member of our family. And he's already quite a little fellow!'

At the mention of this 'little fellow' she seemed to forget everything else. And the baby was very sweet. His face was already well formed: he had the round face of his mother, and his eyes were like Lao Liu's – big, lively and intelligent. She obviously saw Kuaile as her real grandson, for O Ran had been raised by her and Lao Liu called her 'Mother'. There was a note of pride in her voice as she spoke, this little boy was her own descendent.

'So who is feeding him, now that O Ran's away?' I asked. 'He still looks very well.'

'I am!' Mother said. 'Grandpa Whiskers occasionally sends someone here with rice flour and brown sugar. He loves the brown sugar! If only O Ran and Lao Liu could see him, they'd be really pleased! Have you seen them yet?'

'It was O Ran who told him to come here,' Aunt Apricot answered for me. 'But she is as busy as ever and couldn't come.'

'And what about Lao Liu?' my mother asked. 'He hasn't been here at all yet.'

I looked at my mother in silence, unable to think of the right thing to say. My lips began to tremble a little. But then, as before, Sister Apricot came to the rescue and said quickly, 'You know Lao Liu moves around all over the place. How can Chunsheng be expected to meet him in times like these?'

'I haven't even seen Grandpa Whiskers!' I said. 'I thought he'd be up here with you.'

'He can't afford to rest either, at a time like this,' Aunt Sunflower said. 'What can he do up here? He wants to be down there among the people. Still, he is very concerned about us and often sends someone here to see that we're all right. But you can't have had anything to eat. Come inside and have some food and then we'll all sit down for a good chat.'

We went into the tiny hall, which had become their living room, and sat down on some little stools. Then they asked me all about the people we knew and about our activities. I told them all I knew, though I avoided any mention of Lao Liu.

At first the three mothers looked at me anxiously, not knowing what news I brought about the fate of those close to them. But by the time I had finished telling them all the news they had brightened up and even my mother, who usually wore a look of anxiety on her face, seemed to feel a sense of relief.

'Do you think Wang Jiansheng will be able to get over here some time to see Aunt Apricot and his son?' she asked. Then, turning to Sister Apricot, she added, 'Such a nice young couple like you two – it would be a real pity if you didn't see more of one another!'

A faint blush came to Sister Apricot's pale cheeks and she lowered her head. Then, diverting the conversation to Aunt Sunflower, she said, 'It shouldn't be long before Uncle Zizhong comes to see you. We young people have a long time ahead of us. A short separation like this really doesn't matter . . .'

'You shouldn't talk like that,' my mother said. 'It's all the more important for families to be together during hard times like these, even if they are only together for a day or two. That makes everyone feel better. Even though O Ran isn't here now, Lao Liu really should come over to visit his child – his own flesh and blood! Kuaile can already smile and recognize people. How wonderful it would be if father and son could be together! Chunsheng, when you go back tell Lao Liu that his child is missing him and that he should come here to see us as soon as possible.'

I had originally meant to find a tactful way of breaking the news of Lao Liu's fate to them, but seeing my mother's state of mind, I decided to remain silent. 'How come there are no nuns here?' I said, so as to change the subject.

'There is a nun living here,' Aunt Sunflower said, 'but she's old and can't get up. At times like these, who would come to give alms? And she is too weak to go out begging. When we arrived she had nearly starved to death and she's only alive now because we're taking care of her. She says that we have been sent to her by Guanyin, the Goddess of Mercy.'

173

'This place really doesn't seem like a temple,' I said. 'It's so far away from anywhere.'

'It wasn't originally a temple,' Aunt Sunflower said. 'An old wood-cutter whom Grandpa Whiskers sent up here with some brown sugar and rice flour for Kuaile knew these parts well and told us a lot about the origins of this temple. You remember, Sister Apricot?'

'Yes,' Sister Apricot said. 'It was originally built as a family shrine to a young girl, the daughter of a man who had come first in the imperial examinations. She could read and write, but it happened that she fell in love with one of the family's servants. Her parents had already chosen a suitable husband for her, but she refused to comply. Then her parents, furious at the shame she had brought on the family, sent the servant off to the local magistrate, who exiled him to some distant place. The servant was never heard of again and the girl, hating her family for what they had done, decided to leave them, shaved her hair and became a nun. But her parents would not let her enter a normal nunnery. Instead, they had this place built for her, far from anywhere, and sent a middle-aged widow to keep her company. Later some other women who had had similar misfortunes heard about this place and came here to get away from the world. One woman who came was quite different from the others. She was married and, far from being disenchanted, she loved the world of men. She adored her husband, who went out into the world on her behalf, hoping to come back a great man. Well, he did become a great man, but by the time he came back to the village he had already married another woman. She was so furious and upset that after less than half a year she died of sorrow . . .'

'That's enough, Sister Apricot!' my mother said, lowering her head. 'Those are all things that happened in the past. Let's not think of the past, Chunsheng. It's a rare chance for you and me to be together in a quiet place like this. Why don't we go for a walk in the woods and have a good talk?'

'Quite right,' Aunt Sunflower said. 'You two really should

go out and have a proper chat. In any case, we've got patients to look after!'

With that, Aunt Sunflower and Sister Apricot stood up. I took Kuaile from my mother and went outside. Among the trees I was struck by the freshness and sweetness of the air. In fact, I was always breathing such air when running through the mountains, but had not really been aware of it until this moment. Walking through these still woods with my mother, I felt as if I were in a dream. Memories of the peaceful, uninterrupted life we had once led in our mountain village flooded back into my mind: Lao Liu telling stories each evening in the village square; Aunt Chrysanthemum getting up in the middle of the night and praying to the ancestors for her Mintun's return . . . And Aunt Chrysanthemum seemed to appear before my eyes, for the story Sister Apricot had told me about the woman who had died of sorrow was the story of Aunt Chrysanthemum herself. Although neither Sister Apricot nor Aunt Sunflower knew this, I and my mother knew it well. Yet neither of us could bring ourselves to utter her name out loud.

Mother and I walked in silence through the woods, unable to think of what to say. Only little Kuaile would occasionally babble the new word he had just learnt: 'Uncle, uncle!'

That night I slept in the temple. The following day neither Aunt Sunflower nor Sister Apricot would allow me to leave.

'You're nothing but skin and bones!' Aunt Sunflower said. 'Since you are here, you might as well rest for a day or two. There is nothing here to stop you from relaxing completely for a while.'

'That's quite right,' Sister Apricot agreed. 'In any case, we're running this place precisely so that people like you can get a decent rest. Didn't you hear us say yesterday that we have other "patients" here?'

'Patients?' I asked, my curiosity aroused.

'That's right,' my mother said. 'Grandpa Whiskers occasionally sends wounded people up here to rest for a few days before going back down the mountain.'

'There is still fighting going on all the time down there,' Aunt Sunflower said, 'and sometimes even Grandpa Whiskers has to take command. Everyone must do their part now. All we can do, stuck away in this wood, is help look after the wounded. There are two people in the back room right now. Do you want to go and see them? Maybe you know them.'

I nodded and followed Aunt Sunflower across a little courtyard and into a hut, probably used originally as a store. Inside were two wooden beds, made from a couple of old doors, and on each of them lay a patient, one a fairly elderly peasant, the other a young man little older than myself. They had both been wounded in the legs and arms and had difficulty moving. Nevertheless, they seemed quite comfortable, as their beds had been spread with a thick layer of straw. They both looked at me in surprise as I came in.

'He arrived here yesterday,' Aunt Sunflower said, introducing me. 'He's tired too and needs a rest. Well, I'll leave the three of you to chat.'

After Aunt Sunflower had gone, I looked carefully at the two patients. Both were typical farming people, somewhat heavy and clumsy-looking, maybe even a little dull-witted. In the past all they would have known was cutting the corn and ploughing the fields. But now they had been to war and had been wounded. We looked at one another, a slight sense of awkwardness between us.

'How did you come here?' the older of the two asked. 'You weren't fighting, were you?'

'No,' I replied. 'I am a messenger. The people looking after you here are my friends and relations. For a long time I had no idea what had become of them. I only found them up here yesterday.'

'You must pick up a lot of news being a messenger,' the younger man said. 'What's been going on lately?'

'The more Nationalists there are,' I replied, 'the more the

Order Preservation Corps dare to bully people. Ordinary people like us cannot just let them get away with it all, and our headquarters has decided to regroup our forces so as to launch a concerted attack and wipe them out.'

'I'm glad to hear it!' the younger man said. 'Small groups like ours don't have the numbers or the skill to deal with them. That's why we got injured and are lying here now. It'll be at least a day or two before we can go back down and fight them again.'

'We're not professional fighters,' the older man added. 'How can we be expected to be good at it? Even Grandpa Whiskers had never fought before. But with the enemy all over the place, we have no choice but to take them on. So now Grandpa Whiskers is in command of us. The most we can manage are small skirmishes with the local Nationalist soldiers or the Order Preservation Corps. We need their guns. The last time we fought them, though, the two of us were too slow and got wounded. Do you know Grandpa Whiskers?'

'He is also a close family friend,' I replied. 'I was hoping to see him.'

'Well,' the younger man said, 'that shouldn't be a problem. Can you stay here another day or two?'

'I'm afraid not,' I said. 'I have to get back to the Changshan Mountains as soon as possible. Important things may have been happening over the last few days.'

'If you like, I could take you to see him,' the younger man offered.

'That would be good!' I said. 'Let's set off tomorrow.'

The following afternoon the young man, dressed to look like a wood-cutter, got ready to set off down the mountain. I thus bid farewell to the three mothers. Each of them knew that I could not be there long and did not press me to stay. They all saw me off at the temple gate. As we parted I sensed that each of them had a lot more they wanted to say, though they remained silent. In the end it was my mother who broke the silence.

'Hold him a while,' she said, handing Kuaile to me. 'You've hardly ever had a chance to hold him. And his father had held him even less.'

I took Kuaile in my arms and kissed his face. He seemed to know who I was and smiled an innocent smile. When I gave him back to Mother, Aunt Sunflower and Sister Apricot, trying to dispel the heavy atmosphere, smiled and said, 'Give Grandpa Whiskers our greetings when you see him. We haven't had any news from him for several days.'

With the young peasant leading the way, the two of us headed towards the place where he usually met Grandpa Whiskers. The whole of that night we walked through the area under Nationalist control, but because they dared not come out at night, we encountered no obstacles. The following morning, we took a lonely little path, nearing our destination at about midday. Suddenly the young peasant stopped and peered ahead of him. A small village lay by a stream near the entrance to a valley. At one end of the village stood a row of ancient weeping willows, concealing the houses from someone unfamiliar with this place. Now, though, we could see a cloud of smoke rising from behind the trees. My companion watched it for a moment and then said, 'Something's happened. We'd better get away from here fast!'

He pulled me into some bushes at the foot of the hill and then, backs bent, we followed a little path into a narrow valley where we stopped for a while, getting our breath back. This place was bare and silent and there was not a soul in sight. Only a hawk hovered above us in the sky, searching for prey.

'What's happened?' I asked.

'The smoke above the village looks a bit suspicious,' he replied. 'It looks too thick to be cooking smoke.'

'Oh!' I said. 'There must be houses on fire there. Perhaps the Order Preservation Corps have been burning the place down, taking away the cattle, sheep and chickens. But . . . what about Grandpa Whiskers?'

'Grandpa Whiskers is always very alert,' the young peasant replied. 'He's unlikely to have come to any harm. Let's go and try to find him.'

We slowly walked on between some fields in the bottom of the valley, constantly on the look out. After a while we saw a young shepherd on the path ahead of us. He was neither driving sheep nor cutting wood, but appeared to be looking for something or someone. Hiding behind a tree, we watched him carefully. He must have noticed us because he ducked into a hollow in the hillside as if to escape our gaze. The young peasant at my side had very sharp eyesight and had already recognized the boy.

'Shengzi!' he called. 'It's me!'

At this the boy reappeared from the hollow and ran towards us. We went quickly over to meet him.

'Brother Shuqiang!' he cried as he came up to us. 'We thought of sending someone up to the temple to fetch you!' Then he eyed me a little suspiciously and asked, 'And who is the brother?'

'He's a friend of Grandpa Whiskers,' Shuqiang said. 'He's come here to look for him. Do you know where he is?'

Shengzi was silent. We waited silently for him to reply, so finally he had to say something. Instead of answering Shuqiang's question directly, he said, 'Did you go to Willow Village just now? There's still smoke rising from it. There was a spy around here, you see, and the Order Preservation Corps got wind of our plans. Yesterday, they came up here in the middle of the night with a battalion of Nationalist soldiers to search for us. I was keeping watch at the bottom of the valley and saw them coming. By the time they arrived, our people had managed to get away and were hiding in the hills. But there was one old man who couldn't walk fast enough and was hit by one of their bullets. We quickly carried him to safety. Meanwhile, the enemy, finding no one left in the village, were furious and started burning the place down. They only went away this morning. At first we'd hoped to ambush them as they left, but without anyone to command us we did not know how to go about it.'

Shengzi lowered his head and stopped speaking. Shuqiang turned pale.

'Who was it who was injured?' he asked quickiy. 'Take us to see him at once!'

Shengzi rubbed his eyes, but remained silent. He started off down the path and we followed him with heavy steps. After walking in silence for a while, over several hills and some bare fields, we reached a hillside where there was a brick kiln, and on either side of it, two huts in which the kilnsmen lived, but as there were no bricks near by, it was clear that this place had not been used for a long time and it had a desolate and untended air. Shengzi took us to the entrance of the kiln. Inside lay an old man and at his side were two middle-aged peasants and a country doctor. When we saw the old man, our fears were confirmed: it was Grandpa Whiskers who lay there. A shaft of light coming through the roof of the kiln illuminated his face; he looked deathly pale and his eyes were closed. Had it not been for his long beard, I would have found it hard to believe that this was really my dear old friend Grandpa Whiskers. Shuqiang stood dumbfounded by the entrance. But before long, he regained his senses.

'Lao Ji, what on earth happened?' he asked one of the peasants at Grandpa Whiskers' side.

'The bullet went right through to the left of his stomach,' the doctor replied on his behalf. 'He's been bleeding constantly and there is nothing I can do to stop it. He's lost all his strength now and hasn't even opened his eyes . . .'

The doctor seemed to be at his wits' end. But our shocked and anxious voices seemed to rouse Grandpa Whiskers a little and for a moment he half opened his eyes. He looked at me as I squatted by his side, softly stroking his long white beard. By now there was nothing I could do for him.

'Oh . . . Chunsheng,' Grandpa Whiskers whispered weakly. 'You have come just in time. Now that I've seen someone as close as you I can feel satisfied. I've never done anything great, but I've tried to do what I should in life. Now I can rest more easily. I'm finished now . . . in future it's up to you . . .'

It took him all his strength to utter these words. I wanted to reassure him that we would carry on his work, but it was already too late. He closed his eyes again, never to reopen them. Before long, his wrinkled face and his hands had turned cold. All of us lowered our heads, unable to utter a word.

After a long pause, Lao Ji said, 'Having found the village empty, the Nationalists and Order Preservation Corps aren't likely to go back empty-handed. They're sure to come up here to search for us. We must move away at once.'

We carried Grandpa Whiskers' body to a well-hidden place below some rocks and buried him in the most sheltered spot we could find. Then Lao Ji said a few words of farewell to our old friend and comrade:

'Grandpa Whiskers has passed away. But there are many, many other people of his strength and determination who will continue his work. Already, we are beginning to reap the fruits of his labours in this poor area. The future is ours!'

After he had finished, we all shook hands warmly and bid farewell to one another. Then I returned alone to the Temple of the Three Gods.

CHAPTER 8

'You are two days late, I'm afraid. The Special Regional Committee has already moved on. But you are welcome nevertheless. Sit down and have a rest.'

These were the first words Zheng Xiangyong said to me on my return to the Changshan Mountains. He was the first person I met when I got back to the Temple of the Three Gods. He was sitting in the room Pan Xudong had used as his office, discussing something with Yu Minghan the bricklayer and Wang the Coppersmith.

Sitting down beside them on a bamboo chair, I asked, 'Where have they moved to?'

'Kongji,' Yu Minghan replied.

'How can they go there?' I asked. 'That's a county town, isn't it? There must be a garrison stationed there. Have you really managed to take the place over?'

'They only had about fifty or sixty guns,' Wang the Coppersmith said. 'I made several reconnaissance trips there and got a pretty good idea of their strength, but in the end there was no need to take them on directly.'

'Brother Wang,' I said, 'the way you're talking you sound more like a commander. How come you're so cool about the whole thing?'

'Hey! You shouldn't underestimate us yokels!' Zheng Xiangyong said jokingly. 'Brother Wang is a very accomplished scout – just as you are a very accomplished messenger. Once you've become a real expert at something you can speak with authority. Did you know that all the members of the Red Spear Society in this area have now come over to our side? They still keep their original name, but in reality they have changed and have become Peasant Volunteers. The garrison always had close links with the Red Spears. Once they changed, the garrison no longer had a leg to stand on. Chang Je-an had talks with them and the commanders of the garrison agreed to join our forces. So any conflict was peacefully averted.'

'But what about the local landlords and gentry?' I asked. 'Have they agreed to all this?'

'It's not really a question of them agreeing,' Yu Minghan said. 'They haven't got any soldiers any more, so they have to be realistic. It's really up to us now. Yesterday Pan Xudong, Wang Jiansheng and Chang Je-an invited them to send over a representative to talk to us. In the end they reached an agreement. The peasants will not redistribute the land or start attacking them, though the landlords, for their part, must reduce rents and interest on loans. We will take over the command of the Red Spears, but we must safeguard the property and personal safety of the landlords. Even the head of the county thought of staying on here, but in the end he decided he couldn't trust us and we feel it is probably best just to let him leave.'

'So that's how things are at the moment,' Zheng Xiangyong said. 'The Special Regional Committee took over Kongji right away and moved over there, making it our new headquarters. Kongji is a pretty wealthy place, with three streets and lots of shops. The Special Regional Committee wants to make it into a centre from where we can expand our operations. You'll probably have to move over there yourself, as you're the Special Regional Committee's regular messenger.'

'Yes!' I said excitedly. 'I'd better be getting there as quickly as I can!'

'I'll come with you,' Zheng Xiangyong said. 'The Special Regional Committee is holding an emergency meeting this afternoon and organizers from all the different regions will be there. Kongji is about fifty *li* from here, so we should make it just in time.' Then glancing up at the sky, he said to Yu Minghan and Wang the Coppersmith, 'Let's leave it at that for the moment. I'll be back tomorrow morning at the latest. In the meantime you can start organizing your troops.'

So, without resting for a moment, I set out for Kongji with Zheng Xiangyong. We did not talk much as we hurried on our way, as both of us were rather out of breath, but I did say what an impression these three old members of the Red Spears had made on me.

'You've really come on a long way!' I said. 'You're more like the leaders now. Even the way you speak has changed!'

'We've all got to learn how to take charge of things,' he said. 'People like Jia Hongcai in the Daji Mountains and Big Tree Lu and Sun Nan in the Lianyun Mountains are the same – they just had to learn through experience.'

As soon as we got to Kongji we headed for the old Examination Halls in the south-eastern corner of the town. This used to be the place where the local examinations were held, but now it was serving as the headquarters of the Special Regional Committee. Pan Xudong, Wang Jiansheng, Chang Je-an and most of the organizers from various areas had already arrived. It was the first time I had seen such a complete assembly of representatives since we had left the county town. Things had really been changing fast. The speed at which these people had been brought together from all the different areas was proof that our communications network was now very effective. Many of the representatives had also had to pass through areas under enemy control.

From the expression on everyone's face it was clear that this was to be a most important meeting – a meeting to decide our future military strategy. I sat quietly in a corner listening to the discussion about 'expanding and unifying our actions'. Each person explained the particular plans they had in mind, though everyone agreed that the main aim was the elimination of the Nationalist armies.

By the time the meeting was over, night had already fallen and, under cover of darkness, everyone headed back to his own area. I went to see Pan Xudong, Wang Jiansheng and Chang Je-an to tell them what I had learnt in the old base areas. When they heard about the deaths of Lao Liu and Grandpa Whiskers they fell silent and looked at one another blankly. But they all had so much on their minds at the moment that they could feel little real grief at these tragic events, just as a soldier in battle is barely touched by the death of a close comrade at his side.

An hour after receiving a report from Shangsheng county, the Special Regional Committee took the decision to begin our unified operations. After some underground preparation, the peasants there had staged an uprising and had managed to take the county town. They had cut off all communications with the outside world to prevent Chiang Kai-shek hearing about the event and sending his armies to besiege the town – which would have severely disrupted our overall plans.

With Pan Xudong at its head, the newly reformed Red Spear Society now headed in the direction of our old county town. This force was divided into two sections, one led by Wang Jiansheng and the other by Chang Je-an. They were to take different routes, meeting up with other peasant forces as they went. Pan Xudong and Wang Jiansheng remained together and, as usual, I acted as their messenger.

Our soldiers on this expedition were armed with an assortment of weapons which, apart from the guns handed over by the county garrison, consisted mostly of ancient spears, knives and swords. The force which Zheng Xiangyong led was similarly armed. Jia Hongcai and Uncle Zizhong had managed to assemble a large force in the Daji Mountains, though they, too, were poorly armed. Peasant Volunteers Uncle Pan had organized in the old base area were even less well equipped, possessing nothing but a handful of long bamboo-handled spears. The best-armed forces were those of Big Tree Lu and Liu Dawang in the Lianyun Mountains. During their repeated raids on the Order Preservation Corps they had managed to build up a considerable arsenal of weapons. But it was still unrealistic for us to consider attacking the Nationalist troops directly. Several encounters with the enemy had also given the armies from the Lianyun Mountains solid experience, which formed the basis of our unified action. As agreed at the meeting at Kongji a few days earlier, the various forces would hide in different positions some three *li* from our old county town, awaiting the signal to begin operations.

When we left Kongji, dusk was already beginning to fall. There was not a soul to be seen on the road ahead of us and all around everything was silent. By the time we crossed over into the old base area it was late evening. This was the point at which our forces separated, each following an agreed route. It took some five or six hours of hard marching before we reached the place where our two divisions again came together. We were safe enough from enemy informers, as most of them were forced into doing their job and preferred to find a quiet place to nap rather than face the dangers outside.

Having reached our agreed destination, messengers from the various forces began arriving to report to Pan Xudong. The overall strategy was as follows: the force led by Pan Xudong and Wang Jiansheng was waiting in a low range of hills due north of the town; Chang Je-an's force was hiding in some woods across from the east gate; the forces of hill people led by Liu Dawang and Uncle Zizhong were positioned in a horse-shoe formation on the south-west side, ready to cut off the enemy should they attempt to flee from the town and, in addition, to protect the route to their respective mountain bases. Uncle Pan sent several scouts to keep an eye on the town and make sure that no one entered the gates and alerted the enemy to our operations.

By the time all these preparations had been made it was

nearing daybreak and I could hear the sound of cocks crowing. After the crowing stopped there was a period of intense stillness. The Nationalists and the Order Preservation Corps, through their campaign of terror, had succeeded in silencing every sound. It was as if even the smallest of beetles had withdrawn into its shell, afraid to utter the tiniest noise. This almost primeval stillness seemed to hark back to a world devoid of human beings and practically devoid of animals. Our soldiers all remained well hidden, hardly daring to breathe.

A streak of pink slowly began to appear over the eastern hills. This was like a warning to our troops to remain on the alert and not let the enemy get wind of our activities. We could not afford to risk attacking the enemy head on, for they would certainly mow down our troops with their superior fire-power and inflict huge casualties. Furthermore, the enemy always kept strict guard over the town, enforcing a curfew every evening, and thus preventing us from alerting our supporters inside the town of our plans. This effectively made it impossible to launch a surprise attack at night. So we had come to the conclusion that the only way to wipe out the enemy forces was to lure them out, force them to disperse and then destroy them bit by bit. It was essential that our action take place as rapidly as possible, as by daylight the enemy would quickly see through our strategy – and then anything could happen.

I remained squatting at Pan Xudong and Wang Jiansheng's side, listening as they gave out their orders. They were keeping a careful watch on the eastern horizon, where before long a red sun began to appear. The surrounding hills and trees grew more and more distinct, yet our troops were so well hidden that not a trace of them was to be seen. Pan Xudong and Wang Jiansheng seemed satisfied by our operations so far and nodded at one another meaningfully.

'Chunsheng,' Wang Jiansheng whispered, 'you can now give the signal!'

As planned, I had with me three large firecrackers. I lit the fuse of one of them and a huge explosion shattered the stillness. After a pause I set off the second, and a moment later the third. The trees, the mountains and even the sky seemed to tremble in anticipation after this rude awakening. The sleepy town, too, was naturally roused by the noise and then, to ensure that it was fully awoken, a series of explosions echoed across from somewhere outside the north gate. In quick succession the same noise resounded from outside the east, west and south gates. The explosions sounded very similar to rifles being fired – an effect obtained by letting the firecrackers off inside empty oil barrels – which we hoped would make the enemy suspect guerrilla activity outside the town.

Just as we had expected, the sound of rifles now came from the town itself. These were real guns that were being fired and the sound of our firecrackers ceased. Only once the shooting inside the town had stopped did the firecrackers start up once again. The shooting began again, though this time we saw enemy soldiers running out from all four gates, heading straight in the direction of our men lying in ambush.

'They're sending troops out of the town,' Pan Xudong said calmly. 'They're hoping to wipe out the guerrillas. Everyone get ready!'

'Get ready!' Wang Jiansheng repeated.

I ran off with this order to all the hidden sections of our force and within minutes everyone was on the alert. Then I returned to Pan Xudong and Wang Jiansheng and found them observing the movements of the enemy from behind two ancient pines. A company of Nationalist troops had appeared outside the north gate and was heading rapidly in our direction. They probably thought that there were so few guerrillas that a single company would be sufficient to mop them up. Confident of success, they marched straight into our ambush. Before they had even seen us, we had pounced on them from both sides. Taking them utterly by surprise, we were able to overpower them and grab their guns. It was the guns that we needed more urgently than anything else and, having disarmed them, we were able to drive our captives away like sheep. Meanwhile, the military commanders in the town thought that their troops were still pursuing the guerrillas.

Exactly the same tactics were being carried out by our forces at other points around the town, with similar success.

Although the Nationalist commanders were confident that victory would quickly be theirs and the guerrillas would be wiped out, they eventually began to wonder what was really happening out there. After a long silence, they heard nothing but a few shots and decided to send out another four companies to investigate. But the moment these troops got beyond their commanders' field of vision, they disappeared as mysteriously as before.

After this process had been repeated four or five times, Wang Jiansheng asked Pan Xudong, 'Isn't it time for the second signal?'

Pan Xudong thought for a moment and then said, 'I'd guess that they have already lost about half of their troops. We're strong enough to cope with the rest of them in the town. With all these new guns we've got we should be able to smash them. Give the signal!'

Wang Jiansheng took his revolver from his belt and fired several shots into the air. This time the shots were real and were followed by a thunderous clamour of voices rising from all around the town. Before the enemy had even had time to close the town gates, thousands upon thousands of peasants began pouring into the town. Most of them were armed with little more than an assortment of old knives, spears and swords, though with the backing of the Peasant Volunteers, equipped with the rifles they had just captured, they posed a most formidable force. There were not more than three or four companies of Nationalist troops left in the town and we easily outnumbered them. Before long they had clearly lost the will to fight and lacked even the courage to try and break out of the town.

In this way, the county town, which had for so long been

under the occupation of the Nationalists, returned to the hands of the Democratic Government of Workers and Peasants.

Most of the people who had worked for the Democratic Government but had been dispersed after our break-out from the county town, were now able to reassemble. Everyone got together at the place which had served as the Nationalist army's headquarters, and Pan Xudong held an emergency meeting for all leaders above the rank of brigade commander. The main topic for discussion was how to deal with the captured troops. It was agreed unanimously that all Nationalist commanders above the rank of Company Commander should be executed. Their crimes were already too numerous to list and only by executing them could we satisfy the masses and regain their full support and confidence. As for platoon leaders and ordinary soldiers, they would be released unconditionally. Having won everyone's approval, the decision was immediately carried out.

When the execution squad fired a volley of shots, like firecrackers, just outside the walls, a chorus arose from the crowds in and outside the town: 'Hurrah!' I realized what was happening, but for some reason the sound of the shooting made my chest tighten and a wave of giddiness came over me. However, the feeling quickly passed and before long I regained my senses. This was a revolution. During the heat of revolutionary struggle I, too, had had to kill enemy soldiers.

By that afternoon much of our work in dealing with the enemy soldiers had been completed. The enemy arms which we had captured were checked and counted. Pan Xudong, as overall commander of our unified operations, ordered that all the peasant forces in this region should now unite to form the Workers' and Peasants' Red Army of China. This would rank as the fourth Red Army in the country. The new army would formally come into existence as soon as it was approved by the Party Central Committee. This announcement was again greeted with thunderous rejoicing by the people. Our guns, which now numbered some four to five hundred, were enough to supply a full army. On past experience, one army of ours would be enough to overpower several of Chiang Kai-shek's armies. Within twenty-four hours we had brought about a massive change in our fortunes.

Having regained the county town did not, in itself, mean the automatic re-establishment of our Democratic Government. The revolution had now spread throughout three provinces and the Red Army had been formally set up. This meant that the kind of Democratic Government we had created earlier was no longer fully appropriate. A new government needed to be set up somewhere on the border of all three provinces. Kongji seemed a very sound location, Pan Xudong concluded while discussing our next move with Wang Jiansheng and Chang Je-an. This was agreed and it was not long before we returned to Kongji.

This time we were accompanied by a large number of our comrades, including Liu Dawang, Uncle Pan, Uncle Zizhong, Jia Hongcai the charcoal-burner, Pockmarks the Sixth, Big Tree Lu, O Ran, Ho Shuoru and Peng Wanzhen, Sun Nan, Zheng Xiangyong, Yu Minghan the bricklayer and even people like Sweet Potato and Zhao Dagui, of whom we had had no news for ages. The only people not to come were Li Chengbao and Wang Jingxian, from the south of the county and Jiqing and Pan Mingxun, who were still carrying on underground work in Mazhen county. They were busy trying to block off the enemy in their areas to prevent them infiltrating the old base area again.

None of the new people who came with us to Kongji were familiar with this area. When we arrived, the Special Regional Committee decided to let them all rest for a day, to give them time to familiarize themselves a little. The following day Pan Xudong held an enlarged meeting of the Special Regional Committee in the Examination Halls. As Wang Jiansheng's messenger I was allowed to attend the meeting. Looking around, I saw that everyone was present except Lao Liu. As the person in charge of propaganda, his work was essential. At such an extended meeting, Grandpa Whiskers should also have been there. It was not long before their absence caught the attention of those who had been close to the two men. The general atmosphere at the meeting was one of excitement and rejoicing. Only O Ran, Uncle Pan and Uncle Zizhong looked troubled. I could guess what they must be thinking. They had lived through many experiences and knew that Lao Liu and Grandpa Whiskers had been exposed to constant danger through their work. I, too, felt a sense of grief and uneasiness, uncertain of whether to break the news to them. However, this was certainly not the right moment to do so, as Pan Xudong had just opened the meeting. The aim of the meeting was to discuss our overall plans for future action. Everything had changed so rapidly and there was a plethora of tasks to be attended to. The local organizers were each responsible for their own area but without a clear overall plan it would be difficult to co-ordinate our efforts. Everyone took the opportunity to describe the situation in their area, express their opinion and state their plans. During this lively discussion, Wang Jiansheng's suggestion, above all others, caught Pan Xudong's attention.

'Our work now seems more complex than ever,' Wang Jiansheng said. 'The administrative body we have at present is inadequate to deal with this new state of affairs. Our government needs to be expanded and we need to change its name. In future our government should not only represent workers and peasants, but should represent a broader section of society, including teachers, doctors, shop assistants and so on. These people should all be the foundation on which our government is built. It should be made up of representatives of all the working people, together with members of the Red Army. In short, this means that it should be a soviet government.'

The word 'soviet' was new to all of us and nobody knew

what it meant. Even Ho Shuoru and Peng Wanzhen, despite their learning, seemed unfamiliar with it, as they looked as mystified as the rest of us. It seemed that Wang Jiansheng and Pan Xudong had discussed the matter beforehand and had both come to the same conclusion. Pan Xudong gave us an explanation of this new word, telling us that it meant a government made up of representatives of the people. After thinking about this for a while, everyone began expressing their support for Wang Jiansheng's suggestion.

'So we should hold a meeting of all representatives as soon as possible,' Pan Xudong said, 'and establish a soviet government. There are many things to be seen to straight away. The first is the general redistribution of land. Then there are other matters like bringing key industries and commerce under the control of the soviet government. This will also have an effect on the currency. We cannot allow Nationalist banknotes to be used in the areas under our control, so we will also have to think about establishing banks. In addition, we will have to expand our army. During our battles with the Nationalists many skilled commanders have emerged in our ranks, like Big Tree Lu, Sun Nan, Jia Hongcai, Zheng Xiangyong and Yu Minghan. We should set up an organization specially appointed to run military affairs. It could be called the Military Committee.'

'And we must also set up schools,' Zheng Xiangyong the carpenter said. 'We can't let our children be illiterate. So we'll need to set up a body to run education.'

'What about a department to look after health and set up hospitals?' Liu Dawang said. 'Although we've been victorious, there are lots of people with injuries. At the moment they have no doctors to look after them and no medicines. Many of them are lying at home and some have already died.'

Liu Dawang's urgent tone of voice clearly struck a chord in Ho Shuoru. 'I'll do what I can to help with this problem,' he said. 'I can write to my father to ask him to send some medicines. That should be simple enough for him.'

At this, everyone turned to look at Sweet Potato.

'All you need to do is write the letter,' he said to Ho Shuoru, 'I'll make sure we get what we need. It's much safer to travel over there now.'

'In that case,' Ho Shuoru said, 'I'll write a letter at once.'

'Good,' Pan Xudong said, his grave expression lifting. 'Your family is sure to have heard about the enemy atrocities here. Now you can write to tell them you're safe.'

'Right! I'll set off as soon as you're ready!' Sweet Potato said cheerfully. 'I haven't been down to "The Big City" for ages. I really quite miss the place. Now that we've got rid of the Order Preservation Corps, I can walk there quite safely in daylight.'

'Do you think you'd be able to bring us a printing machine?' Ho Shuoru said excitedly. 'And a radio transmitter?'

'I'm afraid Chunsheng won't be able to go with you this time,' Pan Xudong said. 'We really can't spare him here just now.'

'Never mind,' Sweet Potato replied. 'I've been carrying a shoulder-pole all my life and a few things like that won't be a problem.'

'I can believe it!' Peng Wanzhen said. 'It's just a pity that Lao Liu isn't here at the moment. Without him Shuoru and I have begun to run out of ideas. He has such a wonderful imagination. Do you think you could find him for us?'

Sweet Potato lowered his head, but made no reply. Being a sensitive person, he could not have failed to feel a sense of foreboding at Lao Liu's absence. A pallor spread across his face; soon others became aware of it and, affected by the same uneasiness, lowered their heads in silence. There was a heaviness in the air, which constricted my chest and quite involuntarily my gaze sought out O Ran, whose face was as white as death. She had not lowered her head, but was staring vacantly out at the expressionless sky. Then, all of a sudden, she looked round at the rest of us and said, 'I know where he is. I'll tell you later. Let's get on with the meeting.'

Pan Xudong seemed a little uncertain of what to say.

'Well, we've discussed most of the main questions,' he said finally. 'Now you can all get back and start the job of selecting representatives. We'll hold a congress of representatives as soon as possible. Good. The meeting is closed!'

I went back with O Ran to where she was staying in Kongji. As soon as we arrived she sat down heavily on the bed, staring at me like a stranger. Rousing her from her stupor, I asked, 'Do you really know where Lao Liu is?'

'You should know better than me,' she said blankly. 'You went to the old base areas specially to look for people we lost contact with. Tell me the truth. What did happen to him?'

Even though she had no idea of what had happened to Lao Liu, she had guessed the worst. There was nothing I could do now but tell her the details, including an account of Grandpa Whiskers' death.

'It's not that I wanted to keep it from anyone,' I explained. 'It's just that I had no idea of how to break the news. I didn't even dare tell Mother about it.'

'Let me tell her,' O Ran said, almost with a note of indifference. 'I know how to talk to her. We'll soon be bringing her to Kongji, together with Aunt Sunflower and Sister Apricot, so that their lives can be a bit more peaceful. Then I'll break the news to them slowly, and also let people like Ho Shuoru and Peng Wanzhen know what has happened. What is done is done and there's nothing we can do to change it. We must all be prepared for sacrifice during a time of revolution like this.'

'It's good if you can see it that way,' I said. Then, unable to think of anything else which would comfort her, I left her. But after I had gone out I heard her burst into loud sobs. She had always had so much misery in her heart, yet had I never heard her cry like that before.

The All People's Representative Congress took place at Kongji and lasted for two days. Most of the representatives who attended were workers, peasants and soldiers. The congress established a new soviet government, with several departments, including those responsible for politics, military affairs, the economy, education and health. It also set up a Security Bureau, run by Uncle Pan, and a bank able to issue currency. A special Land Redistribution Committee was set up under Pan Xudong himself, to begin the task of dividing up the land amongst the peasants.

Despite this new period of stability, the situation was still not secure enough to allow us to be caught off guard. It was essential that each department should begin its work at once so as to forestall any untoward developments.

Without Lao Liu it was hard to find anyone suitable to run a propaganda department. In the meantime, therefore, it was decided to set up a magazine to undertake propaganda work. It was called *The Internationale* and was edited by Ho Shuoru, with his wife Peng Wanzhen as assistant. Neither of them was used to working out in the field, as Lao Liu had, so this work, which chiefly involved writing, was more suitable for them. But without a printing machine, their articles could have little effect on the masses.

Just when things were beginning to look a little hopeless, Sweet Potato arrived at the Examination Halls with a heavy load on his carrying-pole. He had just returned from his excursion to 'The Big City' and he found Ho Shuoru and Peng Wanzhen hard at work. He put down his load and unwrapped a bundle of old clothes to reveal a brand-new printing machine and a large quantity of medicines. Jumping up, Ho Shuoru examined this rare and valuable piece of machinery – the means by which he and Peng Wanzhen could now disseminate their propaganda.

'Did my father give you this?' he asked Sweet Potato.

'Who else could afford a machine like this?' Sweet Potato replied. 'He also asked me to bring back some recent newspapers. He said that they contain everything he wants to tell us.'

Newspapers were very valuable to us at this time as they helped us find out more about the movements of Chiang Kai-shek's forces. Ho Shuoru glanced through them but found little of particular interest, so he handed them over to me. I saw that they were published by the Nationalist provincial government and took them straight to Pan Xudong. He took a quick look at them and then said, 'Take a look at this!' He was pointing at a piece of news on the first page. It was a telegram which the newspaper had thought fit to reprint in full:

Our division sent two regiments which, including the local Order Preservation Corps, made up a force of more than 1,000 men, to wipe out the bandits. But due to the bandits' persistence, we suffered a sudden attack and our division lost over half its troops, while the Order Preservation Corps was almost completely destroyed. The power of the bandits and their supporters has increased and they have set up a government and an army. The border area between the three provinces has been almost totally taken over by the Reds. Our base at Mazhen county is in grave danger. Without the assistance of large forces from outside, our division will certainly perish and this county will be lost.

After reading this I looked up at Pan Xudong, hoping for some sort of explanation. Instead he asked me, 'What do you think of it?'

I thought for a while and said, 'The fact that Ho Ludong sent this paper to us shows his concern for us. He must have been hoping we'd notice this piece of news. And of course his son's here.'

'Anything else?' Pan Xudong persisted. 'Think carefully!'

'Could it be . . . that the situation is getting more dangerous again?' I suggested. 'By printing this telegram they are hoping to put all organs of Nationalist power on their guard and alert Chiang Kai-shek to mobilize his troops as quickly as possible. They don't want to lose their last base in our area.'

Pan Xudong nodded and smiled.

'There's something in what you say,' he replied. 'Any other ideas?'

'Er . . .' I became a little hesitant, suddenly remembering the incident when those two men claiming to come from the garrison headquarters had blackmailed Ho Ludong. 'It's hard to say. Maybe they want to scare the business people in the city to get them to contribute money to help Chiang Kai-shek attack us. At the same time, they can profit from these contributions themselves.'

Pan Xudong couldn't help laughing at this suggestion. He was always so busy – preoccupied with so many pressing matters – that this was the first time I had chatted to him in such a relaxed atmosphere and heard him laugh so freely.

'This is really trying to kill two birds with one stone!' he said. 'By making things look so serious, on the one hand, they can put their army on the alert and step up their policy of "encirclement and suppression", while on the other, they can get rich. But there's another thing you haven't thought of: this will also help to scare their masters, the international imperialists. These people are terrified of the Communists and as we expand our influence they are bound to start worrying about the threat to their economic interests along the Yangtze River. Chiang Kai-shek can thus start asking them for more economic and military backing.'

'So,' I said with a laugh, 'that's really three birds with one stone!'

'Anyway,' Pan Xudong said, 'we should be grateful to Ho Ludong for sending us these papers. He's obviously an intelligent man. Quickly, go and thank Ho Shuoru for me. He must have written a good letter to his father to get him to give us much help. Also tell him that now that Lao Liu has left us it is up to them to take on the work of propaganda. You see,' he added for my benefit, 'in the past none of us had much idea of how to fight. But we've already managed to beat the Nationalists, despite all their military training! Even Jia Hongcai the charcoal-burner, Zheng Xiangyong the carpenter, and Yu

Minghan the bricklayer have become skilled commanders . . .
You'd better go quickly and tell Wang Jiansheng and Chang Je-
an to come and see me. Mazhen county is Chiang Kai-shek's
last base here. We'd better root out the Nationalists there
before they have a chance to send more troops in.'

'Yes!' I said. 'We could also do with their guns and ammunition, which I've heard are pretty good. As our Red Army gets
bigger it is going to need more and more weapons.'

'You're very quick off the mark! You have a knack for taking
all factors into account,' he said. Then he stood up and patted
me warmly on the shoulder. 'Now go and fetch Wang Jiansheng and Chang Je-an for me.'

I carried out his orders and then went to see Ho Shuoru. I
found O Ran talking to him and Peng Wanzhen. She had been
appointed by the soviet government to take charge of the
women's organization. They all looked rather depressed when
I arrived and I immediately guessed what they must have been
talking about. We all looked at each other in silence, then I told
Ho Shuoru what Pan Xudong had said.

'That's right,' O Ran said. 'I'll feel much better if you can
carry on Lao Liu's work.'

Neither Ho Shuoru nor Peng Wanzhen said a word and after
another pause O Ran broke the silence by talking about how
they might start their new propaganda effort. We discussed
this until nightfall and then I went to see Wang Jiansheng.

'I was just about to look for you,' he said. 'We have just had
an urgent meeting with Pan Xudong and have decided to
being our new mobilization right away. You must get this
message to all the commanders so that we can reassemble our
forces.'

However, Wang Jiansheng told me to rest for the night
before I set off on this new errand. I was to leave first thing the
following morning.

This time Chiang Kai-shek moved more swiftly than we did.
Our forces were getting assembled, ready to set off towards

Mazhen county, when his armies pounced without warning. The enemy armies came from the three provinces on each side of the soviet area and were sent by the local warlords and military leaders. From the accounts of our scouts we estimated that their force comprised some three divisions, which were about twenty times more powerful in terms of arms and numbers than our Red Army. We did, of course, have the backing of the peasant organizations of this district. Armed with ancient knives, hunting muskets, swords and spears, they made up quite a considerable force, but nevertheless, compared to a properly trained and armed force of some thirty or forty thousand men, the disparity was all too obvious.

The fact that the warlords in the three provinces had at last assembled a united force was a clear sign of how threatened they felt by the establishment of our soviet government. It was also a sign that Chiang Kai-shek was now determined that they should resolve their differences. Their aim was quite clear: the total erradication of all revolutionary activity and the re-establishment of their control. Faced with this grave threat, we had to abandon our original plan of attacking Mazhen county and concentrate all our efforts on the defence of our soviet area.

The headquarters of the Red Army held an emergency meeting to devise a defence strategy. At the same time all civilians were mobilized to resist the enemy and prepared to evacuate the entire area, if necessary, hiding all food and livestock, so as to turn the area into a waste land. In my usual capacity as messenger I was again in constant service, sending vital messages to and from the headquarters.

It was not long before we began to engage with the enemy. The Nationalist forces closed in on us from three directions, the north, south and west. Their target was the town of Kongji itself. Mazhen county to the east had always been the Nationalists' main military base in this area and since it had never fallen and had apparently remained relatively stable, the

Nationalists had not considered it necessary to carry out a policy of military repression there. They were aware of the existence of fragmented and primatively armed peasant forces, but saw no need to take any serious precautions against them, other than establishing a line of defence along the edge of the county to prevent them uniting with our larger forces outside. These 'unlawful elements' in Mazhen could easily be wiped out once the main section of the Red Army had been destroyed. Then the old order could be re-established once more. This analysis of the situation was provided by the scouts sent into Mazhen county by Li Chengbao, the old head of the Peasant Volunteers, and Pan Xudong, Wang Jiansheng and Chang Je-an thought it accurate.

In order to avoid being encircled by the enemy our forces now split up and began to operate independently, with the aim of trying to fragment, weaken and eventually destroy the enemy. Our main force in Kongji was also divided into three sections, each with some 100 guns, and commanded respectively by Pan Xudong, Wang Jiansheng and Chang Je-an. Pan Xudong's force remained in Kongji itself, while Wang Jiansheng and Chang Je-an's forces prepared to ambush areas through which they expected the enemy to pass. I was assigned to Pan Xudong as his messenger.

As Pan Xudong pointed out, this was a quite exceptional situation: priority had to be given to military affairs and every member of the Soviet Government would be involved in the fighting which was to follow. The only exception was Ho Shuoru, who could not be expected to carry a rifle nor to command troops. He also had to take care of Peng Wanzhen. Even though her tuberculosis had been cured, she was still weak and, in any case, she was so passionately attached to Ho Shuoru that she would not allow them to be separated. As Pan Xudong said, 'In a peasant revolution like ours they are a most valuable asset. There are still few people of their learning and intellect among our ranks and they should be given proper protection.' So before the situation became too dangerous Pan

Xudong ordered me to take them and their precious printing machine up into the hills, where they could stay with a peasant family and continue their propaganda work in safety.

The enemy apparently expected us to concentrate all our forces and seemed to be waiting for us to make these preparations before attacking and wiping us out. Three days after Ho Shuoru and Peng Wanzhen had gone into hiding, the Nationalists at last showed signs of restlessness and began sending troops in our direction. Pan Xudong decided to send me out to get a clearer picture of what was going on. Climbing to the top of a pine tree on a nearby hill, I got a good view of the approaching army, an advance party at its head and a huge black mass of troops behind.

When I got back to Kongji I found every shop closed and barely any sign of life in the streets. By this time all the townsfolk had gone into hiding in the hills, taking old and young with them. The only people who remained were Pan Xudong's men, who kept watch over the silent town. As soon as he heard my report, Pan Xudong assembled his troops and we left Kongji. Now absolute silence reigned there – even the dogs had been taken off to the hills by their masters.

A short distance away a range of hills extended in a westerly direction. Pan Xudong led his troops at a quick march towards a peak which lay due south of the town. Just as we reached the top of this mountain we began to hear of shooting coming from the town. Pan Xudong and I looked back. The weather was clear and fresh and the scene before us was of a quiet, pastoral landscape. Pan Xudong did not utter a word – had it not been for the shooting, which marked the start of the fighting, he might have stood there absorbed in a quiet reverie for a long time.

Turning to me, he said quietly, 'They're flexing their muscles to show how strong they are! But it won't be long before they find they're wasting their time. They seem to have learnt their lesson: they aren't burning down the peasants' houses. Let's see what tricks they get up to now! You'd better climb that tree and see if you can get a better view of their movements.'

I climbed to the top of a nearby oak and hid among the leaves.

'You hear that shooting?' I called down to Pan Xudong. 'The advance guard are entering the town. But there are thousands of other troops closing in on it.'

'How many would you say there are?' Pan Xudong asked.

'At least 3,000,' I replied. 'There are troops all over the place – around the town and on the hillsides. Let's rest here while they're attacking the town!'

But just as we sat down the shooting ceased. We looked at one another in silence.

'Well,' Pan Xudong said after a pause, 'we shouldn't let them have a rest! Let's tire them out a bit – get them to waste some more ammunition. Go and tell our troops to come up here. Let the enemy catch a glimpse of us!'

Our force, with its 100-odd rifles, assembled at the top of the hill.

'Let off some firecrackers!' Pan Xudong ordered.

At once a series of explosions echoed around the hills, giving the impression that a sizeable force was up here.

'Shout!' Pan Xudong ordered.

A great cry rose up, reminiscent of the sudden cry of the peasants during the harvest when a storm is approaching and the crops need to be saved. The Nationalist troops looked up at the hills. With their powerful binoculars they quickly spotted us and started firing furiously in our direction. The shout which now rose up from their midst was even louder than our own. Pan Xudong no longer needed me to watch the Nationalists from the top of the tree. We could guess that the enemy commanders were ordering their troops to change direction and start heading towards the hills. But then, as if by magic, silence descended on the hill and we disappeared from view. At the same moment, the forces led by Chang Je-an and Wang Jiansheng let off volleys of firecrackers and started shouting from hills to the east and west of the town. They, however, were careful not to let themselves be seen. The explosions, which seemed to be coming from all over the hills, drew the enemy up on to the bare slopes. Once they were in the hills, their modern weapons would lose their effectiveness, while our forces, made up largely of hill people, would have the advantage on this rugged terrain. Our plan was to lead them by the nose, deeper and deeper into the hills, dividing their forces and making it impossible for them to return to their base. To keep them on the trail of our three forces, we would stop every now and then to let off another volley of firecrackers. Unaccustomed to hill marching, the Nationalists moved much more slowly than we did and after a while we were able to stop and rest. Only once they were within shooting distance did we set off again. All we heard of one another were the sounds of shooting and firecrackers and we rarely caught a glimpse of our pursuers. Every so often, though, our scouts would climb a high hill, let off a few firecrackers and let the enemy catch sight of them. That way we, too, would keep an eye on the enemy.

These hide-and-seek guerrilla tactics were not limited to the three forces under Pan Xudong's command. Other forces led by Liu Dawang, Uncle Pan, Uncle Zizhong and others were employing similar tactics elsewhere in the surrounding hills. Without local guides to show them the way, the enemy's modern wireless sets were of little help in co-ordinating their efforts. They were beginning to get themselves into an almost impossible position. Our total evacuation of the area had even made it hard for them to find anything to eat or drink.

We, on the other hand, had a good network of scouts who knew the hills and we were soon able to begin co-ordinating the various sections of our forces and keep close contact with the local people hiding up in the hills. So although our Red Army was some ten times smaller than the enemy forces and was just as dispersed, we were able to operate as a unified body in this mountainous area. We were extremely flexible and, bit by bit, we drew the Nationalists deeper and deeper into the hills until it was as if they were blind, or lost in a thick mist. They no longer knew whether to go on or to try and pull back.

This state of affairs lasted for some ten days. Day and night the sound of shooting and firecrackers could be heard, but one side rarely caught sight of the other. We were constantly on the move, although in fact we hardly ever went beyond a radius of some twenty *li* and just kept going round in circles. The Nationalist troops on our trail rarely left this area either and we were able to remain a safe distance ahead of them quite easily. Our forces in other parts of the hills were leading the Nationalists on a similar wild-goose chase. According to our scouts, constant hunger, exhaustion and the frustration of this exercise were beginning to take their toll on the morale of the enemy troops.

At this point Pan Xudong ordered all our forces to go on the offensive and attack the enemy. All the peasants hiding in the hills were mobilized to support our effort. After these orders had been received by all our forces and peasant organizations, we allowed two days to prepare for the assault. Our offensive began during the third night, while the enemy were fast asleep. First, our forces quietly infiltrated the areas around the Nationalist encampments. Our section, led by Pan Xudong, was preparing to take on the enemy's main force, which contained the division command. The principle task of the enemy commanders had been to recapture Kongji – which they had in fact achieved, even though the town was completely deserted. About half an hour before our united action was due to begin we moved quietly towards the enemy encampment and lay in wait nearby. The launch of our offensive grew closer and closer. At the agreed moment Pan Xudong gave the order to attack. The sound of firecrackers resounded through the hills, just like the thud of cannon and the crack of rifles. The same sounds echoed across to us from around the other enemy encampments and the whole effect was truly terrifying. Before the enemy soldiers even had time to get up and get dressed, our fighters ran straight in among them, opening fire left and right and throwing hand grenades, and causing total chaos among the enemy.

Pan Xudong plunged into the fray with three very skilful fighters and at once spotted what appeared to be a high-ranking officer. Grabbing him, they quickly established from a solider that he was the Division Commander, and dragged him out. At this moment our Peasant Volunteer force suddenly appeared on all sides, clutching a variety of ancient-looking weapons. Pan Xudong handed the commander over to two of our fighters and told them to take him to a nearby village for 'safe keeping'. Then he turned back to command the rest of our forces, who were fuelling the enemy's confusion and grabbing their guns and ammunition. These weapons were handed straight over to the Peasant Volunteers, who were now streaming in from all sides.

Without their weapons the enemy troops could do nothing but flee into the night. Only a small group of officers and their bodyguards continued to fight. Knowing that they would receive little mercy after the outrages they had perpetrated in the past, they had decided to try to resist. When Pan Xudong saw this, he concentrated his Red Army fighters for the attack. The officers began to assemble their remaining forces in an attempt to open an escape route through the surrounding wall of Peasant Volunteers. These officers were the backbone of this Nationalist army, so it was essential that they should not be allowed to escape. Once we had captured them, we would effectively have beaten the enemy.

This hand-to-hand fighting lasted a whole hour. Finally, however, we managed to defeat the officers. Then, Pan Xudong was supervising the counting of the precious arms and ammunition we had captured, when he was suddenly hit in the back by a bullet. He did not fall, however, and I rushed over to support him. He was bleeding profusely his blood staining my clothes, but he stayed in command of the battlefield and continued to do so right up until the very last Nationalist had been rounded up.

'Don't miss a single gun or a single bullet!' he said to me in a low voice. 'They are the life-blood of our army . . . Now that I've finished my work, I can lie down . . .'

I felt his body slip heavily to the ground. Fortunately, there was an American-style sleeping bag near by and I lay him on it. But by now he had lost so much blood that he lost consciousness; I saw that his eyes were closed.

By this time, Wang Jiansheng and Chang Je-an had arrived on the scene. Their forces had achieved similar victories and they had come to report to Pan Xudong. But it was already too late. His right hand, which lay in mine, was completely cold. Chang Je-an put his palm against Pan Xudong's forehead; it, too, was cold. The three of us looked at one another blankly, not knowing what to say. The fighters around us looked on in silent disbelief. It was Chang Je-an who finally broke the silence.

'We mustn't stop our military operation for a minute. I propose that Comrade Wang Jiansheng at once take over from Comrade Pan Xudong and continue commanding our forces.'

Knowing that we had pressing work ahead of us, the fighters gathered around us broke into a shout. 'We agree!'

After a moment's silence, Wang Jiansheng said, 'We will have to make an even greater effort if we are to make up for Pan Xudong's loss. Our task is more formidable than ever, as this victory over the enemy has taken our historic struggle one stage further.'

CHAPTER 9

After returning to Kongji, Wang Jiansheng held a large meeting just outside the town to celebrate our victory. He took the opportunity to talk about the experience we had gained during our resistance to the Nationalists' campaign of 'encirclement and suppression'.

'This time we have succeeded in destroying two divisions of Chiang Kai-shek's army,' he said. 'But the struggle is not over yet. The Nationalists still have a base inside our soviet area – Mazhen county. Their headquarters are there and the landlords and gentry, like Chumin and Duan Lianchen, can stay there safely, cooking up more evil plots, protected by the Nationalist troops. We must make sure we wipe them out as well.'

'Wipe them out! Wipe them out!' the roar went up from the crowd.

Taking advantage of our high morale, Wang Jiansheng and Chang Je-an quickly returned to the Examination Halls to discuss our next move – the attack on Mazhen county.

'Let me explain the situation,' Chang Je-an said, as soon as they sat down in Wang Jiansheng's office. 'There's a main road leading from Mazhen to 'The Big City'. There's also a telegraph line between the two and so it's easy for them to send reinforcements over. That's why all the landlords dare to stay on there running their headquarters.'

After frowning for a moment, Wang Jiansheng said, 'Yes.

But we can cut their telegraph wires outside the town. And it shouldn't be too difficult to wreck the road. If they send their troops on foot we can lay an ambush for them. We're now strong enough to handle one of their large armies.'

So the decision was taken to begin our attack on Mazhen county without further delay. Wang Jiansheng, who was now commander-in-chief, and the other leaders of our forces quickly made an analysis of the situation: with the arms we had captured from the Nationalists our Red Army was now able to take the enemy on directly. The peasant forces organized first by Li Chengbao and Zhao Dagui, and later by Jiqing and Pan Mingxun, which were operating around the edge of Mazhen county, had already just about destroyed the power of the landlords in their areas. This left the troops based at Mazhen itself in a very isolated position, despite the road and telegraph line which connected them to 'The Big City'.

Our Red Army, together with all the peasant forces in the area, now began to close in on Mazhen county. We no longer had to resort to our old tactics of appearing and disappearing, playing hide and seek with the enemy in order to tire them out. We were now a proper army and we were ready to take on the enemy face to face. The walls of Mazhen county town were very stout, and according to our scouts, the enemy storehouses were well-stocked with food and ammunition. We were therefore hoping that the enemy would come out and fight, so that we would not have to fight them across the walls. With their plentiful supplies, a protracted siege might be to their advantage.

When we were within three or four *li* of the town, Wang Jiansheng ordered our troops to leave a gap in our encirclement at a point along the main road which led to 'The Big City'. This would give the enemy a chance to come out and 'move freely'. The forces of hill people commanded by Liu Dawang, Big Tree Lu, Zheng Xiangyong and Jia Hongcai lay in ambush on each side of the road, to ensure that the enemy did not escape and to block any reinforcements sent up from 'The Big City'.

Even though our encirclement was quite sudden, the enemy troops in the county town were not taken completely by surprise. The annihilation of the forces they had sent to Kongji had made them extremely cautious, and their spies soon got wind of our movements. So before we had reached the walls of the town they had already sealed off the gates. They did not come out, but paraded their military might along the top of the walls. At each crenel along the battlements they placed the most up-to-date German machine-guns and the gates were all heavily reinforced from the inside. Guessing that we would not dare come within shooting range of their machine-guns, they began to bask in self-confidence and shouted at us through loud hailers to surrender. Even landlords, like Chumin, who were now entrenched in the town, appeared on the walls from time to time, helping to command the enemy's defence operations. Sometimes they would peer in our direction through their field glasses, though we remained too well hidden for them to see us. It would have been easy enough for us to shoot them down. Several times I actually aimed my gun at Chumin, but Wang Jiansheng made me curb my desire to shoot. Our command post was below a disused brick kiln, just a short distance from the town and Wang Jiansheng was afraid that any shot might reveal our position and cause the enemy to open fire. The town walls could quite easily withstand our weapons, but our frail cover would never protect us against the enemy's heavy cannon.

This deadlock continued for some three days. The enemy seemed to be waiting for major reinforcements to arrive so that they could break out of the gates and close in on us from both sides. Wang Jiansheng and Chang Je-an began to look increasingly anxious. A number of other commanders thought that we should launch an attack on the town under the cover of darkness, and many of our fighters and members of the peasant forces, losing their patience, now came to express similar ideas. But Wang Jiansheng felt very uneasy about these suggestions. If we attacked the town directly, we would stand little chance of breaking in and capturing it and might incur heavy losses into the bargain. However, if we remained as we were, there could only be two possible results: either their reinforcements would arrive and they would close in from two sides, or we would eventually be forced to retreat. If this happened, it could have a disastrous effect on the popular credibility of our soviet government.

That evening Wang Jiansheng and Chang Je-an held an emergency meeting to discuss ways of breaking the stalemate. Everyone agreed that it was still essential to destroy this last enemy base, though there were many different suggestions as to how this might be achieved.

Our discussions lasted until daybreak. Uncle Pan finally came up with a plan that received the support of all the newer commanders, such as Big Tree Lu, Sun Nan and Jia Hongcai, though there were others who remained doubtful about it. Wang Jiansheng listened to all these discussions, but was unable to make up his mind. So it seemed as if this meeting, too, had reached a deadlock. Just then, one of our guards appeared with our long-distance messenger, Sweet Potato, who had come from 'The Big City'. The purpose of his mission had been to take Pan Xudong's report on the establishment of the soviet government to Master Qiu, for approval by the Party leadership. Now he was returning to confirm that this document had been fully approved. He also had a piece of news for us. Thumping the table excitedly, Wang Jiansheng read this news out aloud:

'"Chiang Kai-shek's negotiations with the two warlords from the north-west have broken down. Both sides are now preparing for war."'

As an ordinary messenger, I rarely expressed an opinion at such critical meetings, but on this occasion I felt impelled to ask, 'How will this influence our attack on Mazhen?'

Wang Jiansheng, in his excitement, hardly seemed to notice

my question and turning to Uncle Pan, he said, 'I agree with your plan. What we really need is time, and now it seems we'll have all the time we need.' Then, turning to the rest of us, he said forcefully, 'Comrade Liu Dawang, please send a scout to make sure that the telegraph line has been properly severed and the main road destroyed. We will use Uncle Pan's plan of attack. Our preparations should begin at once!'

Uncle Pan was put in charge of our preparations. He was assisted by several other guerrilla commanders, such as Yu Minghan, Zheng Xiangyong and Jia Hongcai, whose old skills were useful for the task in hand. Liu Dawang, who had once been a stone-cutter, and Wang Jingxian, a hunter by trade but who had experience of making explosives, were relieved of their normal responsibilities to lend their expertise to the 'project'. The project took up little space – a piece of ground no more than six or seven metres square, only fifty metres from the town walls. But, shielded by a clump of mature trees and surrounded by bamboo thickets and bushes, it was practically invisible from the walls themselves. Despite this, our work still had to be carried out in strict secrecy, since the slightest noise or sign of movement in this no-man's-land could arouse the suspicions of the enemy. A couple of their shells could have wrecked our entire project. Because of this, we could not have many people working on the project at a time. Uncle Pan suggested that no more than thirty men should be involved, divided into two groups of fifteen. One of these groups would be responsible for construction work, while the other would carry materials back and forth. These men would work in three shifts, with five men on each shift.

Uncle Pan's involvement in our long, hard struggle had changed many of his old notions, but there were still a few beliefs which, through force of habit, he was unable to shake off. For example, he believed that one could begin an undertaking like this at a propitious moment, so the time he chose to start digging was at midnight. He began the digging himself and despite the vigour with which he worked, hitting the soil made little sound. His example was an encouragement to the others to work as silently as possible and all five men who made up the first shift were soon hard at work. The plan was first to dig a deep pit and then to tunnel towards the town walls. The first stage, the digging of the pit, would take two days and could only be attempted at night, while the second stage, the digging of the tunnel itself, could be undertaken during the day as well. The entire project would take us about a week. During this time, the rest of our forces could enjoy a rest, though we had to be careful not to relax our encirclement of the town. We would regularly let off a few shots from different sides to remind the enemy of our presence and to make sure the Nationalists did not dare venture outside. All they could do was wait inside for the troops from 'The Big City' to come and relieve them. Chumin and Duan Lianchen would regularly appear on the walls, confident as ever that the time would soon come when they could seek retribution against the Red Army.

So the days passed and we all waited anxiously for the tunnel to be completed. When the seventh day finally came. Uncle Pan asked Wang Jiansheng, Chang Je-an and the other commanders to inspect the work. A very neat tunnel now ran straight up the foundations of the town walls and extended a short way beneath them. The Nationalist troops had no idea of the tunnel's existence. It would have been quite possible to dig up into the town itself, though this would have attracted the enemy's attention, and in any case, it was unnecessary to dig any further.

After the commanders had made their inspection, some of our soldiers who were keeping guard over the site discovered something which aroused their curiosity. Liu Dawang, Yu Minghan, Jia Hongcai and Wang Jingxian, who had been helping to supervise the work, were nowhere to be seen. It was only later that night that this mystery was explained. The three men suddenly reappeared, carrying a large coffin, which they took with them down the tunnel. The coffin was so heavy that it might have been filled with gold. Uncle Pan himself led the way, carrying a torch. They carried the coffin to the end of the tunnel and then laid a long fuse, leading right back up to the entrance. The coffin, it turned out, did not contain gold, but was packed tightly with explosives – the work of Liu Dawang and the others, who had spent the last few days putting together the great 'coffin bomb', using gunpowder, fragments of metal and a dozen or so hand-grenades.

The night before, Wang Jiansheng and Chang Je-an had passed the message around all our forces, urging them to move quickly under cover of night and to tighten our encirclement of the town. Jiqing and Pan Mingxun had also completed their preparations to ambush the main road, just in case any reinforcements should arrive from 'The Big City'. Having satisfied themselves that all was in order, Wang Jiansheng and Liu Dawang returned to the mouth of the tunnel and gave the order to begin the attack.

Uncle Pan, who had been waiting by the tunnel, struck a match and lit the fuse. We waited anxiously for about five minutes. Then suddenly the stillness of the night was shattered by a deafening roar, which rocked the ground like an earthquake. A large section of the town wall collapsed, whereupon our fighters rushed through the gap, shouting at the tops of their voices as they went. The Nationalist soldiers barely had time to wipe the sleep from their eyes and struggle into their clothes before our Red Army was upon them. Our forces were divided into three sections. The one led by Wang Jiansheng would take care of the Nationalist headquarters, while the other two, led by Chang Je-an and Liu Dawang, would deal with the Nationalist troops and ensure that they did not escape from the town. Our scouts had already given us a clear idea of the exact location of the enemy headquarters and of where the various enemy commanders were billeted. As soon as we entered the town Wang Jiansheng's troops sealed these areas off and took all their occupants prisoner. Chang Je-an's troops surrounded all the barracks, preventing the groups of sleepy enemy soldiers from establishing contact with one another and thus forestalling any attempt at resistance. Liu Dawang's troops were meanwhile blockading the whole town, with the Peasant Volunteers at their rear. Their two main tasks were to prevent any soldiers making a get-away, and to ensure that not a single gun or bullet escaped our clutches.

So the last Nationalist base in our area finally fell. The landlords Duan Lianchen and Mao Dehou were both killed in the skirmishes which ensued. Chumin, however, who had been the Nationalist commander's chief adviser, was taken alive. This was mainly thanks to the quick-wittedness of one of his servants, a cook who had previously served him in the Red Spear Society and whom he had always trusted implicitly. Little did he know that this cook had in fact been working for us for a long time. The sound of our explosion shattered Chumin's dreams, but before he had even had time to get dressed, the cook had sneaked into his bedroom and grabbed him round the neck. Then he stuffed some cotton wadding into his mouth, tied him up and pushed him under the bed.

After the occupation of the town had been completed, Uncle Pan went along to fetch him. Since Chumin had survived the fighting, it was necessary to go through certain procedures to deal with this arch-criminal. Uncle Pan chose several of the most reasonable and unbiased old peasants he knew to try him. It was finally decided that as he had spent a lifetime exploiting the peasants and had never known the meaning of labour, he should be sentenced to working a grindstone under the supervision of the peasants. Every day he would have to grind at least 150 pounds of rice. If he failed to meet this quota, he would lose his evening meal and be forced to stand on the spot for two hours.

As for the leaders of the Nationalist forces, those of the rank of battalion commander or above were also spared execution, but instead they would be forced to shift rocks, supervised by a group of tough quarrymen. Commanders of lower ranks were given a general pardon, but required to attend classes to remould their thinking. It was hoped that later they could help to train our soldiers in the use of the new weapons we had captured.

Having completed these operations, the next step was to stabilize our soviet area, restore production and enlarge our army. The arms we had captured in the county town were plentiful enough to equip three conventional regiments. But by the Red Army's calculations, there were in fact enough to arm two of our divisions.

All these tasks needed the active participation of the people, and so it was vital to begin mass movements to encourage production, the construction of the soviet area and enlistment in the Red Army. The most effective way to set such a campaign in motion was to press ahead with our plans for the redistribution of land. Wang Jiansheng and Chang Je-an decided to return to Kongji immediately to begin this work and I, naturally enough, went with them. The defence of Mazhen was left in Liu Dawang's hands.

Before we set out, Wang Jiansheng wrote a report to the Provincial Party Committee, describing the capture of the county town and asking for advice on how to proceed. Sweet Potato had been spending the past few days with the soldiers outside the town, watching from the sidelines. Now that the fun was over he could again set off to 'The Big City', taking with him the report to be delivered to Master Qiu.

The news of our victory reached Kongji even before we did, and the townsfolk were getting ready for big celebrations. Uncle Zizhong and O Ran were waiting to meet us at the gate of the Examination Halls.

'We've brought Mother, Aunt Sunflower and Sister Apricot over here,' O Ran said, as soon as she saw me. 'With all the government departments in the town, housing is a bit tight, so they're staying at Xing Family Village at the moment. It's only about three *li* from here, so we can easily go to see them.'

'Chunsheng,' Wang Jiansheng said on hearing this news, 'you should take a day's holiday! Go off to Xing Family Village to see your mother.'

'I'll let you two off for a day too,' Chang Je-an said to Wang Jiansheng and Uncle Zizhong. 'It's about time you went to see Aunt Sunflower and Sister Apricot.'

Wang Jiansheng grinned.

'How can you give us a holiday?' he laughed. 'I'm supposed to be your superior and Uncle Zizhong is the same rank as you! Only Chunsheng is to have a holiday. The rest of us must get down to work at once!'

As we entered the Examination Halls, everyone was laughing merrily. We really felt like legendary generals returning victorious to report to the emperor.

'I've learnt plenty of things here that I could never have learnt at the Military Academy. You have special experience in mountain warfare – something I must learn from you.'

These words were spoken by an officer called Luo Tongde in Mazhen county, a month and a half after we had captured the town. Wang Jiansheng, Chang Je-an, Uncle Pan and others were holding a meeting to discuss our collective experience and I was allowed to attend. Also present were Ho Shuoru, Peng Wanzhen and a new member of the leadership called Fan Guodao.

During this month and a half all the various departments of the Soviet Government and services such as a bank, an arms repair shop and a hospital had been set up and were beginning to operate smoothly. A big step had also been taken towards achieving land redistribution and all peasants had now been allocated land. The small landlords in our area had been allocated land, too, as they had not directly opposed the establishment of the soviet government and, in any case, their Red Spear Society had later turned into our Red Army.

Nevertheless, most of them remained uneasy about our government and quickly left the soviet area. As soon as the peasants were granted their own land they were filled with enthusiasm for their work and before long the entire soviet area was buzzing with activity. Everyone was in high spirits and there was at last time to sit down occasionally, get to know each other and exchange experiences.

Everyone had a good opinion of Luo Tongde. He seemed to get along well with these rustic Red Army men and his ideas seemed sound. So Wang Jiansheng put forward a motion, seconded by Chang Je-an, that he should assume Pan Xudong's former post of commander-in-chief. Luo Tongde, however, was unwilling to accept this post and insisted that he should act as Wang Jiansheng's assistant, continuing to learn the art of mountain warfare.

'We're really pretty ignorant about military affairs,' Wang Jiansheng said. 'And few of us have had much education. But at times like these we have no choice but to fight, and the scale of the fighting has got bigger and bigger, covering an ever greater area. Now that we are strengthening the soviet area it will be necessary to expand even further. You've come at just the right time to help us improve our work.'

Luo Tongde had had a proper military training. He was, in fact, a graduate of the Huangpu Military Academy, which had originally been established by Sun Yatsen during the first period of co-operation between the Communist Party and the Nationalists in the early twenties, with Chiang Kai-shek himself as president of the Academy. He had not, however, followed the usual path to become one of Chiang Kai-shek's officers. After Chiang Kai-shek betrayed the revolution, he became one of the chief organizers and commanders of the infant Red Army. After discussing Wang Jiansheng's report on the victory at Mazhen and the establishment of the soviet government, the Political Bureau of the Party Central Committee had decided to upgrade the Special Regional Committee to the status of an organization directly under the

218

Central Committee itself. It therefore decided to send two people to direct developments in the region: Fan Guodao, to act as chairman of the Regional Party Bureau, and Luo Tongde, to direct the activities of our armed forces. It was now a week since they had assumed their new duties.

'But,' Luo said, 'the fighting here is almost entirely in the mountains, where the people are poor and backward and communications are poor. The military books I've read say nothing about this sort of warfare. The Red Army started out with no weapons at all and has had to rely entirely on what Chiang Kai-shek could "supply". We will still be dependent on him to expand our army – and he is our most bitter enemy. This really is a pretty strange state of affairs. I have discussed the question of military strategy with Liu Dawang, Jin Bailong, Li Chengbao, Zheng Xiangyong and others, and I think that any graduate of West Point or Sandhurst would be at his wits' end in their situation. These commanders, who were all originally peasants, bricklayers, stone-cutters, charcoal-burners or hunters, have invented a special kind of strategy which guarantees the success of our armies. I've really been most impressed by their wisdom and common sense.'

'Yes,' Fan Guodao said. 'But the situation has already changed. The Red Army here now has over 10,000 guns – up-to-date weapons supplied to Chiang Kai-shek by Britain, America and Germany. Expanding the soviet area should not just be a matter of taking over the mountain areas; we should really begin expanding towards the big cities on the plains, which are the centre of the Nationalists' political and economic power. If we don't do this, how will Chiang Kai-shek ever be defeated? "Rustic" warfare is not going to achieve this on its own. Our Red Army needs to become more of a conventional army and all commanders should be equipped with a proper knowledge of modern warfare. The most important thing, though, is for everyone to embrace Bolshevik thinking. Our revolution is a revolution led by the Bolshevik working class and so the thinking of the working class should be paramount.

The small peasant ideology is a mixture of feudalism and petty-bourgeois capitalism and with such an ideology the revolution can never be victorious. Of course weapons are important. But ideology is even more important. Our struggle has already developed from the hills and the countryside to the big cities in the plains. So our thinking, too, should develop from small peasant ideology to Bolshevism.'

This was the first time that the old members of the Special Regional Committee had heard the revolution expressed in such high-flown ideological terms. I could tell this from the bewildered expressions on their faces. I, too, felt a sense of confusion. I had thought that it was an adequate expression of our proletarian stance to call our government 'soviet'. But now this chairman of the Regional Party Bureau required each of us to adopt Bolshevik ideology. What, in any case, was this Bolshevism? It was probably this word which had left everyone feeling so puzzled. And once this word was turned into an adjective and placed before the word 'Working class', everyone felt even more confused. There was not a single member of our soviet government who came from the 'Bolshevik working class', nor did anyone living in the soviet area itself. All the people here were farmers or craftsmen. Wang Jiansheng's father had even been a landlord – a petty feudal leader – who had been put down by the peasants. It seemed Fan Guodao was steeped in deep and mysterious learning, everyone turned to look at him, but nobody dared to raise a question. Fan Guodao was, indeed, very learned. It was said that he had even taught in a university and had been to the workers' motherland, the Soviet Union, to study the theory of the working class. When he was there he had joined the Communist International. It was therefore no coincidence that the party had chosen him to come here to assume the highest position in the Regional Party Bureau.

Everyone gazed at Fan Guodao respectfully, but nobody had anything to add on the question of Bolshevism, since no one else had been to the Soviet Union or lived among the

Bolsheviks. Fan Guodao, however, seemed a little put out when this important issue was met with silence and he cast a glance hopefully in the direction of Ho Shuoru and Peng Wanzhen.

'I've seen a copy of your *Internationale*,' he said. 'It's a good name. But I'm afraid the contents are a bit too simplistic, only dealing with things going on here in the hills. You should try and raise it to the level of a truly "international" magazine. Don't forget that we're now part of the central party apparatus and so our work is tied to the international communist movement.'

All Ho Shuoru could do was nod his head and mutter, 'Yes, yes!' in agreement. But in reality, he had no clear idea as to what he was agreeing with. An awkward silence followed.

It was finally broken by a distant sound. Everyone rushed to the door and peered up at the sky to see what it was. We saw an aeroplane flying towards us, dropping lower the closer it came. However, the town was surrounded by trees and backed by tall mountain peaks, so before long the aeroplane was forced to climb steeply. Then it banked and flew back in the direction it had come from.

'That's one of Chiang Kai-shek's spy planes,' Luo Tongde said. 'He's been fighting with those two warlords in the north-west to achieve his indisputable superiority in the country. Now he's paying attention to our soviet area again, which suggests that that fight is over.'

'We should have shot it down,' Chang Je-an said. 'At the height it was flying we could easily have shot it down with those new German guns we've got. We could attack it just as we attacked the Nationalists and Order Preservation Corps.'

'We could,' Luo Tongde said. 'but if it was a bomber, we'd have to be extra careful. We must start teaching the people about air-raid precautions.'

'And we must also start getting ready to resist another "encirclement and suppression" campaign by Chiang Kai-shek,' Wang Jiansheng said. 'Once his battle with the warlords has finished, he's bound to start attacking us again – and he's likely to use more force than ever before.'

'That's true!' Fan Guodao said. 'Start making preparations at once! But remember that military affairs can never be separated from politics. These are the basic principles for building up the soviet area and achieving victory.'

With that our meeting ended for the time being. Fan Guodao personally began to take in hand the 'rectification' of our government and army organizations. He redefined the responsibilities of every person involved, putting Uncle Pan formally in charge of security, Uncle Zizhong in charge of intelligence and Ho Shuoru in charge of propaganda. Furthermore, he set up a new Military Commission, appointing himself chairman. Then, in this new capacity he appointed Luo Tongde commander-in-chief of the soviet area, Wang Jiansheng political commissar, and Chang Je-an deputy political commissar. However, both of the latter were free to organize military manoeuvres independently when necessary, as both had exceptional experience. Other commanders, such as Liu Dawang, Pan Mingxun, Huang Yongfa, Zheng Xiangyong, Yu Minghan and Jia Hongcai were also given officers' ranks, within the Red Army. From now on, therefore, the soviet government became 'conventionalized' and the soviet area entered a new era.

The Nationalists' spy planes began appearing in our skies with increasing frequency – a clear sign to us that Chiang Kai-shek had, indeed, freed his hands to prepare for a further attack. His new campaign could begin at any time and so Luo Tongde, Wang Jiansheng and Chang Je-an were busy day and night perfecting their strategies and preparing the troops. As their messenger, I, too, was kept on my feet. For the people of the soviet area the presence of the Nationalist spy planes was the start of a new kind of struggle. Fortunately it was quite easy to hide in the hills. The planes may not have been such easy targets as the Nationalist troops or Order Preservation Corps had been, but so long as they flew low enough it was possible to take pot shots at them with our rifles. And thanks to Chiang Kai-shek, we now had enough arms and ammunition to spare.

One day some troops of the Red Army were training in an empty field in the hills when they suddenly heard the drone of engines coming from the east. The peasants on guard reported this immediately to their commanders. The sound grew nearer and nearer and, according to our recent experience, the aeroplanes would lose altitude as soon as they cleared the hills, to make a close surveillance of the town. The soldiers grabbed several scarecrows, placing them on an exposed hillside. Then they hid themselves among the trees. Just as they had expected, a spy plane soon appeared over the hills. As it neared the open field, the pilot spotted the scarecrows and started dropping down to see what they were. But once he got within range of our guns, the soldiers lying in ambush opened fire. The bullets whistled in all directions and before long the plane began to descend at a steeper angle, finally gliding down to make a forced landing in the field. Fortunately, the plane landed fairly gently, and sustained little damage.

Two young men emerged from the plane's cockpit, both wearing the uniform of the Nationalist air force. Each carried a revolver and they were looking around frantically for some way of escape. It was too late, though, for they were immediately surrounded by Red Army soldiers. It so happened that Chang Je-an had been there at the time, inspecting the troops' exercises. He gestured to our troops not to fire and seeing they were outnumbered, the two Nationalists quickly surrendered. Chang Je-an went over and removed their revolvers, while our soldiers, too, put down their guns.

'What are your names?' Chang Je-an asked them. 'And what do you want around here?'

'My name is Ma Jiajun,' the taller of the two men replied. 'I'm the pilot. And he's called Xu Qimin. He's a technician. They sent us here on a reconnaissance mission.'

'Who are "they"?' Chang Je-an asked. 'And what sort of reconnaissance mission?'

'We're supposed to get information on the topography of this area,' Xu Qimin said, 'as well as on any military manoeuvres around here.'

'But why on earth should they want information on our military manoeuvres?' Chang Je-an asked. 'We're not bandits.'

'They say you are. And they're just about to send troops to surround the area,' Ma Jiajun said.

'But who are "they"?' Chang Je-an asked again.

'Generalissimo Chiang and his new Anti-banditry Headquarters,' Xu Qimin replied. 'We're just responsible for flying and repairing the aircraft and we don't know any more.'

'That's not quite true,' Chang Je-an said a little more sternly. 'If we hadn't caught you today you would have gone back and reported your findings – and probably have been rewarded for your efforts into the bargain. Still, you've been pretty straight with us on the whole. Tell me, how badly has your plane been damaged? Could it fly back?'

After walking round the plane examining the extent of the damage, Xu Qimin said, 'There's a small hole in the right wing where the bullet's gone straight through. But it can easily be repaired and after that the plane should be able to fly.'

'Good!' Chang Je-an replied. 'You can repair the plane and then, if you want, you can go back to get your reward. But seeing as you're here to get information, you had better stay around for a bit to gather all the facts you can. You can pick up much more reliable information on the ground than you can ever get from the air, you know. So for the time being, be my guests and enjoy your stay!'

Turning to me, he said, 'Chunsheng, take our two guests down to the town. They need a rest and something to eat. Make sure they're well looked after! I'll take care of their revolvers for the time being. They are quite safe in the soviet area and have no use for such things!'

So, accompanied by a Red Army soldier, I took them into

Kongji. The news that we had brought down a plane and captured two Nationalist pilots spread fast and Wang Jiansheng had caught wind of it even before we arrived in the town. He had a lavish spread prepared for the two men, making sure they ate their fill. Then he ushered them into a clean and airy room where they could rest. He gave me several days' leave, so that I could devote my time to showing them around and attending to their needs. This was something I was particularly experienced at, as I had once been servant to Young Master Ho Shuoru.

The two airmen seemed rather puzzled by the friendly reception we gave them and soon they started asking me more about the soviet area. I did my best to satisfy their curiosity, taking them to visit places close at hand. Now that the peasants had been given their own land, morale was very high and there was a sense of excitement everywhere. This contrasted sharply with the atmosphere in the Nationalist areas and the two airmen, obviously impressed, asked many questions. Wang Jiansheng and Chang Je-an were kept busy most of the time preparing our defences. But they managed to find time in the evening to sit with the airmen and patiently answer their many questions. The airmen were more surprised than ever when they learnt that these two young men were commanders in the Red Army.

'It's a good thing we were polite to them,' they later said, telling me of their first impressions of Chang Je-an and Wang Jiansheng. 'At first glance they looked just like cleaners at our air force base!'

'The officers in the Red Army are all like that,' I said. 'They're no different from the rest of the soldiers. And the officials in our soviet government, too, are just like the rest of the people, as they all come from ordinary backgrounds. We've got several able commanders who were originally bricklayers, stone-cutters and charcoal-burners. If you don't believe me, just stay here a few more days and chat with some of them.'

'That's what we've been thinking,' Xu Qimin said.

'Well, why not stay on then?' I said encouragingly. 'You're welcome here. You can see that for yourselves.'

Ma Jiajun nodded.

'It seems to be our only choice,' he said thoughtfully. 'After spending so long here, they're bound to think we've joined the "bandits" and they'll kill us if we go back . . .'

So the two airmen stayed on in the soviet area. As they no longer needed my services, I was able to return to my normal duties. To make use of their special skills and the captured plane, the soviet government now decided to set up an 'Aeronautical Bureau', headed by Ma Jiajun, with Xu Qimin as deputy chief.

After the capture of Mazhen county town, the last Nationalist stronghold in our area, the soviet area had entered an unprecedented period of stability. The redistribution of land had boosted the peasants' enthusiasm for their work; the bank had started issuing its own banknotes and the markets seemed more prosperous than ever. A sense of well-being seemed to fill every heart. This was most evident in the case of Fan Guodao, Chairman of the Regional Party Bureau and Military Commission. The 'conventionalization' of the leading bodies of the Party, army, and government, to which he paid special attention, was at last bearing fruit. The activists who had been working all this time in different parts of the soviet area now came to Kongji to take up posts in the new departments. Fan Guodao himself was in charge of allocating these new jobs.

Fan Guodao's sense of well-being was so great that he even suggested that we should model our style of work on that of the Soviet Union, with an eight-hour day and a rest on Sundays. But there were many among us who had never known such a day of rest and, strange to say, the thought of it left a feeling of emptiness. O Ran was one who shared this feeling. This was probably because everyone she knew had a clearly defined post and was involved actively in the construction of the soviet area. But she no longer had Lao Liu, whose great enthusiasm for the revolution had been a constant source of inspiration to her. O Ran, however, kept her feelings to herself.

'Mother, Aunt Sunflower and Sister Apricot really miss you,' she told me one afternoon. 'And of course they miss Uncle Zizhong, Uncle Pan and Wang Jiansheng too. Why don't we go and see them? Xing Family Village isn't far from here.'

'And it would be good to see Kuaile and Little Baldy too,' I added. 'All right, then. Let's go and find Wang Jiansheng and Uncle Zizhong and all go there together. And then there's Ho Shuoru and Peng Wanzhen – they'll want to see them too. Mother is always really concerned about Peng Wanzhen.'

So O Ran and I went off to find the others. Seeing O Ran's cheerful expression, they all agreed to come. It was only about three *li* to the village, so we could get there in an hour, returning to Kongji that night. As we left the town the sun was already setting.

The three mothers were living in a dry-stone farmer's cottage. Each had her own room and in the middle was a room for communal use. In front of the entrance was a large area used for drying grain. This house belonged to an elderly couple who lived alone. On hearing that the three mothers were all relations of cadres, they had volunteered to move into a little adjoining room and invited them to use their house.

When we arrived, we found the three of them sitting round a low table outside the house about to eat their supper. Little Baldy and Kuaile were playing and laughing at their side. As it happened, it was nearly the time of the Mid-autumn Festival and the moon was full. The three women were delighted to see us. Aunt Sunflower ran into the house to fetch stools while Sister Apricot started preparing food for us in the kitchen.

'He's always smiling,' Mother said, carrying Kuaile over to O Ran, 'and he can already walk. But he doesn't yet know how to say 'Mama', because he sees so little of you.'

Little Baldy, meanwhile, just stood there staring at us blankly. He barely seemed to recognize us – not even his father.

Before long, Sister Apricot came out with a pot of buckwheat dumpling soup.

'Help yourselves!' Mother said. 'We made an extra portion of buckwheat dumplings today as we guessed you might come to see us one of these days. And here you are! It just shows that we were all thinking the same thoughts.'

Mother's cheerful expression seemed to hide an underlying sadness. We sat down to have our meal. After such a long period of separation there was so much we all wanted to say. But at that moment no words came to our lips. After gulping down our soup, we stretched out our legs and stared up at the sky.

'The moon is beautiful – so round!' Peng Wanzhen said, at last breaking the silence. 'I'd really like to write a poem.'

'Write one, then!' Ho Shuoru said. 'And if you can't write it down, tell me out loud and I'll jot it down. Tomorrow I'll write it out properly for you.'

Peng Wanzhen, however, gave a little sigh and said, with a touch of melancholy, 'It isn't too hard to find inspiration in times like these. But I'm afraid writing poetry is something that is going to have to wait until after the revolution has been victorious and our lives are back to normal.'

'When that time comes, I want to sit down and write novels,' Ho Shuoru said. 'I'll never forget all that has happened here. I'm no good as a story-teller, but I can at least write an account of the revolution here. I must do this, if only for the sake of my friends . . .'

'Well, you are both educated people,' Uncle Pan said. 'In the future you'll become writers and poets. But I've never had such hopes. All I want is a good, tame ox to walk with me in the hills and look at the rich harvest.'

'I didn't even finish at middle school,' Wang Jiansheng said. 'I'm still far from literate and can only just write a simple letter. All I hope for is a job as a door-keeper in one of our new modern factories.'

'And I have no skills to offer,' Uncle Zizhong said. 'I just know a bit about herbal medicines. When the country starts its socialist reconstruction, I'll be quite happy if I'm allowed to go and collect herbs. Then I'll feel satisfied with my life.'

Maybe this sudden outpouring of personal feelings, so removed from our present reality, had something to do with the magical effect of the moon, as it hung, round and full, in the night sky. But they quickly returned to their senses and everyone laughed out loud. The atmosphere grew more lively and everyone forgot that they must soon return to Kongji. My mother insisted that we stay the night and everyone agreed, relaxed by the pleasant atmosphere.

So we all spent a night at this dry-stone cottage, a night reminiscent of a long-forgotten family life.

Early the next morning we returned to Kongji. When we got there, Fan Guodao's aide was summoning everyone to an emergency meeting. We went straight to his office, but when he learnt of our visit to our families and our overnight stay there, he said emphatically, 'This shows that we must still work hard to rid ourselves of petty-bourgeois tendencies and the feudal peasant mentality. It also proves the need for Bolshevik thinking amongst us revolutionaries.'

We couldn't understand what this had to do with our visit to our relatives. All of us felt confused and just stood there for a while, staring blankly at Fan Guodao.

CHAPTER 10

The emergency meeting was chaired by Fan Guodao in his office. Wang Jiansheng decided that I should attend too, as I might be needed as a messenger. Luo Tongde was already there when we arrived. He looked grave and we could tell that this was to be a critical meeting.

Pointing to two pieces of paper on his desk, Fan Guodao said to Uncle Zizhong, 'These two reports arrived last night. You should have been the first person to see them, but since you were not here, they were passed directly on to me. One of them was brought here by a messenger specially sent by Master Qiu. The other was sent by an underground activist of ours in Suxuan county. Now, let me read them to you. The first reads as follows: "Chiang Kai-shek has completely ceased hostilities with the two warlords in the north-west. The troops under his direct control are now assembling in the provincial capital and are beginning to head in the direction of the soviet area." The second one reads: "A well-armed division of Nationalist troops has entered Suxuan county town."'

To receive such news just as things were beginning to return to normal was something of a shock. But thinking about it more carefully, there was nothing particularly strange about it. By sending spy planes to the soviet area, Chiang Kai-shek had already indicated that he intended to launch a new offensive. Now he was sending his troops against us. Suxuan county bordered on to the soviet area, but it was still under

Nationalist control. Sweet Potato and I had once passed through Suxuan on our way to 'The Big City'. I remembered that the land there was fairly flat – suitable for massing large numbers of troops.

'These two messages have arrived just in time,' Luo Tongde said. 'There's now no doubt that Chiang Kai-shek's latest campaign against us has already started. But we still have enough time to prepare. One problem, though, is that we do not have enough support in Suxuan county. Nevertheless, we can't just wait here until they surround us. We must take the initiative.'

'I think you'll find we have more support in Suxuan than you imagine,' Uncle Zizhong said. 'The influence of our soviet area and the Red Army is very great and Suxuan had already been affected. Our underground work has been effective, not only there, but in all other surrounding areas. The majority of the people support us, or at least sympathize with our aims.'

'Yes,' Wang Jiansheng said. 'That is my reading of the situation too. I agree with Commander Luo's suggestion that we should take the initiative. In the past we have always done this. Now Chiang Kai-shek is sending his most trustworthy troops, which is proof of his determination to wipe us out. We have never tried to meet him head on. It seems that he is hoping that this time we will concentrate our forces to resist him – and then he can wipe us out with his superior fire-power. Therefore we must not do as he wants. We should divide our forces, so as to diffuse the enemy's pressure on us. Once they are dispersed, we will have more flexibility.'

'But what if they refuse to disperse?' Chang Je-an asked.

'We can encourage them to do so,' Luo Tongde said. 'Once they're divided up, they'll have to fight on several fronts, with no easy way out.'

'You mean you want to fight another guerrilla war?' Fan Guodao said. 'That's a primitive way of doing things. It is only relevant in the first stages of the revolution. Our Red Army has now been made into a conventional force. And Chiang Kai-shek is no longer fighting us with his local forces, but is attacking us with his own modern army. The old hide-and-seek tactics can no longer be successful against him. Now that the situation is changing our strategy must change too.'

This caused us all to fall silent. Fan Guodao's way of thinking was quite new to us and bore little relation to our experience. We looked at one another with an expression of incomprehension on our faces. At a tense time like this, the silence weighed heavily on each of us. Looking at our faces, Luo Tongde guessed the reason for our silence. We had all gained our military experience as guerrilla fighters in the mountains. Such a new concept was alien to us and left us speechless.

To break the silence, he said, 'If we were to mass our forces to take on Chiang's crack troops, we would need to consider our position very carefully. Remember that he has very reliable supplies and is backed up by the imperialists.'

As a graduate of the Huangpu Military Academy, Luo Tongde's reasoning inevitably carried some weight. Fan Guodao, therefore, avoided this question for the time being and shifted his glance to Uncle Zizhong, asking, 'You are in charge of intelligence, so you should be able to give us an idea of how big a force Chiang Kai-shek is sending against us.'

Uncle Zizhong, however, was unable to reply and it was again Luo Tongde who came to the rescue.

'The second report said that a division had entered Suxuan county town. That's about 10,000 men – which is about as many guns as we have.'

'Well, it looks as if we're equally matched,' Fan Guodao said. 'But the heroic soldiers of our Red Army can easily crush them!'

'But they will also have limitless reinforcements,' Wang Jiansheng said. 'We cannot afford to ignore this.'

'That's right,' Luo Tongde agreed. 'The division in Suxuan county is only the vanguard and there are certainly massive reinforcements coming up at the rear. So we must begin splitting them up at the earliest opportunity, leading them off into the hills where we can use our guerrilla skills to their best advantage and destroy the enemy bit by bit.'

Now it was Fan Guodao's turn to be silent. After thinking for a while, he finally said, 'Perhaps there is something in what you say. In any case, it is up to you to think out the strategy, as you are commander-in-chief. The main responsibility of the Red Army commanders is to ensure the total annihilation of the Nationalists' campaign against us. Our chief task is the protection of the soviet area and so long as you bear this in mind, you can use whatever strategy you think appropriate.'

So the meeting ended here. At such a pressing moment we could not afford to spend longer discussing the matter. Luo Tongde took us to his office to examine a map of the area and begin planning our strategy. Uncle Zizhong gave a full report of our underground network around the borders of the soviet area. It was finally agreed to divide the Red Army into four sections, which would move across into the three neighbouring provinces so as to confuse the enemy and split their forces, attracting them away from the soviet area itself. At the same time, we could mop up the forces of the landlords in those areas and mobilize the local people to do all they could to slow the progress of the Nationalist troops. Then it would be possible to begin wiping out the enemy bit by bit. Having achieved this, we would also be able to expand the soviet area, establishing our control in areas previously held by the enemy.

Our First Army was commanded by Luo Tongde, with Wang Jiansheng as his deputy. It consisted of 3,000 men in all and it was to head south towards Suxuan county. It looked as if the Nationalists would be making Suxuan their headquarters for this campaign. The Second Army was commanded by Liu Dawang, with Big Tree Lu as deputy. It consisted of 2,000 men and would be heading east. The Third Army, led by Jiqing, with Pan Mingxun as deputy, also had 2,000 men and would head west. And the Fourth Army, led by Sun Nan and Jia Hongcai, had 1,000 men and would chiefly be responsible for the protection of our bases in the Daji and Lianyun Mountains, preventing the enemy from infiltrating those areas. Other commanders like Huang Yongfa, Jin Bailong, Wang Jingxian, Zhao Dagui and Yu Minghan were posted to each section of the Red Army to help strengthen our fighting ability.

Chang Je-an remained in Kongji to command the garrison which stayed on to guard the town itself. He was assisted by Uncle Pan and their force was made up chiefly of the old Red Spear Society, which had been turned into the Peasant Volunteer Force. Uncle Zizhong, too, stayed on in Kongji to take care of intelligence. Working closely with Chang Je-an and Uncle Pan, he collected information from all other areas enabling all our forces to co-ordinate their efforts. This made my job as messenger a lot easier. Wang Jiansheng decided to take me to the front at Suxuan county to help him keep in touch with the situation in other areas. However, with Uncle Zizhong co-ordinating intelligence for the entire area, all I had to do was to keep in regular touch with him and report back to Wang Jiansheng.

Having devised this overall strategy, the leaders of the Red Army lost no time in mobilizing their various forces.

Before the southern army, under Luo Tongde, set out on its march to Suxuan, Uncle Zizhong sent messages to our underground network there, making sure that they made the necessary preparations, secretly mobilizing the local people to remove any opposition which might interfere with our strategy. Secret preparations were made around the area where we were to assemble, which included arresting any suspicious persons and setting up an efficient underground information network to keep an eye on the movements of the enemy. Our forces moved only by night and were so fast and light of foot that not even the people living along our route were disturbed by our presence and we safely reached our destinations before daybreak.

We encamped at three points about ten *li* from Suxuan

county town. Our command post was hidden in a wood near a small hamlet, where the local people, led by our underground workers, had already locked up a few suspicious persons. The surrounding countryside had been thoroughly vetted so we were able to set up camp without the Nationalist garrison or the local landlords having the slightest idea of our presence. The enemy regularly sent out spies, but as far as they knew all of them simply disappeared without trace.

Our camp seemed very calm and quiet, though in reality our activities were mounting by the minute. Apart from our routine preparations, we also had to dispatch political workers to help the underground organize the local people. Most of the information we received about the movements of local landlords came from the underground. It was essential for Luo Tongde and Wang Jiansheng to take all this information into account when planning their strategy and both men were so busy that they barely found time to eat.

According to our informants inside and outside the county town, part of the Nationalist division was still on its way. This was because the county town was not on a main road, so the troops had to cover a considerable distance on foot. The Nationalist officers had to be carried by sedan chair and their carriers walked more slowly than the rest of the troops. However, since the ordinary foot soldiers could not march ahead of their officers, the progress of the entire army was greatly hampered. This situation was to our advantage, as it gave us more time to make preparations, but the enemy would also be using this time to reinforce their base. The county town was quite small and had no proper barracks, so the Nationalists would have to occupy the houses of ordinary folk, driving their owners out of the town. This, of course, only worsened their reputation and left them with no reliable sources of information amongst the people. The town was effectively turned into a fortress, quite isolated from the surrounding countryside. However, the town made a poor fortress. Its walls were flimsy, built from loose stones, and, compared to the walls of Mazhen county town, it would take much less than a coffin-load of explosives to break them down. Small cannon should be enough to do the job.

But at this stage Luo Tongde and Wang Jiansheng kept our forces positioned where they were. This made our soldiers a little impatient and many of them came to the command post to suggest that we storm the city the following morning, offering to join the vanguard themselves. Neither Luo Tongde nor Wang Jiansheng could persuade them otherwise, so they decided to hold a meeting, to which all commanders, as well as representatives, of the soldiers, were invited. At the meeting Luo Tongde described the situation in the enemy camp and explained our own strategy. Finally, he told us why it was still necessary to wait a little longer.

'The Nationalist troops are still on their way,' he said. 'They also have a strategy, though without reliable information it is not likely to be as realistic as ours. Already that division of theirs has got delayed and is hardly living up to Chiang Kai-shek's expectations. They think that because they are Chiang Kai-shek's élite army and we're nothing but a bunch of peasants, all they need to do is march in and our soviet area will collapse. Little do they know that right beneath their very noses the Red Army has been watching their every move, assessing their numbers and seeing just how much they're prepared to spend on this campaign. The Red Army, despite its poverty, is now prepared to go into big business to try to grab all those up-to-date weapons. If we're to realize this, we cannot afford to act in a hurry.'

The meeting generally succeeded in allaying the soldiers' restlessness. But for some reason it was now Luo Tongde and Wang Jiansheng themselves who began to grow restless. The Nationalist armies were still arriving at the county town and although their numbers at any time were not great, they were equipped mostly with heavy cannon and mortars. Some of these guns were pulled by mules while others were carried by coolies and this was another reason for their slow progress.

With the arrival of these weapons, Luo Tongde and Wang Jiansheng had to carefully rethink our position before taking any action. But to remain stationary could also have its dangers. Our eastern and western armies sent daily reports through Uncle Zizhong. They, too, were concentrating their forces and working up support amongst the people and neither had yet been involved in any action.

I now began to understand why Luo Tongde and Wang Jiansheng were beginning to look so anxious. It seemed as if things might be beginning to turn against us. Wang Jiansheng sent me to Uncle Zizhong with an urgent message. Leaving at midday, I ran through the night and arrived at Kongji early the following morning. Uncle Zizhong had been working all night and his eyes looked red and tired.

'You've arrived just in time,' he said. 'I was about to send a messenger to tell Commander Luo that our other armies have now finished all their groundwork and are getting ready to mobilize.'

'Good!' I said. 'Have a look at this letter from Luo Tongde and see what instructions he has.'

After reading the letter, Uncle Zizhong thumped the table excitedly and said, 'That's excellent! Luo Tongde says that what he needs to know is exactly what I've just told you. He wants me to tell the other armies to begin mobilizing simultaneously. Well, we can begin right away. I'll send out messengers at once to give the order to each of the armies. You'd better go back as quickly as you can to report on the overall situation.'

After giving me a couple of rice cakes. Uncle Zizhong sent me on my way and I headed back to Suxuan county. Luo Tongde and Wang Jiansheng were waiting for me. They read Uncle Zizhong's report at once and nodded meaningfully at one another. Now, at last, it was as if their frowns melted.

We began to discover that the enemy were occasionally sending out small bands of soldiers to operate in the vicinity of the county town. Their little excursions were purely experimental, but it was a sign that the Nationalists had finished establishing their base. The townsfolk, who had had to leave the town provided them with little useful information. Had they been aware of the real situation, they could quite easily have sent troops to wipe us out. But as it was, we could begin to take the initiative and both Luo Tongde and Wang Jiansheng seemed more relaxed and confident of success. The enemy now had roughly one division stationed in Suxuan and our other three armies were about to take action in three different places. Chiang Kai-shek would have to dispatch troops to these areas and so it was unlikely that he would send reinforcements to Suxuan. Luo Tongde decided to hold another meeting to instruct our troops.

'Our eastern and western armies have already begun to mobilize,' he announced. 'They have made all the necessary preparations – using the vacuum left after the defeat of the three provincial armies to begin moving into the white areas. They've already managed to wipe out the remnants of those armies and forces of the local landlords. At the same time they have been redistributing land, which has encouraged the peasants to join the Red Army. They have occupied a number of county towns, setting up soviet governments there, and Chiang Kai-shek must know about this. He is sure to send out troops as quickly as possible to try to dampen the flames. This is probably why we haven't seen any more troops arriving in Suxuan. Now we must act quickly to destroy this division.'

Everyone began discussing how we should go about this. Finally, Luo Tongde announced that we would begin our attack that very night.

Just as the sun had set, Luo Tongde gave the order to begin clearing the area around the town of any suspicious persons. Some local activists disguised as farmers and hawkers were sent to walk around the town walls, keeping an eye on the enemy forces in the town and watching for any spies they might send out. A little later that evening they managed to capture a cook who was working for the Nationalist troops. He and several other men had gone out that morning to buy food in the villages, but on his way back to the town our activists picked him up. He had been buying meat for the officers and after a few cups of wine had lagged behind the rest of his comrades. Two of our men who were hiding in a ditch leapt out and one muffled him while the other grabbed his carrying pole. Then they dragged him back to Luo Tongde.

This cook turned out to be open enough. When Luo Tongde and Wang Jiansheng questioned him, he seemed to go into a daze at first. He had never imagined that there could be so many Red Army soldiers right under the noses of his commanders. But after coming to his senses, he decided that there was little point in evading our questions and he began talking very frankly.

'There are three regiments in the town at the moment and another division is on its way from the provincial capital. Commander Huang and his headquarters are based in the county offices. The footsoldiers are all staying in houses or shops. The machine-gun company has been stationed at the Temple of the Town God by the east gate and the mortar company is in the centre of the town, in the offices of the Board of Trade. Commander Huang has his youngest wife with him. She's a real stickler for good food – she only likes tender chicken and suckling pig. The supplies of those things in town dried up after three days, so now we've got to go out every day to get fresh supplies. But where can we be expected to find food like that at this time of year? Today I was in luck and managed to find some. Look at this, sir!' he pointed to the chicken, ducks and two half-dead suckling pigs he had been carrying. Then he looked at Luo Tongde and Wang Jiansheng to see if these two 'sirs' would appreciate his discoveries. But receiving no response from them, he went on, 'I'm just an ordinary cook. But I have learnt to make a few good dishes from my master. I'm always with him, you see. If you, sir, would care for some chicken and suckling pig, I could begin preparing them at once. There's still time to make you a couple

239

of delicious dishes: boiled chicken and roast suckling – I can get it ready for you in a trice!'

Neither Wang Jiansheng nor Luo Tongde paid any attention to this offer. Instead, they simply glanced meaningfully at one another.

'Take him away!' Wang Jiansheng said to me. 'Hand him over to one of our local scouts and ask him to take him to a peasant family. They should give him a meal and let him sleep. But on no account must they let him get away!'

After doing as I was asked, I returned to the command post in time to hear Luo Tongde say, 'The situation that cook described is quite in keeping with what our own scouts have discovered. We should mobilize at once! Attack according to plan!'

Wang Jiansheng then went out, while I stayed with Luo Tongde. From his bag he took a sketch map, based on recent information provided by our informants. He spread it out on his lap, studied it for a while and then said to me, 'Go and see how our preparations are going.'

I ran around our encampment hidden in the woods.

'Everyone is ready,' I said when I got back. 'Each group is beginning to set off. Wang Jiansheng has left with his troops.'

Luo Tongde was silent for a moment. He looked at his watch and then went outside. The woods were now in darkness and even once one left the trees, hardly anything was visible. The Red Army was divided up into battalions and each group of soldiers was now on the move.

'Pass this message on to each battalion commader,' Luo Tongde said. 'We should head straight for the east gate. And silence is of the essence!'

Starting with the easternmost battalion, I conveyed this message to their commanders. Before long, our entire Red Army force began marching on the east gate. Then Luo Tongde ran to the front to command the positioning of the troops outside the town gates. The night was very still, but the Red Army moved so lightly that one could barely detect a sound. Luo Tongde was standing on a low hill before our assembled troops, who were anxiously awaiting the order to attack. He, too, was on the alert and his figure, silhouetted against the night sky took on dramatic, statuesque proportions. He was watching and listening for any movement around the town. Then he raised his head to look up at the sky. It must have been about midnight and the enemy troops would all be sound asleep. Luo Tongde took a revolver from his belt and fired three shots into the air. The reports carried a long way in the still night and, as if in response to this signal, the sound of cannon boomed back from outside each of the four gates. This time, the Red Army was firing real shells – not just letting off firecrackers in empty oil drums, as we had done in the past. The ground around the sleeping town began to shudder, as if a massive army were swooping in from the heavens and closing in on every side.

It took no more than a few shells to bring the flimsy walls tumbling down. Our troops then poured in through the openings and, led by our agents in the town, they headed straight for our three main targets: the county offices, where the Nationalist headquarters were based, the Temple of the Town God and the Board of Trade, where the machine-gun and mortar companies were stationed. The Peasant Volunteers who surged in behind our soldiers numbered some 20,000. They surrounded each of the houses and shops where the Nationalist soldiers were sleeping, which meant the enemy was divided into many isolated little groups.

The Nationalist headquarters were also surrounded. Having barely rubbed the sleep from their eyes, the Nationalists were confronted by darkness and confusion. All they could hear was the boom of cannon outside the town and the chanting of tens of thousands of Peasant Volunteers, who kept up a deafening roar. Utterly unprepared for this sudden assault, the Nationalist soldiers barely had a chance to get into their clothes, still less to light their lamps. In the darkness and confusion they hardly knew what had struck them, and few even bothered to resist. Luckily for them, the Red Army and Peasant Volunteers had no intention of staging a massacre. Our main interest lay in their modern guns and ammunition. All four forces had been instructed that once the Nationalist soldiers surrendered their arms, they should no longer be regarded as enemies. Most of them, after all, came from the common people and many had been forced to join the army. Now, having so easily deprived them of their weapons, our soldiers and peasant volunteers instantly became fully armed fighters, equipped with the most modern of weapons.

The chief target of the Red Army was the machine-gun and mortar companies, for once these were neutralized, our attack on the town would be assured of success. Yet even after they had been taken, machine-gun fire continued to echo around the town. It came mainly from the Nationalist headquarters at the county offices, which had been tightly sealed off by the Red Army. Luo Tongde was there directing operations. He intended to bring Commander Huang out alive. However, the headquarters had guards on duty day and night, and as soon as they had heard the sound of cannon, they had set a machine-gun at the entrance and were prepared to fight. Now they were waiting for Commander Huang to get up and command a 'counter-offensive'. Little did they know that their headquarters had been completely isolated and the small force on guard at the county offices was the only resistance left. The most they could do was fire the occasional round of bullets into the surrounding darkness in a stubborn bid to resist.

Luo Tongde was directing operations from an upstairs window just across from the county offices. Wang Jiansheng, meanwhile, was commanding the neutralization of enemy troops in other parts of the town. I remained at Luo Tongde's side, awaiting fresh instructions. The building we were in was a medical clinic run by the Christian Association; it was the only clinic in the town to have some modern medical equipment and a few Western drugs. A platoon of Nationalist guards had been stationed downstairs, but our soldiers had disarmed them immediately and now one of our own platoons kept guard outside the building. The three doctors who had once run this clinic had long since fled and only a young nurse remained. This nurse, it turned out, was happy to tell us what she knew about the Nationalist headquarters. Quite voluntarily she had gone straight to Luo Tongde and had even explained the precise position of each machine-gun. Judging from what we could see, her description seemed quite accurate.

There was a period of silence, when all sound of gunfire ceased. Luo Tongde took this opportunity to question the young nurse further.

'Do the county offices have any telegraph equipment?'

'They ran a cable out of the building just after they set up their headquarters there,' she replied, 'but I don't know whether it's a telegraph.'

'We cut off one line outside the town before we attacked,' Luo Tongde said. 'But I still need to know whether there are any wireless sets to communicate with the outside.'

'I'm not sure,' she said, 'and I really wouldn't like to make a guess. But seeing as this is such an important command post, it wouldn't be surprising if they did have a radio transmitter. And if they do, it is quite possible that they are holding out now to give Chiang Kai-shek time to send bombers over. There have been several reconnaisance planes flying over in the last few days and I've heard that it only takes about an hour to fly here from the Provincial Capital.'

'You're right!' Luo Tongde said, his face becoming tense. 'What you say makes sense. What is your name?'

'Han Jielian. I'm a nurse.'

'But you seem to have quite a head for politics – as well as for military strategy. Where did you learn it?'

'I knew you'd ask that!' she said. 'And there's no reason to keep anything secret. I was sent here by the underground to keep an eye on the Nationalist headquarters. Knowing that you'd come, I stayed on. Once everything's over, I'll move on to some other place. Now you know it all!'

'I see,' Luo Tongde said. Then he turned to me. 'Go down at once and order our guards to throw hand-grenades into the county offices. Hurry! Not a second must be lost!'

As I ran downstairs, Luo Tongde's plan became clear to me. Having abandoned our plan to take Commander Huang alive, we would have to blow up the headquarters and then evacuate our forces from the town before Chiang Kai-shek's bombers arrived. This way we would at least have achieved our main objective . . .

As soon as I had passed on the order, there were loud explosions in front of the county offices, and the building itself began to crumble, amidst the rattle of machine-gun fire. The Nationalist guards were trying to protect their Commander by shooting their way out of our encirclement. Luo Tongde rushed down to command our soldiers who were blocking the Nationalists, in a last attempt to seize Commander Huang alive. In the narrow street bullets whistled in all directions. Then the county offices collapsed in a heap of rubble and amid the dust and confusion it was almost impossible to distinguish friend from foe. As a result, Commander Huang and a few of his guards managed to escape and we sustained quite a number of casualties. Most of the enemy guards were killed in the fighting, but the few who got away used their sub-machine-guns to escort their commander to safety outside the town. Before long, all trace of them had been lost.

By this time it was already getting light and in the distance we heard the drone of an engine. Before long, a light aircraft appeared overhead. It was undoubtedly a Nationalist reconnaisance plane, sent to assess the situation. Chiang Kai-shek had probably already received a message from Commander Huang and wanted to check that the town had indeed been attacked before taking further action. By now, however, most of our troops had left the town and were hidden in the surrounding countryside. Even our captives had been forced to take cover, so after circling overhead for a while, the plane turned back the way it had come.

The dust over the collapsed county offices had settled and the narrow street was littered with broken tiles, bricks and bodies. Part of the front of the building housing the clinic had collapsed. Luo Tongde was leaning against the lopsided door-frame staring at the carnage before him, a look of terror in his eyes. His face was as white as a sheet. I had never seen such an expression on the face of a Red Army fighter, but suddenly he staggered inside and fell limply into a chair. He tried unsuccessfully to raise himself with his right hand. Han Jielian, who had been picking up some medicine bottles from the floor, rushed over to him.

'Aiya!' she cried. 'You left arm is injured! Why didn't you call me?'

Only then did I notice that Luo Tongde's left sleeve was soaked in blood and I rushed over to help them.

'It's nothing,' Luo Tongde said, in a voice very much weaker than the one in which he issued commands. 'The skin has just been grazed by a bullet. It's the shock. I'll be fine in a while.'

Cutting open the sleeve, stiff with congealed blood, Han Jielian took a look at the wound, crying out in shock.

'Aiya! It's a nasty wound!'

'Don't worry!' Luo Tongde said with a forced smile. But the smile simply accentuated the look of pain on his face. 'The bone hasn't been broken. I can still move my hand. I'll be fine after a short rest.'

'No,' Han Jielian said firmly. 'Until now you had hardly noticed you were wounded because you had to keep command. But now that the fighting's over you need proper care.' Turning to me she said, 'There's a bed in the back room – it hasn't been damaged. Help me carry him in there!'

By now Luo Tongde lacked even the energy to refuse. Even though the wound was not critical, he had lost a lot of blood and could no longer stand up. Han Jielian found some surgical spirit and cotton wool and began cleaning the wound. Then she applied some cream to stop the bleeding and dressed it with bandages. Finally, she gave him an anti-tetanus injection in his right arm – though in Luo Tongde's case this was barely necessary. It seemed that this young nurse really knew what she was doing. Moreover, she obviously had some feeling for her patient.

'The fighting is over,' she said. 'You can rest now. Don't move. I'll get you something to eat. You need to get your strength back!'

'You're in command now. I'll do as you say!' Then turning to me, he added, 'Go and fetch Wang Jiansheng. Tell him I've been slightly wounded and will be out of action for a while.'

I found Wang Jiansheng outside the town, reassembling our troops, dealing with the prisoners war and assessing the numbers of captured weapons. I gave him my report and for a moment he remained silent, his face growing pale. Then I noticed a red scar across one side of his forehead.

'What? Have you been wounded too?' I asked.

'It was close!' he replied. 'A bullet grazed my forehead and burnt a few hairs on my head. If it had been a fraction lower, it would have gone straight through! This is my memento of our attempt to catch Commander Huang. As it was, he managed to get away!'

'A draw's a draw!' I heard a voice behind me say. 'There was no way we could catch them with their sub-machine-guns. We just had to clear the way for them!'

Looking round, I saw that this was none other than Pock-marks the Sixth, the old dough-stick seller. It was ages since I had last seen him and with a mixture of surprise and delight I shook his large, rough hand. His face looked as fat as ever, but all those pock-marks which had given him his name were no longer obvious.

'I've often thought of you,' I said, 'But I never imagined I'd find you here. What are you doing?'

'Frying dough-sticks, as usual,' he said, laughing. 'After we lost the county town I came over here and again went into business making dough-sticks. I've been doing pretty well! Those Nationalist officers really like my dough-sticks!'

'No wonder you're looking so prosperous!' I said. 'If I hadn't known your voice I would hardly have recognized you. How come you look so different?'

'That's my secret,' Pockmarks the Sixth said with a grin. 'But it's really very simple. Every morning after washing my face I mix some starch with a bowl of rice porridge. Then I rub it in with some oil and that makes my face smooth and shiney! This turns me into the fat and prosperous manager of a dough-stick stall. Nobody would ever suspect that I've been doing underground work!'

'What nonsense!' Wang Jiansheng said. 'It's not because he looks like a fat and prosperous manager. He's like Lao Liu – he's really smart at working on his own. As soon as he got here he took the initiative, found some new supporters and got things going himself. He made a big contribution to our attack on Suxuan. Why do you have to stand around joking? There's so much to be done. I'll pass my work on to you for the moment, Old Sixth. I'd better go and see Luo Tongde at once. He's been injured.'

'What? Luo Tongde's been injured?' Pockmarks the Sixth said. 'Go quickly. Just leave everything here to me.'

We hurried to the clinic where Luo Tongde was lying. He had something to eat and had fallen asleep. Han Jielian was sitting by his side. She gestured to us to keep quiet. Luo Tongde, though, became aware of us and before long his eyes opened. His face still looked very pale, but a knowing smile formed on his lips.

Before we had a chance to speak, he said to Wang Jiansheng, 'There's nothing serious the matter with me. I'll be fine after a sleep. I just wanted you to come over to tell me the situation inside and outside the town.'

Wang Jiansheng gave him a detailed report and then added, 'There are two important tasks ahead of us: the first is to restore order, redistribute land, set up a peasant force and establish soviet rule; the second is to deal with the prisoners of war. We captured at least four or five thousand soldiers and there are also over a hundred officers below the rank of battalion commander. I plan to hand the first task over to Pockmarks the Sixth. He'll organize the local activists to get it done as quickly as possible. I'm taking care of the second task myself. Most of the Nationalist soldiers are peasants who have been press-ganged into the army. After a bit of re-education they'll be able to join the Red Army. As to those officers of lower ranks – they've all had a modern military training and so we should be able to turn them into instructors. What do you think?'

'That sounds excellent!' Luo Tongde said. But this will take some time. Nevertheless, I think Chiang Kai-shek will probably allow us some time now, as he is unlikely to send more troops. And if Liu Dawang and Jiqing have the same success as we've had and destroy his other armies, then we may have even more time to spare. We should use this opportunity to do everything necessary to consolidate the power of the soviet government. You and Comrade Pockmarks the Sixth should stay on here to see to all this work. I must get over to Jiqing and Liu Dawang's forces to see how they are doing. It's essential that they should be successful too.'

'But you must wait until your wound has healed,' Wang Jiansheng said. 'It won't matter if you delay a day or two. If they'd been having any trouble there, we would have heard about it already.'

'No,' Luo Tongde said. 'I can't wait any longer. This is a critical moment! Don't worry. The blood's already dried and I can start off at once.'

'Certainly not!' Han Jielian broke in emphatically. 'You've got to change the dressing every day, otherwise the wound will go septic and then you'll be in trouble . . . Perhaps I could come along with you.' Turning to Wang Jiansheng, she said, 'Please tell Comrade Pockmarks the Sixth that I have to leave. He's my superior.'

'Very well,' Luo Tongde said. 'Thanks to you I'm fine now.' Then he said to me, 'Chunsheng, how about staying on here? Wang Jiansheng needs your help.'

'All right then,' Wang Jiansheng said. 'With such a responsible nurse to take care of you, I feel more easy. I'll arrange for a platoon to accompany you.'

Han Jielian managed to persuade Luo Tongde to rest for one night at the clinic before setting out. Then early the next morning he left with Han Jielian and a platoon of Red Army soldiers. They headed for Liu Dawang's army which was fighting in the east. Then they went on to Jiqing's front in the west. Meanwhile, Wang Jiansheng and Pockmarks the Sixth began establishing soviet rule in Suxuan county.

The work of setting up soviet rule and distributing land to the peasants in Suxuan and the two neighbouring counties continued for some two months. Everything went very smoothly and after a while Wang Jiansheng took me with him back to Kongji. One after another Luo Tongde, Liu Dawang and Jiqing also returned to Kongji. They had achieved similar successes on both the eastern and western fronts. Now Fan Guodao held an enlarged meeting of the Regional Party Bureau, at which each commander gave his report and plans were made for our next move.

After the meeting Uncle Pan encouraged Wang Jiansheng, Uncle Zizhong, O Ran and Jiqing to pay a hasty visit to their families at Xing Family Village. The atmosphere in Kongji seemed so relaxed and happy and Uncle Pan's spirits were so high that it would have seemed wrong to refuse. So in the end, we all went along with him.

The three mothers, Little Baldy and Kuaile were so delighted to see us all that it felt as if Spring Festival had arrived. With the atmosphere of rejoicing we brought with us, we all had a feeling that heaven was here at last.

'This reunion of ours is really a little victory celebration!'

Uncle Pan said. 'We've expanded our soviet area and enlarged the Red Army – that alone calls for a celebration!'

'Yes,' Jiqing said. 'It was a pretty big victory for our troops. We wiped out one Nationalist division and a training unit. Liu Dawang's force did the same. So between all three sections of the Red Army, we captured over ten thousand guns – far more than we'd expected!'

'You've forgotten to mention the 10,000 Nationalist soldiers we won over!' Wang Jiansheng said. 'What would be the use of guns alone? These soldiers have all had a good military training and once we've reformed them they'll make very useful Red Army fighters. We also gained a lot of new experience during our battle.'

When the three mothers saw our high spirits, they too felt that this was indeed a very special occasion. If only Grandpa Whiskers and Lao Liu had been with us too! They cooked us the best meal they could manage. The only person who remained silent was O Ran, who sat there with her child, Kuaile, kissing him again and again. Uncle Zizhong sat to one side, turning something over in his mind. Then he pulled Little Baldy over to him and began stroking his little bare head. Perhaps because he had not actually been at the front, he felt he had little to say.

We spent that night at Xing Family Village. Uncle Pan suggested that Wang Jiansheng and Uncle Zizhong should retire early, as they probably wanted to 'enjoy a bit of family life'. Uncle Pan, Jiqing, O Ran and I were all single and so we had no need for privacy. In any case, we were all too full of excitement to sleep, and so we just sat around chatting outside the front door. In the beauty of the moonlight we could scarcely help our thoughts drifting back to the old life in the mountain village. We chatted for a long while. Then Mother, fearing that Kuaile would catch cold, took him inside to sleep. At night Kuaile wanted to be with no one but his grandmother.

The next day was very clear and bright. As soon as we had finished our breakfast, we all set off for Kongji. Just as we arrived at the Examination Halls, we met Chang Je-an, who said excitedly, 'Where did you all get to last night? I've been looking for you everywhere! I've got some great news: Luo Tongde and Han Jielian have got married. Since this is an exceptional time, they just had a simple celebration – a cup of tea and a few peanuts. Now I'm off to arrange some work for Han Jielian. We're going to expand the hospital for wounded soldiers and I plan to make her head nurse. She'll begin tomorrow. Now, I must be on my way . . .'

I had been one of the first to meet Han Jielian and before long I had introduced her to all the others. Whenever we could spare the time, we would sit and chat about everyday things – a sign that life in the soviet area was beginning to return to normal. Even so, we could not afford to relax our vigilance. As Luo Tongde, who was still nursing his wounded arm, put it, 'This stability can only last for a short time. Chiang Kai-shek is not going to give up his campaign against us so soon. We must use this time well to build up the soviet area and improve the Red Army.'

In other words we should not only work hard to improve the lives of the people in our area, but should also continue full steam ahead with turning the Red Army into a conventional force. This was very much in keeping with the ideas of Fan Guodao, head of the Reginal Party Bureau and chief commissar of the armed forces. But in both these areas, it was actually Wang Jiansheng and Chang Je-an who took most responsibility, as they were familiar with the local people.

It was essential to monitor the distribution of land, to ensure that no disparities occurred. This work now had to be expanded throughout the enlarged soviet area, so that all the peasants would be sure of receiving their fair share of land. In addition, there were schools and factories to be built, currency to be issued and the local economy needed to be revived. Most of this work was supervised by Chang Je-an himself.

Wang Jiansheng, meanwhile, worked with Luo Tongde to

improve the Red Army. Our forces in the whole area had expanded dramatically, both in terms of arms and of men. But there was an urgent need to improve military and political training. This involved visiting many different areas to inspect the work that was going on. Naturally I was to accompany Wang Jiansheng and Luo Tongde on this tour of inspection.

Before we left, Han Jielian used some of the money she had saved while working at the clinic in Suxuan to buy some meat and vegetables and cook us a 'farewell dinner'. She invited Uncle Pan, Uncle Zizhong, O Ran and Chang Je-an to join us. Luo Tongde, naturally enough, acted as host.

'This must be the first time you've been able to sit down for a proper meal!' Han Jielian said, like a real housewife. 'Now I want you all to have a chance to relax and enjoy yourselves. It is you, through your bitter struggle, who have made it possible for us to relax like this. Just enjoy yourselves! At any moment something new could happen to keep you all on your toes!'

Luo Tongde smiled.

'Our generation was born to struggle,' he said. 'Our country is so vast and Chiang Kai-shek has so much backing from the imperialists – who knows when our struggle will end? And now there is a new factor: Japanese imperialism. The Japanese are no longer working through their local agents, but are fighting directly on Chinese soil. On 18 September last year they started a skirmish in the north-east and after only a few days they took over all three north-eastern provinces. The area they've occupied is many times larger than Japan itself. And Chiang Kai-shek, far from resisting them, just moved his troops over here to try to wipe us out. Now the Japanese are taking advantage of this situation to try to push across into North China. At the moment we cannot really afford to concern ourselves too much with this, but we should at least be aware of what it means. Our greater task is to change from a class struggle to a struggle for national liberation. Our experience so far is just a beginning and there will be even tougher fighting ahead. What we've achieved so far, though, is utterly essential, and we must build on it to work together with the Red Armies in other areas, to create a massive united force for the liberation of the people . . .'

'Oh!' Wang Jiansheng said. 'What you've just said is exactly what most of us are thinking. We just lack the ability to express it so well. Our aims are to liberate our people and make China into a modern socialist country. This is bound to be a long and arduous task!'

So this meal of ours turned into another lively meeting. The next day Luo Tongde, Wang Jiansheng and I left Kongji in very high spirits. We visited several areas to organize the restructuring of the armed forces. At the same time we took the opportunity to inspect the work of redistributing land and establishing soviet government. First we visited the area in the east, where Liu Dawang's troops had been operating, then we travelled along the borders of the soviet area to the west, where Jiqing's base was. Finally, we had to go up to the Daji Mountains and the Lianyun Mountains, where Jia Hongcai, Big Tree Lu and Sun Nan were working.

CHAPTER 11

Having completed their work in directing the reorganization of the army, Luo Tongde, Wang Jiansheng and I returned to Kongji. The recent Spring Festival had left a feeling of merriment in the air. It had been the first time the soviet area had celebrated a festival in peacetime. The coldest spell of the year was now past and the weather was growing warmer; or, as the local saying went, 'When the solstice is five and six nines away, the trees by the riverside start to grow gay.' Buds were indeed beginning to sprout on the weeping willows along the riverbanks and this added to the festive atmosphere and general sense of well-being. There was no news of military manoeuvres by Chiang Kai-shek to dent our high spirits: it seemed, for the time being at least, that he was acting less brazenly.

After its reorganization, the army was now divided into three main sections, each operating in their respective areas, east, west and south. The headquarters were in Kongji, with Luo Tongde as commander-in-chief and Wang Jiansheng as his political commissar. When necessary, however, Wang Jiansheng wold also take the responsibilities of a commander. The Red Army consisted chiefly of infantry, though there were now artillery, machine-gun and mortar batteries besides, made up chiefly of Red Army men who had been trained by reformed officers of the Nationalist army. On an area of low-lying land just outside Kongji we had also constructed a small landing-strip, so that the plane we had captured earlier could at last be put to some use and the Aeronautical Bureau finally become a credible entity.

Fan Guodao, too, was able to use this period of peace to implement some reforms in the leading bodies of the government and army. His main purpose was the 'consolidation of the leadership of the proletariat and the Bolshevik party spirit'. The old Security Bureau was expanded and a new chief of security, trusted by Fan Guodao himself, was appointed. He also established a 'secret service', equipped with the most modern weapons we had captured. This was, in fact, a special kind of army unit, though it operated quite independently of the army. Uncle Pan, who had been in charge of security, was now transferred to the logistics department to take care of supplies.

After this enlargement of the Security Bureau, Uncle Zizhong's secret intelligence work was no longer of much importance. However, far from being transferred to some other post, he became a victim of this Security Bureau. Wang Jiansheng and I only discovered this a day or two after we returned to Kongji. We had first been to see Uncle Pan and he took us to look for Uncle Zizhong, so that we could all have a little reunion. He had also planned to see O Ran to suggest we find a free day to go and visit our families in Xing Family Village. However, when we reached Uncle Zizhong's office, the whole place, including his bedroom, was empty. We saw that all his clothes had been turned inside out. The guard on duty then told us that the Security Bureau had taken him off just before daybreak that morning.

'What is going on?' Uncle Pan asked in surprise. 'What could he have done wrong? He did his job really well during our last resistance effort. He should be commended for this, not arrested! Jiansheng, go and talk to Commander Luo and find out what's happened. We'll wait for you here.'

In his surprise and concern for Uncle Zizhong, Wang Jiansheng rushed off to find Luo Tongde. We waited in suspense for a long time, unable to utter a word. Everything felt so peaceful and happy in the soviet area. This event came as a great shock – especially since the person involved was one of our close comrades and friends.

The two hours we waited felt like an age. Finally, we heard Wang Jiansheng's voice and realized that the person he was with was none other than Uncle Zizhong. Filled with relief, Uncle Pan and I leapt up to meet them. But as soon as they came in we saw that Uncle Zizhong's face was deathly pale. Wang Jiansheng stood before us with a dazed expression on his face.

'What on earth is going on, Zizhong?' Uncle Pan asked.

'Chairman Fan Guodao suspects me of subversion.'

'Subversion!' Uncle Pan exclaimed. 'On what evidence?'

Then, coming out of his stupor, Wang Jiansheng answered on Uncle Zizhong's behalf, 'I went to find Luo Tongde and we went to see Chairman Fan Guodao together. Fan Guodao said that we now know that the Nationalists used three divisions and two training units during this recent campaign against us. As the person in charge of intelligence, Uncle Zizhong should have done all he could to find out the true scale of the enemy attack, instead of which he went home to see his wife. After that, he failed to report back. As Fan Guodao put it, this isn't just an expression of "peasant and petty-bourgeois liberalism", but was "clearly a deliberate act" which required immediate investigation. Luo Tongde and I tried to explain Uncle Zizhong's situation, insisting that he was deeply loyal to the revolution and that his failure to find out the exact strength of the enemy forces was simply the result of limited information. This, alone, did not warrant investigation. Both of us said we were prepared to take responsibility for him and – on this understanding – we finally managed to get him released.'

'So that's the end of the case!' Uncle Pan said with a sigh of relief. 'Just forget it, Zizhong. Luckily Chairman Fan has now relieved you of your responsibilities, so you can turn your attention to something else. You could go to the hospital to mix medicines – that's your field . . .'

'That's not the end of it!' Wang Jiansheng broke in. 'Fan Guodao said that when the bourgeoisie, the oppressors, are reaching their final hour, they will try to stage a counter-attack, using all sorts of tricks to sabotage the work of the revolutionary forces through their agents. He said that these were Lenin's own words and were the undeniable truth. The Soviet Union has to carry out purges constantly to get rid of class enemies working from within. This work is as important as our fight with the enemy. To forget this would be to betray the revolution!'

'But how could Zizhong be linked with any class enemies?' Uncle Pan asked in astonishment.

Wang Jiansheng was silent for a moment. Then he went on, rather more hesitantly, 'Chairman Fan explained this too. He said that Comrade Zizhong does not come from a proletarian background. He was really the assistant of a capitalist who owned a medicine store, which makes his class status quite clear . . .'

At this, Wang Jiansheng broke off. Perhaps he was connecting Uncle Zizhong's situation with his own 'class origins'. Uncle Pan lowered his head with an air of bewilderment. I, too, began to feel confused. According to such an analysis, almost everyone we knew was suspect. Even poor peasants like Huang Yongfa and Jin Bailong, who had at one time been members of the landlord's Red Spear Society, could now be suspected of being 'class enemies'.

I dared not take the logic any further. The others, it seemed, were having the same thoughts and an oppressive silence fell between us. Then Uncle Zizhong, who had been quiet and downcast all this time, suddenly straightened his back and said loudly, 'Chairman Fan represents the Party Central Committee and the international communist movement and everything he does is in the interests of the revolution. The class struggle has now reached such a critical point that it is the duty of every revolutionary to keep the strictest vigilance. Strict organization and discipline are the only guarantees of our success and so I am prepared to abide by Chairman Fan's decision. As before, I'll happily accept whatever task the Party gives me and do my work with the utmost loyalty. I'll see this work as the Party's test for me. A true revolutionary should be willing to accept any such test . . .'

Uncle Zizhong's speech succeeded in dispelling the melancholy which had descended and before long we began to liven up again. Wang Jiansheng shook Uncle Zizhong warmly by the hand and said, 'I understand you even better now, Zizhong. You really are a fine comrade!'

Everyone knew that this period of tranquillity was merely the lull before the storm. There was a tension in the air, reminding one that the struggle could not be relaxed for an instant. We had to use this time to the full to make all the necessary preparations – to have wasted it would have been a kind of defeat in itself. Experience had taught us all this and so we now threw ourselves, heart and soul, into the tasks before us. Amid this hectic activity, the tremors caused by what had happened to Uncle Zizhong gradually faded and were forgotten.

At the centre of all our work were our preparations for war. However, this was not purely a military matter; it included extensive work amongst the people, since the people and the army in the soviet area were inseparable. Without those who were its eyes and ears, the army would barely be able to operate at all; and, of course, without the army, the Nationalist campaign to surround and suppress us could never have been defeated. Luo Tongde, Wang Jiansheng, Chang Je-an, Uncle Pan and O Ran were kept fearfully busy in both these fields. They made further progress in strengthening the organization and strategy of the Red Army, turning the forces led by Liu Dawang, Jiqing and Big Tree Lu in the Second, Third and Fourth Armies. The force operating around Kongji was named the First Army and was commanded by Wang Jiansheng, as Luo Tongde was appointed commander-in-chief of all the armed forces. A thorough analysis was made of our old guerrilla strategy of 'hide-and-seek' and the principles of large-scale mobile warfare were now adopted.

In the civilian field, the most important task was to boost production, based on the principle of every peasant owning and working his own land. The purpose of this was to ensure that every person was adequately clothed and fed, while creating a surplus for the maintainance of the army. The old Peasant Volunteer Force was expanded to improve the security of each region and aid the Red Army. Women, too, were now encouraged to get together to expand cottage industries and strengthen the supply-lines to the armed forces. Their work included stretcher-bearing, transport and providing moral support for the troops.

The preparations we were making soon proved to be more than justified. They were neither the result of a nervous disposition nor the expression of miraculous foresight. Before long Nationalist spy-planes began to reappear in our skies and this was a clear enough indication of their intention to launch yet another campaign against us. Reports from various sources, including the newspapers Sweet Potato brought back with him from 'The Big City', were further proof of Chiang Kai-shek's intentions. The short respite we had enjoyed was simply an indication that Chiang Kai-shek had been tied up in some other battle-front – in this case, the area in which the Party Central Committee was located – and could not muster sufficent troops to fight us as well. But he was certainly aware of how our soviet area and our Red Army had expanded and he would inevitably launch a fresh offensive before long.

Pockmarks the Sixth, who was in charge of the defence and consolidation of Suxuan county, managed to capture a Nationalist spy who had been sent into the soviet area. He sent him under escort to Kongji, but on arrival, Fan Guodao's Security Bureau, which dealt with internal matters only, decided that this was a case for the army high command and promptly had him transferred there. Wang Jiansheng was responsible for his interrogation and he found out, as we had suspected, that Chiang Kai-shek was massing his armies around 'The Big City' and was personally in command of preparations for a fresh offensive.

'He is sure to use bigger forces against us than he did last time,' Luo Tongde said, after hearing Wang Jiansheng's report. 'Although our Red Army now has about 30,000 guns, it is still going to be a hard task to beat them if they attack us with twice that number.'

'If that happens,' Wang Jiansheng said, 'of course we won't try to take them on from fixed positions. Maybe we will still have to fall back on guerrilla tactics.'

'The problem is that guerrillas can only operate on a small scale,' Luo Tongde explained. 'If the enemy troops are very concentrated, guerrilla tactics are of little use. And if the enemy were to come in and wreck the soviet area, it will be a very hard job to replace our losses. So we must try to defend the soviet area and ensure that the lives and work of the people are not harmed. We should use the concentration of the enemy forces to our advantage.'

'So you mean we should surround and destroy them? Wang Jiansheng said doubtfully.

Luo Tongde laughed.

'Ha! That's a pretty romantic idea! We could probably do that with two or three hundred thousand troops. But this time, I think we'll have to use a combination of guerilla tactics and large-scale mobile warfare. And if necessary, we may also have to fight from fixed positions. We cannot use one single method. We can use the mountains to our advantage to run circles around the enemy, disperse them when necessary and concentrate them again when this is in our interest. When we think we can beat them, we'll attack and destroy them bit by bit. But when we're not sure of beating them, we should retreat, hide for a while and then lead them somewhere where we can attack more effectively. With no support from the local people, they'll find it very hard to get intelligence. We, on the other hand, are very flexible and can take the initiative. So I think that as long as our forces can co-ordinate their efforts, we will be able to beat them – even if Chiang Kai-shek decides to send forces three or four times greater than ours.'

'Yes!' Wang Jiansheng said more confidently. 'Let me think about what you've said. Generally, I agree with your plan and I'll inform each commander that they should begin co-ordinating their work. It will be too late if we wait until the Nationalists begin their attack.'

'You're right,' Luo Tongde said. 'We can't afford to wait at all. I'll go and report to Chairman Fan right away, as we need his agreement first.'

I was constantly at Wang Jiansheng's side, so I was present at this discussion. Sometimes, when he was too busy to do so, he would ask me to keep a written record of such talks. Now we waited together for Luo Tongde to return from his discussions with Fan Guodao. He finally arrived back after dark.

'Chairman Fan generally approves of our strategy,' he said. 'But he stressed that in the future our main targets must be the cities. The final victory of the revolution depends on winning the big cities. If the Soviet Red Army had not taken Leningrad and entered the Winter Palace, the reactionary government could never have been overthrown.'

'Well,' Wang Jiansheng replied, 'I think it's a bit early to start worrying about the big cities. The Winter Palace was bombarded by the navy. We haven't even reached the banks of the Yangtze River – let alone taken any gun-boats!'

'This isn't really the time to discuss that problem,' Luo Tongde said. 'We need to get on with the job of working out our strategy in detail and then notify all army units. There is no time to hold an enlarged meeting.'

Wang Jiansheng took up a pen to start writing an outline of the new strategy while Luo Tongde sat opposite him and made his suggestions. Suddenly another thought struck him.

'A plan alone is not going to be enough. We need to set up an intelligence and communications base and I suggest that you should be in charge of it. It should be here, at the army high command office. Now that Zizhong has been relieved of his post, there's no longer anybody to take care of communications in Kongji.'

Wang Jiansheng stared at Luo Tongde for a moment, but he said nothing. Then he began writing furiously. The strategy had to be completed that evening and sent by night to each section of the Red Army.

My work now began to intensify once again.

My first errand was to go to Suxuan county, where Pockmarks the Sixth was operating, for his army unit was directly under the supervision of the First Army. I made sure that he received the plan of action and instructions in person. He could barely read and after looking at the instructions uncertainly, he asked me to explain them to him. I told him what Luo Tongde and Wang Jiansheng had said and at once he began clenching his fists excitedly. Pockmarks the Sixth was at home fighting the Nationalists.

Though a dough-stick seller by trade, years of underground work had turned hin into a very capable organizer. His former network of business acquaintances was very useful when he began operating in this area and during our attack on Suxuan county town his underground activities had proved invaluable. Having been made battalion commander by Wang Jiansheng when he returned to Kongji, Pockmarks the Sixth was now taking care of the defence of the new region and the consolidation of soviet power.

'This time we need to strike first and gain the upper hand,' he said. 'That way we can mess up all their plans.'

'Well, that's up to you!' I said.

'Tell Commanders Luo and Wang that they can rely on me!' he said. 'I know what I'm doing. And I'll make sure their instructions are carried out!'

Then I went off as quickly as I could to deliver the instructions from the army high command to the Second, Third and Fourth Armies. This took me three days and two nights in all. When I arrived back in Kongji, a messenger from Pockmarks the Sixth had just come with an urgent piece of news: the previous evening Chiang Kai-shek had launched a large-scale attack on Suxuan. Given the disparity in numbers, Pockmarks the Sixth had decided to evacuate our troops and no casualties were incurred. They had moved to the enemy's rear, where they were harrassing them and blocking the way for Nationalist reinforcements.

'That is essential!' Luo Tongde told the messenger. 'We must prepare to head for Suxuan at once. We must seize this opportunity to occupy the hills around Suxuan. With such a massive force at his disposal, I doubt whether Chiang Kai-shek has even thought of this. So next time you make contact with us, look for our command post outside Suxuan – probably somewhere near Jigong Hill. Your underground workers should be able to locate us.'

Before leaving, Wang Jiansheng and Luo Tongde placed the defence of Kongji in the hands of Chang Je-an. They also asked me to go to the Fourth Army again to tell Big Tree Lu, Sun Nan and Jia Hongcai to move their forces over to the borders of Suxuan county to reinforce the First Army. The area in which the Fourth Army normally operated – the Daji and Lianyun Mountains – was wild and remote and could be adequately defended by the Peasant Volunteers. In any case, it was most unlikely that the enemy would venture into this area.

I went with the Fourth Army as it marched by night to a place in the hills called Redbud Mount, some twenty *li* from Suxuan county town. Then I rushed over to Jigong Hill to report on these manoeuvres. Wang Jiansheng returned with me to Redbud Mount to take a look at the terrain and set up a communications network between our two armies. When this work was complete, we both went back to Jigong Hill. We arrived to find Pockmarks the Sixth giving Luo Tongde a report on the preparations of his troops and the local peasant forces. While he was there, Wang Jiansheng quickly held a meeting with our local scouts to set up a communications base. So now the machinery for resisting the Nationalist attack was all in operation.

The Nationalist forces were apparently quite unaware that two sections of the Red Army had already surrounded the area they were occupying. Early the day after Pockmarks the Sixth's forces had left the county town, the local people got wind of the new Nationalist campaign. They began to organize at once, passing on information and keeping the enemy manoeuvres under close surveillance. Again, the county town had turned into an island. All the Nationalists knew was that Pockmarks the Sixth's forces had disappeared into the mountains and dared not show themselves. Little did they know that the main might of the Red Army, which they were seeking to destroy, was at that very moment surrounding them.

Our bases at Jigong Hill and Redbud Mount gave us effective control over Suxuan county town. Unaware of this, the Nationalists settled themselves in the town and then began to send out battalions to make trial incursions into the soviet area in search of the main force of the Red Army. They spread out in several directions, fan-like, going further and further afield. We were able to get intelligence about their manoeuvres very quickly through our local scouts. Wang Jiansheng would report this information to Luo Tongde and discuss our counter-strategy.

'The Nationalists are being more cautious this time,' Luo Tongde said after he had heard the latest report. 'It looks as if they plan to carry out this campaign in two stages. The first is to destroy our guerrilla forces in every area; the second is to find our main force and cut it off.'

'Well,' Wang Jiansheng said, 'This time we can afford to let them know that we've got large forces here – right in front of their noses. We have over a division here and we are as well armed as they are.'

'In that case,' Luo Tongde replied, 'we should be as cautious as they are. All we know for certain at the moment is that they have set up a headquarters in the town and that they have a little more than one division. Their commander-in-chief, Bai Ledao, has learnt from the mistakes of his predecessor and is busy strengthening the town's defences and not taking any risks.'

'Yes,' Wang Jiansheng confirmed. 'One report says that they are building blockhouses, to prevent the Red Army from moving into the areas under their control and to launch attacks from there. It looks as if Chiang Kai-shek is now trying to use the ancient strategy of Sunzi: advance gradually, entrench at every step and finally strike hard and sure.'

'Chiang Kai-shek doesn't necessarily understand the strategy of Sunzi,' Luo Tongde said with a smile. 'He comes from the Red and Green Gang and probably can't even read the classics. It's said that he has invited German officers to advise him – so his tactics probably come from the German Sunzi, Karl von Clausewitz. Well, we can use the suggestions of their German advisors to our advantage, moving cautiously and hitting hard and sure. But Sunzi also said: know yourself and know the enemy and victory will be yours. We must find out exactly how much Chiang Kai-shek has staked this time. Now that you are in charge of intelligence, I hope you'll be able to put a figure on it.'

Luo Tongde smiled again. Wang Jiansheng smiled too, and I, sitting quietly on one side listening to the conversation, could barely resist smiling as well.

Before long we had indeed 'put a figure on it'. In keeping with their strategy of 'moving cautiously and hitting hard and sure', the enemy sent a battalion towards the central soviet area. But the guides they took with them were mostly unreliable good-for-nothings. In the past the local people had shown little respect for the enemy troops, giving them a thrashing whenever they caught them off guard. This time, however, things were different. At first the Nationalists were allowed to move quite freely without any sort of harrassment. Then as soon as they entered the area of open fields near Jigong Hill, which lay on the main route to our soviet heartland, the Red Army swooped down from the hills on either side and encircled them. The battle lasted barely an hour before the entire battalion was captured alive.

The battalion commander was taken off to a little hut below a hill near the main highway. Luo Tongde's curiosity was aroused and he took me off to have a quick look at him. It turned out that this commander had also graduated from the Huangpu Military Academy during the time that Chiang Kaishek had been its president, though he was many years below Luo Tongde, who had been in the first year. Since the two men were graduates of the same academy, Luo Tongde guaranteed him his life on the strength of 'old school tie' providing he revealed all he knew about Chiang Kai-shek's current campaign. If he agreed, he would be released and allowed to return, after which he could claim that he had escaped without revealing any secrets. He finally nodded in agreement. So the two 'schoolmates' and Wang Jiansheng spent two hours talking together over several cups of tea.

We learnt that Chiang Kai-shek's strategy was as follows: he planned to take the initiative by splitting up his forces. He had divided his armies into three sections which would attack the soviet area simultaneously from the three neighbouring provinces. The section in Suxuan commanded by Bai Ledao was the First Route Army and constituted the enemy's main force. Their aim was to sweep right across the soviet area and attack Kongji itself. The other two sections planned to attack precisely those areas in which Liu Dawang and Jiqing's Second and Third Armies were operating. The entire enemy force consisted of six divisions and two training units. The First Route Army under Bai Ledao was made up of two divisions and two training brigades, but so far less than a division had reached Suxuan county town. The rest were still on their way, which accounted for the rather slow progress of the campaign.

This situation was true of the other two sections as well. Chiang Kai-shek's thought that if the troops at the frontline could achieve a victory, there would be no need to bring in the rest. However, the night before, Bai Ledao had received a telegram from the recently established Anti-banditry headquarters in 'The Big City' saying that the two sections of the Red Army in the east and west of the region were pushing outwards and had already captured four county towns outside the soviet area. So before the Nationalists had been able to surround our area, our forces had already broken through to their rear. This had taken Chiang Kai-shek by surprise and he was now determined to treble his forces, making a total of eighteen divisions.

'But it seems that you haven't yet tried to push outwards on this side,' the commander concluded. 'Nevertheless, Bai Ledao felt uneasy and so he sent me out with this battalion to investigate. We never expected our whole battalion to be captured like this. You seem to have quite a big Red Army here. Is this your main force?'

Luo Tongde smiled and said, 'You're not far off the mark! Well, we're from the same school and you've been pretty straight with us. So let me be straight with you too. This is one of our main forces. But we have no plans to enter the white areas because your main force is based there now, isn't it? This is our main entrance and we intend to keep it guarded.'

'Our forces will become stronger and stronger, though: two, three, four divisions . . .' the commander said. 'How can you possibly hold out against us?'

Luo Tongde did not answer directly, but simply said, 'Well, we wouldn't expect eighteen divisions of your Generalissimo Chiang to sit around doing nothing. We know they will come – two, three, four divisions . . .' Then, changing the subject, he went on with emphasis, 'Now, we will keep our promise and release you. But I'm afraid that your troops will have to stay here as prisoners of war. Please forgive us for this. Chunsheng, take the commander to the guardhouse and make sure he gets a meal. After that, he is free to leave.' Then he turned back to the commander and said, 'I'm sorry we can't see you off in person, commander. Let me wish you a safe journey!'

After I had carried out Luo Tongde's order, he and Wang Jiansheng were still talking and the atmosphere seemed very relaxed.

'Sending him back is really sending Bai Ledao some free information,' Wang Jiansheng said. 'Now they know all about us.'

'Yes,' Luo Tongde replied. 'But the information we got was much more useful. They have wireless sets and can get information quickly. They even knew that secret information about our own troop movements. We had no idea about the success of Jiqing and Liu Dawang have been having. By breaking through the enemy encirclement and taking four county towns they have effectively messed up Chiang Kai-shek's plans and it will take a huge army to deal with them. This means that the forces they have here will be weakened.'

'So we should break out too,' Wang Jiansheng said. 'That way we can disrupt Chiang Kai-shek's plans even more effectively. Once we get behind the enemy we can turn round and we will have them surrounded. The main problem with this plan is that it would badly disrupt the life of the soviet area and cause major losses. So, on balance, I suggest that we stay on here, attacking them each time they send their troops. This way we can destroy them bit by bit. So let them come!'

'How will we destroy them bit by bit?' Luo Tongde asked.

'Well, if Bai Ledao sends out a unit, we'll attack it like we did just now,' Wang Jiansheng replied.

'The problem is,' Luo Tongde said, 'that now they know where our main force is, they are not likely to keep coming in dribs and drabs. They will probably try to tackle us head on with all the men they've got. But our troops are very capable and so long as Liu Dawang and Jiqing can draw things out a little longer in their areas, we should be able to take Bai Ledao's troops on on the battlefield. Of course it would be better not to fight in this way. But if they do send out all their forces, our First Army can tackle them head on, while the Fourth Army goes round to their rear and reoccupies Suxuan county town. Then they can attack the enemy from behind, which will change the entire situation. This can only work, though, if we have enough troops at our disposal. The battalion we just captured was well-armed. Go and check the number of weapons captured. Then start talking to the captives to heighten their class-consciousness and persuade them to turn their guns on their masters. Don't forget that it is not just weapons we need from Chiang Kai-shek. We need his troops as well. In fact, we are not here to wipe the enemy out so much as to convert them, since most of the ordinary soldiers are working people who were forced into the army.'

This 'conversion' of the enemy troops was a vital matter, on which the strengthening of our fighting capability depended. Wang Jiansheng went off to begin this work and so the conversation between the two men ended.

Bai Ledao now knew the position of our main force, but he had little idea of the exact strength of our army. The best that he could do was make an estimate based on our ability to overpower one of his battalions. The only other piece of information he had to go on was that the arms captured by the Red Army during the last campaign were enough to equip a division. However, this division was evidently now split into three sections, two of which were pushing out of the blockade. As far as Bai Ledao knew, the Red Army forces were fairly thinly spread and the 'main force' might consist of no more than 5,000 men. What he did not know was that the force which was lying in wait at Redbud Mount alone numbered over 5,000 men.

Bai Ledao's reinforcements began to arrive unit by unit. A number were ambushed near Redbud Mount, but the majority arrived safely in Suxuan county town, swelling the existing ranks. Feeling confident that he now had sufficent numbers,

Bai Ledao at last decided to begin the campaign in earnest. This time, however, in keeping with Chiang Kai-shek's new strategy, they did not try to storm the soviet area *en masse*, but first strengthened their front line in Suxuan county. Now they turned their attention to the hills which lay right on the front line and the first area they took an interest in was Jigong Hill itself, proof that the commander we had released had gone straight back and made a report to Bai Ledao. They sent out three battalions and two machine-gun companies, with the intention of taking Jigong Hill and setting up a guard post there from which larger forces could advance into the interior to begin their mopping-up campaign. Chiang Kai-shek had talked of 'entrenching at every step, suppressing as we advance' and now the theory was being carried out.

The Red Army command post at Jigong Hill was quickly informed of these new troops' movements by our agents in Suxuan county town. Wang Jiansheng led a force down the mountain to set up an ambush on either side of the main road, while Luo Tongde remained at the command post to defend the hill. I stayed with Luo Tongde, ready to pass messages between the two commanders. They had guessed that this was the prelude to the Nationalists' mopping-up campaign.

The three enemy battalions were massing at the foot of the mountains, with the obvious intention of taking Jigong Hill. This was very much what Luo Tongde and Wang Jiansheng had anticipated so they had a plan of action ready. We had set up several machine-gun posts at strategic points along the road and a line of defence was in place. This was not purely defensive, however. It was to act as a magnet, luring the enemy up the hillside, where they could be wiped out with relative ease.

Luo Tongde stood on a rock, calmly observing the movements of the enemy forces below from the cover of a large pine tree. The three battalions made no move to climb the hill, but remained where they were surveying their surroundings. After a while, they let off several volleys of rifle fire. This, however, met with no response and merely seemed to intensify the stillness of the empty landscape. Confident now that the coast was clear, the soldiers laughed nervously and began to climb the hillside. The hills here were stony and covered in thorny bushes – difficult terrain for people from the plains. Like navvies pulling boats upstream, they began to chant little southern songs to keep up their strength. It was a fine, bright day and the air was warm and pleasant. All around the landscape was calm and picturesque. From their chanting we could tell that they were already in high spirits.

Suddenly, this cheerful song was interrupted by the harsh rattle of machine-guns: the chanting soldiers were within range of our guns. It was followed by the crack of rifles and the shouts of Red Army soldiers – a great chorus of peasant voices, like the call to save the harvest before a storm. This great roar alone was enough to terrify the enemy and the Nationalist troops stood in stunned silence. By the time they had realized their predicament, they were being mown down by our guns. At the same time Wang Jiansheng's forces left their ambush and sealed off the enemy's rear. Now the local Peasant Volunteers moved in from all four sides, their chorus even more deafening than before. As we closed in, the enemy became less and less mobile and did not know where to point their machine-guns. Finally, they were so tightly surrounded that the enemy troops had no choice but to surrender.

The 'prelude' to the Nationalists' campaign thus ended as dusk was falling. Many of the soldiers in the three enemy battalions threw down their guns and tried to escape, taking cover among the trees and bushes. Once they had dropped their weapons, the Red Army soldiers would usually turn a blind eye and let them escape. When the battlefield had been cleared and the number of captured guns assessed, Luo Tongde, Wang Jiansheng and several other Red Army commanders sat down to discuss this latest engagement. Two regiment commanders and three battalion commanders all came out with the same idea: they suggested that we should attack the county town at once, before further enemy reinforcements arrived. This way we could ruin the enemy's strategy and put an end to Chiang Kai-shek's present campaign.

With a faint smile Luo Tongde said, 'I had a similar idea, but I don't think it is the right plan. Our main aim is to destroy Chiang Kai-shek's élite army and not simply to take a county town. We must use every opportunity to achieve this. This is a good moment now. We have the exact conditions we need to destroy them bit by bit. Now that we've wiped out another of Bai Ledao's forces, Chiang Kai-shek is unlikely to admit defeat. He is already sending eighteen divisions and is sure to send still more. Bai Ledao has almost certainly requested further assistance. So let them keep on coming – we'll just tackle each unit as it arrives. If we were to take the county town in one go, Chiang Kai-shek would have to stop sending backup troops. That way, we could reap the benefits of a single victory, but we would lose many other advantages.'

'So you mean we should encircle the town?' several men asked.

Luo Tongde nodded and said, 'That's right. I've had this plan all along. We now have the strength to do it – especially since Bai Ledao has concentrated all his troops inside the town. So we'll form a tight circle around it and each time reinforcements arrive, we'll wipe them out.'

Everyone looked at one another and then nodded in agreement. So every strategic point around Suxuan county town was occupied by the Red Army and the town was effectively sealed off. Bai Ledao remained in his headquarters, bottled up like a turtle in a jar. He knew by now that he was powerless to act and his only hope was that Chiang Kai-shek would quickly send reinforcements.

Chiang Kai-shek did indeed send reinforcements but not very many, since he had to fight on the two other fronts. First he sent three regiments, which fell into an ambush of our Fourth Army before they even reached their destination and were quickly dispersed. The Nationalist troops ran back to the white areas, though they did not realize at the time that our underground activists there were already organizing Peasant Volunteer Forces who were hungry for weapons. In the wild countryside, they were easily able to split the fleeing soldiers into little bands, surround them and disarm them. Freshly armed, these new volunteer forces became a detachment of Big Tree Lu and Jia Hongcai's Fourth Army.

Two weeks later, the second group of reinforcements arrived, this time about a division in total. We received the news that they were on their way well before they entered Suxuan county. The new Peasant Volunteer Force in the neighbouring white area had staged an uprising in their county town, managed to disarm the local garrison, overthrow the old county government and establish soviet control in its place. When the Nationalist division passed through, it was subjected to constant harrassment from this new section of the Red Army. Forced to change it strategy as a result, the enemy soon became bogged down in a futile attempt to wipe out the peasant forces, who would disappear without trace and then reappear whenever the enemy was preparing to march.

This game of hide-and-seek continued for some time and in the end the enemy troops were so exhausted that their commanders had no choice but to cease operations and regroup before setting out once again to relieve Bai Ledao's forces in Suxuan county. But before they had even had time to catch their breath, in the dead of night the Red Army forces under Big Tree Lu and Jia Hongcai crept up and launched a surprise attack from two sides. Faced by this sudden onslaught, and surrounded on every side by a roar of peasant voices, the enemy troops panicked and ran into the undergrowth, where they were easily broken into small groups and disarmed. So the second attempt to relieve Bai Ledao's troops ended before the division had even set foot in Suxuan county.

No doubt Bai Ledao was in close contact with his superiors, requesting reinforcements to relieve him. And no doubt promises of reinforcements were granted. But each time they arrived, they were wiped out before they managed to reach their destination. Bai Ledao's officers could often be seen up on the town walls with their binoculars, scanning the horizon for any sign of Nationalist troops. But they were always disappointed and it was clear that their state of mind was less than cheerful; they were, in fact, growing terribly nervous. There was nothing they could do except strengthen their defences even further.

Luo Tongde and Wang Jiansheng went near the town to take a closer look at the situation. In view of how nervous its occupants were, they decided to tighten the blockade and move the Red Army to positions just beyond range of the enemy machine-guns. Bai Ledao would never dare to break out and so we were able to spare a large number of troops to go and assist Big Tree Lu and Jia Hongcai's forces.

It was now increasingly unlikely that Chiang Kai-shek would send a huge force to Bai Ledao's aid, though nor was he likely to give up the fight completely. Our present strategy of staying in Suxuan county to destroy the enemy units as they arrived would relieve pressure on the other fronts and be easier to execute than the mobile warfare we had always practised in the past.

'But we must have adequate numbers,' Wang Jiansheng said in a meeting with Luo Tongde.

'Well,' Luo Tongde replied, 'we may be weaker than them in numbers, but we are much stronger fighters. We're now even strong enough to fight them directly in certain circumstances.'

Less than two weeks later a direct confrontation did occur between the two sides. Hating any sign of weakness, Chiang Kai-shek now sent three divisions in our direction. His plan, it appeared, was to relieve the troops in Suxuan county town and to follow this with a massive mopping-up campaign. As in the past, these new forces were attacked half way by our Fourth Army, though the disparity in numbers meant the Red Army forces were soon forced to divide in two and make for the mountains. Thinking that these were advance guards of the Red Army's main force, the enemy also divided into two sections to pursue Jia Hongcai's and Big Tree Lu's forces. Having lured them into the mountains, the Red Army soldiers were once again able to display their mountain skills and before long had turned round and beaten the enemy black and blue. Many of the Nationalist troops fled back to the plains, where they regrouped but lacked the numbers, or the morale, to press on to Suxuan to relieve Bai Ledao.

Chiang Kai-shek had by now lost some five divisions on this front. However, Wang Jiansheng and Luo Tongde came to the conclusion that he was almost certain to attempt another attack, using even greater numbers of men and weapons.

'We really need to expand our own forces,' Luo Tongde said, 'if we are to stop them effectively and eventually defeat them altogether.'

I was entrusted with a most urgent task: to send new instructions to Liu Dawang and Jiqing and inform them of the situation here. It was hoped that they would spare as many men as possible to come and reinforce our troops in the Suxuan area.

Liu Dawang and Jiqing had, in the mean time, been continuing their expansion into the white areas, developing underground work and mobilizing the local peasants. With the formation of volunteer forces, they were now able to make 2,000 men available, commanded by Liu Dawang himself. Backed by these extra forces, Luo Tongde was able to make adjustments to our strategy, dividing our forces into three main sections, each of which was positioned at a strategic point along the route to the white areas. Jia Hongcai and Big Tree Lu's troops lay in wait at the very front. Second was Liu Dawang's force. The third front was guarded by the troops under Wang Jiansheng's command, who stayed encamped some ten *li* from the county town to ensure that Bai Ledao's troops did not attempt to break out.

Before the arrival of the next wave of Nationalist troops, the whole area seemed very quiet and peaceful. Taking advantage of this temporary calm, Luo Tongde made an inspection of the forces on each of the three lines. I accompanied him on this tour.

I listened to the discussions between Luo Tongde and the soldiers. Most of them were peasants, wood-cutters or the like, as poor as can be imagined, who had joined the revolution in the earnest hope of changing their lives. Their conversation took me back to the days when I had lived among those people. At first, armed with nothing but knives, hay-forks and spears, they had begun to tackle the Order Preservation Corps and small groups of Nationalist soldiers. Now they were armed with modern weapons and had managed to encircle one of Chiang Kai-shek's main armies. Put like this, it all seemed a little like a fairy-tale, and seeing the soldiers holding their smart German, Czech and Japanese rifles only added to the sense of the miraculous. Our troops still wore nothing but the ordinary clothes they had used to wear in the fields, distinguished only by their red armbands. Only the captured Nationalist soldiers who had come over to the Red Army looked anything like conventional soldiers, for they still wore their old uniforms, minus the Nationalist insignia on their caps. It was also something of a miracle that these ex-Nationalist soldiers now obediently took orders from Jia Hongcai, who used to be nothing but a common charcoal-burner.

'He is like a true friend – quite unlike those Nationalist officers who spent all their time beating and cursing us!' Such was the comment of a company commander from the ranks of the Nationalist army who had come over to us after being captured. 'He's really smart – a lot more intelligent than most of those Nationalist officers! At first he lured our entire division up into the hills, breaking us into little groups and making us lose all sense of direction. Then his forces swung round and attacked us, leaving us no escape. In the end we just had to surrender. Joining him is the only way to victory. All soldiers want to fight to win – especially if they are fighting oppression and corruption.'

Even the words of this company commander had the ring of the miraculous about them!

Despite all this, the problem of numbers was real enough. As Luo Tongde expected, Chiang Kai-shek now sent his strongest and most trustworthy crack troops to fight us. The terrain here was unsuitable for tanks and armoured cars, but he ensured that his troops were equipped with the most efficent weapons at his disposal. With such a force, he imagined, it would be simple enough to crush us and there was no need to take extra precautions against possible ambushes. The threat alone would set us running.

However, when this massive army had travelled about half-way to Suxuan county it encountered a large-scale ambush, contrary to the expectations of its commanders. The modern weapons which our fighters now wielded forced the Nationa-lists to divide up to increase their mobility. They were thus put on the defensive and it was relatively simple for us to manipu-late them in the way we wanted.

About a third of the Nationalist troops were dispersed by our front line. At the second line, another third were dispersed and most of them were later broken up and encircled by the Peasant Volunteers. Armed with their new modern weapons, the Peasant Volunteers were full of confidence and fought a vigorous battle to ensure that not a single enemy soldier escaped. Without an escape route at their rear, the remaining third had no choice but to continue their march towards Suxuan county town, though by now they were like birds in a trap. With little difficulty Wang Jiansheng's forces were able to wipe them out. According to the captured Nationalist officers, this latest Nationalist offensive had consisted of five élite divisions.

Wang Jiansheng went to discuss the fighting with Luo Tongde.

'According to reports from all our intelligence posts, Chiang Kai-shek has already lost seven divisions on our other two fronts alone. As you know, he has also lost about nine divisions here. This means that he has just about expended all the forces he had allocated to this campaign. There isn't much more he can do at the moment. There is only Bai Ledao left and it would be a simple enough matter for us to deal with him right away. I suggest we blow up the walls and attack the town tomorrow. What do you think?'

Luo Tongde shook his head. 'We should attack him, but I don't think it would be wise to blow up the town walls. Last time we did this Commander Huang managed to escape. We must make sure we capture Bai Ledao alive. We need to think of a way to get them to open the gates and come out, so that we can capture them in the open where it is hard for them to hide.'

'But how are we going to get them to do that?' Wang Jiansheng asked.

'We'll make him come out!' Luo Tongde said with a smile. 'We still have that plane we captured. I'm sure that Ma Jiajun and Xu Qimin at the Aeronautical Bureau must be getting itchy feet by now. Let's give them a chance to display their skills!' Turning to me, he said seriously, 'I want you to go to Kongji tomorrow to give an important message to the head of the Aeronautical Bureau. Jiansheng, we need to think carefully about this.'

At this point I realized that neither of them had eaten a thing for the past day and a half. As their messenger and general helper, it was up to me to see that they were properly fed. And to tell the truth, I was feeling very hungry myself. While they were writing their message, I went off to find the cook.

'Go back and tell Commander Luo that we will set off at the exact time he requires,' Ma Jiajun said, after he had read the message I had delivered. 'And please thank him for giving us the chance to do something useful.'

I at once set off on my return journey to the headquarters in Suxuan county. When I got there the following afternoon, Luo Tongde and Wang Jiansheng immediately mobilized the troops to tighten our blockade of the county town. Then shots were fired into the air, as if giving the signal to attack the town, which threw the troops in the town into a panic. They hastily erected machine-guns on the walls and began shooting sporadically at us. From time to time Nationalist officers would appear on the walls, peering at us through their binoculars. Their predicament was obvious enough to them. The only piece of flat ground was outside the west gate; from there the road led towards the Provincial Capital but it looked as if our encirclement was weakest at this point. In actual fact, this 'weakness' was a deliberate part of our strategy.

The night the sporadic shooting continued. Just before dawn our troops began to intensify their shooting and as the sky began to lighten in the east, the sound of machine-gun fire echoed around the walls. This, again, was intended to give the impression that the Red Army was shortly to begin its attack in earnest. In reality, the Red Army made no move at all, but the threat set the Nationalists on edge. They started shooting wildly in all directions, but dared not leave the town. Then, at about midday, an aeroplane appeared in the sky, from the direction of the provincial capital. The sight was greeted with a cry of joy from the soldiers in the town, who appeared on the walls with red flags and other signals to attract the pilot's attention. Doubtless they thought that this plane had been sent by Chiang Kai-shek to bomb the Red Army and break the siege. To their surprise, the plane did not fly low over the Red Army troops, but made straight for the town itself. It circled it once and then began firing at the ground and dropping bombs. The explosions drowned the shouts of the enemy troops. The plane then flew very low, dropping dozens of leaflets telling Bai Ledao's troops to surrender and assuring the soldiers that the Red Army would guarantee their safety. Finally, the plane banked round, revealing the words 'The Lenin' painted on its fuselage, and then headed off in the direction of Kongji.

The fact that the Red Army had an aeroplane was news to Bai Ledao. He now knew that defeat was inevitable and that

Chiang Kai-shek would not send any more troops. But he refused to surrender. Opening the west gate, he tried to stage a break-out through the section of our encirclement which appeared weakest. However, not far from here two Red Army units were lying in wait. There was no way the enemy could escape us now. Had they sprouted wings, we would still have been able to capture them. Bai Ledao himself was disguised as a common street-seller fleeing for his life. Our net, however, was so fine that he was caught with the rest and before long his troops revealed his identity.

Jia Hongcai brought Bai Ledao up to our headquarters himself. When Luo Tongde and Bai Ledao saw one another, both men seemed a little dazed, as if this was not the first time they had met. It transpired that this commander had been one of Chiang Kai-shek's brigade commanders during the Northern Expedition in 1926, when the Nationalist and Communist Parties co-operated to fight the northern warlords. At that time Luo Tongde was a platoon commander under his leadership. Now, despite their differences, the two men could barely resist a chuckle of recognition.

Just then Sweet Potato arrived from Kongji. He began whispering in Wang Jiansheng's ear and, standing beside him, I heard the following piece of news:

'Uncle Pan sent me here on a personal errand, as he has some urgent news for you and Commander Luo. Uncle Zizhong was arrested again the day before yesterday and was immediately executed by the Security Bureau as a "class-enemy element". Chang Je-an was also arrested on the charge of being a spy. You must both return at once to sort things out.'

So that very afternoon Wang Jiansheng and Luo Tongde handed over their responsibilities to Liu Dawang and Jia Hongcai and set off for Kongji, taking Bai Ledao with them under military escort. I went with them.

CHAPTER 12

Even though Luo Tongde and Wang Jiansheng were perplexed by the news Sweet Potato had brought, they still hoped to enjoy the victory celebrations in Kongji. Chiang Kai-shek had again been defeated and the eighteen divisions which had formed his latest campaign had been neutralized. In addition, the soviet area had expanded and the Red Army was stronger than ever before, largely due to the many Nationalist soldiers who had changed sides. During the period of peace which would follow, the soviet area would again be able to give more attention to the task of reconstruction. However, when they arrived in Kongji, Luo Tongde and Wang Jiansheng found little rejoicing. They saw only sullen and anxious expressions on the faces of their colleagues, though few people would be drawn into conversation. The person most affected by this depression was Uncle Pan. He was the first person to come to greet the two commanders.

'How could Chang Je-an be a spy?' Luo Tongde asked incredulously as soon as he saw Uncle Pan.

'Oh!' Uncle Pan let out a sigh. 'Some agents from the Security Bureau picked up a Nationalist spy somewhere. When they searched him they found a letter addressed to Chang Je-an from someone called Qiu Qunying, who turns out to be a former schoolmate of Chang Je-an in 'The Big City'. At that time they both believed in the revolution. Then Chiang Kai-shek betrayed the revolution and wrecked the United

Front and this Qiu fellow joined up with the local warlord and became a minor official. In his letter he said that Chiang Kai-shek was inviting Chang Je-an to come and take up a job in his government. This was all a plot by the Nationalists, but somehow the blame fell on Chang Je-an himself. I really hope that you'll go along to back him up and get him released. There is nothing more I can say. I no longer seem to have any influence in these matters.'

'How could they possibly believe such a plot?' Wang Jiansheng said, in dismay.

Luo Tongde sat staring at the top of his desk, resting his chin on his hand. He remained thoughtful for a while. Then the guard came in to announce that Fan Guodao had come. Luo Tongde and Wang Jiansheng went to the door to meet him. Uncle Pan meanwhile made a quick exit through a side door, while I hastily prepared some tea for this high-ranking but unexpected guest.

'I welcome you on your victorious return!' he said, his face wreathed in smiles. 'Your success against the enemy is unprecedented! It has consolidated and expanded our soviet area and is also of benefit to the Central Soviet Area in its struggle against the Nationalists.'

When he sat down, I offered him a cup of tea and then stood to one side. Luo Tongde managed to force a smile, while Wang Jiansheng just stared at Fan Guodao's conceited face in silence.

'Chairman Fan,' Luo Tongde said, coming straight to the point. 'I hear that Comrade Zizhong has been executed. It is also said that Comrade Chang Je-an has been arrested. What is going on?'

Fan Guodao's expression darkened.

'Comrade Tongde,' he said, 'you should not call those two men "comrades". They are enemies. We are now fighting two battles, one with the Nationalist armies, the other with the counter-revolutionaries in our midst. We've achieved victory on the military front, but the purge of the counter-revolutionaries has only just started. The enemies among us are far more dangerous than the enemies outside. If we don't eliminate them, all our military victories will come to nothing. When it is about to meet its end the bourgeoisie will do everything it can to make a last stand and send in people to wreck the revolution. Comrade Stalin, in his great wisdom, began cleaning up these elements long ago. How can we afford to relax our vigilance when even the Soviet Union, which is much greater than us, still has to keep it up?'

'But it is still important to investigate the case and go through the proper formalities,' Luo Tongde said. 'Comrade Je-an has been working in this area ever since the beginning of the revolution. How could he have been arrested, when so many people can vouch for him? I ask you now: please have him released at once. I will act as his guarantor.'

'Let me remind you again,' Fan Guodao replied, 'the word "comrade" should not be used lightly. And you cannot act as guarantor for any internal enemy. This is a matter for the Security Bureau alone. In any case, Chang Je-an was executed at dawn this morning, putting an end to a great scourge in our ranks!'

Luo Tongde and Wang Jiansheng both turned white. A pallor spread across Fan Guodao's face too, but for a different reason. He stared into Wang Jiansheng's eyes as if trying to read his thoughts. Finally he broke this unpleasant silence. Changing the subject, he said forcefully, 'Now let's turn to military matters. Our victory has brought about a fundamental change in the military situation on both sides. Chiang Kai-shek has just about lost his last stake. What he has left is inadequate to launch another attack against us and is barely enough to defend his own territory. So our main military opponent will now be the imperialists who have been backing him. The victory of the world revolution depends on the defeat of imperialism. And the victory of the Chinese revolution depends on the elimination of the agents of imperialism. The time has come to tackle them directly, so they are to be our next target. We must first capture Chiang Kai-shek's strongholds and his capital. The success of the revolution depends on capturing the cities and we have now reached the stage where we can start doing this. We should aim for the big cities!'

'Well,' Wang Jiansheng said, 'it looks to me as if we'll still need to fight the enemy in the countryside for some time to come. The countryside is so vast and most of our soldiers are country people. The situation here is really to our advantage when dealing with such a well-armed enemy. So far we have only bitten off part of Chiang Kai-shek's army and because of the backing he gets from the imperialists, he is still a pretty tought opponent. It would not be wise for us to underestimate his strength.'

Fan Guodao scowled at Wang Jiansheng.

'We mustn't make the enemy seem greater than us,' he replied. 'That would serve only to boost their morale while dampening our own. This is a basic question of principle. Now is the time to begin attacking the centre of Chiang Kai-shek's power – the capital, Namjing itself!'

'Chiang Kai-shek's capital is hundreds of miles from here,' Luo Tongde argued, 'and is separated from us by two Nationalist-controlled provinces. The success of the Red Army depends entirely on the support of the people in our base areas. Without the support of the masses we would really be in trouble. And Chiang Kai-shek and the imperialists will do all they can to protect the capital.'

'That is rightist thinking!' Fan Guodao reprimanded him. 'What strength do the Nationalists have now? I must warn you once again: do not boost the enemy's morale while dampening our own!'

The conversation ended here. To try to relieve the awkward silence which followed, I went around filling up everyone's teacup.

'We captured the commander-in-chief of this campaign, Bai Ledao,' Luo Tongde said, changing the subject. 'We brought him with us to Kongji and now he's being kept in the guardhouse of the headquarters. How do you think we should deal with him?'

'Why didn't you execute him at once?' Fan Guodao said. 'He is one of our most evil enemies. Killing him would boost our morale and set the international imperialists trembling!'

'Hm . . . we don't usually kill prisoners of war,' Wang Jiansheng said. 'That is one of the principles of the Red Army.'

'Capturing him was no easy business,' Luo Tongde added. 'Now we plan to make the most of him.'

'What can he do for us?' Fan Guodao asked angrily. 'His death would be the best service he could give our army.'

'What we mean,' Wang Jiansheng said cautiously, 'is that he can be used to help the Red Army in a concrete way. For example, most of our soldiers have only the clothes they used to wear working on farms. And we need salt and medicines from the white areas too. The currency we've issued here cannot be used outside and has to be changed into silver dollars. If we were to talk to Bai Ledao's family, we could guarantee his life, providing that they supply all we need. This would also be in keeping with our principle of not killing prisoners of war.'

Fan Guodao scowled once again.

'Please yourselves!' he said indignantly. 'It was you who caught him.'

'But we need the chairman's approval,' Luo Tongde said. 'We must make sure that everything we do is in the interests of the people and the soviet area.'

Fan Guodao turned round and left without replying.

Luo Tongde and Wang Jiansheng looked at one another in blank dismay. There was nothing they could say about the conversation which had just taken place. Just then Uncle Pan appeared from the side door.

'I heard your conversation,' he said. 'So the Security Bureau has already killed Chang Je-an . . . If this is the way the Communist International wants us to do things here, it shows that they know very little about China. What sort of leadership is this?'

Wang Jiansheng hastily put a finger to his lips to stop Uncle Pan from saying any more.

'Uncle Pan,' Luo Tongde said, 'it is our Party's principle that the minority obeys the majority, the lower ranks obey the higher ranks and the local areas obey the centre. Strict discipline is the best guarantee of our success. We mustn't forget this, especially at such a critical time. There is something I would like you to do, as you are now in charge of supplies. Our troops do not have enough clothing and with the Nationalists' blockade, the people are running short of salt and medical supplies. I would like you to talk to Bai Ledao and get his family to arrange for us to be provided with proper uniforms and silver dollars.'

Uncle Pan said nothing. Head bowed, he left the room to set about this new task.

That evening, as dusk was beginning to fall, he returned to the headquarters where Luo Tongde and Wang Jiansheng were discussing the overall plans for the Red Army. Following their recent expansion, the various sections of the Red Army in our area would become the Fifth Army. Uncle Pan now reported on the work he had just completed.

'Bai Ledao said he hoped that as a former member of his army, you would show leniency to him and not have him killed,' Uncle Pan explained to Luo Tongde. 'He agrees to every condition. I told him, on your behalf, that we never kill prisoners of war after they have laid down their arms. There is no reason why he should be an exception. He wrote a letter on the spot to his family in "The Big City", asking them to get hold of 200,000 uniforms and 30,000 silver dollars, to be handed over at a time and place decided by us. I will send Sweet Potato to make all the necessary arrangements.'

'That's good, Uncle Pan,' Luo Tongde said. 'Your promise not to have him killed was quite correct. It would be wrong to kill prisoners after they have laid down arms. You're quite right in sticking to the Party's principles, Uncle Pan. Now don't let things worry you too much. Just get on with your work. I'll leave this in your hands – we all have faith in you.'

Despite Luo Tongde's reassuring words, Uncle Pan could not help thinking about what had happened. One evening, when I had finished my work and had nothing urgent to do, Uncle Pan asked me and O Ran to go with him to Xing Family Village. He had already spoken to O Ran about this but had not yet told me his reason for going. On the way he said, 'We are not just going to pay a visit this time. We are going to help your mother, Aunt Sunflower and Sister Apricot to move. This is just between ourselves – there's no need for you to breathe a word of it to anyone else. The revolution is important, but we mustn't forget our responsibilities to our families. Uncle Zizhong and Chang Je-an are both gone. This means that their families are also in a dangerous position. They can't really understand what is happening, especially your mother and Sister Apricot, and I'm afraid they would not be able to cope with the present situation. So I think we should move them to a safer place, while we are still able to do this.'

Then I noticed that O Ran was sobbing. It was too dark for me to see her tears, but I could sense her grief. It was unusual for her to show such emotion. Since she had joined the revolution she had never wept openly in our presence. She had not even cried when she heard the news of Lao Liu's death. Neither of us could find any words to comfort her and the best I could do was talk of practical matters.

'Will they agree to move?' I asked. 'Where could they go on such a dark night as this?'

'You needn't worry about that,' Uncle Pan said. 'I went to see them on my own last night and told them the news about Uncle Zizhong and Chang Je-an. There was no point in hiding anything from them. They'll still be bitterly upset – just as the rest of us are. Anything can happen at a time of revolution and having committed ourselves, we must be prepared for such tests. Don't cry, O Ran. Be brave!'

O Ran stopped her sobbing and with new strength in our legs, we quickly reached Xing Family Village. The three mothers had already got ready for their move. Uncle Pan had asked two peasants, who had been scouts under his command, to come and help. We found them waiting for us at the end of the village. The three mothers, Little Baldy and Kuaile greeted us with blank expressions. They knew why we had come and having handed us their few possessions, we set off together. We all had our own private thoughts and no one uttered a word. I remembered the very first time we had moved house. Mother and I had left the village where I had been born, taking our watch-dog Laipao with us, to go and join my father in 'The Big City'. Now it was as if our family's history was being repeated – but how different things were this time!

The place where the three mothers were moving to was a small wood-cutters' hamlet hidden deep in the hills, not far from a place called Dragon Taming Ridge. Very few people ever came here and being so hidden, poverty-stricken and far from Kongji, it was unlikely to attract anyone's attention. It was essential that we return to Kongji before daybreak, so, having settled the three mothers into their new home, we prepared to set off on our return journey.

Before leaving, O Ran held Kuaile tight, kissing him again and again. Uncle Pan patted Little Baldy on the head and said, 'Grow up quickly, my little fellow! You should feel proud to have such a fine father.'

At these words Sister Apricot suddenly burst into tears. Uncle Pan was soft-hearted and found it hard to bear this weeping. He urged us to leave straight away. The three mothers saw us off at the end of the village. Uncle Pan lacked even the courage to look back at them.

'It seems that Chairman Fan has made up his mind,' Luo Tongde told Wang Jiansheng. 'The Red Army is to start heading east – straight towards Chiang Kai-shek's capital.'

The two men were sitting in the headquarters of the Fifth

Army discussing Fan Guodao's latest orders. I was taking notes for Wang Jiansheng as they talked, to help him remember exactly what had been decided. The two men were soon to be parted: Luo Tongde was to visit the various sections of our army and begin to gather our forces in preparation for our push to the east. Wang Jiansheng, meanwhile, was to remain in Kongji to command the defence of the soviet area. In reality, he was simply replacing Chang Je-an.

'Chairman Fan has said again and again that the Communist International calls on us to take the big cities,' Wang Jiansheng said. 'He has had a Bolshevik training and has a very strong sense of discipline. He is very resolute in carrying out the orders of the Communist International and, having given his word, there is no way he will change course. We, on the other hand, have grown up in the feudal countryside and we are bound to be influenced by Confucius's "Doctrine of the Mean". This makes us feel that Fan Guodao's way of going about things is too extreme. I think we should thoroughly criticize our peasant mentality – otherwise there is no way we'll be able to carry out his orders.'

Luo Tongde was silent for a while.

'What do you mean, "peasant mentality"?' he said. 'Don't deride yourself like that! We are working in the Chinese countryside and we can't completely go against the realities which exist here. You began setting things up here, transforming the Red Spear Society, making agreements with the smaller landlords to get them to reduce rents and interest, then gradually building up the Soviet Government and expanding the Red Army, until finally, we were able to achieve these victories. These are the realities of the present stage of our revolutionary development. This is Chinese-style revolution. A proletarian revolution should of course be led by the working class. And the Chinese revolution is part of the world proletarian revolution. We know that Chairman Fan thinks that now the Red Army has reached its present strength, the time is ripe to start taking the big cities, where there are large numbers of industrial workers. Once we are there, we can unite with them and bring the Chinese revolution into line with the international workers' revolution. He thinks that Chiang Kai-shek's army is now only of secondary importance and that the Red Army should take on the imperialists directly. Seen from this point of view, his approach is quite logical.'

'Do you really think Chiang Kai-shek's army is now only of secondary importance?' Wang Jiansheng asked. Luo Tongde was silent for a while.

'To tell the truth,' he said finally, 'I don't see things that way. We may want to take on the imperialists directly, but the imperialists are not interested in fighting directly with us. They would much rather act through their agent, Chiang Kai-shek. This is the main reason they have been giving him an endless supply of arms and financial support. Only the Japanese have a different plan. They feel that Chiang Kai-shek can only represent the interests of American imperialism in China, so they decided to act themselves and occupy several of our provinces. Chiang Kai-shek put up no fight at all and has pulled back his troops, bringing our nation to the edge of destruction. If we are to fight directly with the imperialists, then it should be with the Japanese. This should be our next aim. If this is what Chairman Fan meant, then he would be quite correct. The Party Central Committee has, in fact, already called on Chiang Kai-shek to end his attacks on the soviet areas and launch a concerted attack, together with the Red Army, on the Japanese invaders. If this were possible, there would be no need to attack the big cities, at least for the present.'

'This is a very important matter,' Wang Jiansheng said. 'Why don't you bring it up with Chairman Fan?'

Luo Tongde smiled bitterly.

'I have discussed it with him,' he said. 'But Chairman Fan said that this way of thinking was just a product of the "peasant mentality", which is, by nature, conservative and short-sighted. He said that we must change this way of thinking and that taking the big cities is a question of ideology.'

'That makes it sound as if we could just walk straight in and take Nanjing tomorrow!' Wang Jiansheng said.

Luo Tongde made another grimace, at which Wang Jiansheng could find nothing more to say.

'According to the Party's principles,' Luo Tongde concluded, 'the lower ranks should always obey the higher. Whatever we feel personally, we must carry out the orders of the Party leadership. I'll be leaving here shortly. You stay here and make a good job of looking after the defences.'

Just before he left, Luo Tongde received a personal instruction from Fan Guodao: all the Red Army commanders were to come to Kongji and make use of this peaceful interlude by attending classes designed to rid them of their 'peasant mentality' and heighten their proletarian consciousness.

When he told Wang Jiansheng about this, Luo Tongde said with a laugh, 'At least you won't feel lonely here. There will be plenty of old comrades to talk to. I quite envy you this rare chance!'

Thus the two comrades parted. I remained with Wang Jiansheng to give him whatever help he needed.

Not long after this the high- and middle-ranking commanders of the Red Army began arriving in Kongji, among them Pan Mingxun, Big Tree Lu, Sun Nan, Zheng Xiangyong and Yu Minghan. All of them were close friends of Uncle Pan and myself and their arrival gladdened our hearts. Everyone felt that this opportunity to get together and attend classes in Kongji was indeed a sign of the progress of the revolution. But having been in Kongji for a few days, they were surprised to find no sign of Fan Guodao's promised classes. Instead, a special 'Committee for the Elimination of Counter-revolutionaries' was set up, based on the Security Bureau but directly under Fan Guodao's control. Its function was to 'clean up the class ranks, protect the achievements of the revolution and carry out the proletarian revolutionary line'. The day after it was set up it began its operations. The first person to come under investigation was Wang Jiansheng. He was immediately relieved of all his duties. This left Uncle Pan and me utterly stunned. Neither of us doubted for a minute that Wang Jiansheng was, and always had been, totally loyal to the revolution.

'The leaders could never falsely convict a good person – and Chairman Fan is directly responsible to the central leadership of the Party,' Uncle Pan said, in an effort to console both himself and me. 'Since Wang Jiansheng was born into a landlord's family, it is right that he should be investigated now. But I'm quite sure that he'll quickly be cleared and let out. We must trust the Party leadership!'

Despite his words, I saw that Uncle Pan's face was pale, revealing a certain feeling of dread. I could not bring myself to reply.

The following day we received the news we had been dreading: before daybreak that morning Wang Jiansheng had been taken out of the town and executed by firing squad. And then the day after that there was news that Pan Mingxun, Big Tree Lu, Sun Nan, Jia Hongcai, Zheng Xiangyong, Yu Minghan and several other commanders had been arrested by the Security Bureau and were being held for 'investigation'.

This time, Uncle Pan could find no words to explain away these events. I felt utterly confused. My mind quickly turned to Jiqing, who had not come to Kongji this time. Luo Tongde had no doubt decided against sending him to Kongji, considering the fate of his father, Uncle Zizhong. Pan Mingxun and the others, though, had all come from poor, labouring backgrounds and there seemed to be no reason whatever for their arrest. I could find no way to console myself, though I dared not imagine that Chairman Fan, the representative of the Party Central Committee, could make mistakes . . .

My confusion was heightened by yet another piece of disturbing news: O Ran, Ho Shuoru and Peng Wanzhen had been arrested too. Peng Wanzhen had once been married to the traitor Qiu Qunying and Ho Shuoru had been the young master of a capitalist family in the city, so it was understandable that they should be targets for investigation. But how could anyone have any doubts about O Ran? When I went to see Uncle Pan he, too, was at a loss to offer any explanation and simply stared at me blankly. Images of Lao Liu, Kuaile and my mother began to appear before my eyes. Would my mother hear of O Ran's arrest? And if she did, how would she take this news? I shuddered. Then I remembered how we had moved her and the other two mothers to Dragon Taming Ridge. Tucked away there they would be unlikely to get any news. My mind began to feel a little lighter.

But it was not long before there was more terrible news. Ho Shuoru was executed two days after his arrest on the grounds of committing counter-revolutionary crimes. Peng Wanzhen, too, was executed, because she had been married to Qiu Qunying and was accused of spying for the Nationalists. In this way many of the people I had been close to, and many whom I had known less well, disappeared in a very short space of time, leaving barely a trace behind them. Only Ho Shuoru and Peng Wanzhen ghoulishly reappeared as targets of criticism in the 'reformed version' of the *Internationale* magazine they had edited:

The pages of the old magazine were loaded with the peasant mentality, which effectively made it a propaganda tool of the petty bourgeoisie. Petty-bourgeois and bourgeois thinking are very much the same in essence: they are both forms of counter-revolutionary ideology, running contrary to the working-class ideology which the *Internationale* should represent. This meant that much vicious, poisoned thinking had spread throughout the ranks of the cadres and masses. If serious measures had not been taken against these counter-revolutionary activities, the revolution itself would have been put in jeopardy. From now on, the first task of this magazine is going to be the eradication of these pernicious tendencies . . .

Reading this, Uncle Pan and I began to understand why commanders like Pan Mingxun, Big Tree Lu and Yu Minghan, who came from peasant backgrounds, were being liquidated. Their peasant mentality was thought to be bourgeois in essence and therefore they could never be loyal to the revolution. They represented the infiltration of the reactionaries into the revolutionary camp. It was therefore natural enough to want to try and eliminate this 'hidden scourge'. This was how Fan Guodao's argument went, and I saw an expression of pain darken Uncle Pan's weather-beaten face: with this sort of logic, it was hard to avoid the conclusion that almost every one of us could be labelled a reactionary or a spy.

Yet despite the constant sense of terror we now felt, the days passed fairly quietly. Then one day, quite unexpectedly, O Ran was released from detention. She lost no time in finding Uncle Pan and me and began to answer our anxious questions.

'I couldn't bear interrogation and torture any longer,' she said. 'So in the end I just had to find a crime to confess to, to prove that their investigation was right. In the end I admitted that I belonged to the Reorganization Wing of the Nationalists, who had opposed the Communist Party after the two parties had split up.'

'But you've never been a member of the Nationalist Party!' Uncle Pan exclaimed.

'They said that Lao Liu had joined the revolution during the period of co-operation between the Communists and the Nationalists. Everyone who joined up then had something to do with the Nationalists and since I was Lao Liu's wife, I must have had something to do with them too. Then they said that they were lenient to anyone who told the truth and would release me if I confessed. They said that my connection with the Nationalists was like the venom of a snake: once the venom had been extracted for all to see, the snake could harm no one.

If I confessed, I could be released and serve as a negative example, useful to the cause of the revolution.'

'Sister O Ran!' I cried, unable to say anything else. I felt like weeping. But I knew that O Ran disliked seeing us weep.

'O Ran!' Uncle Pan said, now with a touch of severity in his voice. 'How could you be so careless, confessing to a crime you never committed?'

'It wasn't carelessness, Uncle Pan,' she replied. 'And I didn't confess just to save my own skin, either. For the first time I remembered that I am a woman and a mother. I must recognize my weaknesses. I could not bear to leave my child, Kuaile. Mother is growing old. She seems to have aged even faster since Lao Liu died. She won't be able to look after Kuaile very much longer, so it will soon be up to me to raise him. I'm sorry, Chunsheng, Uncle Pan. I've become a poisonous snake and been expelled from the revolutionary ranks. All I can do now is go into hiding and look after my child.' Then, lowering her head she added, 'Please try to forgive me. I'm too weak. Han Jielian, who was also interrogated, really put me to shame. She was accused of being an agent of the imperialists, because she had worked in a missionary clinic. They said that she had married Luo Tongde so that she could spy on the revolutionaries. But she was so strong that they never got a confession from her. In the end they executed her last night.'

Again there was nothing we could say.

'Did she say anything to you before she died?' Uncle Pan asked.

'Yes. She told me that on no account must her sacrifice be revealed to Luo Tongde, as it was essential to the revolution that his work should not be affected. Please make sure you keep this promise too. Also, be sure not to let any news of me get around. Now that I'm no longer able to work, I plan to go quietly back to Mother's place and look after Kuaile. Mother was always so good to me; it is now time for me to go and be a good daughter and a good mother. I'll be leaving at once. It might not be good for us to see each other again for a while.'

O Ran then left us. Shortly afterwards, a scout came from Luo Tongde, telling me to go and join him, as he was in need of an 'experienced messenger'. He also told Uncle Pan to go at once to a place on the border between the soviet and the white areas to arrange the hand-over of uniforms and money sent by Bai Ledao's family. Once he had done this, he should go directly to where Luo Tongde was now working, to help with logistics work. Luo Tongde would have realized by now that something untoward had befallen his close comrade, Wang Jiansheng, and he probably wanted us to leave Kongji so that we could be at his side. He would have no idea, though, of the similar fate of his wife, Han Jielian. At tense times like these, it was quite usual for husbands and wives to be out of touch for long periods of time – and this was even more true in the case of a responsible, high-ranking commander like Luo Tongde. Remembering O Ran's instructions, I made my way to his remote headquarters.

By the time I reached Luo Tongde the retraining and reorganization of the Red Army had just about been completed. The First Army, commanded by Luo Tongde himself, was a motorized division comprising some 20,000 men. This was our main force and so the general headquarters were based here. The Fourth Army, which was our second main force, was still based in Suxuan county, from where it could head due west to strike at 'The Big City'. A large force was essential to us now and so the next major step was to increase political work in the regions around the soviet area, spreading our field of influence and creating a protective ring around the soviet area which would help to defend it while our troops were on the move.

Now that Wang Jiansheng and Chang Je-an were no longer with us, the vital work of mobilizing the masses fell to Luo Tongde himself. Our Red Army now numbered some 50,000 men and without the support of the masses it could not realize its full potential as a fighting force.

Some time after I had arrived, Uncle Pan and Sweet Potato

appeared accompanied by a whole convoy of trucks laden with supplies. At this Luo Tongde felt a sense of relief. We entertained them at his headquarters with tea and cigarettes. For me, they were both like family and honoured guests.

'Did Bai Ledao's family send us all he promised?' Luo Tongde asked.

'Look at all those trucks out there!' Uncle Pan said. 'They're full of uniforms. We got 200,000 altogether, as well as 30,000 silver dollars. It wasn't easy driving on the mountain roads. First we went to Suxuan and gave Jiqing 10,000 uniforms. Then we drove to Kongji, where we spent two days. We counted out the silver dollars and handed them over to Chairman Fan and also unloaded a 100,000 uniforms to be kept in reserve there. After that we went to the Second and Third Armies, each of which took 10,000 uniforms. Now we've got 70,000 left. Please check this number is right.'

'That is excellent!' Luo Tongde said, praising Uncle Pan and Sweet Potato's work. 'You've saved me a great deal of extra work. At the moment we don't need that many uniforms up here – 20,000 will be enough. The rest we can store in some hidden cave. It is better to store them outside Kongji at dangerous times like these. Up to now our troops have always worn tattered farm clothes. Now they will look quite different! This is sure to impress the enemy!'

Luo Tongde laughed heartily at the thought. He had not laughed like this for a long time. Then, remembering something, he said, 'Well, it seems that Bai Ledao is a man who keeps his word. His family are pretty reliable!'

'Of course,' Sweet Potato said. 'They were hoping to buy his life . . .'

'Oh, yes,' Luo Tongde broke in. 'We must release him at once. As a defeated commander and a prisoner of war, Chiang Kai-shek isn't going to have much faith in him any more. In any case, I promised him he would be released – and we must keep our side of the deal too. We must go and discuss this with Chairman Fan!'

Uncle Pan lowered his head, his face pale. Sweet Potato remained as he was, but there was a hint of tension in his face. Luo Tongde was very sensitive and quickly realized that something was amiss. He remained silent for a while.

'You seem troubled by something,' he said at last. 'What has happened? Don't worry – you can speak freely to me.'

'There is no need for you to go to speak to Chairman Fan,' Uncle Pan said. 'As soon as we brought all the goods to Kongji, Chairman Fan ordered the security Bureau to take Bai Ledao out and execute him.'

Now it was Luo Tongde who turned pale. For a long time he said nothing, staring at us as if we were strangers. Finally, he restored his composure and said with a note of sadness, 'The Red Army has never killed prisoners of war. Now we ask a favour from someone and then take his life. What sort of behaviour is this? Uncle Pan, you are to look after the logistics here, so there's no need for you to go back to Kongji. And Sweet Potato: we could really do with such an able messenger as you up here. At the moment Chunsheng has to manage alone. So you should stay here too.'

Sweet Potato smiled naïvely, almost like a child.

'I'm best at running errands,' he said. 'Especially when it means going into the white areas. But I'm afraid there won't be much call for this sort of work in the army. I'd like to make one more journey first. I hope you'll let me go.'

Sweet Potato's request sounded a little mysterious and we all looked at him with curiosity.

'Is it a private errand?' Luo Tongde asked. 'Where do you plan to go?'

'Well, you could say it's partly private. I want to go to "The Big City".'

'Who are you going to see?' Uncle Pan asked. 'Is it Master Qiu?'

'No,' Sweet Potato said. 'There's no need to see him any more, now that Chairman Fan can make decisions for the Regional Party Bureau. I want to go and see Ho Ludong. He gave us a lot of things, and each time I made the arrangements. Although he is a capitalist, he was willing to give us his son, Ho Shuoru. He was also very generous to us and he showed me much hospitality at his home. Now that Ho Shuoru has gone, I feel it is up to me to go and offer some sort of explanation. Of course, I don't need to say directly that we executed his son.'

'Is that all?' Luo Tongde asked.

Sweet Potato nodded miserably.

'Yes, that's all,' he almost sobbed. 'Once I've done this I'll feel a little happier about things. I have felt this strong urge to go and see Ho Ludong for the past few days. It is beginning to stifle me.'

'I agree,' Luo Tongde said. 'You can go whenever you wish.' Then turning to Uncle Pan he asked, 'Do you have any requests, Uncle. You look as if there is something you want to say. Feel free to speak.'

Uncle Pan looked blankly at this commander-in-chief, his Adam's-apple bobbing up and down nervously. Luo Tongde, however, looked at him with such a sincere and determined expression that before long he stopped swallowing and said with a heavy sigh, 'When I took the silver dollars to Chairman Fan's office I heard two things I couldn't quite understand. Ma Jiajun and Xu Qiming, the two heads of our Aeronautical Bureau were both executed by the Security Bureau, together with Bai Ledao. The reason was that they had been Nationalist officers – "the most evil of counter-revolutionaries". Now, it seems, people at all levels are being charged with counter-revolutionary crimes. Just before we left Kongji, the Security Bureau suddenly went to Huangshu Village to arrest the village cadres. The local people then revolted and beat back the Security Bureau's special task force. This certainly isn't the end of the matter – there may well be arrests and executions going on there right now.'

All Luo Tongde could say to this was, 'Stay here with me. I need you . . .'

Neither Uncle Pan nor Sweet Potato made any response. But their silence was a form of consent. Just then a scout entered carrying an urgent document. When he read the contents, Luo Tongde could not hide a frown. Uncle Pan and Sweet Potato had been getting ready to leave, but seeing his expression, they sat down again and looked at him anxiously.

'This is an instruction from Chairman Fan,' he said. 'He wants the Red Army to strike while the iron's hot and begin marching east, to take Chiang Kai-shek's capital. He thinks that Chiang Kai-shek's forces are ready to collapse and that he should not be given a breathing space to enlist the support of his foreign backers and launch another attack on us. We should not lose this chance of striking the final blow. This will be a vital contribution to the world revolution.'

'When are we supposed to start?' Uncle Pan asked.

'Right away,' Luo Tongde replied.

'This is too hasty,' Sweet Potato said. 'The Red Army has only just finished reorganizing and yet it's supposed to set out at once.'

'But this is an order!' was all Luo Tongde, commander-in-chief of the Red Army, was able to say.

It soon transpired that Fan Guodao's order came a little late, for Chiang Kai-shek had assembled an even larger force than before and was launching a new offensive. Just after Luo Tongde had transferred troops to our area to begin the 'push to the east', as Fan Guodao had instructed, urgent messages began reaching us from the other three sections of the Red Army. Chiang Kai-shek now had an overwhelming force, which was bearing down upon the soviet area. This army had appeared so quickly and unexpectedly that it had already managed to occupy many strategic areas. Our armies had lost the ability to take the initiative and were facing the danger of being surrounded. The Nationalists had changed their tactics and were using a large number of aircraft to reinforce their ground forces. Aerial bombing was not only a danger to our troops, but caused a good deal of harm and suffering to the ordinary people.

Luo Tongde was deeply shocked by this alarming news. He now decided against transferring troops from other units for the 'push to the east' and instead began dividing up the force directly under his control so as to reinforce each section of the Red Army. This was, of course, in blatant contradiction of Fan Guodao's orders. Ironically, just at this critical moment, another urgent message arrived from Fan Guodao. After reading it, Luo Tongde mulled it over and then wrote a short reply, which he handed back to the messenger. I saw that his expression had grown even graver and handed him a cup of tea to help ease his mind a little.

'Quickly pack up my things,' he said, swallowing his tea. 'We must leave right away. Fan Guodao has a change of strategy. We must move our troops over to Suxuan county at once, as that area is in the greatest danger, being the main gateway to the soviet area. Chairman Fan wants us to go there to block off the enemy. I've already had news from Pockmarks the Sixth and was thinking about the situation over there. This is a very important change in strategy and we must start carrying out Chairman Fan's orders at once.'

'Are we going to use the same tactics as before?' I asked, 'First surrounding the town and then dividing up to wipe out the enemy bit by bit? Surely they won't be stupid enough to fall for that a second time.'

'That's just what I've been thinking,' Luo Tongde said. 'That Chiang Kai-shek dares to try to attack the soviet area again from there proves that he must have some new strategy up his sleeve. Anyway, the best way to find out is to go there ourselves. So, quickly, go and get everything ready. We must leave at once!'

Before long we were on our way. Our troops travelled by night and before daybreak we arrived at the edge of Suxuan county. Before we had had a chance to stop to rest and decide our final strategy, a local unit of the Red Army came to meet us. Their commander asked to see the commander-in-chief, and Luo Tongde came forward to greet him. It happened that the commander was none other than my old friend, Pockmarks the Sixth. We could see from the look on his face that the situation here was becoming very grave. He wasted no time in coming to the point.

'The Nationalist troops arrived here quite suddenly,' he said. 'They pounced on Suxuan county town with three divisions. Before they took the town, they occupied the two main areas of high ground nearby, Jigong Hill and Redbud Mount. Their numbers were just too great and they had very powerful guns. They also had a strategic advantage over us. Luckily we left the town in time, so we were not surrounded. We've now split our troops in two: one section led by me and one by Jiqing. For the past two days we've been fighting on the move. When one of our scouts told me that a large Red Army unit was heading in this direction, I guessed it must be you, so I brought my troops straight up here to meet you. Jiqing's troops were over in the west of the county fighting a guerrilla battle and so they're cut off from us. But now that we've got a bigger force, we can try to block off the Nationalists and then find a way to get in touch with Jiqing again. Whatever happens, we must not let the Nationalists get inside the soviet area. This is going to be our main front.'

'It looks as if it will also be Chiang Kai-shek's main front,' Luo Tongde said. 'Do you have any idea yet how many troops they have this time? From what you've said they seem to be pretty ferocious!'

'We're getting some idea now,' Pockmarks the Sixth said. 'After we pulled out of the county town they sent a force after us. We fought back and wiped out one of their battalions. We also captured a wounded officer, whom we brought up to an old temple in the hills, hoping to save him. Unfortunately he was too badly wounded, but before he died, he was so moved by our sincere efforts to save him that he told us all he could about the numbers of Chiang Kai-shek's troops. He said that

Chiang Kai-shek has sent thirty-six divisions over, most of which are his own crack troops. These are divided into three sections, which have surrounded the soviet area. The campaign headquarters is in "The Big City" and there is a branch headquarters in the Provincial Capital to the east. Chiang Kai-shek himself is the commander-in-chief. The left-hand section is made up of ten divisions and is closing in on the south-west of the soviet area. The middle and right-hand sections have twenty-six divisions and five brigades, with over 300,000 men, as well as four airborne divisions. The right-hand section is now threatening the areas where our Second and Third Red Armies are operating. But the middle section, commanded by Chiang Kai-shek himself, is the one we are facing on this front. It must have at least sixteen or seventeen divisions, not counting the aircraft.'

'Chiang Kai-shek knows that this is the main way into the soviet area,' Luo Tongde said. 'That is why he has sent such a huge force. He probably wants to wipe out our soviet area in one go. Then he can go on to wipe out the soviet areas in the south-west and finally concentrate his forces on the Central Soviet Area in the south-east. This shows that he still has a huge army at his disposal – it is not just a "secondary force". We must do all we can to deal with it. Have you sent this information to Chairman Fan?'

'Yes,' Pockmarks the Sixth said. 'I sent an urgent message to him yesterday. He must have given you the order to come here after getting my message.'

Luo Tongde nodded.

'Yes,' he said. 'We must set up an intelligence centre here right away. Then we can begin monitoring the enemy's movements. Chunsheng, go and find Uncle Pan. I'll stay here to talk to Comrade Pockmarks.'

I went off at once to fetch Uncle Pan. When we got back, Pockmarks the Sixth was still telling Luo Tongde about the information he had got from the injured Nationalist officer. He had a splendid memory and could almost recite by heart what the officer had said.

'Chiang Kai-shek's strategy this time is like this: first to crush the main force of the Red Army, then to enter the soviet area, wiping out the Red Army along the way, keeping all sides blocked off to prevent us from escaping and finally wipe us out altogether.'

'So it seems that Chiang Kai-shek doesn't plan to try to wipe us out in one go,' Luo Tongde commented. 'He wants to secure each foothold, first destroying our main force and then surrounding us for the final extermination campaign.' Turning to Uncle Pan, he went on, 'You see, Uncle, Chiang Kai-shek is really serious this time! I'd like you to start taking care of intelligence work, as this is vital to our strategy. Logistics are not so pressing at the moment. Comrade Pockmarks and Jiqing are commanding forces around the edge of the county and it will be essential to keep in touch with them. Also, we must get in touch with Kongji and the other sections of the Red Army. It is essential that we do not lose contact and break up.'

'I now understand what you mean, Comrade Tongde,' Uncle Pan replied. 'I'll begin this work right away!'

Just then, Pockmarks the Sixth's messenger returned from Kongji. He rushed in and gave Pockmarks the Sixth a letter from Fan Guodao. As soon as he had read it, Pockmarks the Sixth passed it on to Luo Tongde. 'Here,' he said, 'Chairman Fan wants me to give you these instructions.'

Luo Tongde began to read the contents of the letter out loud:

'"Since Chiang Kai-shek's forces have already occupied Suxuan county town, you should now do the utmost to control them and surround them. This will draw other enemy troops to the area, which can the be wiped out unit by unit."'

After reading this order, Luo Tongde gave a slight sigh, which he quickly tried to hide with his hand.

'These are the tactics we used last time,' he said. 'But they are already out of date. The situation now is quite different. There's no way we'll be able to surround the town. And

Chiang Kai-shek's back-up forces are enormous – not just reinforcements like before. Even if we mustered all our strength and surrounded the county town, we would simply be playing into Chiang Kai-shek's hands, as he could attack us from two sides with his back-up forces. But if we don't draw his main forces over here, they are sure to storm straight into the soviet area itself . . .'

Luo Tongde seemed perplexed by this dilemma.

'We could divide the Red Army up into several units, as Jiqing and I did,' Pockmarks the Sixth suggested. 'Then we could fight a guerrilla war along the borders between the soviet and white areas, splitting up their forces. We could gradually hack away at them, making it impossible for them to follow their campaign through to the end.'

Luo Tongde thought for a while.

'There's a lot in what you say,' he said. 'But we will still need to lure them to a certain point before we can begin splitting them up. So we will have to send one large force to surround Suxuan county town, while the rest get prepared for mobile warfare in the hills. Good! Let us agree on this strategy. We mustn't waste any more time! The Nationalists must know of our arrival and they will be planning to surround us right now. So we should try to divide them up as soon as possible.'

Luo Tongde set this new strategy in motion: one portion of his troops would be used to confront the enemy directly, while the other would prepare to fight a guerrilla war in the hills.

The Nationalist armies could not have known the intentions of the Red Army, but they seemed to have an idea that our main force was located somewhere along the front in Suxuan county. To us it looked very much as if the Nationalists were beginning to carry out their strategy of entrenching step by step and holding on firmly to their base while they waited for further reinforcements. Apparently they did not intend to storm us directly, but planned to close in on us from all sides

305

with large numbers of troops. However, their plans were somewhat disrupted by the Red Army taking the initiative and moving into the hills to begin fighting a guerrilla war.

Mobile warfare now became the order of the day, not only in the area around Suxuan, but also in the areas where the Second and Third Red Armies were operating. Uncle Pan's Intelligence Centre, located in an out-of-the-way hamlet, not far from Luo Tongde's headquarters, became the destination of many a messenger carrying urgent news. In the face of Chiang Kai-shek's superior weaponry and the suddenness of the attack, all the mobile units of the Red Army could do for the time being was to try to divert the enemy forces away from the soviet area, launch raids against them or lure their smaller units into the hills where the terrain was to our advantage. We would only take these units on if it looked as if they could be beaten. Otherwise, our troops would disappear into the hills and hide until the coast was clear. These tactics could at the most bring the enemy to a halt. They could never succeed in wiping them out or forcing them to retreat. The entire Nationalist army was some seven or eight times larger than the whole of the Red Army in our region, and in addition they had the support of their air force. At their rear, foreign powers gave them constant backing.

Luo Tongde was fully aware of the great responsibility he carried. His main aim was to counter Chiang Kai-shek's strategy of 'securing each foothold and hitting hard and sure' with a strategy of 'holding firm and obstructing the enemy'. This way, he hoped, the main force of the enemy would get bogged down around Suxuan county and the military situation could be turned to our advantage. As it happened, our delaying tactics were successful for about a month.

The military situation did indeed change fundamentally during this time, but not in the way we had hoped. Luo Tongde was not quite taken by surprise, though what happened was on a scale well beyond his control. One day, Uncle Pan suddenly appeared at Luo Tongde's hide-out.

'Chairman Fan has just sent an urgent message,' he panted. 'It was so urgent that he didn't even write it down. I got it verbally from his messenger: Kongji is under serious threat. Pull back our main force from Suxuan county at once. The enemy are approaching Kongji – get ready to engage with them to defend the town.'

'Kongji is under threat?' Luo Tongde repeated. 'Did you get any more details?'

'Just before Chairman Fan sent this order,' Uncle Pan said, 'we received an urgent message from the Third Army. Chiang Kai-shek has sent eight divisions to attack their front, with bombers to back them up. The Third Army cannot hold them back any longer and some of their units have already been surrounded by the enemy. The Nationalists' main force is now bearing down on Kongji itself.'

Luo Tongde looked up at the sky. He was silent for a while, and then he said, more to himself than to us, 'Well, I suppose this isn't entirely unexpected. The enemy have always had the advantage of numbers. But up until now we have always managed to make something from nothing and gain the upper hand. In the end, it is the people who fight wars that count most. If experienced people like Wang Jiansheng, Chang Je-an, Big Tree Lu and Jia Hongcai were still around, things would be very different.' Then, turning to Uncle Pan, he asked, 'Are those two messengers still here?'

'Yes,' said Uncle Pan, 'I told them to stay until I'd reported to you.'

'We'll set off for Kongji tonight,' Luo Tongde said. 'They can act as our guides. Send messengers out at once to tell Pockmarks the Sixth and Jiqing of our decision. They should stay on here and do their best to delay the enemy. Also send messages to all our units to get ready to leave here at midnight. We'll follow the two messengers and try to catch up with the enemy forces before they reach Kongji.'

We left very promptly. Uncle Pan and I stayed with Luo Tongde. We marched as fast as possible and just before daybreak saw the Nationalist troops some way ahead of us. They clearly had not expected us to appear so quickly at their rear and, making the most of the situation, Luo Tongde gave the order to attack. Unprepared for this sudden assault, the two regiments at the enemy's rear quickly fell. However, their vanguard was made up of four divisions which regrouped in a horseshoe to launch a counter-attack. It was still not light and Luo Tongde decided it was best to withdraw our forces and hide in the hills before making a detour to Kongji.

The suddenness of our attack threw the enemy into confusion and resulted in few losses on our side. The Nationalists were forced to halt for a while to reorganize themselves and await the arrival of reinforcements to ensure the complete destruction of our main force. Meanwhile, Luo Tongde was able to lead his troops safely into Kongji.

When Fan Guodao and Luo Tongde met, we could not help noticing that the Chairman looked extremely anxious and dispirited. He spoke no more of the Nationalists as a secondary force, nor of our 'push to the east'; instead, he called for the Red Army and the soviet government to withdraw at once from the soviet area to 'conserve our forces'.

'But how can we just abandon the soviet area, when so many have given their lives for it?' Luo Tongde asked. 'We have the strong support of the masses here. This area will always be our revolutionary base. Even if Chiang Kai-shek's forces are as great as we fear, we can at least divert them away from here for the time being and reduce the pressure on our local forces around Kongji. The troops under me could then cross over into the next province to the west, where there are many local warlord armies, and lure the enemy away from here. Our Second, Third and Fourth armies can meanwhile stay here and split up to begin a guerrilla war. Then we can fight our way back again when the time is right.'

Faced by a huge enemy army on all sides and the Nationalist troops practically banging at the gates, Fan Guodao had been thrown into a panic and could think of nothing better than an immediate withdrawal. He had not even considered whether we should ever return. But now he saw that Luo Tongde's plan was the only possible way out. He had neither the time nor the inclination to discuss the matter any further and so made this the urgent decision of the Regional Party Bureau and the army high command. The order that went out read: 'The main force of the Red Army will withdraw to the west. All other troops and cadres should remain in the soviet area and continue to resist the enemy.'

That same afternoon the Regional Party Bureau and army high command left Kongji, accompanied by the main force of the Red Army under Luo Tongde. They all assembled at Dragon Taming Ridge, near where my mother, Aunt Sunflower and Sister Apricot were staying. Everything had happened so quickly that Luo Tongde had had no opportunity to try to see his wife. In any case the Security Bureau had told him that the hospital in which Han Jielian was working had been moved to a safer area a day or two earlier. Uncle Pan and I remained with Luo Tongde. Sweet Potato had disappeared during our attack on the Nationalists and so far we had no idea what had happened to him. We spent that night near Dragon Taming Ridge, intending to begin our march to the west early the following morning. The Nationalists knew little about our movements and for the time being remained outside Kongji, neither daring to attack the town nor trying to pursue us.

That night everyone slept very peacefully. The surrounding mountains were quiet, adding to the calm which descended on us. It had been a long time since the Red Army had enjoyed such a tranquil night. I alone found it hard to sleep. I couldn't help thinking of my mother, O Ran, Kuaile, Aunt Sunflower and Sister Apricot. The distant journey I was about to embark on would be a highly unusual one. I had no idea when I might see them again. In the end, I only managed to catch a little sleep just as dawn was beginning to break. Then Uncle Pan woke me up.

'Get up quickly!' he said. 'We want to set off early so as not to disturb the local people. I've already packed your things for you. Let's go together.'

I had slept in my clothes, so I stood up, rubbed my eyes and set off with Uncle Pan straight away. Our advance troops had already left. Before we had gone far, my mother suddenly appeared at the side of the road with Kuaile in her arms. I ran over to her and looked at her in silence. I felt tears well up in my eyes.

'Boys shouldn't cry on parting,' she said softly. But I could see that her eyes, too, were moist. 'Last night Uncle Pan came over to tell us that you would be setting out early this morning. Now I can see you before you go. Hold Kuaile for a minute – he's also one of the family.'

I took Kuaile and kissed his face. He cried, 'Uncle!' and then I returned him to my mother's arms. Mother took him and kissed him on the head, as if trying to avoid my eyes.

'Why hasn't O Ran come?' I asked. 'I'd really like to see her. We grew up together . . .'

'How could she come?' Mother said, raising her head. 'You are about to set off on a journey for the revolution, she . . . she has been thrown out of the revolutionary ranks . . .'

'Yes, Mother, I understand,' I said. 'I have Uncle Pan with me now. You needn't worry about me.'

'Sons can always get along in the world,' she replied. 'I'm sure you will be fine. And don't you worry about us either. Now, get going. Uncle Pan is waiting for you!'

Uncle Pan lacked the courage to face my mother again. He just stood at a distance watching us. Then I returned to his side. We had fallen behind the rest of the troops and we had to hurry to catch them up. And so our distant journey began. Mother stood at the side of the road, telling Kuaile to wave his little hand at us.

Our troops were so well disciplined that our passage barely roused the local people from their sleep. The quiet mountains looked down on us. I felt as if they, too, were close to me, like my mother. For it was in these mountains that I had spent my childhood, grown to maturity and taken part in countless struggles. How could I bear to leave them now? But as Luo Tongde had said: *we shall come back again!*

EPILOGUE

In fact, this main force of the Red Army did not come back. It led Chiang Kai-shek's forces through the mountains, crossing two provinces and finally wearing them out and shaking them off. Eventually it reached the border between Szechuan and Shaanxi provinces in west China, an area long controlled by local warlords. Here it began to establish a new soviet area and remained there right up until 1935, when it embarked on the world-renowned Long March. During the Long March it joined up with the Central Chinese Red Army. By this time the Japanese fascist armies had already penetrated deep into the Chinese heartland and were threatening the very survival of the Chinese nation. The Red Army went through numerous hardships, finally reaching the north-west of China. There it began confronting the Japanese directly, which in fact marked the start of the anti-Japanese War. Meanwhile, the Red Army forces which remained in the old soviet areas continued to lead the masses in a protracted struggle which lasted until the founding of the People's Republic of China in 1949.

Luo Tongde became a marshal in the army of the new People's Republic. Fan Guodao, his personal ambition as 'the leader' of the Chinese revolution frustrated by the disgraceful blunders he had committed morally, militarily and politically, made contact with the Nationalists at the end of the Long March and finally went over to them and got himself a position in their secret service. As the highest leader of the old soviet area his only claim to fame was his extermination of over 2,000 Red Army officers and men during the three months of purges over which he presided. This figure does not include the local cadres who were killed. After Chiang Kai-shek's government collapsed, Fan Guodao fled to Hong Kong and finally moved to Canada where he lived out the rest of his life. He died in a charitable old people's home.

During the Long March Uncle Pan, whose health was by now quite poor, caught a serious bout of malaria and died in the wild marshy countryside. He had always longed to return to his home in the north before he died, so as he breathed his last breath Chunsheng and another Red Army soldier turned him round so that his head was facing north. This symbolized the return of his spirit to his old home.

Chunsheng, the narrator of this trilogy, later became a writer, for he considered all the ups and downs he had experienced warranted recording, as a small contribution to the history of New China. His mother died barely half a year after he set off on the Long March. Kuaile was taken care of by O Ran. She constantly felt guilty about having allowed Fan Guodao's Security Bureau to label her with the crime of belonging to the Nationalists' 'Reorganization Wing'. Having been stripped of the right to take part in the revolution, she hid herself away in the countryside, scraping a living as a dressmaker. But she never lost her faith in the revolution. She placed all her love and energy in Kuaile, her son, hoping that he might continue in the footsteps of his father, Lao Liu, learning as much as possible in his spare time and getting ready to make a contribution to the people's lives. After the founding of the People's Republic, Kuaile passed the examinations for the first group of Chinese students to go and study in the Soviet Union. He later became one of the country's leading nuclear physicists.

As for Chunsheng's brother, Zhao Jue, he went to Shanghai and began doing underground work there among the local workers. But he was betrayed by a renegade while taking part in a strike and arrested by the Nationalist authorities. As punishment, they dragged him to a place called Longhua, on the outskirts of Shanghai, and buried him alive.

Sweet Potato, who had been cut off from the Red Army during Chiang Kai-shek's last campaign against the soviet area, did what he had yearned to do: he secretly returned to 'The Big City' to tell Ho Ludong of his son's death and try to offer him some sort of consolation for his grief. Unfortunately, Ho Ludong's son-in-law, Chen Chuqing, a senator in the Provincial Government, had just been made an advisor to Chiang Kai-shek's Anti-banditry Headquarters. This promotion owed much to his connections with several foreign banks, which enabled him to procure considerable financial assistance for Chiang Kai-shek. Hoping to demonstrate his staunch opposition to the communists, he reported to the Anti-banditry Headquarters that Ho Ludong had been having secret dealings with the Communist Party. When the agents came to arrest Ho Ludong, Sweet Potato was there too. Both men were tied up and taken away. Two days later, they were each placed in a sack weighted with heavy stones. The two sacks were then thrown into the Yangtze River.

Pockmarks the Sixth was also cut off during the Nationalists' last campaign. He fled into another county in the white area and again started underground work, creating new party members and setting up an information network. In this way he was able to help supply the people still fighting in the old soviet area with salt, medicine and arms. After the founding of the People's Republic he became an official in the Ministry of Commerce, later turning to foreign trade and making a contribution to the development of China's trade with the rest of the world.

Jiqing did not take part in the march to the west, but remained in the old soviet area to command the remaining Red Army forces fighting a guerrilla war. At first they grappled with the Nationalists, but later Japanese troops entered the area and they began to fight them as well. The Japanese invaders were not much luckier than the Nationalists and apart from occupying Kongji and other towns, they made few inroads into the countryside, which remained firmly in the hands of the masses. They often sent out troops to sweep the area and during one of these raids, Aunt Sunflower was shot down while running for cover in the hills. Jiqing later became a commander in the Chinese Air Force, making a major contribution to the founding of New China's air defences.

Sister Apricot managed to survive the war against the Japanese and the civil war between the Communist and Nationalist Parties. After the Liberation, as a result of the extreme-leftism of the time, she was labelled a 'member of the landlord class' during the period of land reform and was only allocated a meagre amount of land. To help make ends meet, her son began learning carpentry from an old carpenter who lived near by. Later, he became one of the best-known craftsmen in the area. After the end of the Cultural Revolution and the fall of the Gang of Four, which marked the end of a long period of extreme-left politics, Sister Apricot was rehabilitated and named as the widow of a martyr. As a result, the local government gave her a pension of twelve *yuan* a month. Little Baldy managed to make a fairly good living from his carpentry, so Sister Apricot was able to enjoy a relatively peaceful old age.